MISERY BAY

A MYSTERY

CHRIS ANGUS

YUCCA

Yucca Publishing books may be purchased in bulk at special discounts for sales promotion, corporate gifts, fund-raising, or educational purposes. Special editions can also be created to specifications. For details, contact the Special Sales Department, Yucca Publishing, 307 West 36th Street, 11th Floor, New York, NY 10018 or yucca@skyhorsepublishing.com.

Yucca Publishing® is an imprint of Skyhorse Publishing, Inc.®, a Delaware corporation.

Visit our website at www.yuccapub.com.

10 9 8 7 6 5 4 3 2 1

Library of Congress Cataloging-in-Publication Data is available on file.

Jacket design by Karis Drake
Jacket photo by Tomasz Zajda and Dollar Photo Club

Print ISBN: 978–1-63158-083-3
Ebook ISBN: 978–1-63158-090-1

Printed in the United States of America

For Jim

MISERY BAY

1

ARRETT STAMPED HIS FEET IN a vain attempt to create some warmth in his toes. The last time he'd been in Point Pleasant Park, it had been a sweltering ninety-five degrees and he'd been tossing back bottles of Keith's Ale with Lonnie following a Saturday afternoon baseball game. That was the first time it had struck him that the park swelled out into Halifax harbor like a woman's breast, the point a perfect nipple. Of course, it could have been the beer.

He could see the breakwater through the steady rain pelting his jacket and dripping off the brim of his Calgary Stampeders cap. During working hours, the area was a busy port. Behind a chain-link fence, hundreds of railcar-sized containers rose five and six high against a backdrop of enormous orange and white cranes that towered a hundred feet into the sky, their tops disappearing into the fog. They stood like mute, alien sentinels, something out of H. G. Wells.

A freighter, engines pounding, moved stolidly through the gloom, past George's Island, heading for the North Atlantic. He could just make out the name on her bow, *Ward of the North*, cribbed from a famous book about the city of Halifax.

The fog-softened lights of Dartmouth, Halifax's poor twin city, floated on the opposite shore like army helicopters preparing to land

and take on the cranes. Streaks of rain emerged from a stainless-steel sky, as devoid of depth as the inside of an aluminum pot. The pock-marked surface of the bay gave the entire scene the look of a pointillist painting crafted by an artist with just a single color on his palette.

Alvin, all five foot seven inches of him, stood hunched against the rain, a cigarette glowing in his mouth. "Shit for weather," he said. "Whole summer's been nothing but one hurricane after another. Never seen anything like it." He took the smoke out of his mouth, hocked up an enormous green gob, and spat it on the ground. "Shouldn't be long now," he said.

"Provided your tip was accurate," said Garrett. He had his doubts. Alvin was enthusiastic for a rookie barely two years on the force, almost gullible, though no one would say that to his face. He had a fuse as short as his stature and, for a little guy, threw a wallop of a punch.

Instead of answering, Alvin grabbed his forearm. A black sedan was entering the park. They watched it pull up to the break-water a hundred feet away and flash its lights twice.

"That's it," said Alvin. He spoke softly into his radio. "All units move in."

Garrett started forward, but Alvin grabbed his arm again. "No one's responding. Christ! The radio won't work. It's too damn wet."

They stood uncertainly, staring at the car. Out on the water, the engines of a fishing boat started to rumble. Then the vessel appeared out of the gloom, moving toward shore.

"Guess it's just you and me." Garrett sensed Alvin's tension in the dark. He was wired like a radio tower. "Take it easy, okay?"

"No problem," Alvin replied.

"Wait till the boat makes contact. We want to establish the rendezvous."

Crouching low, they began to duck-walk across the open lot. There was no cover except for the gloom, but it was enough. The boat continued to angle in, its engines starting to churn, reversing to slow down. A line flew out to one of the men on shore and a moment later, the second man opened the car door.

They were halfway to the black sedan. Suddenly, the entire parking lot was bathed in brilliant light from several high-powered floodlights on the boat, catching them frozen, like Br'er Rabbit stuck in Tar Baby.

In an instant, pandemonium split the night. A man cried out, the craft's powerful engines roared, and the water began to roil fiercely. The man who had opened the car door had hold of a child. He hesitated in indecision, then picked the girl up and threw her onto the deck of the boat like a sack of potatoes before leaping back into the sedan. The car's tires screeched as it reversed away from the water.

"They're getting away!" Garrett yelled. He crouched on one knee and fired at the vehicle's tires. One shot, a second, then Alvin was in his line of fire, racing toward the car.

"Damn it, Alvin. I can't shoot! Get out of the way!"

But the young Mountie was already near the car as it spun in the gravel. The driver shifted into forward, then hit the gas hard. The vehicle spun 360 degrees, coughed once, and the engine died.

They were on it in an instant. As the driver struggled to restart the engine, Garrett fired two precise shots into the rear tires, deflating them instantly. A moment later, he and Alvin stood on either side of the car, pistols pointed at the driver.

"Get out, now!" Alvin yelled.

Garrett could see the driver looking at them. He was a heavy-set, sallow-faced fellow. He said something to the man sitting in the passenger seat. Garrett couldn't tell if anyone else was in the car, because the windows were tinted.

Alvin yelled again and brought his pistol right up against the car's window, which was a mistake. If he fired, the glass would shatter and likely injure him. Fortunately, the fellow raised his hands and Alvin opened the door, grabbed him by the arm, and yanked him out. He sprawled onto the ground.

Garrett did the same to the other man. Three police cars roared into the park, screeching to a halt around the vehicle. Officers swarmed over the men, the entire scene lit up again, this time by police car headlights and floods.

Garrett poked his head into the car and looked in the back. Five girls in their early teens stared at him with wide eyes. They were dressed as though planning a midnight beach party in the Caribbean, with lacy, see-through tops over short shorts and high heels. He held up his police badge.

Instantly, the girls started to chatter. They piled out of the back of the car, all jabbering at once in a language he'd never heard, holding onto him for dear life.

"Alvin, help me out here."

His partner put his gun away and came forward, still puffed up and excited at the biggest arrest of his career. He listened to the girls for a moment, then held up his hand and shouted, "SHUT UP!" at the top of his voice.

The girls went instantly silent, staring at this new menace with open fear on their faces.

"Take it easy," said Garrett. "They're spooked enough. Any of you speak English?"

The girl who looked to be the oldest, maybe fourteen, raised her hand like a schoolgirl. "I speak," she said.

"Where were they taking you?'

She shrugged. "We do not know. We go where they send us and do what they say. There was party on private boat in harbor."

Garrett wiped his forehead and stared sadly at the girls. Alvin's tip had suggested a transfer of illegal immigrants coming into the country. But these young women had clearly been employed for some time already, probably by the escort service they'd had under surveillance.

"What nationality are you?" he asked.

"We are all Ukrainian girls," she answered, proudly. "They told us we would have good jobs and be able to send money home to our families."

"Same old story," said Alvin.

"All right," Garrett said "We'll take you to headquarters. You won't be charged. What's going on here isn't your fault. We'll try to put you in touch with your families." He reached out a hand and gently touched the smallest girl's head. "You're going home," he said.

He turned to an officer. "Get them into a car pronto. They're not dressed for this weather." Several of the girls were visibly shivering. "And tell the Harbor Police to board and search any craft in the area that looks likely." He stared out at the disappearing fishing boat and swore.

Without a word, he jumped into the sedan and turned the key. This time, thank god, it started.

Alvin stared at him through the window. "What are you doing, Garrett?"

But there was no time to answer. The car leaped forward, forcing two officers to jump out of the way. The vehicle made an awful sound and was hard to control as the deflated tires shredded. Garrett knew the channel here. The boat would pass around the end of the breakwater, just feet from one of the towering cranes. If he got there in time, he might pull it off. All he could think of was the small child who'd been thrown onto the deck.

The car was powerful and flew across the parking lot, tires spraying bits of hot rubber into the night. It crashed through a padlocked gate and careened out onto the breakwater. Twilight had given way to blackness. Garrett prayed that the men on the boat would be concentrating on the narrow passage they had to negotiate. The car ground to a halt, fishtailing, in front of three huge boulders that blocked further progress. He was still thirty yards from the end.

He could see the boat beginning to change its tack, concentrating on the narrow channel, edging in closer to shore. There just might be time. Sprinting the remaining distance, he timed his leap and crashed onto the deck, rolling and coming up hard against a metal bulwark that took his breath away.

Groaning, he looked up to see two men in the wheelhouse. They were concentrating on their course maneuvers and hadn't seen his little melodrama in the dark. But another man had. A depressingly large fellow stood on the open deck, one hand holding onto the girl as though she were a doll, the other grasping an ugly-looking steel hook at least three feet long. He tossed the girl to one side and advanced on the intruder.

Garrett barely had time to stand up and take a painful breath before the man was on him, swinging the hook down in an evil arc. It missed by inches, struck the side of the boat, and flew down the deck.

Garrett reached for his gun, only to discover it was gone, lost somewhere in his tumble. Then the big man was on him, landing a crushing blow that glanced off his shoulder as he ducked at the last instant. His entire arm went numb.

The man turned away and went after his hook. Garrett looked around desperately for some sort of weapon. There was a pole with what appeared to be a weight on one end. Some sort of fishing implement. It looked like a perfect club. He grabbed it and almost fell over backward. The thing must have been a float of some kind, probably made of cork. It wouldn't knock the foam off a latte.

His adversary retrieved the hook and advanced once again, pausing long enough to glance at the wheelhouse. He yelled as loudly as he could, but the men inside were insulated by the enclosure and the noise of the engines. They couldn't hear him.

There was nothing Garrett could use as a weapon. In desperation, he picked up a coil of rope and flung it. Miraculously, the coils ensnared the man, catching on the hook and tangling his arms.

In an instant, Garrett was on him. He looped one end of the rope around the man's middle and used it to fling him off the boat into the water. Maybe he could swim, maybe not. He couldn't care less.

He stood, staggering slightly, still feeling the numbness in his arm where the man had clubbed him. The girl huddled on the deck. She might have been eleven years old. He approached her slowly, trying to speak in soothing tones, because he was certain she couldn't understand English. She said something unintelligible and shrank away from him. Men had never meant anything but pain and suffering in her brief life. Garrett was simply one more.

He stopped and made a gesture for her to stay where she was. Whether she understood or not was unclear. He turned his attention to the wheelhouse where the two men were still oblivious to the events on deck.

They were now exiting Halifax harbor. Garrett could see the black silhouette of McNabs Island, home to many World War II installations, where heavy submarine cables and nets had once stretched to Chebucto Head. Only one Nazi U-boat had ever made it through the netting, by following in the wake of a ship. It had then proceeded to torpedo a Canadian warship before making its escape.

The harbor entrance faced south, and Garrett could feel the boat turning northeast, heading straight for Ireland. He knew Alvin must have contacted the harbor patrol, so at least someone would be looking for them. What he had to decide was whether it made more sense to hunker down and wait for help or try to overpower the two men by himself. The decision wasn't all that difficult. He was sore all over from the leap onto the boat and the blow from the man on deck. He couldn't find his weapon in the dark. The men could wait.

He eased over to the girl, who stared at him cautiously like a wounded animal. He avoided touching her and sat a few feet away. "Well, darlin', it's you and me. Let's hang out for a while and see what develops, okay?"

She started to cry and his heart melted for the poor creature. He shuffled over to her and put out one arm. After a moment, she moved in, and he hugged her tightly, talking to her in a low voice. "We're going to be just fine . . . just fine," he said over and over.

Twenty minutes later, a Coast Guard cutter and a harbor patrol boat loomed out of the darkness. Simultaneously, a helicopter appeared and hovered overhead, bathing the scene in light. Alvin had called in the cavalry.

The fishing boat slowed, her captain aware there was nothing he could do against such a force. Twenty minutes later, Garrett and the girl were wrapped in blankets and sitting in the warm cutter, drinking hot chocolate and smiling at one another.

2

"DEPUTY COMMISSIONER'S LOOKING FOR YOU," said Martha, her eyes avoiding him.

Garrett stopped in front of her desk. "As you can clearly see, I'm not here."

"He said to be sure to tell you that you *were* here and that you should get your F-ing blank the F up to his office." There was a smile at the corner of her mouth.

"I assume he did not actually say, 'F-ing.'"

"He was more colorful, but a demure, overeducated, highly trained personal assistant is not aware of the meaning of such language."

"You are all of those things except the first, Martha." He sighed. "Thanks."

He took the stairs two at a time, satisfied that the effort produced no discernible limp, nodded at two officers, and presented himself at his boss's door.

Alton Tuttle had been Deputy Commissioner for six years. He was the Royal Canadian Mounted Police Commanding Officer in Nova Scotia, known as "H" division. In Halifax, as in many municipalities outside of Ontario and Quebec, the RCMP was hired on a contract basis to provide police services in rural areas. Recently, local police commissioners had been considering ending the relationship, giving local RCMP officers the option of transferring to the municipal force. The business had been controversial and was one reason Garrett had decided to retire. He despised the bureaucratic runaround.

Tuttle sat at his desk, unlit cigar in his mouth, head buried behind a stack of files. He was in his mid-fifties and wore a navy dress shirt, sleeves rolled up, the shirt tight across his bulging abdomen. He'd been a muscular high school wrestling champion three years running. But the years sitting at a desk had taken a toll.

"Nice of you to drop by," he said.

"Martha said you wanted to see me . . . in somewhat more colorful terms. I figured you wanted to rehash things again," Garrett replied in a tired voice. "Frankly, it's all been said. I'm on my way out, Alton. You know that. Twenty years on the Halifax force is enough. I'm tired of people who can do this sort of stuff to young girls. I'm tired of people who can do this sort of stuff to me. My retirement, my garden, and my boat await me."

Tuttle scowled at him. "Damned if I can understand young officers these days. You're forty-two years old, for Christ's sake. Most experienced sex crimes officer I've got and you want to hang it up while you're still in diapers." He spat the cigar onto the desk, where it spun around, stuck to a piece of paper, and slowly began to spread a brown stain. "The guy who invented pensions ought to be shot. What the hell are you going to do with yourself—grow pansies all day?"

It was an old conversation, one Garrett had no interest in rehashing. Besides, he didn't much care for pansies. He also wasn't a young officer. His title was Special Constable with expertise in prostitution. The nature of the job allowed him to go without uniform, working primarily undercover.

Seeing there would be no reply, the Deputy Commissioner sat back in his chair. "I'm going to make one more effort with you,

Barkhouse," he said. "What you need is a break from the big city. Get back to the hinterlands—use your damn boat too, if you want."

"What are you talking about?"

"Misery Bay." Tuttle scratched himself.

Something clicked in the back of Garrett's head. He'd grown up outside the little coastal village. The memories that flooded back were good, but he hadn't returned since his parents had died six years ago. He kept up by reading the *Eastern Shore Chronicle*— who died, who got married, who was lost at sea. Lately, the papers had taken on a more sinister tone—coastal smuggling, illegal immigrants funneled into prostitution, bales of drugs washing up on the shore and in fishermen's nets.

"I gather from that wistful look on your face, you've followed what's been going on in the old hometown," Tuttle said. "We've got Halifax pretty well buttoned up, but crime is like one of those dolls you push over and it bounces back. One of the places it's bounced back lately is Misery Bay. I want you to go down there, establish a police presence. Place is too small for an official headquarters, but you'll have full cooperation of the RCMP and Coast Guard."

Garrett stared at him. Retirement had not been an easy decision. As tired as he was of the city grind, the truth was he feared being bored more than just about anything. He wasn't at all sure he could survive simply fishing off his boat every day, puttering in the garden, and staring out to sea from the deck in the evening. Alton had a nasty smirk on his face, and he realized his boss had been planning this for some time.

"There's a woman down there by the name of Sarah Pye." Tuttle found his cigar, picked it up, and stuck it back in the corner of his mouth. "Her husband had his own private investigation business. We hired him to do some undercover work for us. Locals got wind of it and set him up. Planted heroin in their house. Everyone knew it was a setup but the proof was there and he got two years in prison. He was killed while he was inside."

Garrett whistled. "Never heard a thing about it."

"We kept it as quiet as we could. But things are out of control down there. The good citizens, few as they are, have been raising a stink and demanding we station an officer in the town. You're it."

"You can't order me to do this, Alton. I'm retiring."

"It's your hometown, Garrett. You know the people. You going to throw them to the wolves?"

3

THE EASTERN SHORE HIGHWAY WAS the sleepiest bit of road left in the province. Tourists had long since descended on the rocky, forested bays of Nova Scotia. Four thousand miles of coastline, the brochures read. For a while it had seemed the two hundred miles or so from Halifax to Canso was the only stretch yet to be discovered. No longer.

Tiny fishing villages swept past Garrett's window: Musquodoboit, Ship Harbor, Mushaboom, Tangier, Spanish Ship Bay, Marie Joseph. Most consisted of a few plain houses, a dock piled with lobster traps, maybe a tiny Ma and Pa grocery. The highway was narrow, two lanes, heavily patched. But signs of encroachment were everywhere. New homes sprouted on seemingly every headland with a view.

The Germans were coming.

In the past decade, German tourists had discovered Nova Scotia with a vengeance and were about as excited as Columbus must have been upon sighting Hispaniola. Like most of Europe, Germany had virtually no wilderness. As a result, her citizens were completely gaga over the rocky, remote, and—best of all—cheap oceanfront property to be had just a short flight across the big puddle. Already they had bought up every available yard of coastline from Yarmouth to Halifax. Now they were beginning to move farther up the Eastern shore. Even Misery Bay was getting in on the act. A developer had bought up several headlands sticking out into the ocean, run a gravel road out to the end, and put up lot numbers and For Sale signs. Sixty thousand dollars for a few acres and a rocky spit.

The real estate boom seeped up from the south like a poisonous red tide. Paradise, the slick brochures promised; magnificent, windswept forests sweeping down to rocky coastlines. Well-to-do Germans bought it hook, line, and sinker. Invariably, the lavish advertisements showed sparkling sunshine and swimsuited revelers everywhere.

It was all a lie. Oh, it was beautiful enough, if you liked that sort of thing, but sunshine on the Eastern shore could be as elusive as a snowfall in the Sahara. Heavy coastal fog and a cold rain sometimes set in for weeks at a time during the summer months. The water was a frigid fifty degrees in August. Garrett had once encountered a bewildered, bikini-clad German woman on a beach south of Halifax on a hot July day. As he passed her, she said in halting English: "Summer is late coming this year, yah? The water—she is very cold."

He hadn't had the heart to tell her that this was the best it would ever get. She'd have to buy a wetsuit if she wanted to swim.

Ten miles from Misery Bay, he began to pass people he knew. There was only the one road and everyone traveled it in one direction or the other every day. He recognized Dwayne Stewart's red hair as his old classmate drove by in his small car. Then Lissa Publicover passed driving her father's Nova Scotia Power truck. Next came a blue pickup he recognized immediately as belonging to Roland Cribby, one of the neighbors of the old Barkhouse homestead.

No one returned his wave. He hadn't been down this stretch in six years and had lost his membership card. Might as well have been a German tourist. He'd insisted to Tuttle that he didn't want to arrive in a police car, so he drove his own nondescript blue Subaru. Another part of the deal was that he would continue to operate out of uniform. "Get me in practice for being a civilian," he'd explained, "and I can operate at least a little bit undercover."

"Hard to establish a police presence," Tuttle had fumed, "if no one knows who the hell you are."

"Humor me," Garrett had said. "Word will get around."

In the center of town, easily missed if one drove over thirty miles an hour, he pulled in to the tiny grocery store. Perched at the edge of the sea, it had a rickety dock sticking out the back into the ocean. Last he knew it had been purchased by an Iranian couple who lived above the store with their two children. One family member or another was on duty from six in the morning until ten at night. He paused outside to admire an enormous bush of pink roses. The flowers grew wild all over the province and bloomed riotously in July.

Inside, the shelves were barren as usual. No fresh fruit or vegetables. There were canned goods, white bread, racks of potato chips and candy bars, a cooler with whole milk only and soft drinks. Behind a makeshift counter in the back, pizza and hoagies were offered. A slender, olive-skinned girl of perhaps fifteen worked the oven. She stared at Garrett with haunted eyes, as though she could already see the entire rest of her life stretching out before her.

The man standing at the cash register was dark with a bristling mustache and brooding eyes, but he smiled at his potential customer and spoke perfect English.

"Help you find anything?" he asked, as though every item in the store couldn't be seen from where he stood.

This was the center of town, and Garrett knew word would spread quickly if he stated his purpose.

"Name's Garrett Barkhouse." He held out his hand. "I'm going to be the new RCMP officer stationed here in Misery Bay." The girl glanced quickly at him.

The man looked stunned for a moment, then smiled broadly and took the offered hand.

"I am Ali Marshed. You are none too soon. My place was broken into last week. Didn't take much—candy, soft drinks—just kids probably, but there's a rowdy bunch living up Ecum Secum way. Think they own the town."

"One of the things I'll be looking into," said Garrett.

The screen door slammed and a voice said, "There I was, aboot ta turn inta the gr'aage when I coulda swore I seen Garrett Barkhouse drive by."

Garrett winced at the familiar voice, turned, and offered his hand to Roland Cribby. The scallop fisherman's hands were rough and callused. It was like grabbing a horse's hoof.

"Been a while, Roland."

By any stretch of the imagination, Cribby was an unusual-looking man. He stood almost six feet tall and was lean as a beanpole with a permanent stoop that made him seem shorter. He wore a stained T-shirt and sweatpants that were six inches too short. As long as Garrett had known him, which was since they were in high school together, he'd walked with a limp, the result of one leg being slightly shorter than the other. The stoop wasn't related to his leg but rather to a lifelong insecurity around people, as though he were constantly trying not to be seen. He had a reputation for telling stories about himself that were wildly inflated.

For years, Roland made a tenuous living diving for oysters and scallops from the bottoms of the ocean bays. The hours spent in the frigid water without a wetsuit, which he refused to use, had given him arthritis and eventually forced him to cut back on the pursuit. He'd turned to taking tourists out in his boat for sightseeing and deep-sea fishing. The arrival of the German summer homeowners had given his business a boost.

"Wa'll now, must be five, six years. A'w'ys kept an eye on the old place, though. Sure 'nough knew ya'd come back some day." He glanced down at Garrett's leg. "How's the foot?"

"Still missing," Garrett said. And to change the topic, "The old place make it through the winter?"

"Standin'—jest. Livin' room floor slopes 'bout thirty degrees. Laid some tar paper over the kitchen roof two summers ago. A'w'ys meant ta send ya a bill, but I didn't know how ta reach ya."

"Appreciate it, I really do. Let me know what I owe you."

"So you be stayin'?" Roland jackknifed his lean frame into one of the heavy wooden chairs by the door. Even sitting down, the stoop was pronounced.

"He's going to be our local RCMP rep," Marshed said.

"That a fact? Wa'll, ya mebbe seen we can use one. Ma's some tired o' the boys comin' by squealin' their tires late at night. I had ta take a couple of 'em out behind the woodshed and teach 'em some manners."

Garrett looked at him skeptically. Roland never confronted anyone if he could avoid it. He was an inveterate coward.

"'Sides," the fisherman said, pausing for effect. "We could use som'un ta keep an eye on the Ar-teests."

Garrett blinked. "Who?"

"New neighbors downta the wharf. Three of 'em bought the new house on the old Whynot lot. Poured a ton o' money on it. Looks like a Las Vegas whorehouse, ya ask me. Partyin' at all hours. Keeps Ma awake."

Roland had lived his entire adult life with his mother. She was in her seventies and a semi-invalid who rarely left the house. Garrett hadn't seen her in probably twenty years. He glanced at his watch. As usual, five minutes in Cribby's company was enough to remind one of a pressing engagement.

"Well, good to see you, Roland. Got to be going."

Roland stood up, opened the screen door and let Garrett go ahead of him. "Don't be a stranger," he said, limping off to his car. Over his shoulder, he added, "Ya want ta know anything 'bout those kids—or the Ar-teests—jest give a holler."

4

A MILE OUT OF THE tiny village, he turned into Misery Bay itself. The gravel road wound through spruce forest, then skirted a large bog. He passed the overgrown track that led to where he'd be staying in the old family home. The trees lining the lane had begun to close in, and he wondered if he'd be able to make it through when the time came.

The cove road split in two and then split again as he approached a small wharf, one branch heading off into the woods. A half dozen fishing boats were tied up to the lee side of the dock. When he was a boy, the boats would never have been sitting idle at mid-morning. But the fishing industry was shut down, literally fished out of existence. Now the boat owners lobstered during the two-month season or scraped together a few tourists or Germans, wanting to go deep-sea fishing. Mostly, they collected unemployment.

He found Sarah Pye's small white cottage on a point a hundred yards from the wharf. He knew the house. It had belonged to friends of his parents years ago. He pulled the car into the driveway and walked up a path that all but disappeared under a colorful mat of deep purple lupines. They were one of his favorite flowers, and he stopped to admire them.

A voice almost beside him said, "Well, you can't be a local. They don't admire flowers all *that* much."

He looked around and saw a straw hat emerge from the dense mat of flowers. Its owner bent over to retrieve a wicker basket filled with gardening tools, removed the hat, and turned to look at him.

"You looking for that whale?"

She seemed very young. Tuttle had given the impression she would be middle-aged, after all the things that had happened to her. But the inquisitive eyes that stared out from beneath a mound of auburn hair, flecked with tiny bits of lupine pollen, were youthful and sharp.

"I'm sorry?"

"Most of the tourists want to know how to find it. You'll need a boat, I'm afraid. It's on one of the offshore islands—Heron Rook."

"Uh . . . Ms. Pye? I'm Garrett Barkhouse. Deputy Commissioner Tuttle said you would be expecting me."

A frown touched the corner of her mouth. "Oh."

She bent down and picked up a pair of gloves and placed them in the basket. Without looking at him, she said, "I suppose you'll have to come inside, then."

The house was small, as he remembered it, filled with sunshine and flowers. The kitchen sparkled in that spotlessly clean Nova Scotian manner. She didn't offer a chair but instead went right to work making tea. He stood awkwardly beside the kitchen table, a Spartan, wooden affair that nonetheless looked out on a spectacular vista of ocean and islands.

Finally, just as the teapot began to boil, she turned and looked at him directly. Her eyes were set off by a handful of freckles on either side of her nose, and he realized these were part of what made her look so young. Now, however, he could see a few creases around the eyes. She was small, not quite petite. He guessed she might plausibly be in her early thirties.

"Ms. Pye, I know it's worse than late for an RCMP officer to be stationed here. . . ."

"Oh, God, will you please stop calling me that. Do you know how strange it sounds to hear someone say Ms. in this neck of the woods? I don't even hear it much in Halifax. Anyway, my name is Sarah."

"Sarah, then . . . I . . . I want to express my sympathy for what you've been through. I've only just learned about the incident from my Deputy Commissioner, but it sounds bloody awful."

She stared at him. "Tuttle sent someone who doesn't even know what went on here?"

He sighed. "Manpower is limited, Ms . . . uh . . . Sarah. It's why there hasn't been much of a police presence on the Eastern shore in recent years. To be honest, the only reason I'm here is because it was the one way Tuttle could think of to keep me interested in the job. I was about to retire. I'm not totally in the dark, however. Truth is, I was born and raised here, though I haven't been back in years. I read the papers, though."

"The papers." She shook her head slightly. "Yes, they worked hard to keep the details of my husband's death out of the papers." She took a plastic bag out of a bread box and placed several scones on a plate. Then she put the plate on the table and for the first time offered him a chair, though it was only with a quick motion of her hand.

He sat gratefully and took a bite out of a scone. It had fresh-picked blueberries in it and was close to the best thing he'd ever eaten. In a moment, tea appeared.

She poured for both of them, then sat across from him. "You don't look like a local," she said, her head tilted to one side.

"You're not exactly what I expected either."

"Why did they send you here?" she said abruptly.

"I guess I don't have to tell you that things have turned pretty ugly in Misery Bay. Seems like whenever we crack down in Halifax, the criminal element just moves up the coast. It makes sense.

Hardly any police presence here at all. Anyway, your husband was doing undercover work for us when he died. Did you know much about what he was working on?"

Her eyes saddened and he was afraid she might cry, but instead she said, "There are drugs everywhere here. Bales of marijuana wash up on shore nearly every week. They toss them overboard if the Coast Guard stops the boats. And of course other drugs, cocaine, crack, heroin, angel dust, pills of a hundred kinds. It was the drug business that finally got Patrick. They planted heroin in the house here and then got word to one of the officers they owned. We could deny it all we wanted. Made no difference. They planned all along to kill him once he was in the penitentiary. To send a signal."

He could think of nothing to say. "Sorry" seemed totally inadequate.

"So my question to you is, do they own you too, Mr. Barkhouse?"

He stared into her sad eyes. "Sarah, it makes me mad as hell to think of a fellow officer doing that. If I can accomplish just one thing while I'm here, it will be to find out who that was and bring him to justice."

She met his gaze. "I think I almost believe you, Mr. Barkhouse."

"Thanks. Could you begin by calling me Garrett?"

They finished their tea and then walked down the dirt path to the wharf. The sun was a gauzy halo behind a light vale of fog, though it was warm enough.

"What did you mean when you asked if I was here to see the whale?"

"A dead whale washed up on Heron Rook Island about three years ago. A big one, a humpback, I believe. I've been out to see it in my kayak. First year the smell was so bad, you didn't want to get within half a mile of it. But now, it's deteriorated to the point that only bones are left. Whale bone can be valuable to native carvers, and of course the tourists all want to take a piece home with them as well. Most of the new German homes around the cove have pieces of vertebrae and so forth on their mantels." She stared out at the islands. "A sad end for such a magnificent creature."

"That happen a lot—whales washing up I mean?"

"Quite a few in the last several years." She stopped on the pebble beach next to the wharf and poked a stone with her foot, pushing it around in a tight circle. Controlled. It was the sort of thing Garrett couldn't do with his new eighteen-thousand-dollar foot.

"Patrick had an idea they were being used to bring in drugs. You know, kill a whale, stuff it with drugs, and tow it to an island in the dark. Stinks so bad no one wants to get near it. When it's safe, they go in and take out what they stashed. But he never proved it, and I think it was probably unlikely—way too much work for those sorts of people. They don't like to work. It's what the business is all about really. Not having to do real work."

"I suppose you know Roland?"

She grinned. The freckles seemed to leap about her face like the spray of freshly poured seltzer.

"Everybody knows Roland. That's his house set back from the wharf. Of course, you know that, having grown up around here."

"I ran into him on my way into town."

"Lucky you. He mention our Ar-teest problem?"

He raised an eyebrow. "It came up."

"It always does with Roland. They're really quite nice, you know. From Wolfville. An ex-university teacher at Acadia, his wife and a woman friend—all artists. They pooled their money and bought the big house in the bay that circles in behind Roland's place."

"Next door to Roland." He shook his head. "Talk about your poor real estate locations."

"Well, they're not exactly next door . . . across the narrow inlet there, though Roland's back porch looks right over their home."

She nodded out the window. "That would be too close for me. Some days I'm very glad I have a hundred-yard buffer. The artists have created something quite elegant. You passed the house on your way in. It's completely modern and about as out of place as you could get in a little fishing cove like this. Three stories high, round like an early Shaker barn, with circular redwood decks all the way up. High-end furnishings, fancy art, a studio work space. It's way beyond Roland's comprehension. He was hostile to them from the start. It's been very hard on them to have him as a close neighbor, and I gather the whole thing has escalated. Ingrid claims Roland dumps his fish carcasses in the sea behind their house. It causes an awful stench. They had a trench dug at the edge of their property for drainage that unexpectedly blocked Roland's ability to pull his scallop boat onshore to winter behind his house. So Roland built a barn and used it to store his bait in an old cooler. He placed it at the edge of his property line, twenty yards from Ingrid's house. The motor faces their bedroom window. He runs it day and night and it's so loud they can't sleep."

"I'll talk to him. That will stop."

"Would you do that, really? That would be a very good thing."

"Roland's always been something of a bully—even when he was a kid. He's skinny but wiry and stronger than he looks. It's all toothless, though. He's about as powerless an individual as there is—no money, fewer friends, poor health and precious little backbone. He backs down if anyone at all confronts him. You might want to tell your friends that. Fact is, if they got a solicitor to issue a threatening letter or two, that would probably put an end to it."

Her eyes appraised him. "Maybe you really did grow up here," she said. "I sort of suggested the same thing to Ingrid, but they don't want to make waves, you know? They just want to be left alone. Her husband still works part-time at Acadia and he's gone a lot, leaving it to Ingrid and Grace to deal with all this. The last thing they need is a reputation as unpleasant city people who go to the police for every little problem."

"Roland's not a little problem. Especially if he happens to be your neighbor. I can't imagine having him right next door. Half a mile from my home was always way too close."

"You actually lived here in the cove, then?"

"Up the overgrown lane where the road circles the bay. The old family home's been closed up for years. I haven't even seen it yet. Came straight to see you first."

"Of course! I know the house. Used to belong to Jim and Beatrice Barkhouse."

"My parents."

Her face lit up. "My God, I'm finally starting to make the connection. Beatrice was a good friend. She had the most wonderful flower gardens. Many of my own came from her. She always talked about you, but she called you . . . Gar."

"Lot of my friends in high school called me Gar. She picked it up."

"I remember you at her funeral. You were the boy who stayed beside Jim the whole time."

"Hardly a boy. I was well into my thirties."

"And Jim died so soon after."

"Six months. He just couldn't imagine life without her. I tried to get him to come live with me in Halifax but he didn't want to leave her grave. He went there every day."

"I remember—it was so sad." She gazed pensively into the bay. "So you're alone, then."

"Only child. They wanted more but couldn't. I'm hardly alone, though. They both came from big families. I've got elderly aunts and uncles and hordes of cousins scattered all over the province. I was spoiled rotten when I was growing up. Even more so after I was injured." He swore under his breath at the slip.

She spoke the familiar words. "Injured how?"

Even after a dozen years, he hated telling the story. "It was a long time ago. I was serving in the war in Afghanistan. Pretty mundane, really. Roadside bomb killed three in my platoon and neatly took off my right foot above the ankle. I was the lucky one."

As everyone did upon hearing the story, she glanced quickly at the foot and then carefully avoided looking at it again. Fact was, one of the few—very few—things he actually liked about Roland was that he never failed to mention the foot. No *pussyfooting* around with Roland. She surprised him, though, by not changing the subject.

"I didn't notice it at all. I suppose you have a prosthesis?"

He looked at her for a moment, then reached down and lifted his pant leg, exposing the metal shaft. "They call it an "intelligent" prosthesis. Closest thing to a real foot on the market. Microprocessors, a gyroscope, actuators, software to replace muscle function. My dad used to say I had more brains in my foot than my head."

She laughed delightedly, her entire face lighting up. "That sounds like something Jim would say, all right." She put one hand on his arm. "I'd like to come up and see the old place some time, if you wouldn't mind. I spent many hours there. I've missed their company."

Before he could reply, a boat appeared around the headland, moving fast. It clearly had a powerful engine, and as it throttled down and angled into the wharf, Garrett recognized the man waving from behind the wheel: Tom Whitman, Coast Guard patrol for this part of the Eastern shore. He expertly maneuvered the craft in and jumped onto the dock, holding a line, the engine still sputtering.

"Hi Gar—Mr. Marshed at the grocery said you might be over this way. I could use a hand. Got a report of a possible smuggler coming into Ecum Secum harbor."

"Sure, Tom. Tom Whitman—Sarah Pye."

"An old high school friend, I suppose," Sarah said.

"How'd you know that?" asked Tom, holding the boat easily as it rocked in its own wake.

"I was just telling her how the guys sometimes called me Gar," said Garrett.

"Did you give her the whole nickname?"

"That's all right, Tom." He jumped onto the boat's deck. "I'll take a rain check on showing you the house, okay?"

"Not so fast," she said, those lips firmly set. "What's the whole nickname, Tom?"

He grinned. "It was Gar-goyle—because he had so many goyl friends."

Her eyes washed over him, and he looked away.

"Really?" she said.

"It was a long time ago," he said. "Thanks a lot, Tom. I've a mind to let you handle this by yourself."

Tom threw the rope on the boat and jumped aboard. "Better get going before my crew jumps ship."

5

THEY MOVED QUICKLY OUT ONTO the bay, passed Dougal's Island, then turned southwest toward the Eastern Shore Islands Wildlife Management Area. Their destination was no surprise. The maze of islands gave perfect cover for smugglers. There were a thousand coves to hide in. Ten thousand.

"How far out?" Garrett asked.

"About ten miles according to the source. It's a small fishing boat, but they're apparently fully equipped—EPIR, WSR, GPS, pulse Doppler—heading southwest, probably planning to turn into one of the bays and unload whatever their cargo is for transport to Halifax."

"Where'd the tip come from?"

"You kidding?" Tom stood at the wheel, spray from the bow flying past him. Garrett wore the yellow slicker Tom had given him. Most tips proved to be bogus—and always anonymous—but they all had to be followed up.

"Anyway," Tom said, "Not too many fishing boats sport all that hardware these days. Not enough legit business to pay for it. That alone's a sign it could be for real."

It was four in the afternoon and the spruce-covered islands were beginning to thrust their shadows across the ocean, like accusatory fingers, though the sun wouldn't set till after eight.

There was plenty of time to check things out—provided they could locate the craft in the surrounding archipelago.

Tom pored over the map as he steered. "I bet they're heading for Rupert's Island. It's got a deep-water channel between two rocky ridges. Perfect cover for a cargo transfer."

Garrett nodded, though it all seemed like a long shot.

It took thirty minutes to reach the island. Tom angled the cutter along the sliding rock ledges that plunged straight down into the depths and past a small spit attached to a tiny peninsula.

Garrett scanned the horizon with high-powered binoculars. There was something barely visible in the distance. "What's that?" he said.

Tom followed his finger. "It's an oil rig, past Lighthouse Point. Went in about two years ago. Part of the Sable Island group that discovered oil in the '90s."

"I didn't know there were any in this close."

"That's the closest one to the mainland, and it's probably seven or eight miles from here. Outside territorial limits. It raised something of a stink, I can tell you, being so close to the wildlife area and all. But it was included in the original contract and no one could stop it."

He throttled down until they were almost silent as the cutter rounded the point and they saw the boat. She was at anchor, a forty-footer crammed, as Tom had said, with radar and antennas. They could make out what looked like a much smaller craft tied up to one side.

"They'll see us any second," said Tom, "if they haven't already picked us up on radar. Might as well announce ourselves."

He pressed the throttle and the engine roared to life as they bore down on the boat. Thirty yards off her port side, Tom cut the engine back and turned on his loudspeaker.

"Attention fishing craft. This is the Coast Guard. We are coming aboard to inspect you."

Suddenly, the engine on the smaller boat sputtered. They heard a series of sharp popping sounds, and a few moments later, the sleek-looking speedboat tore past them, angling away into the islands at very high speed.

"Son of a bitch!" Tom thrust his own throttle to maximum, and they raced after the other craft, but it took only a minute to realize that even the powerful cutter was no match for the incredible engines of the speedboat. He cut power with a muttered curse and turned sharply back to the fishing boat.

"Holy Christ!" Garrett stared at the speedboat that was now just a speck in the distance. "They must be doing seventy miles an hour in that thing."

"We're always outspent in that department," Tom said flatly. "Those SOBs have more money than we do and they spend it on power. It's their escape hatch—that boat is top of the line. Hell, they're probably ten miles away already." He picked up his radio phone. "I'll call it in, but no one's going to find them."

They angled in to the larger craft; Garrett jumped aboard and tied the cutter fast. Despite all the expensive equipment, the boat itself was nondescript, stripped down, practically devoid of any attempt to provide comfort or décor. The owners clearly didn't want to attract attention and were prepared to abandon the craft if need be—so why waste money on niceties?

"Think they already offloaded their cargo?" Garrett asked.

"Possible. Though there wasn't much time between the tip and our arrival. That speedboat couldn't hold more than two or three people. There's got to be something here to justify abandoning the larger boat."

They quickly searched the wheelhouse. It had been stripped of papers, permits, everything. Garrett went below and came back shaking his head. "Nothing."

"It doesn't make any sense," said Tom, exasperated.

"Perhaps . . ." suggested Garrett, "they planned to pick something up instead of dropping off. Maybe we got here too soon. But if that was the case, why run off?" He raised his hand. "You hear something?"

Above the pounding of the surf against the side of the ship, there was a faint sound, like a low murmur.

"It's coming from over there." Tom pointed to the far end of the front deck, where there appeared to be a large white tarp. They hadn't noticed it at first because it was the same color as the deck.

Cautiously, they approached the tarp. The heavy canvas seemed to be moving slightly, sort of twitching. Tom pulled his revolver out. He nodded to Garrett, who reached down and threw the covering to one side.

Tom took a step back. "Mother of God!"

Garrett just stared, unable to move. Lying facedown on the cold decking were the bodies of four young girls. They had each been hastily shot once in the back. They wore shorts and simple shifts on top. They all had long, black hair and olive skin.

One of the bodies quivered.

"This one's still alive!" Garrett dropped to the deck and turned the girl over, cradling her in his arms. She was clearly Asian, not more than thirteen years old. Her eyes flickered open and stared at him blankly, then the light went out of them forever. He felt for a pulse, knowing it was a waste of time. Gently, he lowered her body next to her companions.

"Sick bastards." Tom leaned on the railing, looking like he was going to throw up. "Why'd they have to do that?"

"No loose ends. The girls might have been able to finger them or at least give information about their pipeline. These kids were probably destined for the escort services in Halifax. From what we've seen lately, Asians have been increasing in popularity."

31

Garrett stared out at the evening sunset. It was beautiful and peaceful and made a mockery of the scene on the deck. "I can't stomach this," he said bitterly. "If we hadn't shown up, these poor girls might still be alive."

"Maybe," said Tom. "But after a few weeks of what life had in store for them, they might have preferred to be dead."

He knelt, put one hand on the head of one of the children for a moment, then pulled the tarp back over the tiny bodies.

"I can probably navigate her back to port," Garrett said quietly, "if you follow behind in case I have any trouble." He thought about Tuttle's comment that he'd be able to spend more time on his boat in his new job.

This wasn't the sort of recreational boating he'd had in mind for his retirement.

6

BALES OF MARIJUANA WERE ONE thing. The bodies of four young girls were another altogether. The media had a field day. There was no way to keep something like this under wraps.

Deputy Commissioner Tuttle was on the phone to Garrett half a dozen times in twenty-four hours. "I said get a handle on things, Garrett. Not start a bloody damned war! Reporters want to know your role in this, whether you're representing a police presence on the Eastern shore or just happened to be in the old hometown. What the hell's going on?"

"You know as much as I do," said Garrett. "I've only been here for two days. Haven't even seen my house yet, but I sure want to thank you for easing my way into retirement."

There was silence on the line. Then Tuttle's tone changed. "Look, I'm not throwing you to the wolves, okay? We're going to investigate the hell out of this—see if we can find out which of the services might have been expecting some new blood. The public is up in arms. It takes things to a new level when these lowlifes start executing little girls."

"Yeah, right. They don't mind that little girls are raped by filthy old men on a regular basis. *That's* just business."

"Maybe you *have* been working this sort of thing too long," said Tuttle. "You're not going to change human nature, you know that. All we can do is hold the line." He paused. "You got anything on that fishing boat yet?"

"The registration number on her bow was false, of course. We're trying to track down the serial numbers on the engine. She must have slipped outside the legal limit and retrieved her human cargo from a freighter offshore. Next step was to offload the girls to a smaller boat that could dock at any of several hundred wharves along the Eastern shore between Halifax and Canso. It's a needle in a haystack. We'll have autopsies by day after tomorrow, and the fingerprints have been sent to CPIC, for all the good that will do."

CPIC was the Canadian Police Information Center, a computerized index of criminal justice information. The US equivalent was NCIC, the FBI's National Crime Information Center.

Tuttle just grunted. Young girls of thirteen or fourteen, from mainland China or maybe Thailand originally, had almost certainly never been fingerprinted in their brief, tortured lives. Another dead end.

"Just let me know if you find anything I can feed these blood-sucking reporters."

Tuttle signed off and Garrett headed to his car. He hadn't slept in forty-eight hours. His head felt like the inside of a trash compactor.

He headed down the coast road and turned into Misery Bay. A few minutes later, he was bumping slowly up the hummocky lane to the old Barkhouse homestead. The house was set in a meadow filled with wildflowers and surrounded by tall spruce.

Despite the traumatic events of the day, a kind of peace settled over his shoulders. There was a lot of family history in this place. It was good to be home.

As Roland had promised, the old house listed even farther into the meadow than he remembered. The building consisted of two steep-sided roofs connected by a low passageway. The passage had been the source of most of the leaks over the years. He could see where Roland had put on new tar paper. Despite his arthritis and limp, which would seem to limit his movement, the fisherman remained a damned good carpenter. The job was well done, and the inside was dry and relatively clean for a place that had been boarded up for years.

He carried his belongings into the downstairs bedroom and spread out his sleeping bag on the aging spring mattress. It would have to do until he could find time to replace the bed and get proper bedding. Despite his near exhaustion, sleep was slow to come. The face of the girl who had died in his arms danced before him when he closed his eyes. A pretty girl, only a child. It took a long time for the *why?* to drift away.

When he woke, he had slept through the evening and into early morning. In contrast to Halifax, where a hundred sounds threatened to wake him, the quiet of the sleepy meadow in the deep spruce was like a narcotic.

He lay in bed, gradually becoming aware of what could only be described as a gnawing sound. Then he caught movement and watched as a gopher poked its head out from an opening in an old wall panel.

"Well, hello. Nice to have company. Even yours."

His foot ached. He would never get over the strangeness of an ache in a part of his body that no longer existed. Phantom pain. The tiny, almost electrical spasms he felt were a signal that the foot was acting up. He took three Advil to get ahead of the pain, then attached a fully charged lithium-ion battery to his new foot and inserted it into its prosthetic socket. Good to go for another thirty hours.

He puttered around, cleaning the little kitchen, as the phantom ache slowly dissipated. He started a fire in the wood cookstove and primed the pump. The water that issued forth was clear and tasted like nectar. It came from the nearby tarn out on the bog and always had a slight bogweed flavor. It was a flavor he'd grown up with, like the wonderful, tangy bakeapple berries that grew on the bog.

With coffee and a bagel brought from Halifax—two days old now but still better than anything he could buy locally—he sat on the little deck off the kitchen and stared at the wildflowers dotting the meadow. The birds chattered noisily as the sun grew higher. A whiskey jack landed in the lilac bush a few feet away and begged some crumbs. The bird squawked suddenly and flew away.

"Sorry." Sarah walked into the opening in front of the house. "Your friend didn't like my arrival."

She held a walking stick in one hand and had on a green flannel shirt tucked into loose-fitting jeans. Her straw hat was perched at an angle, and she carried a plastic bag in her free hand.

"Scones," she said, gesturing with the bag. "I'll trade you for some coffee."

"You're on." He stood, suddenly aware that he was only wearing shorts. Sarah looked at his foot, real interest in her eyes.

"Wow, that's pretty elaborate, isn't it?"

"The original bionic man." He flexed his titanium heel and headed inside, returning in a moment with a steaming mug.

They sat side by side on the porch, sipping and nibbling at the scones.

"I heard about what happened," she said quietly. "It must have been horrible to find those poor girls. It's so remote and peaceful here . . . hard to believe such awful things go on behind the scenes."

"I didn't sleep too well. Kept seeing them, you know, especially the one who was alive for a few moments." He stared out at the woods. "My boss says I've been doing this too long."

She touched his knee lightly. "Maybe he's right, Garrett. If it interferes with your sleep, it might be time to think about doing something else."

"I want to sometimes. It's why I decided to retire. But then I think there aren't many who have as much experience at this as I do. I've dealt with prostitution most of my career. I can stop some of it; maybe help a few of these poor girls. And if I don't, who will?"

"What's going to happen?"

"It'll be a pretty big investigation. I'll have to go to Halifax for some of it. I'm not sure how much yet." The whiskey jack returned to its perch. Garrett broke off a piece of scone and threw it on the ground, where the bird eyed it suspiciously. "In the meantime, I have other things to do. Thought I'd make a visit to Ecum Secum this morning."

"Multi-tasking Mountie, huh?"

He smiled. "Guess I'm it for law enforcement around here, or will be once the hubbub surrounding the killing of those girls dies down." He thought fleetingly of Roland and the Ar-teests. One more thing to deal with.

"Like some company?"

"I'm . . . uh . . . not supposed to take civilians along on an investigation."

She tilted her head at him. "I used to do this stuff with my husband, Garrett. I know when to get out of the way. I could be helpful. I know my way around here better than you do. You're half a decade out of date. Besides, I know some of the troublemakers at Ecum Secum."

"Fact is, I knew the scene up there pretty well in my former life," he said.

She cocked an eyebrow.

"It was essentially a commune," he began, but then was saved by the sound of an ATV growling its way up the lane. The smelly beast roared into the opening in front of the house. Its rider stared at them and then killed the engine. Before he dismounted, Garrett was on his feet.

"Keith! Good to see you!"

His neighbor had red hair, a bit of a pot belly, and was pushing seventy. He grinned at them. "Heard you were back," he said. "Didn't expect to see you too, Sarah. More troubles with our new artist's commune?"

She grimaced, but couldn't help smiling at Keith. "It's hardly a commune. Just three people who want to be left alone. It appears all troubles lead to our trusty Mountie's door."

Keith shook Garrett's hand and sat on the edge of the porch. "You really going to live here?" he asked, shaking his head. "Your outhouse is probably more waterproof—or at least it was till Old Man Publicover went to war on it."

Garrett looked puzzled and Sarah laughed.

"It was the highlight of last hunting season," she said. "Harold Publicover took to coming up here and sitting in the outhouse with the door open. He said it was a good place to look for deer up the meadow, and he couldn't walk very far. Well, one evening he didn't come home for dinner and his . . . current . . . wife, Etty, phoned around and then got several of us to go looking for him. We ended up here and found him. He'd fallen through the outhouse floor and gotten stuck. Couldn't move a muscle from the waist down. Took all six of us to pull him free."

"Good Lord!" Garrett said, barely stifling a laugh. "Was he hurt?"

"Only his pride," said Keith. "And he said the best buck he'd seen in ten years came right up and stared at him through the open door and all he could do was stare back."

"Don't think I know Harold's current wife," said Garrett. "What's that? Number three?"

"You're way out of date," said Keith. "Etty is number five. Old Harold's pretty well fixed, and he's looked like he's had one foot in the grave for twenty years. All the old ladies on the Eastern shore have been playing musical chairs, vying to be the one he's married to when he finally kicks the bucket, so's they can inherit. But he keeps outliving them."

Keith segued seamlessly into one of his patented soliloquies. He was the self-appointed cove historian. An amateur genealogist, he knew the lives and histories of everyone for twenty miles in either direction on the cove road, as well as most of the nautical history, coastal tramps, fishing lore, and shipwrecks. Keith knew it all.

"Roland's brother said he was going to come up and fill in the hole so no one else got hurt. But Jennifer, his wife, told him to stay clear, it wasn't his business. She's from over Smith's Cove way, you know. Her dad and I went to school together. He married a Heemer down to Marie Joseph and they're a tough lot."

"A Heemer?" Sarah asked.

It was Garrett's turn to smile. "That's not the real family name, but it describes everyone who comes from Smith's Cove. Had to do with a brawl that occurred there years ago. Two guys from Halifax went into the wrong bar and insulted one of the locals. The local punched one of the outsiders a couple of times and then when he fell down, one of the other locals yelled to his friend, 'Don't hit heem, keek heem,' and damned if he didn't. They've been called Heemers ever since."

"Like I was saying," Keith went on as though no one had interrupted him. "Roland's brother's wife's father worked in the crab factory 'til he accidentally sliced off his thumb. Got a good settlement from the company and opened a gr'aage. Never was worth a damn to change a tire with only four fingers though. He hired Riley Vogler to do most of the work. Riley's family owned five hundred acres behind Roland's house, stretching back to Barcomb's Head. Roland had set his eye on the land—mostly bog. Said he was going to turn it into an international golf course like St. Andrews in Scotland and make a fortune. He had an idea how the tourists would flock in to stay at the fancy inn he was going to build, so's they could hit golf balls across the headlands and over the tarns. Darnedest thing you could imagine, golfers chasing tiny white balls through the fog in gum boots and rain slickers."

Garrett stared at him in amazement. "I never heard about it. So that's why Roland spent so much time on borderlines and tax maps. I never could understand why he was always arguing about who actually owned what on the bogs. Never made a lick of sense to me."

Keith nodded. "He wanted to nail down the property, thought it was his ticket to fame and fortune. When Riley's father sold out to a developer without telling anyone, I thought Roland would have a stroke, he was so upset. His dreams of presidents and prime ministers playing golf in his backyard went down the drain."

"That's pretty unbelievable," said Sarah. "But it just might explain his attitude toward his neighbors. Before Riley sold the land, Ingrid bought up several lots in order to protect them from further development. Roland was probably afraid that would undermine his scheme."

Garrett glanced at his watch and then at Sarah. "Look, I'm going up to Ecum Secum. Keith, will you keep Sarah company for a while till I get back?" He raised a hand as Sarah started to say something. "Maybe you can help me, okay? Just let me make this first contact on my own. Then we'll see."

She stared at him for a moment, trying to determine if she was getting the brushoff. Then she shrugged. "All right."

7

Ecum secum consisted of half a dozen home-built cabins spread over ten hilly acres where the group grew organic vegetables for sale at farmers' markets around the province. At least that was the way it was twenty years ago, the last time the place came on Garrett's radar screen.

He'd had a girlfriend who lived there. Ellie was the original flower child with long, cornrowed hair and a deep all-over tan, the result of going topless and sometimes completely naked when she worked in the gardens. She'd been a big draw. Most of the men in the area stopped in to buy fresh produce on an almost daily basis. Their wives, not so much.

It took all of six months for Garrett to realize that the only thing they had in common was sex. He bailed out. Two years later, he ran into her and she had two naked babies and had put on thirty pounds. He couldn't help wondering how the produce business was faring.

It was a twenty-minute drive to Ecum Secum. The approach, he remembered, was up a steep dirt pathway to the first and largest cabin. He realized things had changed the moment he saw the driveway. The dirt track had become a wide strip of asphalt lined with carefully trimmed plantings, each surrounded by wood chips. An equally well-crafted stone fence lined both sides of the driveway. A professional-looking sign read: ECUM SECUM HAVEN: REDIRECTING TROUBLED YOUTH.

It was the first of several surprises. The largest cabin had been replaced by a modern three-story home that sprouted wings in every direction. On the roof, an assortment of antennas and satellite dishes poked out. Parked in front was a pair of expensive motorcycles, known as crotch rockets in biker parlance. He wondered what part they played in redirecting troubled youth.

The other cabins looked more or less unchanged, including the one that he and Ellie had rocked late into the night with their bawdy activities. Still, the overall impression was of a tidy and shipshape organization, as unlike the hippy commune he remembered as one could possibly imagine. Either organic farming or redirecting troubled youth appeared to have grown lucrative in the intervening years.

He parked in a carefully delineated space in front of the house and went up to the front door. Before he could ring the bell, a voice from inside a fenced garden said, "Help you?"

A man sat on the ground picking asparagus. He wore only a pair of worn blue jeans hanging low on his gaunt frame. Garrett went over and leaned on the fence.

"Asparagus looks good," he said.

"Can't buy it. Goes to farmers' market. They got a contract."

"Anyone in charge here?"

He stopped picking and stared at Garrett more closely. "Sort of," he said slowly.

"Can I talk to him?"

He stared for maybe ten seconds, as though trying to absorb the difficult question. Finally, he said, "Lloyd."

Garrett waited.

The man went back to picking.

"And where might Lloyd be?"

An earthy finger sliced the air. "Up back."

It appeared the asparagus picker had used up his entire vocabulary, so Garrett walked around the house and followed the path leading to the next cabin.

There were several more small gardens. Most had one or two remarkably untroubled-looking youths weeding away. He rounded one small cabin and stopped dead in his tracks.

A well-built, blond-haired man with a tidy blond beard and a tidy blond mustache and wearing a tiny blond pair of bikini bottoms that made him look almost naked was standing on a patch of mowed lawn directing what appeared to be an exercise session. Facing him were some twenty young boys and girls, none more than fifteen. They also wore bathing suits and were making a go of following the calisthenics of their leader.

"Come on, Lila," said the blond man. "Pick up your feet and for God's sake stop scowling. It's not going to kill you."

The girl mouthed a silent "fuck you" but made an attempt to raise her feet an inch or two higher.

"*That's* better," said the man. He threw himself to the ground and began to do pushups, his lean and tanned body rippling in the sunlight. Garrett saw pure envy from the young boys and something harder to describe on the faces of a few of the girls, with the exception of Lila, who continued to exhibit total boredom with the routine.

The man had graduated to one-armed pushups, flipping from one hand to the other effortlessly. On one of his flips, he saw Garrett. He put both hands on the ground and bounced back up to his feet. "Eric, you take over for the run. We appear to have a visitor."

A pimple-faced boy jogged to the front and the others followed him off on a path that disappeared into the surrounding spruce.

"Help you?" he asked, coming over and wiping himself off with his T-shirt.

"You Lloyd?"

He nodded. "Don't think I know you," he said. "Thought I knew everyone around these parts. You a tourist? We only deal with young people here."

"I'm Garrett Barkhouse, the new RCMP officer for this section of the coast."

There was a slight hesitation, as though Lloyd was readjusting some little speech he'd had at the tip of his tongue.

"Glad to meet you," he said, offering his hand. "Be good to have some law and order in these parts."

"Some of your neighbors seem to think you could use some up here."

Lloyd smiled thinly. "I know there have been a few burglaries in town. My kids had nothing to do with it. We teach them to obey the law. People see our sign and figure trouble comes from troubled youth. But it's not always the case."

"Actually, I used to live here," Garrett said.

"Really?"

"That cabin back there," he said, pointing. "Stayed about a year with my girlfriend—almost twenty years ago."

"Before my time, I'm afraid."

"I understand you still sell to farmers' markets."

"Yes, we've been quite productive in that regard. It's pretty much what's paid for our new buildings and facilities . . . that, and the small amount of provincial aid we get for taking in troubled kids."

A striking blonde woman appeared on the porch of the cabin and said something in German. Lloyd looked annoyed, answered abruptly, and the woman disappeared inside.

"You speak German here?" Garrett asked.

"Most of the staff does. Last few years I've hired mostly workers from Germany. You can't find good help locally. I tried bringing people in from Halifax but it was the same story. Canadian kids, American kids, they're spoiled, you know. Actually, it's worked out quite well. The foreign workers set a good example for the challenged kids we deal with."

"Work ethic, huh?"

"Something like that."

Lloyd was too smug for Garrett's taste. He still had his shirt off, proud of his tight, muscular frame and not the least bit reluctant to show it off. He certainly seemed to enjoy exhibiting himself to the youngsters.

"We're trying to track down information on a fishing boat that was found offshore the other day," said Garrett, showing him a photo of the boat. "Ever seen her?"

He glanced at the picture. "Nope. Probably smugglers though. We get our fair share passing along the coast here. Pretty close to Halifax. I've found bales of marijuana on the shore myself."

"Did you turn them in?"

"Nope. Had a bonfire on the beach and cooked it. I don't allow any illegal substance here."

"How about alcohol?"

"Especially not. Our kids are all under the legal drinking age."

Garrett stared out at the cultivated gardens alternating with manicured lawns and wood-chipped paths. "You should have turned the drugs over to the RCMP," he said.

"What RCMP? Wasn't any around till you showed up. I don't have time to haul freight to Halifax. We generally police ourselves. Besides, RCMP mentality always assumes the worst and they would have blamed our kids for having the stuff."

Garrett nodded. That was probably what would have happened, all right. Just like the local people blamed the kids here when anything turned up missing. Much as he'd taken a disliking to Lloyd, he couldn't fault what he was doing here.

Lloyd looked at the picture again. "Say, isn't that the boat the papers said had several dead children on it?"

"The very one."

"Sick bastards. It's people like that that make our work here necessary. A number of our kids were involved in prostitution."

"In Halifax?"

"Based there. Escort services in the city deliver anywhere in the province, just like pizza."

"I'd like to talk to the girls who were in the profession," said Garrett.

Lloyd tightened. "I'm not sure I can allow that. They're trying to forget all about those times. It's not easy for them."

"I'm sure it isn't. But given what they've been through, I doubt a few questions are going to upset them. And it might give us a lead that could help save other girls from getting sucked into the business."

Garrett watched as Lloyd tried to think of some way to refuse to help.

"Look, we need help. It won't take long. I don't want to have to do this through legal channels, but I will if necessary."

Lloyd shrugged. "I'm not trying to be difficult. Uh . . . you have some sort of ID or something? I didn't realize Mounties operated out of uniform."

Garrett showed his badge. "Trying to keep our provincial presence low-key for now. Till I feel my way around. Doesn't always pay to advertise."

Lloyd was thoughtful for a moment. "How about I let you talk to Lila Weaver? She's been here a while and is pretty self-contained for a fifteen-year-old. She spent two years at a service in the city— Sweet Angels Escort Service."

Garrett nodded.

"You wait on the porch. I'll try to catch up to them."

He turned and jogged off. Garrett watched his taut little butt, barely concealed in the bikini briefs. The man verged on exhibitionism just being around young girls in that outfit.

He climbed onto the porch and sat in a green plastic Adirondack lawn chair. It was almost twenty minutes before Lloyd reappeared, followed mopishly by a sweating and obviously less than thrilled Lila.

"Lila, this is Mr. Barkhouse. He's a Mountie and wants to ask you a few questions."

Lloyd started up onto the porch, heading for another plastic chair.

"I'll handle it from here, Lloyd," Garrett said.

Lloyd paused abruptly at his dismissal, started to say something, thought better of it and disappeared down the path.

Garrett looked at Lila and then at Lloyd's disappearing frame. "He ever put any clothes on?"

Lila hooted. "He'd prance around starkers if he could get away with it." She climbed up onto the porch and leaned against the railing. "Not that he's got anything I haven't seen."

Garrett looked at her world-weary eyes. Fifteen years old. It was already clear that any semblance of a normal future, falling in love, marriage, a job, and kids was going to be a very long shot for this girl. She was right. There wasn't much she hadn't already seen.

"You get to read any papers here?"

"What, you mean newspapers? Hell, no. They don't let us see nothin' from outside." She waved a hand that took in the entire surroundings. "Looks pretty, don't it? But it's just a cage all the same. No bars, but if you run away, they catch you before you make it halfway to Halifax. There's only the one highway running to town. I've got to stick it out here another six months. It's nothing but a bloody reform school. They make us get up at six and do calisthenics, for Christ's sake. Like that's gonna prevent us from wanting some pot. Then they force us to swim—and the water's fucking cold! Then we spend the day listening to stupid motivational speeches or working in the gardens. It's the pits."

He nodded. "The life you were leading was probably lots more fun."

She sniffed. "You get used to it. One trick's pretty much like the next. Sometimes you get one's crazy in the head, wants stupid stuff, you know. But you learn how to deal with it."

He considered this and said, "Lila, there was a boat found off-shore the other day. It had four young girls on it, we think headed for the escort services in the city. When we stopped them, the men on board killed the girls and got away."

Her face turned white. "Bastards," she said softly.

"Exactly. I know you've been out of the scene for a while. But anything you might be able to tell me about how the services got their supply when you were there might help save other girls from going through what you did—or worse."

She looked out at the gardens. Even though she was sweaty and tired, her stringy, blonde hair unkempt and her face flushed, Garrett could still see why a pimp would want to latch onto her. She had a button nose, small mouth, and deep, wide-set eyes. She had long, slim legs and for her age was very well developed. She would have been a good moneymaker.

"If I help you, can you get me out of here quicker?"

"I can't make any guarantees, but I'll look into your case and help if I can. That much is a promise."

She nodded. "Lloyd said he told you the name of my service?"

"Sweet Angels."

"Some hoot, huh? If we were angels, I'd sure like to see the other guys—you know, the ones live a little farther down. But that's how they told us to market ourselves. Sweet angels who will do whatever you want."

"Who ran the business?"

"Margaret Allen was her name. Big Margaret. She had the biggest butt I've ever seen. She was all right, though. Took care of us okay, long's we did what we were told. Her old man was a different story. Hank was his name. 'Bout fifty. He had some other job and wasn't around a whole lot of the time. He let Margaret run things, but he'd come by couple times a month to sample the merchandise. The girls hated him 'cause he liked it rough and he beat one girl half to death when she was slow to do what he told her."

"Any idea where the girls came from?"

"We got a delivery three, four times a year. They always came by boat. We knew 'cause a lot of 'em were so seasick when they first arrived they could hardly walk. Hank cured 'em of that right quick and then they couldn't walk because of all the screwing they did in the first coupla weeks. They threw the new girls in at the deep end, if you know what I mean. Twelve, fourteen tricks a day right off the bat. Hank called it *conditioning*."

"What nationality were the girls?"

"All over the block. When I first came on, Russian girls were really big. The Slavic look, you know? Then we had a lot of spics. Just before I left, they were moving to more Asians—you know, Oriental types."

"Can you tell me anything at all that might help me track down their sellers?"

Lila thought. "We weren't told anything, but we girls talked among ourselves a lot. It was the only way we had to pass the time. I remember one thing. A coupla girls said they thought they'd been rescued at the end of the boat trip because there was a cop on board. But nothing happened."

Garrett couldn't conceal his shock. "How did they know he was a cop? Was he in uniform?"

"Not full Mountie gear. He had the hat, though, and wore a cop belt—you know—with night stick and handcuffs. Oh, yeah, and he had a badge of some kind."

"Did they say if he was armed?"

"Uh . . . I think so. At least one of the girls said something about a pistol."

The partial uniform was strange. Maybe he was on special assignment or possibly from some other government agency. He could have been undercover, but then why have any Mountie stuff at all? Could he have been a cop undercover, pretending to be a pimp pretending to be a cop? Garrett shook his head at the idea. It made no sense.

"Okay. Anything else you can think of ?"

"Yeah—'bout a year ago, we had a large group of spic girls come in. Must have been fifteen of 'em. They told us they'd come by plane. A big private jet. I guess it was a pretty cushy deal. Lots of food on board and fancy seats. A couple of the girls even got alcohol when they were brought into a private room. 'Course they had to have sex to get it."

"Did they say who with?"

"All they said was a coupla older guys."

He sighed. "All right, Lila. You've been a big help—I mean it."

She nodded, looking up at him with her wide eyes. "You won't forget about trying to get me outta here?"

"I won't forget. And Lila? They're not spics, they're Hispanics."

8

ROLAND TURNED HIS PICKUP INTO his driveway and stopped just past the bait barn. The engine for the cooler ground away in a satisfyingly loud manner. He listened to it for a moment, grunting in satisfaction.

He took two repaired scallop rakes out of the truck bed and tossed them to one side. His front yard was an amalgam of trash, dilapidated boat parts, heaps of plastic buckets, rotting fish nets, two old refrigerators, and several piles of dirt, one almost twenty feet high.

The original house was a small log structure. Years ago, Roland's father had stuck a modern two-story addition onto the back, creating a spectacularly ugly mismatch. This was Roland's space, where he could get away from Ma and spend hours immersed in chatrooms on his computer. Though he worked with various helpers doing carpentry and taking out sport fishermen, none of the workers cared for him and left him alone the rest of the time. His sole social outlet was through his computer friends, people he would never meet.

He banged into the house and his mother called from the living room, "Did ya remember ta do the shoppin'?"

"Yeah, Ma. I got the stuff." He unloaded the bags of groceries on a counter overflowing with dirty dishes. Rose, his mother, had always maintained a spotless home, but she'd been injured in a fall years ago. Her mobility had been greatly reduced as a result and now arthritis had set in. Her husband, Roland's father, quickly tired of caring for her and left. Now Rose could only get about with a walker and was unable to do much housecleaning. Roland was hardly a good substitute.

She plodded slowly into the kitchen, pushing her walker. Inactivity had turned her into an enormous woman, nearly three hundred pounds. She wore a pink housecoat that billowed around her stump-like legs. A half-burned cigarette dangled from her mouth. She stopped when she saw her son.

"That awful woman banged on the door this mornin'. Screamin' 'bout the noise. I din't answer." She paused to breathe heavily.

"Don't worry 'bout it, Ma. There's nothin' they can do. I'm a fisherman by trade an' I'm allowed ta keep my bait in a cooler."

This seemed to satisfy her. She stared at the little pile of groceries. "Where's my haddock?" she asked.

"Weren't none, Ma. No fresh fish at all today." He looked at her sad face. She could still pluck his heart strings with her obvious suffering. She was the only woman in his life. Always had been and always would be. When she died there would be no one on this earth who would care about him one whit. Sometimes that thought overwhelmed him to the point that he nearly cried.

He sighed heavily, then tried to smile at her. "Never guess who I ran inta, Ma. Garrett Barkhouse. He's goin' ta be the new RCMP officer in the area. I tol' him ta drop by 'n see ya."

Rose had no friends either. Her only visitors were Roland's cousin, Hank, his wife, and two kids who stopped by once a month. The truth was she didn't much like the visits. The kids were unruly and destructive. She and Roland had developed a system over the years. They each had their space, she in her La-Z-Boy surrounded by piles of craft supplies. She made knick-knacks and table mats for sale to tourists. Roland spent his time upstairs in the back room with his computer.

That was their life.

"Garrett? Yeah, I 'member him. A'w'ys used ta pick on ya when ya was little."

He winced. He and Garrett had tussled once or twice when they were in high school. He'd hated Gar because everything always seemed to work out for him. He got good grades, was a good athlete and as for the girls . . . well . . . they just went for him. It used to drive Roland crazy. Still, Gar had always tried to be neutral to his neighbor. When they clashed, it was because Roland brought it on, almost in spite of himself. He actually appreciated what he'd heard from others, that Gar never said anything bad about him behind his back.

"Aw—that was a long time ago, Ma. He don't seem like sech a bad guy now."

"Then you get him ta come 'roun' here and tell those La-de-dah ar-teests next door ta leave me alone. Bad 'nough I havta listen ta their silly parties on their back deck, all their nudie, artsy friends from Halifax sunnin' themselves nekkid."

"Aw, Ma, you can't see nothin'. It's the back side o' the house." Roland knew because he'd tried every way he could think of to get a look without success. Once, he'd brought his boat in close as he pretended to take a wide approach around the wharf, but they all covered up when they saw what he was doing.

He slipped past his mother down the narrow hall and closed himself into his room. Sometimes, he just needed to be alone. Heck, maybe it wouldn't be all bad once she died. He'd have the whole place to himself with no one needing constant help and errands run. Course, he wouldn't have anything to do all day once fishing season was over.

He flipped on the computer and sat in front of the screen, stooped over as usual. Maybe today he'd meet someone new online.

9

ARRETT STOOD NEXT TO ALTON Tuttle, who leaned into the podium in the RCMP Press room as if the tiny microphone might somehow hide his bulk from the assembled reporters.

"You identify the girls yet, Commissioner?" shouted a petite, meticulously dressed woman with an insistent, shrill voice.

Tuttle had on his hangdog, I'm-the-most-maligned-man-on-earth expression that Garrett knew so well. "That's *Deputy* Commissioner," he said. "Those poor girls were no more than thirteen, obviously Chinese in origin, probably from poor peasant families. There's no record of their fingerprints and unless . . ." he paused. "Until . . . we find who did this to them, it will be difficult to identify the victims."

"Do you know why they were being smuggled into the country?" came another shouted question.

"We have no proof at this point, but it seems obvious they were destined for the prostitution business. We've noticed a trend toward younger and younger girls. The lowlifes engaged in this sort of activity appear to have decided it's easier to train kids who have never known anything else for the task. One thing is certain. They sure weren't brought here to be adopted by loving parents."

The adoption of Chinese baby girls was big business in North America. It had always struck Garrett as bizarre. Chinese girls had two ways to get to the promised land of the New World: as the much-loved, adopted children of affluent Canadian and American families, or as prostitutes. There was no middle ground.

"Who's in charge of the investigation, Commissioner?"

Tuttle waved a hand at Garrett. "One of my best men. Garrett Barkhouse. He's also the man who found the girls and very nearly captured the perpetrators."

Garrett winced. The only thing he and Tom had captured was a face full of spray as the high-speed powerboat left them in its wake. He still felt guilty that their appearance on the scene was probably responsible for the girls' deaths.

The reporters turned their hungry eyes on the new face, and Tuttle moved subtly away from the microphone, forcing Garrett to take his place.

"Mr. Barkhouse," cried one reporter, "Have you traced the girls' destination yet? Do you have any leads that point to Halifax escort services?"

"We will be following that line of inquiry. And yes, we do have some leads that I obviously can't tell you about, as it would also inform the perpetrators."

The piercing voice of the tiny reporter rose above the din. "The *Deputy* Commissioner said you nearly caught the men who did this. Was your handicap responsible for your inability to catch them?"

Garrett nearly choked. "My handicap has never interfered with my ability to do my job. Just as your voice, apparently, hasn't interfered with yours."

The crowd burst into laughter. It was clear the woman was not much liked by her colleagues. She gave him a venomous look.

Tuttle leaned in and said, "We'll keep you informed of any new developments in the case. Thank you for coming." He gave Garrett a none-too-gentle push and they exited the room as another volley of questions surged after them.

"Great job," Tuttle growled as they moved down the hall. "You've given Kitty Wells every reason now to dog your ass in this case. She's tiny, but she's a pit bull. She'll make you pay."

Garrett shrugged. "She was going to do that anyway. Showing us up is how they get the most out of the story."

"So," Tuttle said, pausing for emphasis, "*do* you have any leads?"

"There's one or two things I'm going to look into here in the city."

"All right. Look into them. I don't want to know what they are for now. Gives me plausible deniability—like Nixon." He stopped in front of his office and met Garrett's eyes. "But you better get something fast."

"Fast isn't going to happen, Alton. Even when we had those SOBs in our sights, we couldn't catch them because they had outspent us on hardware. We get tips all the time, but they don't do any good. Somehow we've got to catch them in the act. Short of calling out the Canadian Navy for every anonymous phone call, that's not likely to happen. We've got to figure out how to sneak up on these fishing boats. That's hard to do in a Coast Guard cutter."

"You suggesting we need someone undercover?"

"Wouldn't hurt, but it's hardly feasible. They run a closed shop. Tighter than the Mafia ever was. They don't trust anyone. And if you cross them . . . well . . . there's never a second time."

Tuttle blew a cloud of smoke into the air, a disgusted look on his face. "Let me know when you find out anything . . . if you ever do." He turned and disappeared into his office, slamming the door in Garrett's face.

Garrett stood, choking on the smoke, and wondered for the hundredth time why he hadn't taken his retirement when he had the chance.

He went over to an empty desk and picked up a Halifax phone book, turning to the yellow pages. There were fourteen pages of escort services. A few had full-page ads with color pictures and graphics. Others consisted of little more than a single line with name and phone number. These were the freelancers, housewives looking to turn a trick or two a week for rent money. He found Sweet Angels in the mid-range, a small box ad with a line drawing of a man and woman kissing and the words: *Unique, Personalized Service. We accommodate ANY interest.*

He jotted down the number and then placed a call to the phone company. In two minutes, he had the address. It was on lower Barrington Street, along the waterfront.

Halifax had changed from the sleepy, provincial city of the 1950s to the busy, cosmopolitan tourist juggernaut of today. It boasted one of the busiest and most fascinating waterfronts anywhere, full of trendy restaurants and nightclubs, street musicians, museums, shops, and wharves lined with tall ships, best known of which was the famous Bluenose II, which sailed the seas but spent much of its dock time in Halifax. The city reminded him of San Francisco, with its steep hills and throbbing waterfront. He could sit on the lawns of the Citadel, the famed eighteenth-century fort that dominated the landscape, and watch sailboats float ethereally between the walls of tall buildings.

The address turned out to be a nondescript apartment building. There was no sign or any other evidence of the business. Escort services required little but a phone drop to carry out their lucrative concern. He climbed up the stoop and pressed a bell that was marked, simply, APT 5. At once, a woman's voice came over the intercom.

"Who is it?"

"Uh, I heard I could get a girl here," he said. Nothing ventured.

There was silence for a moment. Then, "You heard wrong." The intercom went dead.

He pushed the bell again, holding it down.

"Who the hell is it?" said the voice again.

"Police," he said. "Open the door."

The buzzer went off immediately.

Inside, there was an elevator with an OUT OF ORDER sign on it. He swore. Too many stairs caused his foot to ache. He plodded slowly up the five flights and rapped on the door.

A woman he identified at once as Big Margaret answered and stood, hands on bountiful hips, looking him up and down. Lila hadn't exaggerated. She did indeed have one of the biggest butts he'd ever seen. He stared past her into the apartment. In contrast to the decrepit building, it was elegantly furnished.

"Don't look like no cop," said Big Margaret. "Whataya want?"

"I'm looking for Hank," he said.

"What's that loser done now?"

"He here?"

"Naa. I haven't seen him in weeks."

Garrett managed to slide past her into the apartment.

"Hey, I didn't invite you."

"How's business?" he asked.

"What are you talking about? I live here."

"Your phone number is listed for Sweet Angels Escort Service."

"We run a legitimate business. It's completely legal. We provide escort company for people who need a date to attend some function or somethin'."

"Right." He looked around the room and found the telephone on a coffee table in front of a couch facing a huge flat screen TV. Also on the table was a pile of address books. He went over and began to leaf through them.

"You can't do that without a warrant," Big Margaret said indignantly.

"I'm investigating the deaths of several young girls—you may have heard about it on the news."

"What? Those babies? We don't hire no one 'cept young women over twenty-one."

"You won't mind then if I take these address books of yours and just make sure of that."

He watched her anger rise, but she controlled herself. She'd been in the business a long time and was used to a roust by the police.

"There's nothing in there but friends of mine, and none of it would be permissible in court without a warrant."

"Maybe," he replied. "You want to take that chance?"

She waddled across the room and sat in a fancy gilded chair. She said nothing and just stared at him, waiting.

"I'm not interested in you, Big Margaret."

Her eyes grew large as she realized he knew her name—her phone name. Her Madame name.

"I said it before . . . whattaya want?"

"I don't see any Chinese names in your book."

"Don't have any Chinese. Our girls all come from Europe, Russia mostly. They're working to support their families back home."

"Where would I go for a Chinese girl?"

She looked away.

"All right." He began to gather up the books. "I'll be sure to have these returned to you if there's no illegalities, as you said."

"Madame Liu," she said quickly.

"Where is she?"

"I don't keep track of every one of my competitors. And if she finds out you got her name from me, I'll deny it."

"What's she call her agency?"

"Madame Liu's Lulus."

"Cute." He stood up. "I'll be back if you're lying to me or if I decide you called Madame Liu to warn her about me. Understood?"

She nodded, relief washing over her that he didn't intend to take the books.

He left without another word, taking a deep breath once clear of the building. How people could make a living this way always seemed incredible to him. Big Margaret operated solely through her telephone. The girls were lodged somewhere else. Madame Liu, he felt certain, would be closer to her young girls in order to have better control over them. Before he went for her, however, he needed some backup.

10

SARAH DROVE SLOWLY PAST ROLAND's house. She was returning from shopping in the city. It was a rare, hot summer afternoon, the sun high in a crystal sky, the ocean sparkling with reflected light. She'd been enjoying the day until she got here. The Cribby household—mother and son Roland—always left her with the creepy sense that she'd suddenly been transported to a third-world country. Over the years, she and her husband had been friendly to Roland and his mother, but it was an effort that paid few dividends.

She pulled into Ingrid and Grace's driveway just past Roland's and got out of the car. At once the sound of Roland's refrigerator cooler assaulted her. It was hot and the compressor was working overtime and overloud. Evidently, Garrett hadn't had time to deal with this particular problem.

Ingrid came out the door and waved. She and her husband Leo were in their fifties. Along with Grace, a much younger thirty, the three had pooled their resources to purchase their elegant home in what was supposed to be a peaceful fishing cove.

"Hi Sarah. Welcome to paradise!" she said, yelling to be heard over the generator. Ingrid was silver-haired. She wore a bikini and sported an all-over leathery tan that she had probably started working on in high school. She was a freelance writer and illustrator. Her husband still taught art courses at Acadia part-time, and Grace was a self-employed artist.

"I wanted to tell you," Sarah said, "that our new RCMP officer, Garrett Barkhouse, told me he would get Roland to stop with the motor."

Ingrid's face lit up. "Do you really think he will?"

Sarah looked out at the bay. "I've only known him a few days, but yes, I really do."

"Well hallelujah! Let's have a drink to that." She turned and led the way into the house.

Although the home was beautiful, with a spectacular living room, a circular wall of windows facing the island view, and high-priced art and sculpture, it nonetheless was always a bit of a shock to Sarah. She'd known the picturesque little fisherman's house that had once graced the spot on the inlet.

When the cottage was sold, everyone speculated over who had bought it and how they might spruce the old home up, since it had been empty for several years. It was a shock when the dozers came in one morning and flattened the place. The building that rose in its stead was modern, full of glass and redwood decking, and, most disconcerting of all to the others who lived in the cove, round. That fact alone caused endless speculation and derogatory comments.

Still, she supposed it was progress of a sort. The tiny little homes of the fishermen were cold and drafty, the living rooms, kitchens, and bedrooms tinier still. The Germans had set the trend when they arrived, building new, modern homes with thermopane windows, super insulation, and high-efficiency furnaces.

They passed through the living area and out a sliding glass door to the deck, where Grace, a petite, startlingly beautiful blonde, greeted Sarah warmly. She also had a bathing suit on. It was practically a required uniform whenever the sun made its all-too-infrequent appearances this wet summer.

"Roland's going to be made to stop with the engine," Ingrid announced with a flourish. "We're going to drink ourselves into a stupor to celebrate."

"Oh my God," said Grace. "What'd they do? Threaten to take away his fishing license?"

"Nope," Sarah said, collapsing on a chaise lounge. "Our new Mountie's going to reason with him."

"Well he'll be a bloody magician if he can pull that off," said Ingrid. "Like reasoning with a ball-peen hammer."

"A very skinny ball-peen hammer," said Grace. She giggled and shook the ice in her drink. Evidently, they'd begun the celebration before the arrival of the good news.

Ingrid handed Sarah a Manhattan. It was the house drink and Sarah had never been here when there wasn't a pitcher standing by.

"Have you heard from Ayesha?" Grace asked. "I haven't seen her in almost a week."

Ayesha was the daughter of Ali Marshed, the Iranian who ran the grocery. She was fifteen and going through something of a teen-age crisis. Grace had taken a liking to the girl, immediately recognizing that she was depressed. She hired Ayesha to help in their garden. The pay was good and the girl's father hadn't objected. For the past several weeks, she'd arrived in old jeans and chamois shirt and seemed to revel in getting herself as dirty as she possibly could. Seeing how much escaping from the dreary little store meant to Ayesha, they had all taken to her.

"Hmmm," Sarah said. "I saw her in the store yesterday and she was kind of quiet, barely said hello. I wonder if something's happened."

"I bet that bastard Roland has been bending Ali's ear again about what a bad influence we are on the girl," said Ingrid with a snort.

"You *are* kind of a scary looking broad, Ingrid," said Grace with a laugh, but Sarah could tell she was concerned.

"I'll see if I can talk to her when I stop at the store tomorrow," Sarah said. "Usually Ali's not there late in the afternoon."

Conversation turned, as it inevitably did, to the neighbors.

"I actually saw Rose the other day," said Grace.

"You didn't!" said Ingrid.

Grace raised her right arm in a mock two-fingered salute. "Scout's honor. She hobbled out onto the back deck with her walker. First time I've seen her in a year. I think it's actually the first time she's been outside in all that time. God, she was even bigger than the last time I saw her."

"Did you talk to her?" Sarah asked with interest. The houses had rear decks that were close enough for conversation.

"You could call it that, I suppose. I called hello. I think she grunted. Or maybe it was a wheeze. I'm not sure. Anyway, soon as she saw me, she galumphed back inside like she was afraid I might contaminate her."

Sarah sipped her drink and stared out at the islands. A fishing boat was coming in on the late afternoon tide, its engine chugging in a slow, repetitive thrum. The boat turned around Dougal's Island and angled obliquely toward them.

"Christ!" Ingrid swore, sitting up. "Here he comes again. Looking for an eyeful." She jumped out of her chair. "Well, I'll give him one."

She jumped up, went to the deck railing and tore off her bikini top. She put her hands above her head and did the bump and grind.

The boat was now less than thirty yards out and Sarah could clearly see Roland at the wheel. He had a pair of binoculars up to his eyes.

"Oh, come on, Ingrid," Sarah said. "You're just encouraging him."

"No, I'm pissing him off," she replied, still bobbling her large breasts. "He'd rather see Grace doing this, so I'm just irritating him."

Grace got up and went over beside Ingrid. For a moment Sarah thought she was going to take her top off too. But she just put her hands on her hips and glared out at the boat. After a moment, Roland put down the eyeglasses and turned the boat around the little headland that separated them from the wharf.

"Guess he didn't like the show," said Ingrid, putting her top back on. "What an asshole."

Sarah wasn't sure she cared for the show either. She finished her drink, made her excuses and left. She hadn't realized how tense the whole relationship between Roland and his neighbors had become. She made a mental note to tell Garrett to get to work on the generator issue soon or there was going to be real trouble.

11

LONNIE BACKUS WAS GARRETT'S COUSIN. One of more than a dozen, not counting second cousins. They'd grown up together, hung out since they were kids, and gotten into trouble as teenagers. They once set fire to an abandoned barn in the winter, then drove a Ski-Doo far out onto the frozen bay and watched it burn to the ground. The two boys had never been caught for any of their escapades, which was fortunate, since if they had, it would likely have preempted any career in law enforcement for Garrett.

Both of them had gone into enforcement, of a sort. Lonnie was a longshoreman on the docks in Dartmouth and had become an enforcer for the unions. Strong-arm stuff, though generally all anyone had to do was look at Lonnie and they'd do whatever he said. He was six-foot-four and solid muscle with a bull neck that emerged from his shirt collar like a wedge of oak.

When Garrett entered the military, Lonnie tagged along, because, he said, he had nothing better to do. In the army, he was the go-to guy, the strongest and most reliable. Garrett once saw him strike a member of the Taliban, a giant of a man in his own right, so hard during close hand-to-hand combat that he killed the man. Another time, in a dispute with a member of their unit who had a black belt in karate, he watched Lonnie simply stand

and take every blow the guy could throw at him. He hadn't even grunted. Then he picked the guy up and threw him twenty feet. That was the end of the fight.

They served together in the same unit and fought in the mountains around Kandahar. It was Lonnie who fashioned a tourniquet and cradled Garrett's head after his foot was blown off. Ever since, the big man had helped Garrett out whenever possible. Everything from chiding him over his phantom pain to offering backup when Garrett got in over his head with the RCMP and needed to stretch the legal limits.

So it was hardly surprising that once again Lonnie had offered to go along on a legal-limit-stretching bit of after-dark sleuthing.

Garrett had decided to try a different tack with Madame Liu's Lulus. Instead of confronting Ms. Liu directly, they staked out the brothel, which was located in an upscale part of Bedford Basin. Set back on extensive grounds, the house fronted on the basin, which was filled with small pleasure craft. The building was a spectacular, rambling Victorian with at least a dozen bedrooms, if he had to make a guess. Very posh accommodations. The clientele was certain to be upscale.

Lonnie sat in the car sipping a Keith's Ale and watching a cold rain spatter the windshield. "How long we going to sit here?" he asked.

"You got someplace better to be?"

"Kandahar would be someplace better."

Garrett felt a twinge in his phantom foot. "Every time you mention the war, my foot starts to ache."

"Suck it up," said Lonnie. "I can't mollycoddle you along the rest of your life. Besides, you don't even have a foot. So how can it hurt?" He refused to accept the concept of phantom pain. Lonnie dealt in the world of real pain.

"Mollycoddle?"

"Let me know if I use words too big for you."

"Car coming."

They sank into their seats, which in Lonnie's case meant that his entire head and shoulders still showed. But the car brushed past them in the rain and turned into the sweeping driveway. It was a black limo, the windows heavily tinted.

"That's a clue," Garrett said.

"Funny, I thought it was a limo," said Lonnie. "What are we going to do?"

"Take a hike."

"Shit. These shoes are brand new."

"Little mud's good for them—help break 'em in. You carrying?"

Lonnie stared at Garrett as though he'd asked if he had a left nut.

"Okay, just keep it holstered is all. What we're doing isn't strictly legal, you know, without a warrant."

Lonnie smiled. "You Mounties do have your limitations."

They ran from the car up the driveway and huddled under a rare chestnut tree. The rain wasn't heavy, just cold, like little icy needles against their skin. They could see the limo parked in front of the entrance, which was bathed in light from the foyer.

"I'll go 'round the right. You take the left," Garrett said. "Just look in the windows. See what you can see. Meet back at the car in ten minutes. We'll reconnoiter."

"Always wanted to add Peeping Tom to my extensive resume," Lonnie grunted, but he lumbered off.

In fact, the house might have been designed for Peeping Toms. There was plenty of cover, with numerous shrubs delineating carefully mowed lawns and big, twelve-over-twelve windows. Garrett stayed wide of the foyer, in the shadows of the trees, then parked under one of the windows and peered inside. The room was empty, as were the next two that he checked. Finally, he came to a larger space. It was an enormous living room with a stone fireplace, leather loveseats, and dimmed lighting. A Chinese woman and man stood in front of the fire talking. They were quite intent about whatever it was they were discussing.

The man turned and called something toward a hallway that disappeared out of sight. In a moment two more men entered, along with three young Chinese girls.

Garrett stiffened, but the girls seemed entirely at ease. They bounced down onto the leather couches, giggling and talking to one another. The Chinese woman went over and stared at them. She said something and the girls immediately stood up and took off their clothes. The woman looked them over, then turned abruptly and crossed to a desk, where she unlocked a drawer. She handed a wad of bills to the man. He nodded once, gestured with his head to one side, and he and the other men left.

Garrett had seen enough to know what had transpired. The girls had just been sold to Madame Liu. He'd have to figure out what to do about that at some point. But right now what he wanted more than anything was to follow the man who had sold them.

He jogged back across the lawn, cursing when his prosthesis landed in a large, soggy puddle surrounding a flower bed filled with some kind of fertilizer. Probably cow manure with his luck.

Lonnie was already back at the car waiting for him.

"You're late," he said.

"Nice to be missed. Get in. We're tailing the limo when it leaves."

They sat in the car for about a minute before the big car turned slowly out of the drive. Lonnie said, "Something stinks."

"I know. The guy in the car just sold three girls inside. But I don't want to move in now. I'm hoping they'll lead me to someone—maybe a bad cop."

"No. I mean something stinks. *You* stink."

Garrett looked down at his shoe and realized it was covered in manure. "My new cologne," he said. "Deal with it, and get going. I don't want to lose those sons of bitches."

That was unlikely. Lonnie had been a tank driver in Iraq. He could make anything with a cylinder purr like a pussycat. You hadn't lived till you'd seen him on a Harley. He looked like an elephant riding a motor scooter. It had always amused Garrett to watch his cousin squeeze himself into a tank. It was a very tight fit, but Lonnie had absolutely no problem with claustrophobia.

They kept an easy distance behind the big car. Though there was little traffic this time of night, the rainfall made it unlikely they'd be spotted. They followed Route 2 along the shore of Bedford Basin all the way downtown, hooked up with Barrington Street and funneled onto the Angus L. Macdonald Bridge that took them across the harbor to Dartmouth.

Garrett looked down on the warships of the Canadian Navy parked just off the bridge access, their turrets drifting in and out of a fogbank. The lights of the city twinkled in the mist along both shores. A steady rain made the scene as dismal as could be.

"Typical Halifax weather," Lonnie groused.

"A wonder Governor Cornwallis didn't turn around and go home when he got here," said Garrett. "Hell of a lot better weather in the old world." But they both knew there was more to it than that. Halifax had one of the best protected ice-free harbors in the world.

They turned left on Victoria Road, right on Woodland Avenue, passed through the rotary, and ended up on the shore of a small body of water called Lake Micmac. The limo pulled into a small private parking lot. Lonnie drove past and pulled over to the side of the road.

By the time they got out of the car and crept back, they discovered what was happening. The occupants of the limo had boarded a small launch at a dock and were motoring out onto the black lake. In a moment, only its running lights could be seen.

"Damn! We've lost them."

"Maybe not," said Lonnie. "Wait a minute."

They watched the boat's lights dwindle and then heard its engines cut back.

"Going to that island," said Lonnie. "We can always come back in daylight and check it out."

Garrett nodded. If it was a private home, it was certainly well isolated, the kind of place someone might want if he was up to no good.

"Okay," he said. "We'll be back."

12

I F LONNIE AND GARRETT WERE going to get on that island, they'd need transportation. A standard kayak wasn't feasible for Lonnie. He was wider than the cockpit. At an outfitter Garrett knew on the outskirts of the city, he purchased two solo kayaks, one with an open cockpit for Lonnie. He paid for them with an RCMP voucher. Tuttle was going to love that.

He took the boats straight to Sarah's. She wasn't home, so he went out alone for a test run. When he got back an hour later, she was waiting on the pebble beach by the wharf.

"I was thinking about calling the police," she said, as he pulled up and stepped out of the boat. "But then I remembered you *are* the police and I couldn't very well report that you were missing to you."

"Elementary, my dear Watson." He shook off his life jacket and tossed it and the paddle into the boat. Then he pulled the kayak above the high tide line.

"What happens when you get the bionic foot wet?"

"Never a good thing, but it stands up pretty well under most conditions."

"Where have you been?"

"Doing a little recon out beyond Heron Rook Island."

"There's a storm supposed to be coming in," she said. "Left-overs of that hurricane that hit down in Florida. One of them anyway. Been a busy season that way. You don't want to be out when something like that makes landfall."

"Wouldn't be the first time," he said.

She raised an eyebrow. "You've done a lot of kayaking then?"

"Long time ago, when I was in my twenties. Fact is I was kind of into it. Kayaked around the entire province of Nova Scotia. Took three years. I got so I could replace a broken rudder cable in a gale."

She looked suitably impressed. "So what sort of recon were you doing?"

"I'll tell you in exchange for a scone and a cup of tea."

Inside, Sarah went about making tea while Garrett put an obscene slab of butter on his scone.

"I've actually got two avenues that might require a little boating," he said. "One is checking out an island on Lake Micmac in Dartmouth, whose owners probably don't take kindly to trespassers."

"And the other?"

He stared out at the ocean. "We can't catch those SOBs in a Coast Guard cutter. They can hear us coming for an hour."

"So you're going to sneak up and ram them with your kayak? Good plan."

"Well, you got the 'sneak up' part right. Not so sure about the ramming part."

"You won't do that alone, will you?" The concern in her voice was real.

He stopped eating and looked at her. "No, I won't. Probably Tom and maybe one of my cousins will go along. Anyway, nothing can happen until we get the next tip. Then, we'll see. But . . ."

"What?"

"Would you go for a paddle with me this weekend, take along a picnic, maybe check out that whale?"

She brought his tea over and put it on the table. Then she lingered, putting one hand on his shoulder. "Are you asking me out on a date, Garrett, or just wanting company to help you find the whale? It's been a long time and I can't really tell."

He looked into her eyes and studied the set of those thin lips. Then very slowly, he pulled her down and kissed her. She hesitated at first, then relaxed and put the requisite amount of effort into it.

When they separated, she stood up, her hand still on his shoulder, but squeezing a little tighter. "I guess that means it's a date, huh?"

"Pretty *and* smart is my favorite combination in a woman."

13

ROLAND WAS SEETHING AS HE pulled his boat up to the wharf. God damn Ar-teests were insufferable. They were trying to make a fool out of him, which of course was the result of his efforts to catch them, especially Grace, sunning themselves. Ingrid's naked body did nothing but anger him. She was actually making fun of him by exposing herself. He felt the anger rise in him like bile.

Ingrid was the worse of the two, hands down. He couldn't imagine what her husband saw in her. He didn't find her angular features and large breasts the least bit attractive. But Grace was something different. He couldn't keep himself from thinking about her. She was just so incredibly beautiful and had been a part of his fantasies from the moment he first laid eyes on her.

He finished tying off the boat, carried the handful of bait fish he'd caught to his cooler, and deposited it inside. He listened to the satisfyingly loud roar of the compressor. Maybe he could tweak it a bit louder still. Trouble was he didn't want to burn out the motor. He decided to leave it alone for the time being.

As soon as he entered the house, Rose called from her room. "Whad'ya catch?" she said.

"Nothin' but bait fish, Ma. There's nothin' left out there. If it wa'nt fer the scallops, we'd be eatin' seaweed all winter long."

"It's the seals," said Rose. "Critters eat all the fish. Them and the oil rigs fouling the water."

It was a long-standing belief that seals were responsible for the declining fish industry. In recent years, fishermen had taken to shooting the creatures on sight. It was nonsense, of course. The local industry had simply fished out the banks, in consort with the big factory ships from Japan and Russia. Seals had nothing to do with it—except to suffer along with everyone else.

"Did I tell ya," Rose said, "I saw Grace out on her deck. I swear all she had on was a pair o' Kleenexes shaped like a bikini. I don't know what we done ta deserve havin' ta live next ta a house full'a perverts." Her voice petered out and Roland knew she'd lost the energy necessary to continue her conversation yelling from the other room.

Good thing. He didn't want to hear about it. He cursed his luck at having missed Grace. He limped up the stairs and down the tiny, narrow hall to the room at the back of the house. This was where he had the best view of his neighbors. Rose never came upstairs. She was too fat and crippled.

He had a chair set up where he could sit and just stare at the house next door. There was a set of binoculars on a table next to him. At night, he'd sit in the dark waiting for a light to go on in any of their windows. He'd only gotten a glimpse or two, though. It was as if they knew what he was doing and avoided activity at the rear of the house. Which only served to make him even more frustrated.

He heard a car coming round the cove but didn't get up. No one ever visited them. It might be a delivery, of course. He ordered fishing equipment through parcel post and Rose was always getting stuff for her crafts.

When the car turned into their driveway and he heard the engine stop, he hoisted himself out of the chair, took one more look at the neighbors' house, and went to see who it was.

"There's som'un at the door," Rose yelled needlessly.

Roland opened the door and stared at Garrett. He was so surprised at the visit, he was nearly speechless. He hadn't really expected Gar to stop by as he'd asked. No one ever did.

"Hi Roland," Garrett said. "Glad I caught you home. Can I come in?"

"Can I do somethin' for ya, Gar?"

"Been wanting to talk to you is all. Thanks for the roofing repair on the old house. It's a real nice job. Hundred dollars cover it?"

"Sure." Roland took the money in Garrett's hand.

"Can I say hello to your mother?"

Roland led the way into his mother's room where she sat like an immense Buddha behind piles of wood, fabric, and paints. The rest of the room was filled with stacks of various craft supplies, old magazines, and discarded boxes of chocolates. The strong odor of her presence hung over everything. She was so heavy and immobile that she rarely bathed.

"Hello Rose," Garrett said. "How are you getting along?"

"Had better days," she grunted. No one offered him a chair, which were all piled high with debris anyway. "Glad you're here, though. Mebbe you can do somethin' 'bout those disgustin' Ar-teests next door. A'w'ys prancin' about wit' no clothes on. Me and Roland is tired of it."

"Uh-huh," Garrett said, not believing a word of it. Roland would be the last one to protest any girl going naked within his line of sight. But it gave him an opening. "Well, I'll certainly talk to them about that, Rose. We want to keep the peace amongst neighbors."

"Neighbors, horseshit!" Rose said. "All their druggy friends from the city hang out here. Ya need ta git a warrant and search the place. It's full'a illegal stuff."

"Well, I'm here to make sure no one breaks the law, and I'll keep an eye on them, you can count on it." He took a deep breath. "But while we're on the subject, Roland, I've come to tell you you've got to either fix or turn that compressor off. Hell, I couldn't hear myself think when I got out of the car. It's way beyond any legal decibel level."

Roland's face turned red. "I got a legal right ta keep my bait from spoilin.'"

"Come on, Roland. You and I both know why you're doing this. It's simply to aggravate your neighbors. You don't even need bait this time of year and when you do, you can store it at the fisherman's co-op. Now you have a right to keep a cooler here if you want. But the only way I'll allow it is if you get a new compressor and insulate it so there's no sound coming from it that will bother people."

Roland was nearly spitting in frustration but, true to form, he wasn't about to confront the police. The fact that it was Garrett who represented the authorities only made it worse, because Garrett knew Roland was all bluster and Roland knew Garrett knew it.

"Now, I'll give you a week to correct the situation. After that, I'll put a provincial police lock on the thing and you won't be allowed to use it—fair enough?" Garrett decided to leave it there. He could see Roland was boiling.

"Well, it was nice to see you, Rose. You're looking fine as usual." He headed for the door, more than ready to breathe some fresh air. "Thanks again, Roland, for the roofing job. I'll see you around." He let himself out, already hearing Rose lay into her son. He wondered for the hundredth time how a man could live his whole life with his mother. Garrett had loved his mother but wouldn't have wanted to live with her.

"Ya can't put up with that, Roland," Rose was saying to him. "Ya got a right ta keep your fish. Whadd'ya gonna do about it?"

"Aw, Ma . . ." was the last thing Garrett heard as he stepped off the porch.

14

"READY? LIFT." GARRETT RAISED THE back of the Wilderness Systems double kayak off the roof of the Subaru, while Sarah struggled with the front.

"Watch out for the antenna," he said.

"God, it's heavy," said Sarah. "I've always used a solo. What's this thing weigh?"

They carried across the pebble beach and set the boat down, half of the craft in the water.

"About a hundred twenty pounds." He hesitated. "But I've got the paddles, life jackets, lunch and two bottles of a very nice Cabernet in the cockpits, so it's probably more like one forty."

She swatted him. "Asshole! No wonder. I've a mind to make you load it by yourself when we get back."

It was Friday morning. A few wispy clouds scudded rapidly across the sky, seemingly whipped by an invisible force, for there was no discernible wind at ground level.

"You want bow or stern?" Garrett asked.

"Doesn't matter, but she'll probably trim better with you in the back."

They stepped into the spray skirts, and after Sarah was in place in the bow, Garrett pushed off.

Sarah sat back comfortably in her seat, slipped the skirt over the gunnel, and closed her eyes, enjoying the sensation of floating.

"I love this," she said. "I always feel like I'm on an invisible plain, poised between sky above and water below. But it's a plain we could ride right round the world if we wanted to."

"Pretty philosophical for so early in the morning."

She turned and gave him a dazzling smile. "I'm just glad to be doing this, Gar. Thanks for asking me."

"So it's Gar now, is it? Getting a little familiar, aren't we?"

"I'm feeling a little familiar," she said. "I might even call you Gar-goyle before the day is out."

They headed straight out past Dougal's Island, then Barrel Island and Seal Island. Sarah paddled with an easy and fluid motion. Clearly, she had done a good deal of this. She directed Garrett to head northeast beyond Seal Island and, after an hour or so, they were approaching Heron Rook, where the whale had washed up several years before.

"I don't smell a thing," Garrett said as they neared shore.

"Yes, the smell's long gone. We might still pick up a bone or two, though, if it hasn't been completely picked over."

But when they landed, the site was utterly clean, with no sign of the whale at all.

"That's incredible," said Garrett. "It's only been three years, right? There's nothing left at all of a creature that must have weighed thirty tons."

"Ocean's a good cleanser, all right. At least that's how I've always thought of it—as clean. Pristine," she said. "But after hearing about those poor girls who were killed out here, it doesn't seem quite so clean any more. And I hate that."

Garrett carried the pack with lunch as they hiked the length of the island and then waded across a pebbled spit that separated the island from a tiny islet at one end. As they came around the islet and faced the open sea, the wind picked up and breakers crashed against the rocks.

"Let's go up there," said Sarah, pointing to a bluff covered with vibrant green moss and sporting a single weathered and barren spruce, dripping with storm-blown seaweed. Garrett climbed up first, then reached back and gave her a hand.

The view of the outer islands was spectacular and the warm summer wind blew the smell of salt air over them.

"What a spot. I bet you bring all your boyfriends here."

She was quiet for a moment. "My husband and I came here a few times."

"I'm sorry," he said. "Stupid thing to say."

"It's all right." She turned to him, raised her head and gave him a quick kiss. Her breath was sweet and Garrett wanted to linger, but she broke away and said, "Let's eat. I'm starved."

While Sarah dug out the sandwiches, Garrett opened one of the bottles of wine and filled two plastic cups. The moss was as comfortable as a feather bed. They could put their drinks down by burrowing them deep into the thick ground cover. Garrett wore shorts and Sarah looked at his foot with fascination.

"You don't seem to have any trouble with it at all," she said. "Was it very hard at first?"

Normally he hated talking about his injury, but Sarah made it easy to discuss for perhaps the first time in his life.

"It was hard to accept for a long time. Silly, in a way. Other guys lost much more. Multiple limbs, legs right up to the hip. Mine seemed too insignificant to justify a lot of sturm und drang about it. So I kind of bottled it up and just . . . dealt with it. But I went through a period of depression. Almost all the guys who went to Afghanistan suffered depression, PTSD. Some of the most screwed up had no physical disabilities at all. Everything was in their heads."

"Your cousin was with you when it happened?"

He nodded, took a sip of wine. "Saved my life. Everyone else was injured or shell-shocked. I would have bled to death if he hadn't been there."

She rolled over onto her stomach and stared out at the ocean. "Sounds like you two have been close all your lives. It's good to have that, Gar. A lot of only children have no one once their parents die."

"You?"

"Uh-huh. I was an only child of only children. I have no siblings, cousins, aunts, or uncles. My grandparents are long gone. There's no one but me. I have friends, of course, who mean a lot to me, but I think it's why my husband's death affected me so strongly. He was my future in a way, you know? We hoped to have lots of kids."

"Hard to be alone," Garrett said. "Lonnie could identify with that. He's got lots of siblings and cousins. But he's never been successful in finding a woman to love him and start a family with. You haven't met him yet or you'd see why. He's huge. A bull in any china shop. I think he's not bad-looking myself, but women are just scared of him. And I'll tell you, despite what he does for a living, he's got a real heart of gold. If he likes you, he'd do anything for you. If he doesn't . . . best to get out of town in a hurry."

She considered him mischievously. "What about you? Any ex-wives or children kicking around?"

"Nope." Garrett adjusted his wine in the moss. "After I lost my foot, I kind of went through a period where I didn't want to be close to anyone. A depressed, one-legged ex-grunt is a lot to foist on a companion."

"You're not one-legged, only one-footed."

He shrugged, conceding the point.

She wanted to ask him more but felt his reticence. "I talked with Ayesha the other day," she said.

"Who?"

"Ali Marshed's fifteen-year-old daughter, the man who runs the grocery. The ladies living next to Roland thought she was depressed and invited her to come work on their garden. It's been very therapeutic for her, I think."

"That was good of them. I imagine being fifteen and having to work all day long in that dreary little building would depress anyone."

"She hadn't come by to work in the garden for a week, so I went to see her. When Ali's there, you can never talk to her because he forbids it. He's very strict, and I think she's scared of him."

"Really?" He leaned back in the moss on one elbow. "It's not good for a girl to be afraid of her father. You don't think there's anything else going on, do you?"

"What do you mean?"

"Abuse of some kind."

Her forehead furrowed. "I hadn't considered that. We thought she was depressed about working at the store, but I suppose there could be more to it than that."

"She's said nothing to you, though?"

Sarah shook her head.

"Well, perhaps we shouldn't make too much of it. Understanding what goes on inside families is tough. I've seen the dynamics in a lot of families whose daughters went into prostitution, and it's not pretty. But it's also usually not abuse—at least not the official sort. There's plenty of misunderstanding, lack of communication, coldness, withholding of love—all the bad stuff that tears families apart. But that's not abuse, at least in a legal sense. Just stupidity." He took another sip of wine and bit into a sandwich. "Still, it wouldn't hurt to keep an eye out for her if you're concerned."

"I guess you're right. I don't know enough about it. You've been around this sort of thing a lot more, Garrett. Maybe you should come talk to her with me. You might pick up something I've missed."

"I can do that." He tossed the dregs of his drink over the rocks and stared at her until she blushed.

"And I can do this," he said. He put one hand gently on her shoulder and turned her over. He kissed her deeply and felt the passion rise quickly in both of them.

She rolled on top of him, her body pressing against him urgently, as Garrett sank into the moss under their combined weight. He ran his hands under her blouse and felt the firm, slim muscles of her back. She moaned slightly, arching her back upwards, her face toward the sea, and then he felt her freeze.

He stopped. "What's the matter?"

"Garrett," she whispered. "There's something out there—in the sea."

Reluctantly, he rolled her off and turned to look. Floating twenty yards away, washing with the waves against the rocks, was what looked like a piece of seaweed. Except it was black and wispy instead of green and floated heavily in the sea. He knew what it was instantly.

"It's a girl," he said.

15

KITTY WELLS PARKED HER VERY tiny rear end very firmly on the porch steps of Garrett's house. The news of another young girl discovered in the ocean had galvanized the press. This was turning into the type of story that could move an ambitious reporter onto the national scene. She wasn't going anywhere until she got an interview with the man who'd been responsible for finding all of the bodies in question.

Truth be told, she was quite pleased with herself. It hadn't been easy to find the Mountie's out-of-the-way shack. She still smarted from the crack he'd made about her voice during the open briefing with the press. But Kitty Wells prided herself on being a professional. First things first. Get the story. She could always shred the son of a bitch later.

Garrett had no idea how long she'd been waiting for him. The day had been sunny early on, but now a heavy fog blew across the meadow, and though the woman sitting on his steps wore a jacket, he could tell she was cold. Not much insulation on those bones. Well, it would be a cold day all right before he'd help promote her career. He had half a mind to take his *handicap* and kick her off his property. She was so tiny, one good boot would probably do the job. But he chose instead to play the good cop.

"Can I help you?" he asked, pretending not to know who she was. "Are you lost?"

Wells smiled, showing her perfect, little white teeth. Everything about her was perfect, slim, trim, impeccably dressed. Not a man alive could resist her. She oozed sexuality and had used it to advance her career from the very first day on the job.

"Kitty Wells, Mr. Barkhouse. I'm reporting on those poor murdered girls."

"Ah," he said, nodding sadly. "I'm sorry you had to come all the way out here for that, Ms. Wells. I know nothing that hasn't already been reported in the papers."

"Well, you know, a good reporter needs background and context, as well as basic information. It all goes into the hopper." She looked around as though seeing the dilapidated little house for the first time. "Do you actually live . . . in this . . . ?"

"Home sweet home," he said, regarding her without enthusiasm. Much as he disliked this woman, press coverage might be helpful in the case. The more people knew about things, up to a point, the more likely someone might remember seeing something—and that just might present a thread he could begin to unravel. He'd solved more than one case in such a manner.

"Well, you might as well come in." He opened the door and stood to one side.

"You don't lock the place?" she asked with surprise.

"As you can see," he said, stepping past her and turning the lights on in the living room with the sloping floor, "There's not much worth stealing. I've only been here a few days and the place has been closed up for years."

He swept a pile of newspapers off the sagging gray Victorian couch. "Have a seat," he said grandly.

Kitty contemplated the moldy piece of furniture the way she probably looked at a bag lady on the streets of Halifax. She sat primly on the very edge of the object, her knees pressed close together.

"What I wanted to know," she began, "is why you think you've been the only one so far to discover any of these girls?"

He shrugged. "Had to be someone. I get around. It's part of the job, you know."

"Yes, that brings me to my next question. What exactly is your job title here?"

"Not sure they ever gave me one. I was asked by the department to investigate the smuggling on the Eastern shore."

"Found anything?"

"A few threads. It's early, and frankly, dead Chinese girls were not what I expected to find."

She gave her sympathetic look, furrowing the tiny, but very cute, wrinkles on her forehead. No Botox honey, she. "It must have been a shock," she said. "Well, what I'd really like to ask of you, Mr. Barkhouse, is the chance to follow you around while you do your investigation. Kind of an exclusive, you know? In exchange, I'll see that you figure prominently in the coverage. Might get you a promotion."

"Sorry, I'm not interested in a promotion. Fact is, I'll be retiring after this case, so you see you're not offering me anything except another person's safety I'd have to worry about if I got into a tight situation. Not good for you or me."

She nodded and immediately went to her second plan of attack. She stretched and took off her jacket, placing it, somewhat reluctantly, on the tired sofa. Underneath she wore a skin-tight sort of leotard. Though she was not well endowed, what she had was displayed to maximum effect. The outfit was sheer and tight. It showed every curve and outline of her body. Her nipples stuck out quite proudly and she proudly noted that he was looking at them.

"I really wouldn't get in your way, Garrett." She said his name in a sort of breathy whisper, and he could almost hear her phero-mones kick in. "Maybe I could stay here. You have an extra room don't you? Would we have to share a bathroom?" Titillating a man was Kitty Wells's most highly developed skill.

He gave his sophisticated, man-of-the-world smile. "Well . . . yes. It's an outhouse. Only about thirty yards away, though, at the edge of the meadow. It's a two-seater," he added helpfully. "The floor was partially busted a while back by a neighbor who fell through, but I've put some plywood down and it's good as new. Very little possibility of falling through again . . . I think."

Her face registered something between dismay and disgust. "Well . . . uh . . . well, maybe there's a hotel I could stay in?"

"Yes, there's a good hotel down the coast a ways, called Lis-comb Lodge. Maybe that would be best. Honestly, I'd be glad to tell you what I can. It might be helpful to have some of the infor-mation out there."

"Oh, wonderful!" she said, immediately standing. "You won't be disappointed." She put one hand on his arm. "I just *know* we're going to work well together on this."

She slipped her tiny jacket back onto her tiny body. He couldn't believe how much wriggling was involved to achieve this.

"I'll just get settled and then report in to you," she said, making a beeline to get out of the pesthole Garrett lived in.

He stared after her, wondering what he'd gotten himself into.

16

THE DEPARTMENT OF PROTECTIVE SERVICES was on the fourth floor of the provincial government building in downtown Halifax. Garrett knew it well. His grandmother had been a do-gooder of the old school. She'd taken him along with her many times on one errand of mercy or another. "Take care of others and they will take care of you," she'd say, in her own personal version of the Golden Rule.

Of course, the first thing he learned was that the building contained a host of strange people. He could barely distinguish between those giving the services and those receiving them. But his grandmother had been one of the good people. She'd sung *Rock of Ages*, totally out of key, at the funerals of scores if not hundreds of people at Anglican church services. You hadn't been properly buried on the Eastern shore if you weren't laid down with an inspiring, if glass-shattering, rendition by Grandma Barkhouse.

Sheila Vogler had run the bureau for thirty years. Garrett had done business with her many times during his work against prostitution. She was no-nonsense but had a soft spot for children of any stripe or condition. No one was beyond saving in Sheila's book, except possibly the politicians who regularly tried to cut her budget. She was often willing to stretch the rules if it meant helping a child.

He found her in her usual spot, sitting at a desk piled high with folders, each one representing some painful story. When she saw him, she sat back.

"As I live and breathe. Garrett Barkhouse. Thought I'd seen the last of you. Heard you were retiring at the grand old age of— what?—forty-two? Waste of good manpower, if you ask me."

"Well, then, remind me not to," he said, placing himself firmly in the wooden chair facing her. "You sound like Deputy Commissioner Tuttle. You two been dating? Believe it or not, Sheila, there's more to life than saving mankind."

"Like what?"

"Like sex, making money, travel, good food, bungee jumping . . ."

"My bungee jumping days are over." She looked thoughtful for a moment. "I wonder if anyone's ever had sex *while* bungee jumping. Now that might get you in the Guinness Book of Records."

"More likely get you a hernia . . . or a Darwin Award," Garrett replied caustically.

"What's that?"

"Special recognition for people who kill themselves via some utterly inane and stupid activity. Ergo the name, Darwin Award, for improving the human gene pool by eliminating oneself from it."

She smiled. "What's on your mind?"

"Girl named Lila Weaver. Must have come across your desk. Used to work for Sweet Angels Escort Service."

She sighed and spun her chair so she could access a file cabinet. "I'll never understand where they come up with those names. Sarcasm is a skill beyond most of the dirtbags in the profession."

In a moment she came up with the file. Rather than hand it to him, which would have been illegal without a formal hearing, she paged through it.

"Yes, I remember her now. Two years plus with Sweet Angels. Began when she was just thirteen. Most girls who go through at such a young age are messed up for life." She looked up at Garrett. "What's she done now?"

"Actually, she's going through Lloyd's Haven for Troubled Youth down in Ecum Secum. You know anything about his operation?"

She sniffed. "I know he's close to being a pervert himself. Never been charged for anything, but I hear things. He bought the place and converted it about five years ago. Spent a lot of money. Who knows where he got it, but the provincial government wasn't about to look a gift horse in the mouth, budgetary concerns what they are. He doesn't have a record, though. I can assure you of that, or he wouldn't have been able to do it."

"So you're saying he's not making a fortune running the place?"

"Not from the government, he's not."

"Well, that's one interesting bit of information. How have the kids going through been doing, by and large?"

She shrugged. "Some have stayed out of trouble. Some have gone back to the business soon as they were able. Like I said, it's hard to break the pattern. They're just kids, virtually all of them without resources, skills, or a family that gives a shit about them. Once Lloyd—or we, to be honest—spit them out of the system, they've got nowhere to go except back to their pimps."

Garrett stared at the wall. "I know you don't approve of personal tinkering with the system, Sheila. But I'm trying to help another girl and just maybe it will do Lila some good, too."

She said nothing. She'd known Garrett a long time and generally considered him competent. But he had also proven his ability, on occasion, to come up with incredibly stupid ideas. This just might be one of those times.

"There's a girl in Misery Bay named Ayesha. Fifteen. Iranian family, probably clinically depressed. Works in her father's grocery store a whole lot of hours every day."

"That may be illegal right there," Sheila said.

"Sure, but it's a family business and you and I both know it would be impossible to prove anything at all in that area."

She nodded silently.

"Anyway, there may be the possibility that she's depressed for another reason, beyond the endless days making hoagies in that hot, windowless box of a store."

"Such as?"

He shrugged. Here he knew he was on shaky ground, for there really was nothing but speculation. "Abuse maybe. Hell, near as I can see, she's practically a slave. She's almost never allowed out unless it's to work at some other job. She has no friends or social life . . ."

Sheila interrupted. "That's the norm for most Muslim girls, Garrett. We've got plenty of them in Halifax. Their lives are pure exploitation. They work, marry who they're told to, have lots of kids, work some more, and grow old. That's it. The divine teachings of Mohammed. Most don't even go to regular schools. Many courts have allowed them to attend religious schools instead."

"I know all that. All I want is to see if we might help one girl with one problem. I'm not asking to change the divine plan of the universe."

"Changing the divine plan is what I do every day in here, Garrett. Besides having sex, making money, jet-setting around the world, and bungee jumping, that is. What do you want?"

"I want you to spring Lila from Lloyd's clutches for a few days and remand her to my custody. I think the two girls might be good for each other. If they can develop a friendship, something neither one of them has ever had, as near as I can tell, it just might make a difference in both their lives."

Her brow furrowed. "Lila, I can do. No problem. But I can't take Ayesha away from her family and hand her over to you. How are you going to get them together?"

"A friend of mine, woman named Sarah Pye, knows the family. She'll ask the father if she can hire Ayesha to clean house. If we make the offer attractive enough, I have no doubt he'll agree. Then we'll simply put them together and see what happens."

Sheila sighed and picked up the phone. "You really need to get a life, Garrett. Most of these girls are beyond saving, you know."

"Then why do you do it?"

"I'm a lousy bungee jumper."

17

LILA HADN'T BEEN THIS RELAXED in weeks. She sat back in Garrett's car, talking a blue streak. She wore cut-off jeans and a tank top and had shucked her sandals to put her feet up on the dash.

"I can't believe you actually got me out of there," she said. "That's so cool! Did you see the look on Lloyd's face when you told him? I thought he was gonna have a stroke."

"Well, it's only temporary, and I had to pull a few strings to make Lloyd agree. But I really think you can help me out on this."

She grew serious, like a child being told there was work to do. "I understand. You want me to try to find out if this kid is in trouble—maybe with her dad, who might be one sick son of a bitch. Look, I'll be able to tell, okay? I've dealt with enough of these perverts to spot one a mile away."

"You're not going to meet the father, Lila. You're going to have to figure out what's going on strictly by talking to Ayesha. My friend Sarah agreed to put you up at her house for a few days. It's nice, on the ocean, you can relax, go for hikes, whatever you want. And Sarah will get Ayesha to come over as much as possible, on the guise of hiring her to do some cleaning."

She made a face. "Cleaning sucks. I made more money in a weekend than my mom could in a month." She rolled down the window and spat out her gum. "Don't worry. I'll find out what's going on, no problem. You can shitcan the hikes, though. I've had enough galloping around the woods following Lloyd's tight little ass to last me till I'm a zillion years old." She brightened. "Maybe your friend will take us shopping in the city. Nothing helps a bunch of gals get to know each other better than that."

Sarah and Ayesha were planting flowers when they arrived. After introductions, the girls seemed to be getting along, so Sarah invited Garrett inside for tea, leaving them alone.

"I'm a little nervous about this," Garrett said, as they sat at the kitchen table. "It's kind of like a clash of cultures, you know. Lila's about as experienced as they come in the carnal ways of the world, while Ayesha, from what you've told me, is a pretty typical Muslim girl, which is to say, virtually no contact at all with men outside the family."

"That may be the reason it works, Garrett. Opposites attract. Anyway, if Ayesha's being abused, she's got more experience than you may think. It could give them some common ground. We'll just have to see what develops." She got up and poured herself another cup of tea. "By the way, I wanted to thank you for getting on Roland about the compressor. You were right, he backed down as soon as you confronted him. Didn't even wait the week to turn it off. Grace said she saw him removing the bait and driving away with it in his truck. Peace reigneth in the cove and none too soon."

"How so?"

"It was getting a little out of hand. Ingrid was really toying with him, exposing herself on their deck. Roland was asking for it, of course, by bringing his boat in so close, but . . . well . . . I'm just glad it's done."

"Well, it's only one battle. Roland may back off on the direct confrontations, but he's never going to be a guy they can borrow a cup of sugar from. He's pretty much all bluster, but he still knows how to hold a grudge. Sounds like Ingrid was just rubbing salt on the wound. I should probably stop by and talk to them, maybe head off anything more serious."

"Just be prepared to down a pitcher of Manhattans if you go any time after noon."

They were interrupted by the sounds of the two girls screaming with laughter outside. Garrett went over and looked out the window with Sarah. Lila and Ayesha were rolling on the grass, holding their sides in absolute stitches over something.

"I guess that's a good sign," said Sarah.

"You think so?"

"That's the first smile, much less laugh, I've seen out of Ayesha . . . ever. She enjoyed working at the ladies' but was always pretty reserved." She nodded at the girls who had recovered and were now talking intently. "If nothing else, Lila looks like she's a tonic for Ayesha's depression."

Garrett leaned over Sarah and kissed her neck. "Speaking of tonics, we never finished what we started on the island."

"It wasn't very romantic, was it, after finding that poor girl?"

"No. Anyway, I've got to go to Halifax to take care of some business. Maybe we could plan another outing when I get back?"

She turned and looked in his eyes. "Is it dangerous? Your business?"

He looked away. "Probably not."

When he turned back, a single tear was running down her cheek. "What?"

"The way you said that was just how my husband sounded when I asked about something he was working on. He never wanted to worry me either." She pushed him away and went and stood over the stove. "I'm sorry. It's just something I have to deal with. Why the hell can't I fall in love with a man who transports plutonium for a living or something safe like that?"

"Did you say fall in love?"

"Yes, damn it." She looked at him. "I don't commit easily, Gar. Guess I'm just a sucker for a man in uniform."

"I haven't worn my uniform since I got here. It was part of the deal I made with Tuttle. Easier to blend in right off the bat."

"Oh, shut up and kiss me."

Which was precisely what they were doing when the girls came inside.

"Uh-oh," said Lila. "Boy-girl stuff happening." She cocked her head to one side. "Pay attention, Ayesha. This just might be the real thing. It can be hard to tell, though."

Ayesha smiled shyly. "My mom and dad never do that," she said.

Garrett squeezed Sarah's hand. "I'm out of here while I'm ahead of the game. You girls can talk all you want about boy-girl stuff after I'm gone."

* * *

Coast Guardsman Tom Whitman appeared with Lonnie at eight o'clock outside the main gate of the Halifax Public Gardens. Tom had three solo kayaks in the back of his pickup, including one with an open cockpit. With Lonnie sitting in the cab, there was no room for Garrett in the front seat, so he followed them in his own car to Lake Micmac.

They passed the private dock where the men from Madame Liu's had set out and drove another mile down the road to a public launch site.

The lake was a popular place for small boaters, and while it was a bit unusual for people to head out this late in the evening, there were still a few cars in the lot. By the time they approached the island, it was completely dark, with just a sliver of moon to navigate by.

But light wasn't going to be their problem. One entire end of the island consisted of an extensive compound that was lit up like Piccadilly Circus on New Year's Eve.

"I can't believe this," said Tom, as they floated side by side fifty yards offshore. "It looks like the Playboy Mansion on steroids. Tennis courts, swimming pool, some sort of gazebo thing over there. That really big structure could be a gymnasium, for God's sake. There must be fifteen buildings."

"Keep your voice down," said Garrett. "It carries over the water." But he had to admit he was equally impressed with the extent of the grounds. The sheer size of the place was going to make it difficult to investigate thoroughly. And the bright lights were no help either.

They could hear voices and music coming from one of the buildings near shore. As they watched, two men came out a door, followed by several girls. The men were obviously drunk, and they pushed and pawed at the girls as they made their way to a smaller bungalow.

"The honeymoon suite," said Lonnie, but there was an edge to his voice.

"Come on," Garrett said. "We'll go round the back side and land."

On the dark side of the island, they pulled the boats out of the water and hid them in the brush. Lonnie led the way. In Iraq, he'd always been the best at sneaking up on the enemy, a not inconsiderable feat given his size. He could move through the woods like a Passamaquoddy hunter. They circled the compound, then crawled up behind a long, low bungalow that was dimly lit. Once they were in place, Garrett crouched at a window that had heavy bars on it and peered inside.

"What do you see?" Tom asked.

"It's empty. But it's kind of strange. There's probably thirty beds lined up in there."

"Maybe it *is* a resort."

"A high-class place like this is going to have first-class rooms, not dormitory-style sleeping arrangements—with iron bars on the windows to boot."

"Maybe it's for the help," said Lonnie. "Especially if they're illegals."

"I might believe that if I hadn't seen what went on between Madame Liu and the men we followed here." Garrett peered inside again. "I'm getting an idea about this place. Come on. I want to get a look inside the main building."

"Are you nuts?" said Tom. "This place is lit up like Yankee Stadium. We can't get close without being seen."

"Actually, the compound's been empty," said Garrett. "Aside from those two men and the girls, I haven't seen another soul. Come on."

Before the others could object, Garrett raced across the central courtyard. With a muttered curse, Tom followed, while Lonnie brought up the rear like an oversize caboose. They ducked behind a row of shrubs beside the building, then cautiously raised their heads until they could see inside.

Garrett stared in amazement. Inside was a large central fireplace, crackling with logs despite the warm evening. Sitting in chairs facing the flames was the man they'd followed from Madame Liu's and beside him, big as life and actually wearing clothes for a change, was Lloyd.

There was a sudden cracking sound as someone stepped on a branch and Garrett felt the cold barrel of a pistol against his neck. He started to raise his hands, seeing that Tom already had his up. Lonnie was nowhere to be seen.

"Well, what have we got here?" the man said. "Couple of Peeping Toms—or maybe something worse. Step out here in the light." As Garrett started to comply, he caught a flash of movement in the corner of his eye and almost faster than he could see, Lonnie had disarmed the man and laid him out flat with a single blow to the back of the neck.

"Remind me to ask how you do that sometime," said Garrett, staring at the man.

"What do we do with him?" said Lonnie.

"Leave him. I've seen enough to have a pretty good idea what this place is used for."

Tom stared at him. "You wouldn't care to share it with the rest of us, would you?"

"My guess is this is a central clearing house for new girls from out of the country. That's why the dormitory. They keep them locked in there, while they 'condition' them."

"Condition them?" Lonnie asked. He had a funny look in his eyes.

"It's why the rest of the place looks like a Playboy club. They bring high-paying clientele in to help with the processing. I bet it's a pretty popular corporate getaway weekend. Boating, tennis, lounging by the pool and, oh yeah, all the freebies you could ask for."

Lonnie's face was still. He had an aversion to perversion. It was unusual for someone in his profession, but he had a moral streak a mile wide, instilled by his grandmother, who had raised him. "I say we take the place down," he said.

"How the hell do we do that?" asked Tom.

"Burn it to the ground," Lonnie replied without hesitation.

Garrett was tempted to agree with him. But he had the sense they'd just started to pull at a thread of something that might be whole a lot bigger.

"It's an idea, all right," he said. "But let's find out more before we go off half-cocked. I want to see where all of this leads. We've got Lloyd connected, and I'm going to be quite interested to see how he explains his presence here."

18

B Y THE TIME GARRETT GOT back to Misery Bay, it was already morning, a windy, gray Nova Scotia day. He wondered if the remnants of the hurricane Sarah had mentioned might be moving in. The sky was angry and low, which was how he felt after mulling over the professional setup they'd uncovered, designed solely for the purpose of exploiting young girls. He wondered, too, if this whole situation was precisely what Tuttle had in mind as a way of keeping him on the job.

Well, it wasn't going to work. Straightening things out here, if possible, would be his last official duty. Then he'd be ready for retirement and maybe something else new, with Sarah.

He pulled into Sarah's just after nine a.m. There was a strange car in the driveway. As he went up to the door, it opened and Sarah emerged with Kitty Wells in tow, holding onto her dress to keep it from blowing up.

"I've been having a nice talk with your partner," said Sarah, smiling sweetly at him.

"My who?"

"Well, Garrett, we are going to be working together." Kitty came over and put her free hand through his arm and walked him toward her car.

"Look, Miss Wells, we are *not* working together. I said I'd give you any information that I thought could be released. So far there isn't any."

"Oh, that's okay, Garrett," she oozed, giving him a little squeeze. "I'm just working on background. You might be surprised what I uncover. It could be helpful to you. Anyway, I'm off now to meet the people at Ecum Secum. Find out what's what over there. See you all later."

She climbed into the car, letting go of her skirt, which the wind compliantly picked up, exposing a generous portion of thigh. It was an action for the benefit of Sarah, he suspected, as much as himself. He watched her drive off as a way not to look at Sarah for as long as possible.

"What a *charming* girl," Sarah said. "She's been telling me all about how closely you two are working. Practically in bed together."

He grimaced. "Look, I only met her yesterday. She wants to kick-start her national career with the killings here. It was probably a mistake to tell her I'd give her what I could. But sometimes it helps to have someone in the press funnel the right stuff to the media."

"Well, and isn't she the perfect choice?"

He detected a need to change the subject. "How did she get on to Ecum Secum, anyway?"

"She saw the sign on her drive down. 'Troubled Youth' is apparently code to reporters that stands for 'News at Eleven.' She asked me about it and . . ." She looked sheepish. "I'm afraid I told her what I knew about the place."

"Well, maybe it will keep her occupied. I can't really see Lloyd spending too much time explaining his operation to a reporter."

"Oh, I don't know. From what you told me, she's exactly his type. I don't think there's much she wouldn't do to get a story from someone—including you."

"You've got that right. She practically invited herself to move in with me."

"And you turned her down?" She leaned in, the wind blowing her hair about her face and kissed him on the mouth. "There might be hope for you yet."

"I didn't exactly turn her down. It was more like my two-seater of an outhouse that gave her pause." He looked around. "Where are the girls?"

"They walked into town to buy some ice cream. Thank God. It might have really been a mess if Kitty had got hold of them." She looked at the sky. "I hope they don't get rained on."

"Well, thanks for small favors. How about inviting me in out of the weather?"

"Tea?"

"I was thinking of something a bit stronger."

"Why Mr. Barkhouse, it's not even ten in the morning!"

"It was a long night. Give me a drink and I'll tell you about it."

Inside, he relaxed on the couch with a glass of Glen Breton and told her about what they'd found on Micmac Island.

Her eyes grew wide. "Can't you close the place down?"

"It's a possibility. But it's not against the law to have a ritzy resort or even a building with bars on the windows. We have to catch them in the act."

"Sounds like you did just that. Didn't you say there were men and young girls?"

He sighed. "Yes, but we didn't really witness anything except them walking in the compound. Besides, I think it might be better to keep an eye on the place for a while, see what turns up."

"Evidently Lloyd turned up."

"That was interesting, all right. I hardly think he was there to do research on prostitution, so he could better relate to his own girls."

She frowned, and he could see the wheels turning behind those freckles. "Do you get the sense you might be onto something bigger than you expected?"

"Crossed my mind a time or two." He put his glass down. "But this isn't the first time I thought I might be close to breaking a major prostitution ring that didn't pan out. You can't begin to know how good these people are at covering themselves. Part of it is that they can be very well connected politically. Lots of money, top-notch legal assistance, and sexual favors to boot. That can buy a lot of protection." He stood up. "You know, I think I'm going to tag along after our Miss Wells. I want to confront Lloyd anyway, and it just might be interesting to see his reaction to a reporter snooping around."

* * *

He was about forty minutes behind Kitty when he turned into Ecum Secum Haven. He parked the car, wondering where she was, since her vehicle wasn't in the lot. Maybe Lloyd had given her a quick boot. The sky had turned an interesting shade of purple with mackerel clouds blowing high overhead. Still, it hadn't rained and the wind at ground level was sporadic.

In contrast to his last visit, this time there were kids sitting around on the deck of the main house, relaxing and jamming, with one of the boys playing a guitar. They also appeared to be drinking. It wasn't clear what was in their glasses, but the mood of levity suggested something stronger than carrot juice. Lloyd was nowhere to be seen.

As he approached the porch, his suspicions were reinforced as several of the kids slid glasses out of sight. This hardly seemed the atmosphere Lloyd said he tried to promote.

The guitar player stopped when Garrett climbed onto the deck.

"Hi guys," he said, trying not to sound like a cop. "I'm looking for Lloyd. He around?"

The guitar player said, "Lloyd's not around." He raised his glass casually in a mock salute. "While the cat's away . . ."

"While the asshole's away," said a thin girl of perhaps fourteen. Several others laughed.

As a detective of some twenty years' experience, Garrett perceived a possible opening.

"You mind if I ask you all some questions? I'll be honest with you. I'm a cop, but I'm not interested in you personally. I'd like to know more about Ecum Secum Haven. What do you think of the program here?"

The guitar player snorted. "I've been in reform school," he said. "Twice. This is worse."

"How so?" Garrett sat casually on the steps. Just one of the guys. "Seems like a pretty nice place."

"Lloyd's a prick," said the thin girl. "Thinks he owns us. It's a real power trip for him. He prances around with no clothes on half the time."

"No clothes at all?"

"Yeah, that's right," said the guitar player. "He says he's a naturist, or something. But he likes us to see his body. He sunbathes naked on the porch while we have to work in the garden in the front yard."

"Sometimes, he plays with himself," said another girl.

This was developing into an all-together nastier picture than he'd had in mind.

"Have any of you been molested by him more directly than that?"

No one answered. A very blonde girl who appeared to be one of the oldest said, "I think he likes to be looked at, you know? He's an exhibitionist. It's how he gets his rocks off."

"Yeah," said the guitar player. "He's got himself the perfect little setup here. None of us dare say anything, 'cause it would just get us in more trouble than we already are, if that's possible. And who would believe us anyway?"

"I see." He stared at their plain, hopeless faces. Having nothing and no one had led to their being sent here, where they were just being exploited all over again. He was getting pretty ticked off at old Lloyd.

"Anyone happen to notice a young woman drive in, oh, about an hour ago?"

The thin girl nodded. "I saw her. She was real pretty. She asked for Lloyd and went in to his office. They were there for about ten or fifteen minutes, then they came out, got in her car and drove away."

"Any idea where they went?"

Heads shook all around.

"Any other staff around right now?" Garrett asked.

"Greta and Keegan went into town for supplies," said the blonde. "The woman who cleans is somewhere up in the cabins and there's a couple of others out in the gardens. But things generally slow down around here when Lloyd's gone."

He looked longingly at the house. There would never be a better opportunity. "Do you mind if I wait for Lloyd in his office?"

"Suit yourself," said the guitar player, and he began to strum softly.

That, as far as Garrett was concerned, was a legal invitation. He listened to the musician for a couple of minutes, then got up easily and went inside. It was the first time he'd been in the building. A hallway with several doors off it led to a central staircase. He poked his head in two of the doors before finding one that was clearly an office.

Alone, he began a hasty search. The room was big. Lloyd had clearly taken the best for himself. There were two large windows looking out on the garden at the side of the house and a fireplace with a polished mahogany mantel. One whole wall was taken up with shelves filled with various bric-a-brac, largely pictures of Lloyd himself.

He spent some time going through a file cabinet but it was pretty straightforward, records of the kids who passed through the program. In a chest of drawers by one of the windows, he found a digital camera. The viewscreen showed a variety of pictures of the kids, mostly working in the garden and many of them obviously taken through the window of the office. Several pictures showed girls looking straight at the window with wide eyes. He would have bet the farm they were staring at a nude Lloyd who wanted pictures of their reactions to seeing him in all his glory.

The desk was messy, covered with papers and forms. In the center drawer on top of other papers was an address book. He only recognized one entry: Madame L, with a Halifax exchange number.

There was nothing else. He'd gleaned little more than an increased dislike for the man in charge. Yet he couldn't quite believe this entire enterprise was all simply about Lloyd's need to expose himself to kids. He had a perversion for sure. But Garrett continued to feel he was part of something bigger and more sinister.

He was looking out the window when Kitty Wells's car came up the driveway. He glanced quickly about the room to make sure there was no sign of his presence and went back out onto the porch. He had little worry that any of the kids would tell Lloyd where he'd been. He didn't get the impression they told their resident exhibitionist anything at all voluntarily. But he did notice that all signs of the drinks had miraculously disappeared and even the guitar player's instrument was nowhere to be seen. These kids had developed a well-greased cover-up operation. Everything was hidden in just the ten seconds it took from the time the car became visible to Lloyd's climbing onto the porch.

Before he saw Garrett, Lloyd said, "What's going on here? You kids are supposed to be doing garden work. Get cracking."

The crowd of youngsters moved slowly off the porch, leaving Lloyd staring suddenly at Garrett. Kitty had also come onto the deck.

"What are you doing here?" Lloyd asked. "I didn't give permission to talk to my kids. You already took Lila. Now you're after more of them? I'm going to report this to your boss. These kids are here for a reason, you know. To turn their lives around. Your interference is not going to do them any good."

Obviously, the pleasant facade of their previous meeting had evaporated following their little contretemps over Lila. Lloyd glanced at the departing kids and Garrett took the moment to meet Kitty's eyes and shake his head. There was no reason for Lloyd to know they were acquainted. He went over to her.

"Don't believe we've met," he said. "Garrett Barkhouse, RCMP."

She had the presence of mind to play along, giving him her hand. "Nice to meet you, officer." She smiled seductively.

Lloyd observed the interaction with distaste. He'd clearly been enjoying having Kitty all to himself. He stepped forward and took her arm.

"Miss Wells has asked me for an interview," he said, directing her toward the door. "You're not welcome here, Barkhouse."

Kitty winked at Garrett as they disappeared inside, her expression clearly saying, "See? I'm making progress already."

He decided to clear out before Lloyd could see anything that might suggest his office had been ransacked, though Garrett suspected his attentions would be altogether focused on Kitty for however long their 'interview' took. He wondered just how far Kitty would go for information and suspected Lloyd was wondering the same thing.

19

ROLAND SAT IN HIS KITCHEN and stared out at the house on the bay below. He was home alone for the first time in more than a year. Rose had been taken to the hospital for shortness of breath and they had decided to keep her overnight for observation.

He listened to the quiet of the house. Usually, he could hear his mother's wheezing lungs and grunts of exertion whenever she moved. It had become background noise he didn't hear most of the time, like the slap of the waves against the dock or the thrum of his bait cooler.

The shutting down of the cooler had infuriated him and left him trying to think of other ways he might aggravate his neighbors. Damn that Garrett. First trying to bribe him to cooperate by offering money for the roofing job. It was so obvious what he was doing. His old high school classmate had always been smooth and, Roland thought, condescending. How would he like it, he wondered, if he had to live next door to a house full of wild, immoral artists from the city? Grace was nothing but a big tease. Still, he couldn't get over the sight of her staring at him as Ingrid had waggled her breasts on the deck. Like she could read his mind and knew it was her body he wanted to see rather than Ingrid's.

He uncoiled his beanpole frame from the chair, climbed the stairs, and limped down the long, dark hall to his room in the back. He glanced out to see if any lights were on in the back of the women's house. It was dark as usual. They almost never spent any time in that part of the house, much to his anger.

He sat in front of his computer and began to search for information on his neighbors. He'd been crunching websites, Google, Twitter, Facebook, and anything else he could think of for information about them.

It wasn't hard. They all had Facebook accounts and he'd learned how to hack into them. Mostly, they chatted with their web friends about the city and various art functions and shows they planned to attend. The stuff was so boring it practically put him to sleep. But he particularly enjoyed looking at the photos they posted. Grace had a picture of herself sitting on her deck in a bikini, and he spent lots of time looking at that. It felt sort of like he owned her, having that picture, though he would have given anything for an even more revealing shot.

He'd been planning to get one on his own. Pick a sunny day and climb the forested hill on the other side of the inlet until he could see their deck that faced the ocean. There were a couple of spots he'd already scouted where he could look out through the trees. With luck, he might catch Grace in the altogether. He'd even purchased a camera with a zoom lens for the purpose.

The problem was Rose. Her chair faced the window that looked out on the hill. She'd want to know at once why he was going up there with his camera. Even if he hid the camera, there was no real good explanation for him going up the hill. He never went anywhere that required any excessive amount of exercise. So today would have been the perfect time, except it was overcast and cool and no way Grace would be out in anything other than jacket and jeans. He swore. What rotten luck.

111

He copied the Facebook photo of Grace and printed it out. The quality was pretty good. He decided to take it with him next time he went to the city and have a poster-size copy made to pin on his wall. He could sneak it upstairs when Rose wasn't looking, and of course, she never went upstairs.

Roland had never had a girlfriend. Not one. He knew he'd missed out on a major part of life. He simply didn't know how to go about it, what the proper procedure was to approach someone. And of course, he wasn't exactly a prize catch. The only women he'd had sex with were prostitutes, and he didn't give a damn what they thought. That his cousin Hank actually had a wife and family had always grated on him. So he'd fixated on Grace. She was beautiful in a way the professional girls never could be, and she was handy. Right next door.

He turned the computer off finally and went and got two Extra Strength Tylenol for his arthritis. Then he sat in his chair in front of the window. They were all home. He could see their cars in the driveway and a couple of extra ones to boot. Probably had some of their druggy friends over. He fingered the binoculars with one hand and stared, brooding, at the dark windows that faced his side of the house.

20

G ARRETT HAD BEEN AWAKE FOR thirty-six hours and could barely keep his eyes open long enough to drive home. He stripped off his pants and shirt, threw the sleeping bag across his legs, and lay listening to the wind whistle through the eaves for maybe two minutes before he was gone.

It seemed he had only been asleep for five minutes when he began to dream he was a carpenter building a new house. Maybe it was a replacement for this old wreck. He hammered and pounded away for a long time trying to get one particularly stubborn nail into place before his addled brain came far enough out of the fog to realize that someone was banging on the door.

He stumbled up the hillside that was his living room floor to the kitchen and opened the door. Sarah stood there in a rain slicker, her hair blowing about her face.

"Gar—thank God! I was beginning to think you weren't here in spite of your car."

"What's wrong?" He was fast coming out of his grogginess. He'd grown used to being woken from a dead sleep. It was an occupational hazard.

"The girls are gone," she said.

"What do you mean? Gone where?"

"I don't know. I waited a long time and when they didn't come back from the grocery, I went to look for them. Mr. Marshed said they'd bought ice cream sandwiches and were going to walk back. He was pretty angry at me and wanted to know who Lila was. Said he hadn't given Ayesha permission to be with another girl. Jesus, it was like she wasn't even allowed to talk to another human being. Anyway, I told him they probably were just down on the beach and I'd let him know as soon as I found them. But, Garrett—I can't!"

"All right." He put his arms around her. "We'll find them. Where could they go?" He sat her in a chair. "Wait a minute while I get some clothes on."

They drove down to the pebble beach by Sarah's and walked a mile each way, calling for them. No luck. A few drops of rain spattered, but despite the dark clouds, things seemed to be holding off. When they got back to the wharf the second time, Tom was waiting for them.

"Heard you calling half an hour ago, but I couldn't figure out which way you'd gone," he said. "We've got a job."

"I'm a little busy, Tom." Garrett said. "What's going on?"

"We got our tip. Sounds like a good one—possible transit of illegals offshore. Probably beyond Snow's Island. We need to get the kayaks and head out."

Snow's Island was way out, beyond Rupert's Island where the dead girls had been found. They'd planned to use the boats the next time a hot lead came along. It couldn't have come at a more inconvenient time.

"Garrett," Sarah pleaded. "We've got to find them."

Tom looked at them. "Find who? What's going on here?"

"Lila and Ayesha are missing," said Garrett. "We've been looking for them."

"What do they look like?"

Sarah described them and what they were wearing.

"I saw them," Tom said after a moment. "But you're not going to like where."

"Tell us," said Sarah.

"I passed two girls fitting that description probably two or three miles up the road toward Halifax. They were hitchhiking. I would have stopped them but I was in a hurry to find Garrett."

Garrett swore.

"What do you think they're doing?" Sarah asked.

"I'd lay odds that Lila's talked Ayesha into going to Halifax with her. Come on, maybe they're still there."

But Tom put a hand on his arm. "Hold it, Garrett. We've got another job to attend to. Besides, I saw a car pick them up in my rear mirror. That was . . ." He looked at his watch. "Almost an hour ago. If they got a ride all the way, they're halfway to Halifax by now."

"Damn!" Garrett looked back and forth from one of them to the other. They both needed him and God knew he wanted to stay with Sarah. But she surprised him.

"Garrett—you've got to go with Tom. The lives of who knows how many girls may be at risk. Lila and Ayesha aren't in any immediate danger. I . . . I'll go look for them in the city," she said helplessly.

He held her by the shoulders. "No. Listen. You'll never find them just driving around the city looking. It's hopeless. I'll call Lonnie. He'll have a better idea where to look for them. You stay here and be our call center."

She hesitated. It felt like doing nothing, but she knew he was right. She had no hope of finding the girls by herself in a metropolitan area of almost half a million people.

"All right," she said in a resigned voice.

Tom went to get the boats ready, while Sarah and Garrett went inside to call Lonnie. He was initially skeptical that he could find two girls he'd never seen before in a large city, but Garrett told him to start with Sweet Angels Escort Service and Big Margaret. Maybe Lila had some notion of going back to work. He couldn't believe she was doing this. Perhaps Sheila was right. When girls were spoiled so young, there really was no hope for them.

He grabbed the slicker he'd left at Sarah's and then wrote down his cell phone number for her. "I don't think this will work once we get out of the bay. There isn't complete coverage on this part of the coast. But I'll check in when I can."

He led Sarah out to the beach where Tom had positioned the two boats along with spray skirts, paddles, and life jackets. He stopped at his car long enough to pick up his Glock, stuffing the pistol into a waterproof sack.

Then they skirted up and stepped into the boats without saying much. Sarah looked worried standing on the little pebble beach. "Gar—be careful. Are you sure about this? Don't you need more help?"

"Don't worry," he lied. "This is more by way of a trial run. We need to see if using the kayaks will really work as a way for us to get close. We'll use caution if it looks like we're dealing with too large a force. I promise." He avoided looking at Tom and gave her a quick kiss. Then they were away into a rising mist off the bay.

Tom paddled in next to him. "Caution would be a good thing," he said. "Too bad Lonnie's in Halifax. We could use him. But, you know . . . if we get the chance to free some girls from these SOBs, we're going to take it."

"I know," said Garrett. "And I think Sarah knows too. She was married to this, don't forget."

Tom just said, "Yep. I got it."

It was three in the afternoon, a little more than five hours until sunset. It ought to be enough. Tom had GPS navigation equipment that should allow them to keep on course in darkness or heavy fog. And the Coast Guard officer was a good navigator. Garrett, on the other hand, was pretty rusty. It was twenty years since he'd done any serious kayaking. It wouldn't be good to get separated from his companion.

The headland here was dotted with new German homes, most built in the last three years, their yards and boat launches still graveled scars on the landscape. It would be quite a few years before the thin maritime soil replaced the spruce that had been uprooted.

He stared at the houses grimly until he and Tom left the mainland and they fell behind. The change from the emptiness of this place when he was growing up was huge. Still, he knew a few houses didn't change the fact that the North Atlantic could be an unforgiving place. The combination of wind, waves, and swell could quickly put a small boater at risk. Often, the three elements barreled in from completely different directions. A sudden gust could unbalance an unwary paddler. The fourth element of North Atlantic paddling was water temperature. Even in August, it hovered around fifty degrees. Twenty minutes in water that cold could incapacitate, with death close behind.

By any reasonable paradigm of caution, they ought to have backup, someone at least aware of where they were, preferably someone in Tom's cutter, far enough behind not to scare off the smugglers, but close enough to be in radio contact. Trouble was, what they were doing was not reasonable and had not been approved by their superiors. If Tuttle had known what they were about, he would have quashed the idea. Taking on a boatload of desperate smugglers on the high seas in a couple of plastic kayaks was madness. But it was also the only way Garrett knew to get the job done.

Tom was the only Coast Guard officer for this section of coast. There would be no backup unless they got into trouble and called for it . . . assuming Garrett's cell phone worked . . . and there was anyone close enough to be useful.

21

THEY SOON DEVELOPED A RHYTHM, paddling steadily. A heavy mist hung in the air and coated their slickers, not quite rain and not quite fog. The essence of Nova Scotia weather.

Their world was gray, the sky low and filled with bulbous clouds that looked like damp, oversized cotton balls. The heavy light seemed to weigh them down, making every islet a fuzzy gray blob against a horizon line that was nearly imperceptible. Even the occasional squawking gulls seemed like gray phantoms swooping overhead. For the first hour it was quiet, almost deathly calm, with not a breath of moving air. Garrett thought they would make good time.

Then the mist turned to a light drizzle and the wind started to pick up. Soon, small whitecaps began to form, their tops whipped into little windblown waterspouts. Garrett had boated in worse conditions. Still, there was no telling how much things might deteriorate. The wind was coming at them straight on now, the rain stinging their faces. In the back of Garrett's head a little mouse chewed away on the idea that this system could be the outskirts of the hurricane.

His breathing was becoming strained. He wasn't in the same sort of condition Tom was for this. His lower leg ached as his prosthesis pressed against the rudder controls. There was now a sizable ocean swell. The boats rose high in the air and then descended, their noses momentarily underwater before rising again. The wind was against them, while the waves slapped at a forty-five-degree angle. He had to constantly adjust his weight and paddling force, always prepared for a sudden gust that might turn his nose sideways, exposing him to being upended in the frigid water. That was an outcome he didn't want to contemplate. There would be little Tom could do. If he tried to come back and help, which Garrett knew he would, he risked turning over himself.

They stuck close to each island that hove into view, using them as shields against the wind. After what seemed an eternity but was probably a little over two hours, they edged into the protected shoals of Rupert's Island, where they took their first real break. Garrett's shoulders were on fire. There was no wind on the lee side of the island, and the rain let up. It seemed like the weather was coming in bands.

"How you doing?" Tom asked.

"Okay," Garrett lied. "Well, a little sore. I haven't done this in a while."

"The best is yet to come. You sure you want to go through with this?"

He almost said no, but the image of a little girl, shot in the back and dying in his arms, stopped him. Maybe there was another girl like her out there somewhere—in the dark hold of a freighter or fishing boat, huddled, fearful, about to enter into the worst nightmare one could imagine. He and Tom were all she had between her and a living hell.

"Let's do it," he said.

"All right. Try not to fall too far behind me on this next section. This will be open water with no islands for protection until we reach Little Snow and Big Snow islands. There's no turning back once we're into it."

Garrett just nodded, a queasy feeling in his stomach. He hadn't eaten in a long time, and he thought of Sarah's sandwiches, but knew he'd probably chuck anything that he ate right now.

He followed a few feet behind as they rounded Rupert's Island and were met by the fiercest wind yet. There was at least a three-foot chop. Waves hit the rocks like artillery shells, huge plumes of spray whipping high and then disappearing into the grayness. Garrett tried to quarter into the wind. Every few minutes, the combination of a big wave striking at a strange angle and a gust of unexpected wind would send their tiny crafts reeling. Then it was only by paddling fiercely and throwing their body weight one way or the other that they managed to keep upright. Garrett could barely see Little Snow, floating in the mist, a seemingly impossible distance away.

"How far across?" he yelled to Tom.

"About four miles," he cried back. "Little over an hour in calm water. But in this . . . no way to be sure. Twice as much anyway. There was some bad weather predicted but it was expected to stay far offshore. Maybe the wind will shift and help us out."

Garrett doubted it. The law of the sea was immutable: the wind was never at your back.

There was no more talking, unless grunting was considered a form of speech. His mind went numb as he paddled with every fiber of strength he possessed. With no nearby shoreline, it was impossible to gauge if they were making any headway at all, as though they were paddling inside one of those clear plastic Santa-balls, going round and round, nothing ever changing. Every now and then, another wave of weather would surge in and the rain would pelt them, as if someone had turned the Santa upside down in order to stir things up.

Though it was only six o'clock, it seemed later . . . and darker. Garrett couldn't quite imagine being out here after dark. He'd often kayaked under a full moon, the islands casting strange shadows, the moon's glow reflected beneath him. But with the sky overcast, the blackness would soon be complete. Then there'd be no forward or backward, no up or down. He wouldn't be able to see his hand in front of his face. They'd be in limbo, like spirits floating in a world without boundaries, completely reliant on the GPS. The relentless waves would continue to blow in from every angle, but once darkness fell, he wouldn't be able to see them, wouldn't be able to anticipate their force or intent.

He was unable to keep up with Tom. Garrett saw him peek back once or twice to see how he was doing. But the simple act of turning to look back could unbalance even a skilled paddler. To cease paddling for even a moment risked the boat turning crosswise to the waves, a potentially disastrous outcome. Turning around to come back and help was out of the question.

Garrett fell farther and farther behind. The crossing seemed to be taking much longer than they had anticipated. His arms and shoulders had become one large aching mass, indistinguishable from each other.

Then, darkness fell. Not the gradual approach of evening one was used to; rather, it was as if someone turned out a light in a windowless room. Garrett managed to look at the luminous dial of his watch, which read only eight o'clock. The sun wouldn't set for another thirty minutes. But he couldn't see. The clouds must have thickened with the approaching storm to the point of allowing no light at all to penetrate.

Panic rose in his chest. What direction should he go? He could no longer see Tom or the waves and struggled desperately to keep the boat balanced against what were now a series of invisible forces, as if some demonic ogre kept pushing maliciously against his small craft. Only one constant remained. The wind. It had been directly in Garrett's face when he last saw Tom and lined his boat up with the island. He'd have to trust it wouldn't shift direction.

He paddled straight into the teeth of the growing gale, waves now four to seven feet, breaking across his bow and splashing against the boat skirt, sending salt spray into his face. His eyes stung from all the salt, so he had to wipe them against his sleeve constantly. Since he couldn't see anyway, he tried keeping them shut, but that was worse, too abnormal.

His arms felt like two dead things. Blisters on both hands stung from the salt water and the constant rubbing with each turn of the paddle. God knew how much longer he could keep this up. Once his strength failed, he'd be able to do nothing but pray the boat wouldn't flip when he turned and ran before the wind until he struck land. He knew, though, he'd be as likely to blow straight to Newfoundland as back to the coast.

Just when he decided he must have missed the island, conditions suddenly took a turn for the worse, if that were possible. The wind seemed to change direction and then ratchet up as though someone had turned on some mighty celestial wind tunnel. He was in a full-blown gale. He wondered if the hurricane had decided to swipe the province more directly than they'd anticipated. He had never experienced such wind before.

His arms were throbbing and he could do almost nothing. It was so black that paddling made little sense anyway so far as direction was concerned. He had no idea which way to go. He allowed the boat to turn till the wind was behind him, an effort that nearly swamped him. Then he ran before the blast.

At least it was less effort. He used his paddling skills now just to keep the boat straight and to balance against any rogue waves that decided to come in at an angle. He was skimming along, faster than he'd ever gone in a kayak. The little boat rose with the swell and crashed down, almost submerging into the water. It felt like the craft would come apart at the seams. Garrett prayed Tom had found safe haven somewhere. It had been madness to come out here with a storm approaching.

A wave hit him broadside and he threw himself against the side of the boat to counteract its thrust. His movement caused the spray skirt to come loose in the back. He struggled to reattach it as freezing water began to enter the boat with every wave that crested over the kayak. He needed both hands to get the spray skirt back on and was forced to stick his paddle inside the boat. This left him totally at the mercy of the wind, yet somehow he stayed afloat.

When he picked up his paddle again, the boat actually seemed steadier. The water that had gotten inside was stabilizing him, lowering the boat's center of gravity. He didn't want to think about what all that salt water was doing to his bionic equipment. His legs were so cold he couldn't feel anything, not even his phantom foot.

He ran before the wind for a long time. It felt like hours, though he had no way of telling. His watch must have stopped from the salt spray, as the luminous dial no longer worked. Everything was blackness and stinging rain and cold. About the time he decided he must be halfway to Ireland and ought to be on the lookout for freighter traffic, he saw a sudden flash of light.

It was distant and disappeared at once. But he stared at where it had been until he saw it again. There was a quick flash and movement and then it was gone again. He knew at once what it was. Lighthouse Point. He was far out to sea, then, blowing away from the mainland. He strained to see the light again. It was his one chance. If he missed the little island that held the lighthouse, he knew there was nothing but open ocean until the British Isles.

He began to focus on the light, learning its rhythm, adjusting his course each time it appeared. It was difficult to keep on the trajectory he wanted. Even though the light gave a sure beacon, the wind was pushing him away from it. At some point he would have to paddle against the wind in order to hit his objective. For now, he continued to try to quarter his boat against the wind behind him.

For every hundred yards he flew before the blast, he inched his craft a few yards nearer to the light. It was going to be close.

Then he could see the lighthouse itself, almost a hundred feet tall, surrounded by a rocky shore. Waves smashed against the rocks, causing huge sprays of white foam that reflected the light momentarily, then disappeared until the revolving pulse returned. The island loomed suddenly closer. He was moving so quickly before the wind that it was going to be on him faster than he expected.

There was no more time to go with the wind. Now, he had to fight directly into the teeth of the gale. He paddled till his shoulders felt like they were ripping apart, the sinews of muscle ready to leap out of his skin. Still, he was losing the battle. He could see he wouldn't come closer than a hundred yards from the end of the island before the wind carried him off into the night. No matter how hard he paddled, it was fruitless against the fierce blow.

He stopped paddling when he saw he wouldn't make it, his arms and shoulders quivering from the effort. He had a decision to make, and only seconds to make it. Should he leave the boat and try to swim to the island? He was a strong swimmer, though the pain in his shoulders suggested his swimming would be severely handicapped. In the water, he wouldn't be subject to the forces of wind that blew against the kayak. He might make it. Of course, if he didn't, then he'd be floating in the frigid water and his life could be measured in minutes.

In the end, he stayed with the boat. He watched the lighthouse fall away behind him. Now he truly was in the cruel, open North

Atlantic, nothing but thousands of square miles of ocean surrounding him. He replayed his decision not to swim for it over and over. At least it would have settled things quickly, one way or the other. Now he would be forced to spend more hours and even days fighting the storm. But he had no illusions as to the inevitable outcome. Either exhaustion or hypothermia would take him eventually.

22

Tom huddled in the lee of Big Snow Island. He couldn't see much of anything in the dark, but had been able to check his GPS thanks to its illuminated screen. It was the only reason he'd made it to land. He had no idea where Garrett was. He knew his friend had been falling behind and even attempted to slow his rate of paddling so Garrett might catch up, though it endangered his own boat. Turning around was impossible, and in the blackness and noise of the storm, he'd probably have missed Garrett anyway.

He called himself hoarse but the wind swallowed his cry. Garrett was out there somewhere, alone, with nothing to guide him. The possibility he would hit the Snow Islands by chance was slim to none.

He considered his options. He could stay here, try to wait out the storm, then look for Garrett. But the wind showed every intention of blowing all night. If Garrett had overturned and was in the cold water, he was as good as dead, no matter that he had a life jacket on. The frigid water would snuff out his life in an hour at the outside. If he managed to keep the boat afloat, he'd be blown out to sea. Tom tried his cell phone again. There was no service.

There really was only one choice. He had to go back. With the GPS, finding his way in the dark wouldn't be a problem. It was set to guide him straight back to the wharf. It would be an intimidating struggle against the ache that already invaded his shoulders. But if Garrett was on his way to Ireland, Tom needed to contact the Coast Guard and air/sea rescue to try to find him. He realized that being in a kayak without GPS in such seas was worse than being helpless.

It was past midnight when he finally sighted the light of the wharf. Inside the inner islands, the wind lessened but still whipped up whitecaps with grim determination.

As he pulled onto the little beach by the wharf, he was surprised to see half a dozen vehicles and the Coast Guard cutter from the next station down the shore. Men were milling about and then he saw Sarah. She wore a yellow slicker and gum boots and ran to him as soon as she saw him.

"Tom! Thank God you're okay." She scanned the darkness behind him. "Where's Garrett?"

Tom tried to get out of the boat and nearly fell into the water, he was so sore and stiff. "I don't know where he is. When the weather deteriorated, we got separated in the dark. He's got to be way out to sea by now, if he hasn't turned over."

The color drained out of Sarah's face. "That . . . that's why I called in the authorities. I thought you'd be in trouble once the wind picked up. The hurricane has moved closer to shore than anyone expected."

Tom weaved a little as he tried to get his land legs. Arthur Parmenter, his counterpart on the Eastern shore, came over and pulled the boat up for him. "I'm ready to go out, Tom," he said. "Though I'm not happy about it. Air/sea has also been notified and will send out a plane." He looked quickly at Sarah and said softly, "Be a miracle if we find him."

"I'm going with you," Tom said.

Arthur looked at him. "You sure? You look all in . . ." But he could read the determination in the man's eyes. "All right, Tom. We can use your GPS coordinates to give us a direction."

"I can get us to the last point when he was with me," said Tom. "Then it will be guesswork, but he was already pretty tired. He would have soon had to turn and let the wind take him, so we can follow the wind out to sea. I hope to God he remembers he has an emergency flash beacon in the boat. If he sets it, we should be able to see him."

He looked at Sarah. "Any word on the girls?"

She shook her head. "It's a night for disasters," she said. "But if they're in the city they should be all right for a while. Certainly in less danger then Garrett is. I'm going with you on the boat."

Arthur started to say something, then thought better of it. He'd known Sarah for a long time. There was no way she was going to be put off.

23

GARRETT SHIVERED SO FIERCELY, HIS titanium foot rattled against the side of the kayak. His slicker leaked water down his back and into his clothes. The lower half of his body rested in frigid water taken in during his struggles with the sprayskirt. He knew he was dangerously close to hypothermia.

Damned ignominious way for a Mountie to die. He could imagine Tuttle using him as an example to recruits for the rest of his career. *Always prepared* was Tuttle's Mountie mantra. Garrett could hear the lecture: no backup, no communications, no detailed weather reports, out in the North Atlantic in a twelve-foot plastic boat in a hurricane. This man deserved to die, Tuttle would expound.

And Garrett would have to agree with him. It *was* a stupid way to die.

He kept his paddle balanced on the gunnels, dipping the blades as needed to keep the wind at his back, the boat running straight. He wiped his soaking sleeve against his eyes to counteract the stinging salt. When he looked up again, he saw lights on the horizon.

"Can't be Ireland already," he said out loud. "What the hell is that?"

The wind was blowing him straight down on the lights. There was something strange about them. Several appeared to be right at water level, while others floated high in the sky. Was it a ship? Some kind of optical illusion? Whatever it was, it was massive, a huge freighter or oil tanker maybe. He couldn't tell which direction it was moving, and he sure as hell didn't want to be run down by whatever it was. Another nice chapter for Tuttle's lecture: no lights.

Well, he could do something about that. He fiddled inside the cockpit and managed to mount and turn on his emergency beacon. Maybe the skipper of the ship would see him. He almost laughed out loud. The ship captain would be riding a hundred feet above him, looking straight ahead. He'd never see a small light bobbing in the waves at sea level.

He continued to be blown toward the lights and began to paddle to try to get out of the ship's path. But she didn't seem to be moving at all. It was almost as though the ship was at anchor. How could that be possible out in the middle of the North Atlantic?

Then he got close enough to see what the lights were illuminating. He couldn't believe his eyes. It wasn't a ship at all. It was an oil platform, one of the ones Tom had told him had been put close to the mainland against fierce environmental opposition. At that moment, he was ready to shake the hand of the chairman of Exxon or whoever had won that argument.

The wind blew him straight toward the base of the thing, where he could see lights delineating some sort of platform at water level. A landing platform, he assumed. His little craft banged against the steel frame and the boat rose and fell a dozen feet with every swell. Each time he crashed against the structure, he came close to turning over. He tried to time the swells and finally managed to ride one right over the top of the platform. As the water retreated, the kayak sat firmly on the heavy-gauge grating.

Aching from every pore, he pulled himself out of the boat and stood, wobbly, for the first time in many hours. He tied the boat off fore and aft to the platform and looked up. A steel ladder rose fifty feet above him. Damn! More stairs. Worse. A ladder.

His titanium foot seemed stiff and unresponsive. The brains in his foot had been seriously compromised by the cold salt water. Slowly, he began to climb. When he finally pulled himself onto another platform, he collapsed from the effort and looked up to see two men staring at him like he was a ghost from Davey Jones's locker.

"Hey there, mate. Where the bloody hell did you come from?"

"I'm glad to see you too," Garrett said, his voice shaking from the cold. "I was blown out to sea by the storm. Thought I was done for till I saw this place."

"Blooming miracle you washed up here. You look exhausted, all right. And cold. Don't worry. You're in good hands now." They helped him to his feet. Garrett tottered on his bad foot. One man started to put an arm around him, but Garrett motioned he could walk on his own.

The other man said, "Take him to one of the bunks near the workmen's galley. Looks like he could use some food and shuteye. I better tell Craig what's happened." He met the other man's eyes. "Good thing it's a slow night."

"I wasn't sure anyone would be here at all," said Garrett. "Don't they usually close you guys down when a hurricane's approaching?"

Again, the men exchanged looks. "Just a skeleton crew here, mate," said one. "To make sure things stay buttoned up and to pull wayward kayakers out of the drink. We've had one blow after another this year. Busiest hurricane season in decades. This storm wasn't expected to come so close to shore, or there would have been no one here at all."

The first man led Garrett to a small bunkroom. "Take a load off," he said. "You look like you could use some sleep."

"Any chance I could make a phone call? There are probably some pretty worried people wondering what happened to me, and I was with another man who might still be out there somewhere."

"If he's still out there, I don't like his chances," said the man. "Two miracles in one night would be pretty unlikely. Anyway, our phones and radio have been knocked out by the storm. We're on our own, I'm afraid."

It struck Garrett as odd, both that there would still be men on the rig and that they had no working communications, but though the thought nagged at him, he was too exhausted to think straight. The man left and Garrett tiredly removed his prosthesis. He placed it near a heater to dry out the electronics. Ever hopeful. Then he fell into bed and was asleep in a moment.

When he woke, the fury of the storm seemed not to have abated. He lay in the bunk listening. It felt like it was still the middle of the night. There was a throbbing in his phantom foot, which was probably what woke him.

He decided to get up and see if he could find some painkillers. He strapped on his foot and wandered down what seemed like innumerable corridors, up ladders and through various work areas lined with equipment. Apparently he'd been put at a far end of the rig from where others stayed. He found no other bunkrooms, kitchens, lounge areas or even bathrooms.

The rig was huge and an utter maze of pipelines, cranes and steel catwalks. At one point, he found himself outside on a platform that must have been a helicopter landing pad.

Then he was back inside again, in an obviously more luxurious living space. Floors were carpeted, which seemed a bit bizarre in a place where men had to walk around filthy and covered with grease and oil virtually all the time. He tried a door off the carpeted corridor, found a light switch, and then stood, stunned at what lay before him.

Spread out in front of him was a private living space that could have been something straight out of Club Med. The room was large and had a sliding glass door that led to a balcony and a bar recessed into one wall. There was a king-sized bed facing floor-to-ceiling mirrors, leather chairs, and a couch. Maybe he'd stumbled upon the boss's private digs, though it was hard to imagine even Bill Gates requiring accommodations like these on a working oil rig.

"You lost?" asked a voice immediately behind him.

Garrett turned. "Couldn't sleep," he said. He pulled up his pants leg and showed the man his titanium foot. "I was looking for some Tylenol. I get phantom pain in my leg sometimes." He waved a hand at the room. "Pretty posh accommodations. I guess they really take care of you guys out here."

The man snorted. "Not at my level, they don't. Come on, we're close to the medical room. I'll get you some painkillers. You shouldn't be wandering around on your own. Big rig can be a dangerous place if you don't know your way around. You could walk right off an open-ended platform and fall into the sea. It's happened before. My name's Craig, by the way. I'm in charge when they close down for a storm."

Garrett followed him out and down the hall. "How many are still on board?" he asked.

"Just three. You met the other two. Keeps us pretty busy making sure everything's battened down during high winds. Shouldn't bloody be here at all. Too dangerous, but the storm track veered from projections."

"What happens if the main brunt of it strikes you directly?"

"You don't want to know. More than one rig has toppled off its piers in a blow like this."

Like the other two men, Craig wore blue coveralls and a hard hat. He stopped at a cabinet long enough to pull out another helmet and hand it to Garrett.

"Keep this on whenever you're outside. Things fall from great heights around here even on completely still days."

"Thanks."

Next stop was a room that held a small operating table with what looked to Garrett like state-of-the-art equipment.

"Pretty impressive," he commented.

Craig shrugged. He was a big, muscular fellow, maybe thirty-five years old, not your typical donut-eating security guard, Garrett thought. "We're only forty minutes by chopper from the hospital in Sherbrooke, but the chopper can't come in high winds. We have to be ready to treat injuries on our own, everything from acute appendicitis to amputations, if necessary."

Garrett whistled. "That ever happened?"

"Not on this rig. We're still pretty new, but I've been on other rigs where it has."

Craig rummaged through a cabinet and came out with a bottle of Extra Strength Tylenol. "Here you go," he said. "Now I'll take you back to your room."

Though Craig was friendly, even affable, Garrett got the distinct impression the man didn't want him wandering around on his own. For his own safety? Perhaps. But it felt like something more than that.

24

THE TYLENOL HELPED WITH HIS leg pain and he fell into a fitful sleep. It was still dark when he woke for the second time. He lay listening to the wind howl through the rig's superstructure. The platform was alive with sounds, the banshee wail of the wind, creaking and swaying metal parts, periodic banging sounds as though loosened panels or walkways were being whipped about and slammed into the steel frame.

It was all disconcerting, yet Garrett felt nothing but relief that he was no longer out in that awful maelstrom in a plastic boat. He got up and strapped his foot on. It seemed to be working more or less normally. The hours in front of a heater had helped dry it out. It was a resilient bit of technology.

He headed out the door to his room, then stopped and went back for his helmet. Craig was right about that. It sounded like parts were falling from great heights all over the rig.

Out in the open, the wind seemed to be decreasing. He made his way to the more luxurious part of the rig that he'd stumbled upon earlier. He'd been unable to reconcile the room he'd seen. It was simply not the sort of thing any oil rig might have. It intrigued him. He wondered how many such rooms there were.

When he reached the higher-class accommodations, he moved along the plushly carpeted halls, looking into one room after another. There were at least a dozen rooms all more or less like the first one he'd seen. It was astonishing. Then he found himself in a large lounge area with thick leather couches, a bar along one wall, and a pool table. Double doors led to a dining room that looked like a miniature version of something out of the *Titanic*, with a large crystal chandelier and tables set with white linen.

What on earth was going on here? No oil corporation was going to treat their roughnecks to such accommodations. Could it be some sort of show rig, designed to fete high-level oil executives who wanted to tour their facilities?

The first streaks of daylight appeared on the horizon.

He looked at his watch, but it still wasn't working. The salt water had probably done it in for good. It had to be nearing six in the morning. The storm clouds must be diminishing to allow light to come through.

He didn't want to annoy his saviors any more than necessary. They'd been good to him. He made his way back to his own room and had been there just a few minutes before there was a rap on the door. He opened it to find one of the first two men he had encountered.

"Breakfast—if you're interested," he said.

Garrett followed the man to a small dining room off an even smaller galley. There was no crystal chandelier and no linen. Instead, Craig and the other man sat at a wooden table eating bacon and eggs. Craig got up when he saw them and went into the galley and came back almost immediately with a plate for Garrett. It contained hash browns and a muffin along with the eggs and bacon. He put the plate on the table and nodded at a coffee pot.

"Help yourself," he said. "Sleep all right?"

Garrett sat gratefully and dug into the eggs. "Like a baby once I had the painkiller. Thanks. Though I guess I woke up a couple of times. There was a lot of noise."

"You got that right. We've been tying things down all night. You'd think they made this bloody rig with parts from Costco."

"Some of the rooms I saw hardly came from Costco," Garrett said. "Hilton Hotels maybe."

The men looked away.

Craig said, "This rig is state of the art. Whole new concept, really. They bring the chief executives here to show it off. I hear the company has received orders for four similar platforms. Two of them are in Colombia."

Garrett nodded. It was just barely plausible, but he wasn't buying it. Still, if they wanted to stick to the company line, he wasn't going to argue.

"Any luck with your communications yet?" he asked.

"Yes," Craig replied. "I managed to contact the Coast Guard and they're sending a boat to pick you up. They were pretty excited to hear you were all right."

"Did they say anything about the man who was with me?"

"Yes, I spoke to him. Name of Tom Whitman. He was pretty relieved."

As if to affirm the words, they heard the piercing wail of a boat horn.

Craig looked at his watch. "Made good time. Wind must be dying down."

Garrett followed Craig down a warren of levels and walkways all the way to the ladder leading down to the platform where he had landed. He watched the Coast Guard cutter pull up and tie off. Tom jumped onto the deck, looked up and waved. Garrett saw Sarah holding onto the boat railing and she waved also.

He went down the ladder quickly, leaving Craig to follow. As soon as Garrett reached the bottom he turned and said in a low voice, "No need to mention I'm RCMP, Tom." His look took in Sarah and the other boatman, both of whom heard him as well.

Tom gave the slightest nod of his head, and then Craig was standing beside them.

"I'll give you a hand with that," he said, reaching down and untying the kayak. They passed it onto the boat, where Sarah secured it to the railing.

"Well," Garrett said, putting out his hand. "Thanks hardly seems adequate. I'd be halfway to Ireland by now . . . or halfway to Davy Jones's locker if not for you. Either way, I'm in your debt."

Craig shook hands and gave him a little salute. "Glad to be of assistance, mate," he said. "Might check the weather report next time you go for a joy ride."

"I'll do that," said Garrett.

Ten minutes later they were a hundred yards off the rig and Garrett sat on a bench holding Sarah's hand.

"Hope I didn't give you too big a scare," he said.

She squeezed his hand tightly. "I had you in your grave, Garrett. Damned fool thing to do, going out in that storm." He could see her eyes well up. He leaned in and kissed her. "I know," he said softly. "We didn't expect it. The one thing that kept me going when I was exhausted was the thought I'd never see you again." To Tom he said, "Why don't you take a GPS reading on the rig?"

Tom took out his device. "You planning a return visit? I'd say you already used up at least eight of your nine lives last night."

Garrett glanced at Sarah. "I just think it would be nice to put that thing on the charts for the next idiot who comes along." But he gave Tom a look that suggested a greater explanation was to come.

25

A<small>S THEY APPROACHED THE WHARF,</small> Garrett saw Roland's scallop boat getting ready to go out. When Roland saw them, he throttled the engine down and retied the boat up against the dock.

"Jest headin' out to look fer ya," he said. "Heard ya got yeself in a fix."

Garrett nodded. "Appreciate it, Roland. I really do."

For all his bombast and complaining, Roland was a man of the sea and would go out for any man who was lost. Garrett knew this and it was one thing about his old nemesis that he admired. That and maybe his carpentry skills.

They left Roland and Tom talking on the wharf and Garrett and Sarah walked to Sarah's house. When they arrived, Lonnie emerged from a car sitting in the driveway.

"Any luck with the girls?" Sarah asked.

He nodded. "Found them at Big Margaret's. You were right about that, Garrett." He stared at his cousin. "You look like something a rat dragged in. What the hell happened?"

"Long story," Garrett said. "I'll tell you about it sometime. Where are the girls now?"

"I dropped Ayesha at her family's store. Her father didn't say a word to me, just pulled the poor girl inside. I wasn't happy leaving her there, I can tell you. Lila's inside, probably asleep."

"Did they say why they did it?" Sarah asked.

He shrugged. "I think Lila was showing off to her new friend. You know, showing her the big city and all. Someone from Sweet Angels apparently saw them and before they knew it they were hustled off to Big Margaret's. God knows what would have happened if I hadn't shown up when I did. Big Margaret was glad to let them go when I said I worked for you, Garrett. Seems you put the fear of God into her on your last visit. She didn't want anything to do with you . . . not for a couple of girls she can probably replace in a Halifax minute."

Garrett knew it wasn't any fear he had put into Big Margaret but rather the appearance of Lonnie on her doorstep that explained the girls' release. The sight of Lonnie was usually enough to give anyone religion. "Good work, Lon. Thanks."

Lonnie nodded, then yawned. "I'm as beat as you look, chasing two wayward teens across half the province. I'm going to bed. Let me know if you hear anything about how Ayesha is doing."

Inside, they found a sheepish-looking Lila sitting at the table sipping from a stoneware mug. Before Garrett could say a word, she said, "I'm soooo stupid! I don't know what got into me. I've been locked up at Lloyd's stupid au naturel preserve for so long I was desperate to get back to the city. It was stupid and stupider to take Ayesha. Her father's going to kill her."

Sarah filled two more mugs and they sat down with her.

"I'm just glad you're okay," she said, taking the girl's hand. "And I'm glad you weren't heading straight for Big Margaret's on your own."

"God, no!" Lila said. "I didn't think I'd have any trouble keeping away from there. It's a freaking city, you know? But one of Big Margaret's girls happened to see us on the waterfront and before

I knew it, we were thrown into a car and taken back to Sweet Angels."

She started to shake, and Garrett realized she was crying, her tough facade crumbling. "I . . . I was never so scared. I thought they might kill us. I think it's the first time I realized I didn't want to go back to that life. And instead, I'd delivered Ayesha right to them. Big Margaret examined Ayesha all over. Made her strip down and everything. The poor kid was terrified. She would have been put in conditioning that very night if your cousin hadn't shown up."

"All right," Sarah said, stroking the girl's hair. "You're safe now." She looked at Garrett. "Can't you do something to put that awful woman out of business?"

"I can, and I will," Garrett said. "But it's important now to try to tie all these elements together. Maybe we can bring down more than just Big Margaret. Lloyd's in this somehow and Madame Liu and who knows who else." He looked at Lila. "Did you get a sense whether Ayesha was being abused at home?"

"It's abuse in my book," said Lila. "She's nothing but a slave. They don't let her have friends or go to school. The only reason she got to come here was 'cause her dad thought she could make some money."

Garrett looked troubled. "Anything . . . more direct?"

"You mean sex?" said Lila. "No. Her father isn't sexually molesting her. I think when Big Margaret stripped her down it was the first time Ayesha had ever been naked in front of anyone. She was so mortified."

"What difference does that make, Garrett?" Sarah said. "Lila told you how that poor girl is treated at home."

He shook his head. "It's a cultural question. I've talked to the woman in charge of many of these cases in Halifax. Absent direct sexual abuse, there's nothing I can do. Muslim girls are raised differently and the courts have held that the government can't get involved. Keeping Ayesha home for home schooling, making her conform to her family's religious beliefs, and having her work in a family-owned business is just not something open to legal redress."

Lila stared at him. "It's legalized slavery," she said. "That totally sucks!"

"I know. Life isn't fair. That's not something I have to tell you, Lila."

"No way her father's going to let her come back here to work," Lila said. "No matter how much you pay her. Not after what happened." She stared at Garrett with those big brown eyes. He could see the hurt in them for her new friend, but also for herself. "I suppose this means I have to go back to Lloyd's, right?" She shivered at the thought.

Sarah looked at Garrett with indignation on her face. He held up a hand to forestall her.

"No. I won't make you go back there," he said. "It won't be easy, but I'll work something out."

Sarah smiled. "She can stay here as long as she likes."

Lila beamed for the first time. She hugged Sarah tight. "I'll be good. I promise! I never want to go back to the city again. Maybe . . ." she straightened up and wiped tears away from her eyes. "Maybe I can get to see Ayesha somehow. Check on how she is."

Garrett met Sarah's eyes with a questioning look. He wondered if she knew how big a chew she had bitten off.

26

HALIFAX WAS ENJOYING A RARE sunny day, the kind that brought hordes of young people out onto Barrington Street. The grassy slopes of the Citadel were covered with scantily clad bodies and tourists strolled through the Public Gardens, stopping to feed the ducks or take pictures in front of the small model of the *Titanic* anchored in the pond.

Garrett strolled along the dirt pathways of the gardens and sat on a bench, half of which was taken by an elderly woman holding a bag of peanuts and dozing. The park was a frequent location for weddings and he watched as a Japanese couple stood on top of a metal platform backed by flowers while friends took their picture.

He was still feeling relieved that Lonnie had managed to find the girls in time. Big Margaret wasn't scared of much other than the loss of her moneymaking girls. But Lonnie was more than even she cared to bargain with.

Now he just needed to find some way to convince Sheila Vogler to free Lila from Lloyd's gentle control permanently. Sheila had a big heart but was also a stickler for the rules. Garrett had been surprised when she'd agreed to release Lila to his custody in the first place.

Still, there was a lot going on here. Maybe Lloyd and Madame Liu were only part of the story. Garrett felt like he had his hand on a small corner of something and that if he tugged long enough and hard enough, something big and mean and nasty might just pop out. Maybe another visit to Big Margaret would pay dividends.

The married couple was moving on, still celebrating and surrounded by their friends but in that uniquely quiet, respectful, and low-key manner the Japanese have. They would never want to disturb others in the park.

Garrett walked through the large old graveyard in the center of the city and continued on until he reached Dalhousie Medical School, where a longtime friend, a prosthetics specialist named Marcia Chisholm, did occasional work on his foot.

She looked up from her desk and gave him an appraising gaze. In her mid-forties, she remained very pert and attractive despite having three children under the age of ten. She'd been a late bloomer in that department.

"Hi Marcia. How's that stuff about growing new body parts from stem cells coming along?"

"Not next week, but it's coming, Garrett. In my professional opinion, you will be buried with two feet wholly your own."

"Be nice if it happens before I'm on my deathbed." He sat in a chair beside her desk and began to unstrap his foot. "I had a little accident. The thing sat in salt water for several hours. Thought you might be able to give me a tune-up."

"I believe not putting it in salt water is on page one of the instruction manual you were issued when we first fitted you out." She gave him a look. "Someone push you off a pier?"

He finished taking the foot off and handed it to her. She put it on the table in front of her and began a series of diagnostic tests using some serious electronics.

"Doesn't look too bad," she said.

"I attempted to dry it out in front of a heater," he offered helpfully.

"We don't generally recommend home recipes for twenty-thousand-dollar feet," she reprimanded. "Still," she added grudgingly, "I think it must have helped." She replaced the battery, tinkered a bit, and handed it back to him. "Good for three thousand miles or twenty thousand leagues, whichever comes first."

"Thanks. I'll try to keep the leagues to a minimum." He strapped the foot back in place, stood up and flexed it, walked around the room. "Better."

She shrugged. "Didn't do much. See if you can keep from stepping in a vat of hot wax on your next assignment, okay?"

"You'd be surprised the things we Mounties have to do out there in the field."

He kissed her on the cheek and walked jauntily to his car.

Next stop was to see Tuttle. On the way in he ran into Alvin, his former partner who'd been with him during the Point Pleasant stakeout.

"Been missing you," Alvin said.

"I heard you'd moved up. Assigned to that joint commission on illegal substances," said Garrett.

"Well, when you left I had no one to mentor me," he replied with a smile. "You know, steer me clear of the horrors of drug enforcement, keep me in something clean like prostitution. How am I going to learn how to steal a limo and leap onto boats in the dark when you're not around setting an example?"

"Good point," Garrett said. "Though the two areas aren't generally mutually exclusive."

"Tell me about it. It's all intertwined. Maybe we'll work together again. You never know."

They shook hands and Garrett watched him saunter to his car. He was still that wiry little guy, walking with a bit of a swagger. It must have been hard to be little and a cop at the same time.

Tuttle had his jacket off, sleeves rolled up. He was banging on the air conditioner, which had been his favorite office sport as long as Garrett had known him.

"Why don't you keek heem?" Garrett said.

"You keek heem! Do I look like a bloody Heemer? You're the one with the bionic foot." The Deputy Commissioner looked disgusted and fell into his chair. His forehead was damp with perspiration.

"Heard about your little escapade," he said. "Still think plastic boats are the way to go?"

"To be honest, no. Not unless the department wants to buy me my own GPS . . . and a small destroyer to attach it to."

"I'll be sure to put that requisition in next year's budget. You might want to get a weather band radio while you're at it. What a cockamamie scheme. Maybe you *should* retire. Sounds like most of your brain cells have taken a vacation anyway." Tuttle stared at him. "Did you learn anything at all?"

Garrett sat down and took a long breath. "About all I can say for certain is that there seem to be a lot of people doing suspicious things." He proceeded to fill Tuttle in on Lloyd, Madam Liu, Big Margaret, and even the strange accommodations on the oil rig. When he was finished, the Deputy Commissioner stared at him for a while.

"Big Margaret we know about," he said finally. "And Madame Liu, to a lesser extent. High-end escort services. Probably the two of them are in competition, though there seems to be enough business to go around."

"Madame Liu's got some sort of mansion on Lake Micmac," Garrett said. "It might be a good idea to do a raid. See what you find. Underage girls for certain."

Tuttle leaned forward and made a note on a pad. "We'll look into it," he said.

"Not right away," said Garrett. "I'll let you know. I don't want to scare anyone off for a while. Lloyd's in this and I'd like to shut him down. An exhibitionist in charge of a bunch of cowed teenagers is not the best business model. But . . ."

"What?"

"This whole thing smells of some sort of major prostitution ring. We might have a chance to shut down one of the big corridors of girls coming into Halifax and Canada in general. But I need more time."

Tuttle grunted. "Take all the time you need, but you might consider that I'm in the running for Commissioner. You break this soon and it just might help my chances."

"That certainly sounds like a good deal for me all right," Garrett said.

"Just keep moving ahead. I'll get you any assistance you need when you need it." With that he swiveled around and began to go through the pile of reports on his desk. Garrett was dismissed.

As he went out the main entrance, Kitty Wells came up to greet him. She had on a green leather jacket, tight leather miniskirt, and black nylons. She smiled broadly and put her hand through his arm. Every time she did that, Garrett thought, it meant she wanted something.

"How'd you get along with Lloyd?" he asked.

She made a face. "The man's a creep. How someone like that got put in charge of children is beyond me. Might be a whole exposé for my paper right there."

Garrett's surprise showed. He hadn't really thought highly enough of her to think she could see through Lloyd. Maybe there was more to Miss Wells than met the eye.

"To tell you the truth, I was a little worried about leaving you alone with the man. He's been keeping bad company lately, and you should be very careful around him. He doesn't have any scruples and from the way he looks at you, I think he'd have even fewer if he got you alone."

She smiled up at him and squeezed her perfect little body tightly against him. "I believe that's the nicest thing you've ever said to me, Garrett."

He carefully removed her arm from his own. "Just be careful, okay? And while we're on the subject, I'd appreciate it if you didn't latch on to me . . . especially when Sarah's around."

She pouted a perfect little pout. Garrett figured she must practice the look in the mirror. It made her so adorable.

"Oh, you're no fun, Garrett." Then she was immediately all business. "So what exactly is our Lloyd up to?"

"I'm not sure." He considered her. He made a practice of not telling reporters anything. Still, he didn't want her to get in trouble. He decided to give a little in order to make her see the risk of what she was doing. "Listen, this is off the record, understand?"

The pout reappeared, but she was a reporter and would take whatever she could get. "All right," she agreed.

"He's connected somehow with an escort service in Halifax. And the man's an exhibitionist. Exposes himself to the girls at Ecum Secum. That alone would be enough to bring him down and close his 'Troubled Youth Haven,' provided any of his charges were willing to testify against him."

"Do you think he could have anything to do with the girls who have been killed?"

He shrugged. "Anything's possible."

"I appreciate the heads-up, Garrett, I really do. I'm going to visit Lloyd this afternoon. I'll poke around, see what I can find out." She raised a hand at his expression. "Don't worry. I take your warning to heart. I won't be alone with him."

"Be certain of that," said Garrett. "I'm not joking, Kitty. He's a world-class manipulator. If there's a way to get you off alone with him somewhere . . ."

She slipped her arm back into his. "I'm pretty good at dealing with men, Garrett," she said sweetly.

"Men . . . yes. But Lloyd's some kind of animal. Don't underestimate him."

27

SARAH ARRANGED TO HAVE DINNER with Garrett and the two women who lived next door to Roland. Ingrid's husband was away.

"They want to thank you for getting that compressor turned off, and I think you'll like them, Gar. Besides, Ingrid is a great cook."

Garrett arrived about six in the evening, sinking down into the seat of his car as he passed the Cribby household. He'd almost never seen Roland or Rose outside or even at a window. They appeared to hunker down in the back of the house in their respective warrens and never expected visitors. Still, he thought it would be the better part of diplomacy if Roland didn't see him fraternizing with the neighbors. That would simply add fuel to the fire.

Sarah was waiting for him by the wharf, and they went in together. They were greeted warmly, both women insisting on hugging Garrett and thanking him profusely for his efforts on their behalf. As they were led into the sunken living room for the mandatory Manhattans, Garrett was surprised to see his neighbor Keith sitting in a comfortable chair in front of a low table filled with papers and maps. On the edge of the table was a frosted glass that Garrett knew held Pepsi. Keith never drank alcohol. There was no time for it. He took the business of recording the history of the Eastern shore seriously.

Ingrid thrust a Manhattan at Garrett and offered a toast.

"To our whale slayer," she said. "We are forever in your debt and shall sing your praises each night at bedtime for all eternity."

"Wow," said Garrett. "Things must have been getting pretty tense around here."

"You don't know the half of it," said Grace.

"I don't get it," he said. "Why am I a whale slayer?"

"It's what we call Roland," said Ingrid. "Because he's such a whale of a liar."

Garrett nodded his understanding. "I might call what he does embellishment, but it's a small point."

"Embellishment," Ingrid said. "There's a quaint notion. Back before he stopped talking to us altogether, he told me how he used to water-ski around the islands when he was a kid. Said he came around a point once at full speed and there was some sort of catamaran bearing straight down on him, so he bounced off a wave and flew over it. That's one. Want to hear another?"

Garrett laughed and held up his hands. "God, no. I've heard stories like that since I was twelve years old. For the record, Roland has never water-skied in his life. I was just trying to be diplomatic." He stared at the mass of papers on the table. "What on earth are you up to, Keith?"

"Our hosts asked me about property lines, so I brought along some tax maps and aerial surveys of the cove."

"You're looking to buy *more* property?" Sarah said to Ingrid. "I thought you might be selling out and looking for a new neighbor."

She shrugged. "We like it here, despite the whale. But I thought it might be wise to know precisely where the boundaries are between Roland's land and ours. He was furious when we dug the drainage ditch. Said it was on his property, but we had a survey done to prove it wasn't."

"Roland spent a lot of time on surveys of the bogs," said Keith, "back when he was planning his boglands country club. He knows the area inside out. But he was wrong about the location of the drainage ditch."

"I always thought the bogs were crown land," said Garrett.

"Some is, but not all of it. Anyway, when the women bought their extra lots, it pretty much put the kibosh on Roland's plans, crazy as they were. It's why he's been so hostile to them."

"Sheesh!" Ingrid said, "He ought to get down on his knees and thank us for saving him from wasting all his money on that cockamamie scheme."

"Roland knows the cove too well," said Grace. She pointed out a window to the spruce-covered hill above the house. "I think he's been spying on us from up in the trees. It's the only spot that provides a view right down on our deck."

Garrett stared out the window. "You actually caught him doing that?"

"No, but I've walked up there myself when he wasn't around. There are several places where someone cut tree branches to improve the view."

"Who owns the land?" Garrett asked Keith, who just shrugged.

"It's his land, Garrett. Nothing says he can't walk on his own land and trim the trees if he wants to. Much as I don't like it if that's what he's doing, Grace is the one who just admitted to trespassing."

"Can't you do something about it, Garrett?" Sarah asked.

He spread his hands. "Pretty hard if he owns the land. If you actually caught him looking at your house with binoculars . . . maybe . . . but he'd just claim he was bird-watching or looking at the architecture or something."

"I know the bird he's watching," said Ingrid. "It's Grace. As for the architecture—look, we weren't crazy about the design of this place either. It's pretty far out for this neck of the woods. We recognize that, but the price was right and the view is spectacular—at least on the ocean side."

Garrett sighed. The relaxed evening he'd been looking forward to was turning into a legal primer. He met Sarah's eyes and knew she understood how he felt. "I suppose you could build a fence to shield the deck," he said dubiously.

"Damn it, Garrett," said Ingrid. "Reason we moved here was because of the ocean view and the big spruce on the hillside. I don't see why we have to shutter ourselves off just because we live next door to an asshole."

"A whale," said Grace.

"I stand corrected," said Ingrid. "A whale of an asshole."

"I kind of doubt Roland would be quick enough to come up with either the bird-watching or the architecture excuse," said Keith. "He's not the sharpest knife in the drawer, if you know what I mean. Remember when he burned his boat?"

"He what?" Garrett asked.

"It was the highlight of last year's season," said Ingrid. "He'd been doing something in his boat on his way back in after a day of scalloping and the engine caught fire. He tried to make it back to the wharf and almost did, but the fire was nearly out of control. He opened the sea cocks thirty feet from the wharf to try to drown the flames. The boat sank in the shallows but not before it blew against the wharf and set the dock on fire as well."

"How did he get off?" Garrett asked incredulously.

"Jumped into the water at the last moment, swam ashore, and called the fire department. They managed to save most of the wharf. He had quite a time with the insurance company though, figuring out who had to pay for what."

"Only thing not underwater in his fishing boat were the WSR and GPS antennas," said Keith. "He had to bring in a crane and have the thing lifted out, and he spent the whole summer rebuilding and drying out the engine. Had to buy all new electronics."

"My god!" Garrett stared at them. "If it was anyone but Roland, I'd say that was utterly unbelievable."

"Story was all over Misery Bay," Keith went on. "Fishermen were winning drinks in every tavern up and down the coast with that one."

"Can we *please* stop talking about Roland," said Sarah, coming to Garrett's rescue. "I thought you invited us here for dinner, not a Cribby seminar."

"To turn a phrase," said Ingrid.

"You're right," said Grace. "Enough about the whale. We're celebrating the renewed silence of the cove."

So they settled back and talk turned to the wet summer weather, cove news, and as always, with Keith in attendance, local history. He told them about one of the more obscure shipwrecks off Lighthouse Point. There were thousands, maybe tens of thousands of shipwrecks off the rocky coasts of Nova Scotia.

"It's how Misery Bay got its name," Keith said. "The shoals and offshore islands here were a ship's graveyard back in the seventeenth, eighteenth, and nineteenth centuries. Wrecks were so common that bodies sometimes washed up by the score, the way bales of marijuana do today."

"I remember when we were growing up," said Garrett, "Keith found a Native American dugout down in the bay. It had been sunk with big rocks, probably as a way to hide it."

"Really?" said Grace. "That's fascinating. Who do you think it belonged to?"

"Well, we actually raised it from the lagoon," said Keith, "and gave it to the Maritime Museum in Halifax. They determined that it was Mi'kmaq in origin and was close to six hundred years old."

"That what got you so interested in local history?" Sarah asked.

Keith broke into a broad smile. "It was the first thing," he said. "I just sort of got hooked on it after that."

"Maybe Roland sank his boat as a way to hide it too," said Ingrid. "Too bad he wasn't aboard when it happened."

"Can't sink a whale," said Grace.

The conversation threatened to deteriorate into another anti-Roland tirade, but Keith saved the day by beginning one of his patented soliloquies, this one on an elderly woman who lived in the next cove.

"Abbey Whynot," he announced, as though answering someone's question. "Related to the Voglers, you know. Her ancestors were the first settlers at Ecum Secum. Old Martin Vogler built himself a hut on the shore near Balcomb's Lake. I was actually walking around the foundation a while back."

Sarah glanced at Garrett, her face a question mark. He just shrugged. There was no stopping Keith once he got on a roll. Non sequiturs were his specialty.

"Her husband was a whaler," Keith continued, as if this comment justified the conversational turn.

"I met her once," said Ingrid. "A lovely lady. She must be ancient now."

"Ninety-eight . . . last Thursday," said Keith. "It was also her eightieth wedding anniversary. Church had a little celebration and cake for her. Her husband didn't participate. He was killed at sea seventy-five years ago at the age of thirty-four. Whaler went down off the Grand Banks in the blow of '39. Sixteen men killed. Storm hit late on a Friday afternoon and blew for three days."

Garrett couldn't repress a smile. Keith's memory for obscure dates was a thing of wonder. The man had to have a photographic memory and must have spent his evenings pondering old church records and recorded deeds. Of course, it was possible he just made this stuff up, knowing no one would ever question him or try to verify anything he said. But Garrett knew that wasn't the case. Keith simply loved history and enjoyed nothing more than being the dispenser of information.

He let the historian rattle on, relieved that Roland was no longer the topic. But he had a bad feeling about the long-term consequences of the local neighborhood feud.

28

KITTY DID SOMETHING THAT RARELY occurred to her. She actually dressed down for her appointment with Lloyd. She traded her all-leather outfit for a pair of designer jeans, admittedly, but they were the most ordinary thing she owned. She added a plain dark blouse and even eased back on the makeup. It was all a real sacrifice, but when she looked at the results in the mirror, she had to admit she still looked gorgeous. It just wasn't possible to hide her incredible beauty.

She was no fool, and took Garrett's warning to heart. Men found her irresistible, which had often helped her career. Lloyd was a type she'd met before. He looked at her like a lizard sizing up a fly. She knew from the very first moment that he would do anything—even act like a gentleman if he thought it would work—to get into her pants.

Her appointment with him was for late Saturday afternoon, which seemed like a time when there would be plenty of kids and other staff around. But when she pulled in and parked in front of the main building, she was immediately aware that there were no other cars. She saw no kids or staff either, but assumed they were busy back in the gardens or other buildings.

She was halfway onto the porch before she saw Lloyd. He stood buck naked in the window holding a camera. The instant she saw him, the camera flashed, catching her startled reaction.

The next moment, Lloyd stood in the doorway, still with no clothes on.

"I like to work au naturel in the garden when no one is around." He gave her a lecherous grin. "Maybe you'd like to join me?"

Kitty looked straight at him and said, "Sorry, I'm working." She sat on one of the chairs on the porch, paying his glorious prick no further attention.

"I once interviewed the entire Calgary football team in their locker room," she said. "Two-hundred-fifty-pound giants were coming and going with no clothes on the whole time." She glanced down at Lloyd. "Believe me, there was a whole lot *more* to see on that occasion."

Lloyd wilted visibly. He was silent for a moment, then retreated inside. When he reappeared, he wore jeans and a T-shirt. He sat down across from her. "Your loss," he said.

Kitty leaned forward and placed a small tape recorder on the table between them. "You don't mind, do you?" She asked. "I like to be accurate."

"I don't know. Exactly what is it you want to talk about?" He looked thoroughly pissed off and sullen. Exposing himself to an adult had proved less stimulating than it had been for fifteen-year-old girls. Kitty might have passed for fifteen herself, except for her more mature demeanor and presence. She'd been around the block a few times and had dealt with unwanted male attention since she was twelve years old.

"Well," she began. "I wanted to ask you more about your haven for young people. In my business, one has to get around, ask lots of questions. One thing I heard was that you were connected with some of the escort services in the city."

He started to interrupt, but she moved quickly to defuse the question. "My feeling is that it's sort of a requirement of your job. You know, to study the places your kids come out of in order to better understand what they've been through."

Lloyd's look of indignation turned on a dime. "You're absolutely right," he said. "We've had extraordinary luck in turning young kids' lives around. It's important to know where they are coming from."

The man was an idiot, Kitty decided. He'd just exposed himself to her in the most provocative way possible, even taking a picture of her reaction. And now he expected her to believe that he was so concerned about his protégés that he hounded the escort services in order to *study* them.

But it was part of Kitty's professionalism that she'd begun the interview the way she had, complementing his *work ethic*, for Christ's sake. Now Lloyd was back on familiar ground, boasting about himself. God, but men loved to boast in front of a beautiful woman. That small fact alone had gotten her some of the best material of her career. All she had to do was shut up and let her interviewees skewer themselves as they bent over backward in their attempts to impress her.

"I know my way around the services in Halifax," Lloyd said, smugly. "Studied them for years, and of course I know some of the inside story from the girls we have here. I know how those outfits work and the hold they have on their girls."

Kitty had no doubt this was the truth. He'd learned how to exploit young girls, and it made sense that he'd learned that particular skill during his on-the-job training, so to speak, at places like Sweet Angels. She was beginning to feel that, if anything, Garrett had underestimated Lloyd's level of pathology.

"That's interesting," she said, leaning forward, her cute little forehead wrinkling. "How do girls get into the business in the first place?"

"Unfortunately, they're easy marks. Pimps find them in all the usual places, bus and train stops, diners, moping around on the waterfront with no obvious resources. And of course, many of them are brought in from other countries. It's kind of interesting, really." He was clearly back at ease now, expounding on a subject he knew lots about to a beautiful woman who seemed to hang on his every word.

"How do you mean?" Kitty asked, her attention obviously riveted on this fascinating man.

"Well, the foreign girls have grown in popularity in recent years. It goes in waves. Russians were very big for a while, then Hispanics, and the last year or so, it's been all Asians. Hard to know whether the market reflects the customers' demands or the availability spurs the demand. Be an interesting study there."

"So knowing the tricks of the trade, so to speak," Kitty said, "you can come back here and apply what you've learned to straightening these kids out?"

He nodded. "And it's not easy. You wouldn't believe how much a lot of these girls want to go back on the job. They love the work. It's all they know."

That last remark Kitty knew was at least partly true. The girls had no resources, no education, no support from family. For most, the pimp who got his hands on her was the first person some of these girls felt had ever loved her.

She realized Lloyd was back to scrutinizing her in great detail. That she had shown real interest in what he was saying had rekindled his desire for her.

"Take you, for instance," he said. "You could probably never believe you might actually like such a life. But I can tell you, you would be very popular. In a year, you'd be rich. You'd have a stable of regulars, all high-end clients, good-looking guys, rich guys who would treat you nice. Take you out to dinner in the best places.

Hell, I know one girl who was so gorgeous that a guy . . . a wealthy Arab businessman . . . took her to live in Paris."

Kitty looked down. "I guess I can see what you mean. That would be attractive all right for some women."

"Maybe you?" Lloyd asked. He leaned forward, placed one hand on Kitty's knee. "I could make it happen. I know some people. You could make more money than you ever dreamed of."

Kitty was close to feeling panicky at his touch. Why the hell was there no one else around? Still, this was clearly an opening she hadn't expected. He was actually telling her he could introduce her to a high-end clientele, the crème de la crème of the escort services. She needed to play along. Garrett would be proud of her if she uncovered something like this.

"I don't know," she said slowly. "It's kind of an interesting idea. How would I go about it?"

Lloyd leaned back. He nodded at the tape recorder. "Turn that off and we'll talk," he said.

29

GARRETT MET LONNIE ON THE Halifax waterfront. It was the first chance they'd had to talk since his cousin had rescued Ayesha and Lila from Big Margaret's clutches and delivered them home again.

They were in a tiny greasy spoon off Barrington Street. Very greasy. A Louisiana oil spill. But Lonnie liked the place for some reason. He was already seated in a booth, looking like a Tonka truck, holding an ironware coffee mug in his ham-sized grip.

"Better not hold that thing too tight or it will pop," Garrett said, as he squeezed in opposite his cousin.

"Hate these things," Lonnie said. "Look at the size of this finger hole. What kind of normal finger is going to fit into something like this?"

Garrett stared at him. "Normal? Your finger is almost as big around as my wrist. You're lucky they let you sit in this booth. You probably exceed the provincial weight standard for booth patrons."

"Anyone check on Ayesha since I left her at home?" Lonnie asked.

Garrett shook his head. "Haven't had time, though Lila and Sarah may try to scope her out when her father isn't around."

"The man didn't take kindly to my delivering his daughter back to him. Like the girl even being in the presence of any man outside her family was a scandal."

"Yeah, that's part of the cultural thing, or so Sheila tells me," said Garrett. "You're lucky he didn't pop you one by way of thanks for rescuing her."

Lonnie looked at him like he was nuts. He could have bench-pressed three men the size of Ayesha's father. "I didn't tell him anything about where the girls were—not that I had the chance. He just pulled her inside and slammed the door. So if Ayesha manages to keep quiet about it, he probably won't know anything about Big Margaret."

Garrett nodded. "Let's hope. If he ever finds out what really happened, I suspect that poor girl could face a real beating . . . or worse."

"So what's going on with Madame Liu? We going to turn that place upside down or what?"

Garrett drank some coffee. It was black and heavy and made the hair stand up on the back of his neck. Several longshoremen came into the diner and took seats at the counter. They eyed Lonnie cautiously and spoke in low voices. Everyone in this part of town knew who Lonnie was.

Garrett filled him in on his current thinking about a possible prostitution ring. Lonnie listened intently. He hated pimps. It was part of his upbringing, and while his grandmother, if she were still alive, would not have been happy to know how her grandson made his living, Lonnie's surprising moral streak was especially in evidence when it came to pimps.

When Garrett was through, Lonnie grunted. "So we're just going to leave those sweethearts alone?"

"For a while. I want to pull on some loose ends. See what turns up. You want to help?"

"Sure. My boss loves it when I disappear for a week to spend time with pimps."

"I didn't know you had a boss. Thought you said you were some kind of freelancer."

Lonnie tilted his massive head. "I use the term loosely. Most of my work is political. Guys who employ me don't want to know what I really do. They just pay me to solve their problems."

Garrett raised a hand. "Don't tell me another word. I don't want to know either. I'm going to look into this whole pile of dung some more. Why don't you follow Lloyd around for a while? See what he does with his free time."

"Okay." Lonnie looked at his watch. "So when's whatshisface gonna get here?"

Before Garrett could reply, the door opened and a man walked in looking about as out of place as one could in this part of town. He wore a thousand-dollar double-breasted suit, wing-tip shoes, and polarized lenses that he swept off before closing the door behind him, so he could see into the gloomy interior. His hair was flawless, his shave the same, and Garrett would have bet he had a hundred-dollar manicure.

The newcomer saw them and walked the length of the diner counter, glancing uneasily at the men there, and slipped into the booth next to Garrett. There was no room next to Lonnie.

Garrett shook his hand and said to Lonnie. "This is Louis Liotino. He works in the firm of Wanbolt, Hartless, and Noseworthy. Lou, say hello to my cousin, Lonnie."

"Christ, Garrett, your cousin? You sure don't look anything alike."

"I've got a better personality too," Garrett said. "You want coffee or anything?"

Liotino shook his head. "Had lunch already and it took me half an hour to find this . . . establishment. Look, I owe you, Garrett, I know that, and I pay my debts, but sitting in here just about evens the score."

Lonnie's face was expressionless. He disliked high-powered attorneys almost as much as pimps. Didn't see much difference between the two.

Garrett nodded. To Lonnie he said, "Lou's firm represents Global Resources, one of ExxonMobil's partners in the Sable Off-shore Energy Project. I asked him to meet us here to talk about one of Global's rigs."

"The one you visited," Lonnie said.

"Don't know what you're into, Garrett," said Liotino, "or how much I can tell you. But go ahead. Fire away."

"Kind of curious," Garrett said. "I spent the night on one of your rigs, the one closest to shore here off Lighthouse Point."

Liotino raised an eyebrow. "They're not my rigs. We just represent the company. But I wouldn't mind knowing how the hell you pulled that off. I've never been allowed to visit. And I gather it's a pretty popular place amongst company high-rollers."

"I dropped by . . . uh . . . unexpectedly. Rig was closed down for the hurricane but the three guards pretty much had to let me stay. I saw maybe a dozen rooms that looked like something out of Club Med. Huge beds, mirrored ceilings, private bars and balconies. High-end stuff. Kind of wondered if you knew anything about it."

Lou studied his hands. "Global's our biggest client, Garrett. And they're not in too good a mood right now. Yields for natural gas have been declining. The province has taken a hit too. Windfall royalties are off nearly 70 percent from two years ago. What you're asking is privileged information."

"Why I'm wining and dining you in this fine establishment. Give you a chance to even the score between us. You didn't think I was going to ask for the name of your tailor, did you? I already sort of have an idea about this, Lou. I just want confirmation. Because the only reason I can think of for an offshore rig to have accommodations like that is for special customers. *Very* special customers."

Lou sighed. "You've been in this business too long, Garrett. Thought you were going to retire."

"I am. This is sort of my last hurrah, you might say. You know the sorts of things I investigate. Just tell me if I'm wasting my time."

Liotino looked at the greasy counter where the other men sat. It seemed to remind him where he was and he eased his hands back so his suit cuffs wouldn't touch the table surface. "Like I said, Garrett, I've never been invited. But you hear things . . . around the water cooler, you know?"

"What sort of things?"

"Shit. If I tell you this, you got to swear no one ever finds out where the information came from."

"All right."

Liotino looked at Lonnie. "Him too."

Lonnie nodded once, said nothing.

"Okay. Global has a side business. A few of their oil rigs around the world have the special accommodations you mentioned. It's a sweet deal. The rigs are outside territorial waters, so what goes on is pretty much out of bounds to legal authorities."

"And what goes on?"

"They bring special clients in—usually from countries that are interested in purchasing one of their state-of-the-art oil rigs. Executives from Colombia, South Africa, Argentina, as well as from the Middle East. Part of the sales pitch involves a few nights' stay at the high-end rigs, where they are treated to . . . well, you know what they are treated to."

"All the freebies they want," Lonnie said quietly. He put his hands on the table and levered himself out of the booth. Garrett noticed that the metal stretch band on his watch was stretched out almost to its maximum to accommodate his enormous forearms. "Gotta go. Job for one of the politicians. Then I'll latch onto Mr. Exhibitionist. Let me know when you need me, Gar."

He lumbered toward the door, filling the available space between the wall and the counter stools, and that was after the men on the stools all cringed away from him.

Lou shook his head, watching him go. "Not the sort of guy you want to meet late at night outside a bar," he said.

"More than you know," Garrett replied. "Any idea where the pimps who run Global Resources get their girls?"

"Christ, Garrett. You can't call the CEO of one of the biggest oil franchises in the world a pimp."

"Never heard a better word for it. You know anything about the ages of the girls involved?"

Liotino looked sick. "You're not going to believe me if I tell you they're all over twenty-one, are you?"

Garrett just stared at him.

Lou leaned in closer and said in a low voice, "It's the young girls, thirteen, fourteen, fifteen-year-old virgins that these foreign guys like. They don't want to have to worry about getting social diseases. Each girl is only used once. Then they ship them on to an escort service somewhere." He sat back. "Pretty sweet deal. Unspoiled goods. Guaranteed fresh and clean."

Garrett shook his head. "Good thing Lonnie didn't hear that. What I'd like to know is how you can be aware something like this goes on and not want to do something about it?"

He shrugged his shoulders. "Not my business. Besides, everyone thinks solicitors are nothing but pimps anyway. I just try to keep my own nose clean."

"A moment ago you were complaining that you'd never been invited to one of the special rigs. Kind of sounded like you'd go if you got the opportunity."

"What do you want from me, Garrett? I told you what you wanted to know. I have to go. I've got another appointment."

Garrett put his hand on Lou's arm. "All right, thanks for the information. But I'm not cool about your involvement."

"Christ, Garrett! I've got nothing to do with it."

"Far as I'm concerned anyone who knows about this is complicit. One thing. I hear a whisper that you warned anyone at Global about this, you'll be taking the fall along with everyone else."

Liotino stared at Garrett like he was a crazy man. "The fall? Christ, Garrett, you have any idea how powerful these people are? Believe me, you go after them, I won't have to worry about you at all. You'll be spending the rest of eternity encased in cement in the footing of an oil rig in the middle of the ocean."

He stood up, straightened his jacket, and looked at the men at the counter. "Been nice knowing you." He walked quickly past the men and out the door, turning the doorknob with just two fingers to avoid any contaminants it might hold.

30

G ARRETT'S CELL PHONE RANG WHILE he was still in the diner. He was careful about who he gave his number to, so there were only a handful of possibilities. Tuttle was at the top of the list, but it didn't sound like him at all. It was Sarah.

"You had a kind of funny call from Kitty Wells," she said.

"Funny as in hilarious?"

"No. As in worrisome."

He was silent.

"She wanted to get a message to you, and I'd given her my number."

"What's the message?"

"She said she could only talk for a minute. That she was closing in on something substantial regarding Lloyd. Maybe a big break in what happened to those girls who were killed. She sounded pretty excited . . . wired, you know? She said she was going to meet some people and then she'd call again. That's it."

He swore. "She say anything at all about where she was going?"

"Nope. And it sounded like she was really in a hurry. She hung up very suddenly."

Annoying as he found Kitty, Garrett felt a degree of responsibility. She was a reporter and followed where leads took her, but she had no idea what she was getting into by playing Lloyd. And he knew she was playing him. Using her sex as a lure, as she did with every man she met who wasn't a relative or gay.

Only Lloyd wasn't every man.

Still, there wasn't much he could do with the information he had. Kitty had said they were going to meet someone, so they probably weren't going to be at Ecum Secum's Haven for Troubled Youth.

"I'm coming back tonight," he said.

"You don't think they could have gone to Halifax?"

"Anything's possible, but the only place I can think to look is Ecum Secum. Maybe someone there knows something about Lloyd's whereabouts. The kids I met didn't seem to have any hesitation in squealing on Lloyd if they could."

"I'll meet you," Sarah said. "Can you be there by seven-thirty?"

He hesitated, trying to think of some way to dissuade her, but knew it was hopeless. Besides, he wanted to see her. It seemed as though every time they got together, something interrupted them: Tom needing help, the girls' disappearance, then their reappearance, the dead girl on the island. He was feeling in strong need of her company.

There was silence on her end of the line. Then she said, "I know. I miss you too. We better get some quality time together soon, Gar, or I'm going to have to jump the first man I see—oh my god!"

"What?"

"I just saw Roland turn onto the wharf. Listen. He doesn't count, okay?"

Garrett smiled. He could think of some ways to spend quality time as well. "What's he doing?"

"Oh, I don't know. He's always moving fishing gear around or looking for tourists to gouge somehow."

"All right. I'll see you at seven-thirty. You get there before me, stay in your car till I show up. I don't want you anywhere near Lloyd when I'm not around."

He hung up, left the diner, and walked quickly to his car. His foot felt good. Marcia had always been a miracle worker with the thing. He crossed the Angus L. Macdonald Bridge, circled the rotary, and took 107 heading for the Eastern shore. After twenty miles, it turned into Route 7, the two-lane highway that went all the way to Antigonish. He wondered sometimes how the locals didn't go bonkers traveling over this same road day after day.

The familiar landmarks swept past his window. The Gold Coast Restaurant, where he'd gone for lobster with his parents when he was a kid. The new mussel farm near Ship Harbor. They grew the mussels on lines sunk into the bay, and they were the best, biggest, and most succulent shellfish in the province, supplying all the restaurants in Halifax. Then the turnoff at Tangier for Willy Krauch's smoked fish. Willy had a wall of newspaper clippings in the small outlet. He'd supplied smoked salmon to the Queen of England. Garrett loved stopping at Willy's and smelling the wonderful combination of wood smoke and salmon. The old man had been dead for many years, and the business was now run by his offspring who zipped around, incongruously, on ATVs.

His thoughts never wandered far from Kitty. What the hell was she up to? Lloyd would never have bragged about anything to do with the girls who'd been killed, not unless he felt there was no need to worry about who Kitty was going to tell or what she might try to put on TV. And that meant Kitty was in deep shit.

He'd revised some of his feelings about the reporter. She was nosy, oversexed, and ambitious. But he'd experienced some of her persistence and thought she might actually be a pretty good reporter, in her own way. If she thought she had her teeth into something with Lloyd, she'd go after it. He had no doubt about that. And he had no doubt that Lloyd would be just fine with having the beautiful Miss Wells cozying up to him.

He drove with one hand on the wheel and dialed Lonnie with the other. His cousin answered on the first ring.

"I'm going to Ecum Secum to see if I can locate Lloyd. But I want you to look around for him in the city. Highest priority."

"What's going on?"

"I think Kitty Wells, the reporter, may be with him, trying to investigate him. If she is, she's going to be in a world of trouble."

Lonnie grunted. "The reporter on Channel 9?"

"That's the one."

"I can see where Lloyd might be attracted. Good-looking woman. I'll pay a call on Big Margaret. Haven't seen her in two days. She probably misses me."

"Right. Listen, if you happen upon them and Kitty seems all right, don't barrel in and spoil things for her, okay? She might be in control of the situation. Just keep me posted."

He pulled in to Ecum Secum just as the evening light was fading and the deer were beginning their evening parade across the highway. He narrowly missed a doe and her fawn and was glad when he finally saw the sign for Troubled Youth. Sarah sat in her car waiting for him.

She kissed him hungrily and said, "There's more where that came from, big boy."

"Please," Garrett said, "Not in front of the children."

"What children? I've been here for thirty minutes and haven't seen a soul."

He looked around. The place certainly seemed deserted. But if Lloyd wasn't here, then it figured the kids would be having a hootenanny somewhere.

"Let's walk up back," he said.

They passed the more showy buildings near the road and worked their way deeper into the compound. Most of the area around and between the buildings was cultivated with vegetables in long neat rows. Lloyd evidently was a stickler for neatness, so long as someone else was doing the work.

Garrett stopped in front of one small cabin and stared at it, remembering. Sarah gave him a puzzled look.

"What is it?" she asked.

"I used to live here."

"With the girlfriend?"

He nodded.

She made a show of bending over and checking the foundation. "Looks like it survived the pounding."

He gave her a look. "My wild youth. Truth is, I could have been a customer for Lloyd's Haven if Lon and I'd been caught doing some of the stuff we did back then."

She nodded speculatively. "And if you'd been caught, no job in law enforcement, right? And we never would have met." She squeezed his arm. "I'm kind of glad you survived your wild youth."

"What's that?" He was looking up behind the cabin where the woods grew thick. There was a flickering glow above the treeline.

"Looks like a fire," Sarah said.

They began to climb higher. The evening light was fading, but the dirt path was still clear enough. As they neared the glow, they could hear music and then saw dark figures moving around a big fire.

They entered the circle of firelight where about twenty boys and girls were lying around. Most were paired off and making out on blankets. The music came from a boom box and there was a picnic table with food and drinks on it.

"I guess we can safely conclude Lloyd isn't here tonight," said Garrett, disappointed.

The kids gradually became aware of them. Most sat up and stared, but a few couples, pretty close to fully involved in sex, paid them no attention. Garrett recognized the boy who'd been playing the guitar at his earlier meeting.

"Looking for Lloyd," Garrett said. "Guess he's not here, huh?"

The boy waved a hand that took in the booze, food and make-out couples. "Gone for the weekend," he said. He seemed to be the unofficial spokesman when Lloyd wasn't around.

"Any idea where he is?"

The boy considered him for a moment, then looked around the group. "Anyone know where the asshole went?" he asked.

A thin, mousy-faced girl unlocked lips with a heavyset boy long enough to say, "Don't know where he went, but he had company and he looked like he was planning on a good time."

"He had a woman with him?"

The girl nodded. "Real pretty too, but tiny, like a doll almost. You had to feel sorry for her. I thought she might be a hooker, the way Lloyd was holding her arm. Possessive-like."

"Who else but a hooker would go with Lloyd?" said the guitar player.

"Was she being held against her will?" Sarah asked.

"Didn't seem like it," the girl said. "But I only saw them together for a minute." She turned away and locked lips again with the heavy-set boy who was becoming impatient. Pound for pound, Garrett thought, these young teens must be some of the most sexually experienced kids in the province. He glanced at Sarah and shrugged.

"Have a good night, kids," he said, turning away. "Don't do anything I wouldn't do."

There was a sprinkling of laughter and one voice in the darkness cried, "I bet you two do it all the time."

"I wish," Sarah whispered, as they worked their way back down the path, now almost invisible in the dark. When they were out of sight, Garrett stopped suddenly and pulled her close to him. He kissed her hard.

When they came up for air, Sarah murmured, "Trying to set an example for the kids?"

He stroked her hair. "For troubled youth, they looked to be having a whole lot more fun than we are."

31

KITTY STARED OUT THE WINDOW of Lloyd's car. They were in an upscale part of Halifax, near Bedford Basin. Lloyd had volunteered to introduce her to some people who might agree to an interview about the world of child prostitution. He cloaked it all in the guise of research, saying he'd been around long enough to have built up a certain level of trust with these people.

She couldn't quite believe anyone breaking the law would want to talk about it openly, but as a reporter she'd used the promise of confidentiality to score big interviews in the past. People liked to talk about what they did. Even scumbags. It had been a revelation to her when she started out in the business. She was already working on the story in her mind. An exclusive look at how young girls were ensnared in the world of prostitution. Maybe she'd make the national news.

But she was beginning to have second thoughts. Lloyd oozed charm like snake oil. As he drove, he emphasized his points by touching a hand to her thigh, just long enough to send a message.

"Who are we going to see exactly?" Kitty asked.

"Woman named Madame Liu. She runs a service called Madame Liu's Lulus. I called ahead while you were in the bathroom, told her we were coming."

"And she wants to talk about this?"

"Long as no names are involved. I told her all about you. She said she's seen you on TV. I guess she liked what she saw."

Kitty wasn't sure how to take that. She leaned against the door, trying to get as far from Lloyd as possible. She knew she was taking a risk. But that's what reporters did, and she felt a certain safety in her fame. What fool in the prostitution business was going to hurt a well-known figure? It would be suicidal. On the other hand, she couldn't really imagine why they'd be willing to talk to her either. So she was on edge as they turned into the entrance to a large Victorian house with manicured lawns.

Lloyd bounced out of the car, went around, and opened her door, taking her arm proprietarily. "Nice place," he said. "You'll like it. Very upscale."

The door was opened by a bear of a man who seemed incapable of speech. He just grunted and waved them through a foyer filled with Asian statues. Lloyd obviously knew where he was going as he directed Kitty into a luxurious room with leather furniture and a roaring fire.

Standing in front of the fire was an attractive Chinese woman. She looked Kitty up and down, then said to Lloyd, "You've got an eye all right, Lloyd."

Kitty noticed that the huge man who had let them in had entered behind them and now stood to one side, cracking his knuckles, or so it seemed. She tried to assert herself.

"Madame Liu? I want to thank you for seeing me. I can assure you anything you say to me will be held in complete confidence." She held out her hand.

The woman stared at her hand. Then, without preamble, she said to Lloyd, "Let's see the goods."

Lloyd smiled and turned to Kitty. "Take your clothes off," he said.

Kitty blinked. "What?"

"You heard me. I told you we might be able to land you a job, but we got to see the merchandise first."

Her eyes went wide. "I'm here for an interview."

"It's a kind of interview," he replied.

"I haven't got all day," Madame Liu said.

Kitty looked at the woman, then at the giant standing behind her. Her heart felt like a piece of lead. She swung her head around to look at Lloyd.

"You don't want to do this," she said. "You can't believe the trouble I can get you into."

"Oh, I don't think you'll be much trouble at all," said Lloyd, and the way he said it sent a chill right down to Kitty's tiny little toes. "You think you're pretty hot stuff, don't you? Well, let's see how special you really are."

Madame Liu nodded at the giant. "Strip now," she said, "or he'll do it for you."

But Kitty was frozen. For all her worldliness and experience, she'd never been humiliated in such a manner before. She opened her mouth to say that Garrett knew where she was but something stopped her. These were not nice people. If they thought the cops had any idea who she was with, they might decide to just kill her and be done with it.

Lloyd said, "I kind of prefer it when we have to take their clothes off. But any way you want it, Miss Wells, it's going to happen."

A sheen broke out on Kitty's upper lip. She believed him. She was completely helpless here. She could see it in Lloyd's eyes. There was no way she wasn't going to be standing naked in front of these people. Slowly, she lowered her purse to the floor, then stepped out of her shoes. Her hands moved like an automaton as she unbuttoned her blouse. The big guy leaned forward in anticipation. Lloyd settled back to watch with a confident smile, as he saw her resistance collapse.

Kitty dropped the blouse on the floor and began to undo her pants. She could feel her face redden under Lloyd's stare. Then the pants were gone too. Her legs were perfectly proportioned, slim and tanned. She stood uncertainly, as if hoping for divine intervention.

"Come on," Lloyd said. "You should have taken my invitation to do a little gardening with me when you had the chance. Might have been more fun. Now I got to share you."

Madame Liu clapped her hands once, loudly. The sudden noise shocked Kitty. "Everything off!" the woman ordered. "Now." She nodded impatiently to the big man, who started forward eagerly.

Kitty raised one hand, palm out, to forestall him. Then she reached behind her back and unhooked her bra. Her breasts were the least favorite part of her body. She'd always thought they were too small, like those of a young girl, but they were pert and nicely shaped. She saw Lloyd stare at them and take in his breath.

Then she removed her panties and stood with her arms folded across her chest.

"Arms over your head," Madame Liu said, "and turn around."

Kitty complied, feeling like she was in a dream, some sort of exotic sexual nightmare. Except she realized she was excited. More excited than she'd ever been. An incredible warmth came over her, and her entire body flushed red.

Madame Liu nodded approvingly. "You were right, Lloyd. She's pretty special. Some men like that petite little body. It's like one of our thirteen-year-old girls, except with more awareness in the eyes. And the body flush . . . exquisite. I can market that at the highest level."

Kitty had her back to them now and could feel Lloyd's eyes looking down at her narrow waist, her perfect, tiny little bottom. Goose bumps rose on her buttocks. She felt Lloyd's hand on the small of her back and almost leaped out of her skin as he ran his hand lower, caressing the goose bumps. He gave her butt a playful squeeze.

'Not bad," he said. "Not bad at all. I bet you're a real tiger in the sack."

"All right," said Madame Liu. "That's enough."

Kitty moved as if in a dream. She was completely humiliated that Lloyd had exposed her so utterly. He was the last man on earth she would ever have chosen to be naked in front of. Yet she was stunned at how incredibly hot and aroused she felt, on the edge of having an orgasm. She'd never realized before how erotic it was to feel totally helpless. Kind of like all those men she'd teased and tortured over the years with her body and looks and moves. She'd enjoyed that feeling of power and control she'd had over them. Now she had an idea how they felt.

Madame Liu opened a drawer in her desk, took out a fat wad of bills, and handed them to Lloyd. "Let me know if you come across any more like her," she said. "No one knows you brought her here, right?"

Lloyd nodded, stuffing the bills in his pocket. "I'd be glad to start the conditioning if you like," he said.

Madame Liu shook her head, "I'm sure you would. But this one will require some very careful handling. I don't want to waste her . . . use her up . . . before I sell her. I'll get a fortune for her. I have to decide how much work she'll need."

Kitty listened in disbelief. They were talking about selling her body. "You . . . you can't do this," she said. "You know who I am?"

"That's what will make the price so high," said Madam Liu. "Relax, from what you've just showed us, you might enjoy the experience. That body flush wasn't embarrassment. It was excitement, wasn't it?"

The woman nodded to the giant. He put one hand on Kitty's arm and began to pull her toward a door opposite the fireplace.

"What about my clothes?" she said.

"You won't need them," said Madame Liu. "We'll provide clothes when it's time."

"Sorry I couldn't give you a workout, Kitty," said Lloyd, real disappointment in his voice. "But I certainly enjoyed the show. Too bad we couldn't tape it. Now there would be some 'news at eleven' that might have really jump-started your career."

He was still laughing at his own joke as Kitty and the monster left the room. He led her down a corridor and up a set of steps to a bedroom. He groped her buttocks and then pushed her through the door and locked it behind her.

She stood, breath short, still working on controlling the adrenalin that was racing through her veins. The room was spare compared to the rest of the house. There was a bed with a sheet, pillow, and single blanket. A large stuffed chair sat in one corner opposite a plain brown dresser with a vase on top. It held some sort of dried weeds. That was the sum total of the furnishings. No pictures on the walls. There were no windows, no other doors. Not even a closet. She wondered how many other women had been here in the same situation she was in.

She went over and listened at the door. She could hear the heavy footsteps of the man going away and then nothing. She tried the handle. Locked tight. She leaned her weight against it, but since she weighed only ninety-eight pounds soaking wet, it didn't even creak.

There was nothing else to do. Up until the moment she was locked in this room, it might have been questionable whether what had just happened to her was even illegal. She'd investigated rape cases before and knew there were gray areas in the law. She'd accompanied Lloyd here of her own free will. No force had been used. Lloyd had simply asked her to take off her clothes and she had complied. That there was coercion was a given, but she knew coercion was a hard thing to prove.

And the truth was she *had* been aroused by what happened. It was humiliating and frightening, but also the most stimulating and sexually exciting few minutes of her life. She could just imagine how some hotshot solicitor would make that point in court. She had obviously engaged in a consensual sexual experience. Maybe she liked bondage. "Do you enjoy being told what to do, Miss Wells?" the solicitor would say, titillating the court.

Out loud she muttered, "Get a grip!"

None of that mattered now. Once the bedroom door was closed and locked, the crime became kidnapping and she had real fears for her life. They intended to make money off her, and that meant they would never be able to let her go. They would use her to the fullest extent possible and then kill her . . . if the work didn't do it for them. No one would ever hear of Kitty Wells again. Her dreams of national fame as a correspondent would be nothing but a sad footnote about an attractive young reporter who had simply disappeared. It happened to women every day.

She sat in the chair, drew her legs up, and wrapped her arms around them. The room was warm enough, but she realized how strange it was not to be able to get dressed when she wanted to. And right now she wanted to more than anything. How long would it be before anyone missed her? Thank God she'd left a message for Garrett. But he'd have no idea where she was. Then she began to wonder how long it would be before someone came for her conditioning.

32

L ONNIE SAT ON A BENCH in the Halifax Public Gardens. He nearly filled the entire thing just by himself. He held a bag of popcorn and tossed kernels to the ducks and geese that paraded around him.

He was something of a familiar sight to regulars in the gardens. He often came here after carrying out some particularly unpleasant job on the docks. It relaxed him. For all of his frightening demeanor, he was not a violent man. He didn't like hurting people, but somehow his size had connived to make that his profession. Even in Iraq, he'd felt distaste for the things he had to do. He was an anomaly. A man of gentle nature forced to do violent things upon occasion.

It was a living.

Fortunately, those occasions were rare. His appearance and, after a time, reputation made the use of his hands a relatively rare occurrence. Nearly everyone he encountered bent over backward to do whatever he required of them.

His true nature was a vestige of his upbringing. His grandmother had believed in him, and her gentle remonstrances had stayed with him long after she was gone.

He'd just come from Big Margaret's. Though she was a tough and bitter woman, she nevertheless was one of those who blanched at the very sight of the leviathan at her door. She operated in the same underground milieu that Lonnie did and was well aware of his reputation. When he asked her a question, she answered truthfully and fully, hoping only that he would leave as soon as possible.

But in this case, Big Margaret really knew nothing about Kitty Wells. Didn't even know she was a television personality. Knew nothing about Lloyd's little seduction. Still, she offered up Lloyd's name as one possible avenue of interest and, hopefully, as a way to get Lonnie to move on. But she had no idea where Lloyd was and Lonnie believed her. Then she'd given him another lead, one that required some thought, which was why he was here in the park.

He fed the ducks and watched the couples that always seemed to abound in the beautiful gardens. Tourists and young lovers were everywhere.

It made him feel normal to be here among the flowers and birds and honeymooners. He'd yearned for intimacy and normalcy in his own life from the time he was a teenager. His grandmother's admonitions kept him from going to professionals for his sexual needs. He refused to think of himself as some sort of pervert. As a result, he'd had very few sexual experiences in his life. Garrett had tried to set him up with blind dates a few times, but it never worked, and he grew tired of the frightened looks the women invariably exhibited when they saw him.

He watched a young couple as they walked around the dirt pathways holding hands and sighed. That would never be a part of his life. The bleakness of that reality had to be pushed constantly to the back of his mind. He had refocused his life, in odd ways, toward helping people. Working with Garrett gave him an outlet for that part of his nature. It counterbalanced the unpleasant things he had to do. But sometimes it was a struggle not to get angry at the cruel joke life had played on him.

He wanted to help Kitty Wells. It sounded like she might be in real trouble from what Garrett had suggested. But he was stymied about how to find her. Still, he would keep on the trail, and Lloyd's too. About the best feeling he'd had in a while had been when he'd managed to rescue Lila and Ayesha from Big Margaret, and it had been followed by one of the worst, when he'd had to turn Ayesha over to her father. His service in the Gulf had given him insight into the Muslim world and its exploitation of women. And he had hated it, how many of them could only appear in public in full black burqas, faces invisible.

Indeed, their entire lives were invisible. Hidden away from men, not allowed to work, go to school, drive a car, or go out in public, sold by their families to men not of their choosing, only to have daughters they would have to raise in the same manner.

He felt deep sympathy for them, for their constricted lives, not unlike how his own life was constricted. He took out a large handful of corn and threw it in an arc so at least twenty birds came scooting in from all directions.

He watched them and thought about what else Big Margaret had told him.

33

"LET'S GO BACK TO MY place," Sarah whispered to Garrett after their long kiss.

He was in no mood to argue. Though still worried about Kitty, he had no idea how to find her. Sarah was clearly in heat. He felt the same way. Watching those young kids making out had reawakened some of their own youthful passion. They made it back to her house in record time.

As soon as they were in the kitchen door, they began to grapple and peel clothes off. Then Sarah saw the note on the table. She stopped.

"What's wrong?" Garrett asked, nearly panting with longing for her.

"There's something on the table," she said.

He let go of her and picked up the note. It was from Lila. They read it together.

"Where are you guys?" it said. "I don't know what to do. Ayesha called, said her father had been beating her. She was hysterical. I told her I'd walk to her house and be there at nine-thirty. If she could get out, she could come stay with us. Lila."

"Uh-oh," said Garrett. He looked at the clock on the wall. It was after eleven. Sarah looked very worried.

"Come on. We'll go to Ayesha's house. We'll find them."

The little grocery with the home above it was dark and silent. Of course. It was late. Everyone was asleep.

Garrett banged on the door and kept on banging until a light went on inside. A minute later, Mr. Marshed appeared. He was wearing shorts and a T-shirt. He stared through the door at Garrett for a moment, then undid the lock.

"Yes? What is it?" he asked.

"We're looking for Lila," Garrett said. "We have reason to believe she came to see Ayesha."

The man's face grew dark. "That girl is not welcome here. She is a bad influence on my daughter. That should be clear enough after their running away to the city. My family will never live down such a thing." He started to close the door but Garrett blocked it with his foot.

"We need to see Ayesha," He said. "To make sure she knows nothing about where Lila is. If she says she doesn't know, we'll leave."

"It's late. Everyone is in bed," the man said. "You have no right to demand this."

"I have every legal right," said Garrett. "We have information leading us to believe Lila came here. She's a minor. We're concerned for her safety."

This was a stretch legally. In fact, they had no reason to believe Lila was in any danger. But Garrett knew the man wouldn't be completely sure about the law. They could see him struggling over what to do. Finally, he released the door and waved them in.

"I will get her," he said.

He returned a minute later, his face filled with fury. "She's not here," he said. "Her window onto the fire escape is open. Your Lila has taken her away from me. I demand you find her."

Garrett exchanged looks with Sarah. "All right," he said. "We'll find them and I'll bring Ayesha home." He jerked his head to Sarah to leave and closed the door on Mr. Marshed's contorted face.

"Where do you think they are?" Sarah asked. "We didn't pass anyone on the road. Where would they have gone?"

"I don't know. But we'll check the house first to make sure. Maybe they hid from any cars they heard coming, in case it was Ayesha's father."

Sure enough, the lights were on in the house and they found Lila and Ayesha sitting on the couch. One look at Ayesha told the whole story. Her face was badly bruised.

Lila looked at Garrett accusingly. "She's got marks on her body too," she said. "How could you have her sent back there? Look what he's done to her."

Sarah sat down and put her arm around the girl. She'd obviously been crying but seemed to have used up all that emotion. Her face looked blank. Garrett had seen such looks before, on the faces of so many girls who got nothing but pain from those who were supposed to love them.

"We'll have to take you to the hospital, Ayesha," he said.

"I . . . I don't ever want to go back home," she said.

"All right," Garrett said. "There's a process we have to follow. And the first step is to get confirmation from the hospital that you've been beaten. That sets protective services in motion. I'm going to call someone I know and she'll help arrange a place for you to stay after that."

"Why can't she stay with us?" Lila asked.

He spread his hands. "That might be possible. I don't know. There's going to be legal action on this that will take time."

Ayesha seemed to be struggling with something.

"What is it?" Sarah asked.

"My . . . my father . . . threatened to sell me if I ever ran away again."

Sarah stared at her in horror. "What?"

"He said there was a man who wanted to buy me for a wife." Tears began to flow down her face again.

"Garrett?" Sarah was looking at him, her face filled with indignation.

He swore under his breath. What a mess. He'd always thought prostitution exhibited the worst face of humanity. But in some parts of the world, actually selling one's child as a wife, sex slave, and servant was commonplace. It was more horrible than anything, the ultimate betrayal.

But it wasn't legal in Canada. "Your father can't do that, Ayesha. It's against the law in this country. Maybe he was only trying to scare you. There is no legal way he can do that." He gave Sarah a look. "Lila, why don't you get Ayesha ready and we'll drive to the hospital."

Lila took Ayesha into the bedroom. As soon as the door was closed, Sarah started.

"That man's a monster," she said. "Selling his daughter? Beating her? Making her work like a slave? You've got to do something, Garrett."

He nodded slowly. "I will, but it will take time and we may not be able to keep Ayesha here. It might actually be better for her if she went away somewhere rather than remain so close to her father."

He raised a hand as Sarah started in again.

"Listen, what I said to Ayesha was only partly true. Legally, her father can't just sell her. But I suspect he could try to make it happen through coercion. Some sects have managed to skirt the laws on this, citing their religious beliefs. So spinoff groups of the Mormons and others have married their girls off at very young ages to men who already have multiple wives. The courts have had trouble dealing with this." He pulled her close and stared into her eyes. "We'll do the very best we can for her, okay?"

She nodded, a single tear coming down her face. She gave him a little smile. "If for no other reason, Gar, than because we are never going to get into bed together at this rate."

34

M ADAME LIU STOOD AT THE edge of Lake Micmac and watched as a small steam launch approached from the island. This was an important meeting. She'd met the man she thought of as her boss only once before. Considering he was the CEO of one of the world's major oil companies, he remained something of a mysterious figure. She wasn't even sure of his nationality. The man moved about the world on a series of private planes, yachts, trains, and limos, all paid for by humanity's constant, surging need for energy.

That he was a cautious man, she well knew. Their interactions had gone on for nearly a decade before she'd been allowed to meet him in person. That she had been first vetted extensively and, indeed, been financed in ways that linked her own security to his, were all part of the intricate buildup of their relationship. One thing she clearly understood: he was a man in control of what seemed to be an endless supply of money. She hoped to get as big a chunk of it as she could for her new acquisition.

As the boat pulled close to shore, she waved a hand and the giant got out of her car, unlocked the rear door, and pulled out Kitty Wells. The reporter was completely made up and had on new clothes specially bought for her. She'd been bathed and perfumed and had her hair done. There had been no time for conditioning.

When the call came in from Madame Liu's boss for someone special, there had barely been time to get the woman ready. She was a little nervous about tendering an untried prospect. But . . . one did what one could.

The two women climbed into the boat and sat in comfortable chairs. The giant handed Liu a manila envelope, then pushed the boat off and drove the car away. Kitty was hardly sad to see him go, but the boat held several more men and she saw no hope of escape.

They motored slowly toward the island. It was a quiet, warm evening with a full moon. She might have enjoyed herself if she didn't know that whatever was about to happen would very likely determine the rest of her life . . . whether she would *have* the rest of her life.

"When we get there," said Madame Liu, "do not speak unless you are spoken to. There will be several men. One of them is the most important. You will do whatever he says. Do you understand?"

Kitty nodded. She was totally helpless and knew it. Still, the one part of her they couldn't completely control was her mind. She could still use it to try to think of some way to escape.

The little launch puttered into a small cove and a man came out to receive the lines and tie it up. Then he stood to one side and watched the women get out, admiring Kitty in the process. He knew what she was here for.

They crossed a central compound and entered an oversized log cabin that was reminiscent of some of the large Adirondack "great camps" Kitty had seen. Very luxurious.

Inside, four men sat in comfortable chairs around a huge fireplace. They were drinking highballs and looked like members of a middle-agers' fraternity. Kitty felt all eyes fall on her as they approached. Three of the men appeared to be in their thirties or early forties. Two looked of Arabic descent; one was black. The fourth man, Kitty instantly knew, was the one to be afraid of.

He was probably in his early fifties, tall and stockily built. He looked very powerful. He had thick black hair beginning to fleck gray around the temples and wore brown corduroy trousers with a leather vest over a pale maroon shirt open at the neck to reveal a heavy gold necklace. There was a wedding band on his finger. It was difficult to determine his race or nationality. He had a trim mustache and sharp, almost fierce features. Kitty had never seen eyes so black and cold.

Madame Liu went over to the man and spoke to him quietly. He nodded, never taking his eyes off Kitty. All of the men were watching her.

"Let's see the video first," said the man, settling back in his chair.

Madame Liu opened the manila envelope and handed a disc to one of the other men, who put it into a DVD machine and turned on a large flatscreen television. There was a moment of snow and then Kitty took in her breath as she saw herself in her former life.

The video was one of her television broadcasts. It had been taken within the last few weeks. She tried to remember the big news events of that day, but mostly she just stared, feeling totally surreal about her circumstances. The video lasted five minutes, then ended, and the same man got up and turned the machine off.

Now Kitty felt the eyes of the men on her even more intently. The man in charge smiled slightly. "I believe I promised you something special this evening," he said to the others. "Meet Miss Kitty Wells, lately our local news broadcaster. Come over here, Miss Wells."

Kitty glanced at Madame Liu, who nodded for her to comply. She moved forward into the circle of sitting men and faced them. She was beginning to feel that strange warmth again, flowing up from her toes.

"Been something of a life change for you, I imagine, Kitty," said the tall man. "Hard to accept, but it will be easier if you do accept it. You aren't the first good-looking woman whose looks got her ahead in this world. In your new life, it will take you farther than you could ever have imagined."

She stared into his eyes, afraid to say anything. Seeing the images of herself on television, so in control, the center of a busy news studio, had brought home like a lead balloon just how rapidly her circumstances had changed. She was terrified and felt a near paralysis of both mind and body. But there was something else, that strange sense of intense warmth beginning to surge through her.

"Let me put your mind at ease," said the man. "Nothing bad will happen to you here tonight. This is simply . . ."—he glanced at the other men and smiled a hard smile—"a get-acquainted meeting. Madame Liu said she had someone special and you certainly qualify. Your final disposition has not yet been determined."

He paused, his eyes taking in her diminutive size. "You look bigger on TV," he said. "But I suppose we are all smaller in real life. We would like to see just how small you really are. Would you be so kind as to disrobe." He looked away and picked up his drink.

The warmth had now progressed up Kitty's legs and into her torso. She knew what was about to happen and the prospect was as distressful as it had been with Lloyd. But there was nothing she could do.

She began to take off her blouse, looking into the eyes of each man in turn. A moment ago they'd been watching a sophisticated, well-known TV reporter read the news to many thousands of people. Now that same woman was about to expose herself to them utterly. It was an added bit of titillation, a stroke of genius for Madame Liu to bring that video.

Kitty undressed slowly. As she had the last time, she felt a sense that if she could only delay a few seconds, something might save her from this humiliation. But there was nothing, and in a moment she stood naked before the men.

Their eyes ran up and down her body like probing lasers. Madame Liu told her to turn around and she did so, allowing the men to examine her backside. She felt like a prize steer in a stockyard. Two of the men spoke to each other conversationally, pointing out one part of her anatomy or another.

Kitty felt totally out of control. The warmth was taking over, sweeping across her body. She tried to resist but it was impossible. She shuddered as her body flushed red from her toes to her face. The men exclaimed at the phenomenon. The older man stood up and went over to her. He stared at the red flush on her body. He reached out a finger and touched her stomach, watching the momentarily white skin quickly return to red again.

"Quite extraordinary," he said. To Miss Liu, he added, "You were right. She might be a keeper. At least for a while."

35

AT THE HOSPITAL, A NURSE took Ayesha away and Garrett, Sarah, and Lila had to sit in a waiting room.

Lila fidgeted in her chair. "I should be with her," she said. "Ayesha's real sensitive about being seen naked. This is like pouring salt on the wound."

Garrett nodded. "I know. I talked to the admitting nurse and told her the situation. She understands how Muslim women feel about this stuff. A doctor will have to see her to confirm the injuries. But they've done this sort of thing before and will be as caring as possible, trust me."

It took about an hour. When Ayesha finally emerged, she looked completely drained. The doctor brought out some forms and motioned to Garrett, who went over to speak to him alone.

"Normally we have to call in the police," the doctor said, "but I guess that's you." He handed a copy of the report to Garrett. "In my opinion, the girl was quite severely beaten. Whoever did it didn't bother to conceal the damage. Sometimes, you know, they at least make an effort to put the marks out of sight."

"Her father has such complete control over her life, I don't think he ever imagined that anyone might intervene. She doesn't go to public school, has no friends, and almost never leaves the store."

The doctor sighed and glanced over at Ayesha. "There could also be psychological damage. She should have an evaluation on that too. I suggested someone in the report for that." He paused, the sympathy in his face clear. "Does she have someplace to go?"

"We're working on that," said Garrett. "Thanks for helping us out, doctor."

"About the worst thing I see down here in this little rural backwater," he said, "is what families do to each other. It's really amazing. Good luck with her." He turned and walked briskly away.

"Now what?" asked Lila.

"Next stop is to visit Sheila Vogler in Halifax," said Garrett.

"Not tonight it isn't," Sarah said. "It's late and we're all tired. Your contact isn't going to be working at this hour, Garrett. Tomorrow will be soon enough. We're going to bed. Things will look better in the morning."

He wasn't so sure, but Sarah was right about one thing. Ayesha was dead on her feet. All of a sudden, he felt his own eyes grow heavy. "All right," he said. "I could use some shuteye too. I'll present this paperwork to Sheila first thing in the morning and figure out where we go from there."

He made a call to Ayesha's father to tell him she was all right and wouldn't be coming home that night. The man was indignant and began yelling at Garrett, who promptly hung up the phone.

He drove home, his car bumping up the dirt lane to the old house. It was a clear, moonless night and the darkness fell over him like a shroud. When he was little and had been playing too late with his friends, he used to hate having to walk up the lane alone in the pitch dark, coyotes yipping somewhere in the black night. Sometimes he would get Lonnie to go home with him and spend the night. He was never scared of the dark when Lonnie was with him.

With the girls safe for the moment, his attention again turned to Kitty. What had she been thinking, going off with Lloyd? Her experience with men had given her a sense of invulnerability. Men melted before her. She was the one with the power.

Which was pretty bizarre when you thought about it. She was so tiny that any man over the age of fifteen could probably overpower her. She'd learned to use her looks as a way to level the playing field . . . in work as well as play. A pouty lip, a suggestive twitch of her hips, a hand momentarily placed on a man's arm or thigh. These were the coin of the realm in Kitty Wells's world.

He stumbled around till he found the light switch inside the door and saw some small creature race across the kitchen floor and disappear into a hole in the foundation. Terrific. Next it will be bats, he thought. Then his cell phone rang.

"Don't you ever sleep?" Lonnie asked.

"Mounties never sleep."

"I don't even think you are a Mountie. You don't wear a uniform. You don't drive a marked car. Near as I can tell you pretty much do whatever the hell you want. You're just like me."

"There's no one like you, Lon. You'll be glad to hear we've taken Ayesha out of her house. The evidence that her father was beating her is irrefutable, and I've got papers to deliver to Sheila Vogler in the morning that will put the girl in foster care. Sarah has offered to have her stay with her, if that can be worked out."

He grunted. "Might be better if she got a little farther away from her old man."

"I know. We'll see how it goes. Any luck finding Kitty?"

"Big Margaret said she didn't know anything. I pushed her pretty hard. She gave me Lloyd's name but then said that if Miss Wells was in the sort of trouble I was suggesting, there was one man she'd heard of who bought special girls for top dollar."

"Who?"

"She didn't know his name but said she thought he had something to do with Global Resources."

"The oil company? As what? A janitor? Chairman of the Board? The major stockholder? CEO? What? How the hell are we supposed to find him?"

"Global has its Canadian headquarters in Halifax. I called pretending I was a reporter and asked for an interview."

Garrett raised an eyebrow. "That was enterprising of you."

"The woman said their authorized spokesperson was out of the country but that I was in luck. Their CEO is holding a press conference tomorrow . . . that's today already . . . at two o'clock to answer questions about the effects of the hurricane on their operations."

"You get his name?"

"Anthony DeMaio."

Garrett sighed. "All right. It's a start. I need to get at least a couple hours of sleep. Then I'll drive into the city. Got to see Sheila with Ayesha's paperwork. Did you find out where the press conference is being held?"

"Press room at the Holiday Inn. Two p.m. I'll meet you there."

36

I T WAS NINE-THIRTY AND NIGHT had fallen over the cove and myriad islands outside Roland's window. The overcast skies blotted out even the stars. Through his screened window he could hear music coming from the house next door, but all the windows facing his direction were shut and curtained as usual.

His frustration was palpable. Rose had been in the hospital for several days, but she was coming home tomorrow. He wouldn't get another chance home alone like this for who knew how long. He could tell by the muted sounds of the music that no one was on the deck. It was too cold anyway. It felt like the night was going to be wasted from his viewpoint.

Grace floated in front of him on the full size poster he'd had made in the city. Her slim, tanned body and golden hair were the regular nighttime subject of his dreams. She had small features, sensuous lips, and dark eyes that had long ago bewitched him. She was perfect.

If he'd had half a brain and befriended the women when they'd first moved in, he might have been able to see Grace often, just stopping by to be neighborly. And they probably would have been careless about the windows too. But he didn't have a clue how to befriend someone. No one ever wanted to be his friend. And so he had taken the wrong tack and now they knew precisely who and what he was. As a result, he almost never got to see Grace. Sometimes it nearly drove him mad with frustration to think of her being so close.

He gathered up his binoculars and camera with the zoom, put on a black sweatshirt with large pockets and a black fisherman's cap. He made his way down the stairs and out onto the back deck. He stood for a moment listening to the night. There was the sound of music coming from the house next door. Suddenly, the door onto the driveway opened and he heard voices laughing and talking. It went on for several minutes. Then two cars started and began to move slowly out on to the cove road.

It appeared the party was over.

Roland slipped off the deck and began to climb the little trail up into the woods. It was so dark, he had trouble staying on the path. Finally, he wheezed to the first opening in the trees he had reconnoitered and stopped to catch his breath. He was terribly out of shape. He sat all day in front of the TV or his computer. Even when he was scalloping, once his arthritis began acting up, he mostly sat in his boat and let the two young boys he hired do any heavy lifting.

He didn't have a lobster license. They were often handed down through families and could cost upwards of two hundred thousand dollars. Instead, he set traps illegally and emptied them in the evenings after the real lobstermen were through for the day. He wasn't fooling anyone. The joke around the cove was that Roland's favorite dish was "poached" lobster.

He pulled the binoculars out and looked through the trees. He had a perfect view of the side of the house he so rarely got to see. Lights shone from every window and there were no blinds at all to block the spectacular ocean view. He could see people moving around inside.

But it wasn't enough. He had to get closer. He bushwhacked down to the little cove near the back of the house, stumbling over roots and boulders, his gimpy leg no help in the thick brush.

When he was doing something like this, it was as though a part of him went away, like he was watching someone in a movie. A movie with a character he felt vaguely sorry for. What a poor slob *this* guy was, sneaking around, trying to spy on people who had real lives. His feelings of inadequacy were only reinforced when he did this sort of thing. But he craved interaction with people and this was the only way he knew how to get it.

He worked his way to the deck. He could see into the kitchen here. Then, suddenly, he saw her. Grace was standing at the sink washing dishes. She had on a light shift completely open at the back all the way to her waist. Her back was tanned and he could see the slim muscles ripple between her perfect shoulder blades. As she moved about, the sides of the dress billowed, revealing the tantalizing swell of her breasts.

He couldn't believe his luck. He climbed up onto the deck, moving as silently as he could. His limp made his movements awkward, and he worried that the deck might creak. But it was new and solidly built. The kitchen window was open with a screen in place, and he could hear Grace talking to someone.

He sidled along the wall until he was next to the window. He didn't know where the other people were and was afraid someone might decide to come out onto the deck. But he couldn't resist his opportunity.

He peered quickly around the edge of the window. Perfect. He could see the living room beyond the open counter of the kitchen that separated the two spaces. Ingrid and Leo were sitting on the couch facing away from Grace and talking. Grace joined in the conversation as she washed the dishes.

Quickly, Roland pulled out his camera and adjusted it so there was no flash. Then he leaned in and used the zoom to get a perfect picture of Grace's exposed back. He took several quick shots to make sure. It would be a nice addition to his other photo of her.

Then he stood, listening to them. In some bizarre way, he almost felt like a member of the family listening in on a conversation. Besides, maybe he could pick up some information that would be useful in his neighborhood wars.

They were talking about one of the guests who'd just left. Something about what a talented artist he was. Then the conversation turned to plans for the next day. Leo and Ingrid were going into the city to do some shopping. Grace had decided to stay home and work on her tan. It was supposed to be a rare sunny day.

Roland's heart leaped. Rose wouldn't be back until he went to pick her up. What time he decided to do that was up to him. He now knew that Grace would be alone tomorrow, out on the sun deck, maybe even nude. His heart raced just thinking about it.

It wasn't that he intended to confront Grace or hurt her in any way. He was far too much of a coward to do that. He was simply driven by his desire to look at her, to be near her, to take her picture when he could. It was the closest he would ever get to a real relationship. It was sick and he knew it and still he couldn't help himself.

Ingrid was saying something about the whale. What was it? Roland had been the first to discover the beast when it had washed up and had made a good deal of money taking tourists out to see it.

He couldn't quite hear Ingrid clearly. She was the farthest from the window. He leaned in and cupped his ear. She was going on and on. The whale this and the whale that. Leo and Grace were laughing hysterically.

Then he froze. They weren't talking about the whale on the beach. They were talking about him. They were calling *him* the whale. He felt a wave of fury that they would be talking about him that way in front of Grace. And that she was laughing.

He backed away and went down the steps onto the beach again, his face red with humiliation. Who did they think they were? His family had lived in this cove for six generations. What right did they have to come here with their snobby city values and look down on him?

He bumped into a large cement urn filled with flowers. He picked it up in his anger and heaved it out into the ocean, where it sank beneath the waves as the flowers came apart, floating away on the shimmering water surface, illuminated by the lights from the windows.

Tomorrow. Grace would be home alone.

37

KITTY FELT LIKE SHE WAS having an out-of-body experience. Following her display for the cold-eyed man and his friends, she'd been placed in another locked room. At least this time she had her clothes.

It was amazing how helpless it made one feel to be deprived of clothing. The thought of escape seemed somehow insurmountable when one was naked. Of course, her captors understood this implicitly. She'd gotten herself involved with a very sophisticated prostitution ring and these people obviously had lots of experience in controlling helpless women.

Madame Liu was gone. Kitty had no illusions about the woman. She'd shown not a morsel of compassion. But at least she'd been of the same gender. Kitty knew she'd been sold yet again, this time to the man with the powerful build and calculating demeanor. Somehow, knowing that she was now utterly under the control of men and only men was not reassuring.

After a lonely hour, the door opened and she was ushered out by two men she hadn't seen before. They tied her hands behind her back and blindfolded her. Then, one man holding on to each arm, they led her through the compound.

She assumed they were going to another building on the island, but then she heard the lap of water and realized they were loading her onto the little steam launch again. After a short crossing, she was put into a car. The drive was almost an hour. Though she tried to make sense out of the sounds and traffic noises, the truth was she had no idea where they were going.

Then they humped over a series of railroad tracks, she heard a train whistle, and the car came to a stop. The door opened and again she was held by two men.

"Where are we going?" she asked, stumbling as they pulled her from the car. No one bothered to answer. Then she heard a sound she recognized, the thwap-thwap of a helicopter. A moment later she was lifted bodily into the aircraft.

One of the men joked, "She don't weigh no more than an extra-large latte."

"I'd like to give her something extra large," said the other man.

"Yeah, well, keep your hands off, if you know what's good for you. She's above your pay grade."

One of the men gave Kitty's bottom a squeeze. "Can't blame us for taking a little sample."

She was buckled in as the rotors of the chopper began to spin more quickly. Then they were airborne, and Kitty Wells had no idea where on earth she was being taken.

When they landed she could feel the aircraft being buffeted by the wind. They had to settle twice before the pilot felt comfortable and then they were down, the blades whirring down in volume.

The chopper door opened and she was again manhandled out. She was getting tired of being hauled around by men, most of whom copped a feel whenever they felt like it. Which was often. Under the circumstances, however, she was quite certain being groped was better than what lay ahead.

The men led her forward through the wind. Then they were inside. They walked a short distance, a door opened, and one of the men untied her, removed the blindfold, and pushed her into yet another windowless room. She'd had no idea there were so many rooms in the world without windows. She listened as they went away, then looked around.

It was a sort of small lounge, with matching sofa and arm chairs, a vanity with mirror, and pictures on the walls. A door led to a bathroom and shower, also with no window. Practically upscale, she thought, compared to her last space. She could hear the wind outside whistling loudly through the eaves, or whatever. For all she knew she could be in Newfoundland.

She looked in the mirror. Her hair had been blown about and she automatically tried to push it back into some semblance of order. She still wore the elegant clothes Madame Liu had given her. Probably included in the sale price: *One used television anchorwoman, with clothes, $10,000.*

Of course, she had no idea what Liu had paid Lloyd or what the new guy had paid Liu. She only knew the price went up each time.

She was alone for what seemed like hours. With no way to tell time, she curled up on the sofa and waited. Her helplessness washed over her in waves. Whatever came through that door next was going to be very unpleasant. Even if Garrett had some way to figure out what had happened to her, there was no chance at all he could find her. She'd been moved three times. No one in the world knew where she was or what was happening to her.

At work, her assistant would have called her home and her cottage, maybe even her mother. Her understudy would be sitting right now in her anchor chair preparing for the evening news. If she did a good job, it wouldn't be long before Kitty's job would be hers. No one was sentimental in the news business. It was like professional ball players. No matter you hit .400 with men on base last week. What have you done for me lately? An anchorwoman who didn't show up and gave no one a heads-up was of no value to anyone.

She heard a distant sound, like a bee. But it grew and soon another helicopter was clearly preparing to land. Twenty minutes later, her door unlocked and Anthony DeMaio stood there, looking at her intently.

"Going to ask me in?" he said.

"Like you'd go away if I didn't," she replied.

His thin lips spread just enough to give the impression of someone pretending to smile who didn't really know how. He entered the room and sat in one of the chairs opposite the couch.

"Your hair's a little mussed," he said. He ran a hand over his own thick locks. "Always windy out here."

"Where is here?" She said.

He hesitated, then shrugged. "My little home away from home. We're on an oil rig, outside Canadian territorial waters. You could say that what happens here stays here. No higher authority, if you know what I mean."

She felt the sense of panic rise in her again. "What are you going to do with me?"

"Normally, in a situation like this, there would be a line of men coming in to debrief you." He smiled his shark smile again at what he perceived to be a joke. "But I paid a lot for you. Thought I'd sample the goods myself."

Kitty felt her blood go cold. So this was it. Better maybe than what could have happened. She could have been raped by Lloyd and maybe a dozen others. In some queer way, her status as an anchorwoman was still offering her a bit of protection. She was special. They all said that.

"And after that?" she asked.

He stuck his lips out. "What happens after, I guess, will depend on how much you please me. I might want to keep you around for a while. Better for you if I'm happy."

He stood up abruptly. "Let's take a shower," he said. "I'd like you to undress me."

She only hesitated a moment. Already, her sense of self as someone who made her own decisions about such matters had begun to fall away. Paradoxically, even though no one had actually hurt her physically, she still felt completely helpless. The mere threat of violence had stripped away that self-possessed "in charge" feeling she'd had as a television newscaster.

She went over to him and began to unbutton his shirt. He was tall and strongly built. The way he looked down on her and held her eyes with his own made her feel like a little girl in front of him.

He had a thick mat of chest hair, with just a bit of gray beginning to encroach across the area where his nipples were. He was very lean, not an ounce of fat anywhere. She undid his belt buckle, opened the button at the top and pulled down the zipper. The pants fell to the floor and he slipped off his shoes and kicked the pants away. Then he sat down and held up first one foot and then the next for her to remove his socks. He stood back up. She could see he was already aroused.

"Keep going," he said.

She slipped her hands under the sides of his shorts and pulled them down. He sat back in the chair, unselfconscious at his arousal.

"Now you," he said.

She stepped back and took her own clothes off. Somehow it felt different, having him already naked. It was the first time she hadn't had to take her clothes off in front of people fully dressed. She wondered if he'd planned it deliberately in order to make her feel more at ease.

He took her hand and led her into the shower. He liked the water hot and they stood under it together for a long time. She soaped him down all over, feeling him grow in her hand when she got to that part. It was all like something she was watching on TV, something happening to someone else.

Then he turned the water off and they got out and she toweled him down, then he did the same for her.

"Can't wait much longer," he said. He turned her around so her back was to him and pushed her down until she was lying over the back of one of the stuffed chairs.

"I like it from behind," he said.

Then he was in her and she felt that sense of helplessness again. Every bit of what was the private part of Kitty Wells was under someone else's control, like the first time she'd been examined by a male doctor when she was sixteen. He'd been a young doctor and good-looking. It was the first time she had experienced the red flush. The man hadn't said anything, but she could tell he was surprised and probably a little turned on. Even at sixteen, Kitty already knew the effect she had on men. Any man.

Now she felt that same heat rise once again as DeMaio pulled himself deep into her. She groaned and flushed red. His hands squeezed her tiny buttocks and he pushed harder and then came with an intensity that scared her. He made almost no sound, but she could feel the tension in the muscles of his legs as he spasmed again and again.

Then it was over. For the first time in her life she'd had sex with a man she hadn't selected herself, on her own terms. He stayed on top of her, inside her for several minutes, his hands periodically stroking her back and thighs. Then he pulled out and wiped himself off with a towel.

Kitty slid down and sat in the chair, pulling her legs up and hugging them. Her skin had begun to return to its normal color. She was sore but couldn't deny the arousal she had experienced. She was surprised once again how closely humiliation, helplessness, and arousal all played together. But still there was a part of her that seethed. To be treated like a thing, an object of pleasure. A possession. She was angry at herself for being aroused. It ran against everything she knew herself to be. Still, they would never own that final part of her, her anger. Not as long as she had breath in her body.

"That wasn't so bad, was it?" he asked. "I've got the weekend. We'll do that a few more times before I have to leave."

"Then what?" said Kitty.

"Don't know. I might have to put you on my Rolodex."

38

S HEILA VOGLER'S CONCENTRATION ON THE paper in her
hands was total. Garrett knew to keep quiet until she was
through reading. When she did, she sighed heavily and
looked up, her eyes filled with sadness.

"What an awful man," she said. "Why are there so many fathers
like him in the world? Ought to be sterilized at birth, if we could
only identify them."

"No argument," Garrett said. "So, I gather from your reaction
that you agree the girl cannot be returned to him?"

She nodded. "You were right to get her examined as quickly
as you did. There's no question she was beaten. That gives us the
power to take her away, at least temporarily."

"Temporarily?"

"There will have to be a hearing. Depends to a certain extent
on how far the father is willing to go to get her back. Some of them
say good riddance and that's the end of it. But when they hear they
have to pay child support, they often decide to try to get them
back. The girl makes money for him after all, by working in the
store. If he can afford to hire a solicitor, we may have our hands
full. But for right now, I can place her in a home."

"My friend Sarah would like to take her," said Garrett. "They're
already friends and Lila is also staying with Sarah. I think it would

be a help to Ayesha to be in a familiar environment with people she knows."

"Sounds like you're trying to start a haven for troubled youth of your own," said Sheila. "It's taking on a lot, you know."

Garrett waited. Saying anything more, he knew, would only jeopardize the plug he'd made.

Sheila tapped her pen on the desk in silence, then swiveled her chair and picked up the phone. She dialed and waited, asked for someone, then waited some more. Finally, she explained the situation to the person on the line and Garrett heard her say, pointedly, "We're short on available homes right now, right? So, I may take another action in this case." She listened some more, said "Thanks," and hung up.

"All right. It's a gamble, Garrett, but I'll remand Ayesha into your and Sarah's care for one month. Then we'll do an evaluation. The tricky part is going to be school. She's home-schooled. Is that something you and Sarah are prepared to take on?"

He shook his head. "Don't believe in it myself. I'd rather put her in the local high school. Maybe she and Lila can go together. What Ayesha needs more than anything is a little exposure to the real world."

"From what you've told me, she already got a dose of that from her time in the city with Lila." She looked at him disapprovingly.

"Lila just wanted to show her the city. Showing off to her new friend, maybe the only one she's ever really had, you know? She had no intention of going to Big Margaret's. That was an accident of being seen in public. Lila swears she'll never do anything like it again, and I believe her. She was really scared at being drawn back into that."

"And if Lonnie hadn't come along, that's exactly where both girls would be," Sheila said. "I only hope you're reading Lila correctly. Remember what I told you about girls who are prostituted so young. They almost never escape the consequences."

"Doesn't mean they don't deserve the chance."

"You're right. It doesn't. Come back tomorrow and I'll have you sign some papers. You'll have to get Sarah to sign them too. I only hope it works, Garrett."

"You and me both," he said.

He headed in his car to the Holiday Inn near the center of the city. It was a mammoth convention center, one of the ritziest hotels in the province. He parked near a huge open green filled with soccer players and met Lonnie at the entrance.

"They probably require a press pass," Garrett said. "My ID will get me inside, but you don't exactly look like a member of the Fourth Estate, if you know what I mean."

Lonnie smiled. "I'm just a poor reporter who happens to work out in the gym during his spare time, boss."

"Amount of working out needed to look like you might give King Kong pause. Anyway, I want you out here in your car ready to go. Soon as the briefing is over, we need to follow our man. See where he goes."

Lonnie nodded and turned for the car. "Bring me some of those fancy canapes."

Inside, a crowd of some fifty or so news people milled about eating the aforementioned canapes. He'd been right about Lonnie. His cousin would have looked like a body-building ex-convict, a giant midst the blow-dried anchormen, barely-out-of-college environmentalists, and Kitty Wells-sized correspondents.

Garrett spied one of the more rumpled reporters chowing down in a corner. Ernie Sackett had written stories about Garrett's various collars over the years. He lifted a glass of red wine in salute as Garrett came over.

"What are you doing here, Garrett? Slumming? You never come to these shindigs. You take a sudden interest in the safety of offshore drilling?"

"I'm interested in this guy, what's his name? DeMaio? Know anything about him?"

Ernie shrugged. "Global Resources CEO. Usually don't get a direct PR briefing from someone like him. A sign, I guess, that they're feeling the pressure regarding the safety of their rigs that are so close to the coast. The hurricane's sudden move toward shore gave a lot of people the willies, politicians included. No one wants another Gulf Coast-type oil spill. The forecasts have been for one of the busiest hurricane seasons in years."

Garrett nodded, his gaze sweeping the room for any others he might know. He spotted two men in the back who looked out of place, the way Lonnie would have.

"Who are they?" he said, pointing the men out.

"You've still got the eye, I'll say that," Sackett said. "I spotted them right off. Government men. Don't know why they're here. Maybe they have an interest in DeMaio too. Word is he's connected to the wrong kind of people, if you get my drift. Whole bloody company is if you ask me. Connected, I mean. There've been rumors about Global for years. Nobody's proven anything though."

Garrett smiled. "That's why you're here, Ernie. To blow the whistle on 'em."

He tilted his glass in mock salute, then turned as a group of men entered the room and made their way to the podium.

"Which one's DeMaio?" Garrett asked.

"Tall, lean guy in the two-thousand-dollar suit," said Ernie, taking out a small tape recorder.

The new arrivals settled into chairs at the front and waited for the members of the press to be seated. Then a slight, nattily dressed man addressed the crowd.

"Thank you all for coming," he said. "Global Resources is committed to being responsive to the press. The recent hurricane raised some concerns and we're here to reassure the people of Nova Scotia that our rigs are the most advanced and safest anywhere in the world. Our CEO, Anthony DeMaio, will now answer your questions."

Ernie was the first one to his feet. "Mr. DeMaio, we heard there was considerable damage to your rig off Lighthouse Point from the hurricane. Doesn't this affirm what many were telling you when you fought to have that rig placed so close to shore?"

DeMaio smiled thinly. "Actually, the Lighthouse Point rig is not yet fully operational, so there really was no danger during the recent storm of anything like an oil spill. There was some damage from the high winds that has already been repaired."

A woman stood across the room. "So you're saying that once it does come online, there is potential for damage from a storm like this one?"

"Don't put words in my mouth," DeMaio snapped, looking miffed.

It was a more brittle answer than Garrett would have expected. The CEO was probably not a seasoned spokesman who entertained the press very often. This meeting had one reason only and that was to reassure the press and, through them, the public. That meant coddling them, really. DeMaio's superior demeanor seemed out of place somehow.

"Global Resources has an exemplary safety record and we adhere absolutely to all safety and environmental regulations," DeMaio continued.

"Except for the one that says rigs should not be within twenty miles of the coast," said another reporter.

"We received special permission for Lighthouse Point, and the rigors of the environmental impact statements required were severe, over the top really, in our opinion. But we met them all. I would like to point out that none of our other rigs suffered serious damage during the recent hurricane."

Garrett stood. He was no reporter, but having used his credentials to gain entry, he saw no reason not to take advantage of the opportunity. "I wonder if I might ask a slightly different question," he said. "Can you explain why your Lighthouse Point rig has such unusual accommodations? Specifically, why there are Club Med-style rooms?"

DeMaio's eyes seemed to bore into Garrett. "I don't believe that information is accurate. Certainly not to my knowledge. Might I ask where you got this information?"

"I didn't get the information from a source," Garrett said. "I've seen the rooms myself."

DeMaio looked startled for the first time. He leaned over and conferred with the man next to him. Then he straightened himself, almost looking like he was girding for battle. "I'm told," he said, "that there are some upscale rooms at Lighthouse Point that are used for visits by officials from foreign nations interested in our facilities. We are a business, after all, and sell our state-of-the-art oil rigs to nations around the world." He pointed at once to another reporter, cutting Garrett off from asking further questions.

But the explanation didn't wash with Garrett. As CEO, DeMaio should have known about the special accommodations at Lighthouse Point, and Garrett felt certain that he did.

The meeting droned on for another fifteen minutes. Then DeMaio's eyes met with those of the slight man who had introduced him and the man stood and thanked the crowd. Garrett felt DeMaio's gaze wash over him as he left the podium and stopped to talk informally with reporters. This, Garrett assumed, was the schmooze part of the job.

He worked his way through the room over to where the two G-men stood. He nodded to them.

"Didn't know there was interest in this matter by the intelligence services," he said.

"And you would be?" said the bigger of the men.

Garrett pulled out his ID and let the man look at it. He nodded. "I'd say we're both on the same side."

"Question is," said Garrett, "same side of what?"

The man shook his head. "I'm not authorized to say anything." He took out a card and handed it to Garrett. "You can contact this number if you want. Maybe they'll tell you something. Maybe not. Depends, really, on how much influence you have." He turned away.

Garrett stared at the card for a moment. The only influence he had was through Tuttle and usually the Deputy Commissioner wouldn't tell him how to influence the Mr. Coffee machine. He stuck the card in his pocket.

DeMaio was beginning to slip out of the room, so Garrett moved quickly through the crowd and out to where Lonnie was waiting.

His cousin looked at his empty hands. "No food?" he asked in an aggrieved voice.

"Sorry, didn't think about it and if I had, I would have needed a trolley car to bring enough to satisfy you."

Lonnie grunted. "They also serve who only stand and wait," he said.

"And a good job you did too. Keep an eye on the parking garage exit. Unless I miss my guess, DeMaio will be coming out any moment in a couple of Global Resources SUVs."

It took longer than a moment, but eventually three SUVs with the company logo on the side came out of the underground and sped away toward the waterfront.

"Don't lose them," said Garrett.

"Huh," Lonnie grunted. "SUVs? I couldn't lose them if I was driving a tank."

39

LONNIE KEPT A PRECISE DISTANCE behind the three SUVs. He was an expert at blending in with traffic, and it was soon clear that the men in the cars ahead had no expectations of being followed.

"Beats me," said Garrett, "how you manage to be so good at tailing people. Your head must disappear up into the roof for anyone checking his rearview mirror. Ought to be a dead giveaway."

"Least I'm better at tailing than you are at chasing down suspects."

"Hire the handicapped," Garrett said. "You ever actually held down a regular job?"

"Always had trouble getting past the interview stage. Bosses seemed intimidated for some reason."

Garrett just shook his head.

The cars drove through the heart of downtown Halifax to Global's headquarters, a large, mausoleum-like structure on the waterfront. Lonnie pulled over to the curb, and they watched as the three vehicles disappeared into an underground parking garage.

"Now what?" he said.

"What? You expect me to have a plan?"

Lonnie snorted, put the car in park and settled back in his seat, as much as was possible.

"Let's watch for a while," said Garrett. "Any thoughts on Kitty Wells's whereabouts?"

"Nope. But I'd be willing to bet a plate of canapes that if we find Lloyd, we'll find Kitty, or at least can get him to tell us where she is."

"Will you give the canapes a rest?" said Garrett. "Anyway, I haven't had a lot of luck getting information out of Lloyd. He practically kicked me off his property the last time we interacted."

"My interactions sometimes get better results," said Lonnie.

"Don't remind me."

"I just think if you really believe Kitty is in trouble, the longer we fuss around, the worse off she's going to be."

Garrett said nothing. He'd been thinking the same thing. He looked out the window and watched the boat traffic along the harbor. The tiny, nearly round ferries that crossed over to Dartmouth and back chugged along, their wakes the only evidence of direction. An expensive yacht under full sail headed past George's Island, sails snapping in the wind. The *Silva*, a Swedish fishing trawler built in 1947, made her several-times-daily run out around the island and back again with a load of tourists who seemed more interested in the bar constructed in the former wheelhouse than in the impressive sights of the harbor. He could see kids running around on deck. Murphy's Restaurant, with its open terrace on the water, was busy. He wished he were there right now having a schooner of ale and a plate of oysters.

Lonnie's stomach growled. "You keep looking at Murphy's," he said, "I'm gonna have to give this up and go get something to eat."

"Diet would do you no harm," Garrett said, snippily. His cousin had not an ounce of fat on his huge frame. "Let's give it an hour. If they don't come out by then, I'll buy you a beer and we'll call it a day."

Before Lonnie could reply, Garrett suddenly said, "Shit. I don't believe it."

"What?"

"Over there." Garrett pointed. "It's Lloyd."

They stared as the Eastern shore's premier naturist crossed a thoroughfare and made his way into a small public garden.

Garrett started to get out of the car, but Lonnie put one of his mitts on his arm.

"Let me do it," he said.

Garrett hesitated. "All right, maybe you'll have better luck. But don't kill the guy until we find out where Kitty is."

Lonnie gave him a look. "Killing is never helpful," he said. "You'd be surprised how many guys refuse to talk to me once they're dead."

Garrett watched his cousin lumber like a Humvee in need of a tune-up across the road and into the garden. Lloyd had paused to sit on a bench in a small cul-de-sac created by a stand of young maple trees. He unfolded a newspaper and looked like he didn't have a care in the world.

Lonnie sat heavily on the bench, nearly pushing Lloyd off with his bulk. Garrett could see Lloyd's startled look even from where he was. He watched as Lonnie began to talk to him. In a moment, Lloyd tried to get up and leave, but Lonnie put one hand on his arm and fastened him to the bench as effectively as if he'd used a nail gun.

Garrett watched Lloyd look all around, desperate to find a way out. But they were alone in the little park. Lonnie leaned forward and spoke, staring straight into Lloyd's eyes.

Lloyd shook his head and shrugged his shoulders. Garrett could almost imagine the dialogue. Lonnie pressed him harder and then the big hand squeezed so tightly on Lloyd's arm that he grimaced and nearly fell off the bench. Then Lloyd began to talk in earnest. He nodded at Global headquarters several times. All at once, he seemed quite interested in telling Lonnie anything he wanted to know.

Suddenly Lloyd pointed to the sky and Lonnie looked up. Garrett leaned out of the window and looked up too. A helicopter was taking off from the top of the building.

Lonnie stood up, looking at the sky and still with one hand on Lloyd's shoulder. He said something to Lloyd, who looked completely cowed, then walked away. The instant Lonnie let him go, Lloyd scampered out of the park and disappeared down the street.

A moment later, Lonnie got back in the car.

"Okay," he said. "He started out saying he didn't know anything about Kitty Wells. But I . . . pressed . . . him and he finally admitted he'd spent time being interviewed by her but then she left. He said she might have decided to go interview a Madame Liu for a story on prostitution. He said he warned her it was dangerous but couldn't dissuade her. I don't believe that part. If that's all that happened, there would have been no reason for him to deny spending any time with her in the first place. He would have told me straight off. If I had to guess, I'd bet old Lloyd delivered Kitty to Madame Liu himself. I asked him, hypothetically speaking, what Madame Liu would do with Kitty. He said if the woman liked what she saw, she might try to sell her, probably to someone at the oil company."

"Global Resources?" said Garrett. "What for?"

"I don't think that is open to a whole lot of interpretation, Gar."

"What do you mean?"

"If Lloyd sold Kitty to Madame Liu and she turns around and sells her to some guy in the oil business . . . well . . . what do you think?"

Garrett stared at him. "I don't believe it. You're saying they kidnapped a television anchorwoman and sold her into prostitution? Are they nuts?"

"Not prostitution. Sexual slavery. From what Lloyd said, it's common enough with young girls. He actually began talking like he'd done research on the subject, all in the interests of helping his young charges, of course. He suggested the anchorwoman thing would be icing on the cake, that the titillation factor would make Kitty extra valuable. He said Liu would get a fortune for her—*if* his assumptions were correct."

"What about the helicopter?"

"He didn't know who was on it, but he said if Kitty were actually a prisoner, she might be taken out to the oil rig. Evidently, Global has a nice little sideline with girls brought in to entertain potential foreign investors. That was how Lloyd put it. All stuff he said he found out through his research."

"I can't believe you got him to tell you all this just by squeezing his arm," said Garrett.

"There was a lot more to it than that. He knew who I was. I told him if I found out he was holding back on me, I'd find him. Evidently, he believed me." He drummed his enormous fingers on the side of the car and stared up at the distant speck of the chopper now disappearing out past George's Island. "So. You think DeMaio's on that aircraft?"

"Be my guess."

"What are we going to do?"

Garrett shook his head. "I'm not sure. Tuttle would probably get me a helicopter if I asked for it, but outside of Canadian waters, we have no authority."

"Another midnight kayak ride?"

"I don't know. I need to talk to some people about this. About the law on the high seas. The people at Global are going to have influence at very high levels. Sure as hell, more than I have."

"You can waste a lot of time looking into the legality of all this, Garrett. Time Kitty may not have."

"You know how much trouble Tom and I had sneaking up on the bad guys' boats? It can only be that much harder to sneak up on an oil rig. I don't want Kitty shipped out by chopper as soon as we appear on the horizon. We might never get another shot at her. She's been in their hands for several days and it's probably already too late to save her from some pretty nasty stuff. I just hope I can figure something out in time to save her life."

Garrett pulled out the card he'd been given by the two government men at the press briefing. He took out his cell phone and dialed the number. A neutral voice answered and asked his business.

"I'd like to speak to . . ." he read the name on the card. "A Mr. Alfred Nichols."

"One moment, please."

Another secretary answered. No more expansive budget than the intelligence services. This woman was more cautious, however, asking the reason for his call and who he was.

"I'm an RCMP officer," Said Garrett. "Special Constable Garrett Barkhouse, out of Halifax. You can verify that through the Deputy Commissioner if you wish, but this is a matter of some urgency and I would appreciate being able to speak with Mr. Nichols immediately."

Evidently calls like Garrett's were not uncommon in the fluid and rapidly changing world of intelligence. After a series of clicks during a pause of almost two minutes, probably while Nichols was told the situation, a voice came on the line.

"This is Alfred Nichols," said the man. "I'm speaking to an RCMP officer?"

"Yes, sir. I got your number from one of your agents attending the press briefing given by Global Resources just an hour ago. We appear to have a mutual interest in a man named DeMaio. We're following up a missing person, a prominent one; a television reporter who we believe may have been kidnapped by DeMaio."

There was a moment of silence, then Nichols swore. "I don't mean to be obstructionist, Officer Barkhouse, but we've been watching DeMaio's movements, taping his conversations, and investigating him three ways from Sunday for the last six months."

"Can you tell me why?"

"Let's just say we have reason to believe he's connected to some pretty big organized crime elements."

"Does this have anything to do with international sex trafficking?" Garrett asked.

Nichols hesitated. "You appear to be well informed, officer. We believe there may be an international trafficking operation that is run through Global Resources, but it's a tricky situation. I can't tell you all the details."

"I may know more of those details than you imagine," said Garrett. "I think we're on the same side here. The woman we're trying to rescue may be in immediate danger. And as I said, she's high profile. We have reason to believe she may have been transported to one of Global Resources' offshore oil rigs for the purposes of sexual slavery."

Nichols said, "I want to help you, officer. I really do. But we've been trying to build a case against DeMaio for almost a year. We can't compromise that work on the chance you know where your girl is. If you've been involved in prostitution then you should know how difficult it is to build a case for trafficking. Hell, human trafficking wasn't even a Criminal Code offense until 2005. There have only been a couple dozen people charged with trafficking in all of Canada to date and only a handful of convictions."

Garrett knew the statistics. Gang members and pimps had figured out that they could make more money with less risk dealing in girls instead of drugs. The average trafficked woman could make her pimp hundreds of thousands of dollars before he used her up. Some girls had even been sold for sex through Craigslist.

"And I might add," Nichols said, "if she's outside the twelve-mile limit, we have real constrictions on what we can do. That's one reason we've been slowly building up a file on DeMaio. He travels all over the world and most of the time is outside our jurisdiction. His public press briefing today was the first time we've been able to get close to him in months."

Garrett thought quickly. "So you're saying that if she's being held outside the twelve-mile limit, there's nothing we can do to save her?"

"No. If you had some sort of real proof of what was happening on that rig, we might be able to take action. Legally, there's an exclusive economic zone that extends from the outer limit of the territorial sea . . . that's the twelve-mile limit . . . to a maximum of two hundred nautical miles from the territorial sea baseline. A coastal nation has control of all economic resources within its exclusive economic zone, including fishing, mining, oil exploration and any pollution of those resources."

"I'd say trafficking in young girls twenty miles offshore might qualify as pollution," said Garrett. "Moral pollution."

Lonnie grunted. The side of the conversation he could hear did not seem to be going well.

"Again," said Nichols, "It's a matter of proof. The exclusive economic zone cannot prohibit passage or loitering above, on, or under the surface of the sea that is in compliance with the laws and regulations adopted by the coastal state in accordance with provisions of the UN Convention. Last time I looked, escort services were a legal enterprise in Canada, sleazy though they may be."

"We're not talking about an escort service. This is kidnapping, sexual slavery, and trafficking," said Garrett. "I've dealt with this stuff for twenty years, and there is nothing legal about it. I don't care how hard it is to get a conviction. We've had five young girls killed here in the past two weeks."

He could hear Nichols breathing, then the man covered the phone and Garrett heard muffled voices. When he came back on the line, he said, "I appreciate your efforts, Officer Barkhouse. I can't tell you not to continue your own investigation. If you find the proof I've spoken of, I'll be ready to offer you the direct assistance of the Canadian Navy. Until then, I wish you and the woman you seek luck."

The line went dead. Garrett stared out the window. Lonnie's silence next to him finally forced him to look at his cousin.

"We on our own?" he asked.

"Until we get some sort of ironclad, foolproof evidence that Kitty is where we think she is."

"Bloody intels aren't worth the money we give them."

"*You* don't give them money," Garrett said. "You don't pay taxes."

"Most moral thing I do," Lonnie said. "What's the plan?"

Garrett sighed. "The plan is to rescue Kitty Wells. I just haven't worked out the details yet."

40

KITTY STARED AT DEMAIO'S SLEEPING form. They'd had sex half a dozen times over the weekend, always in the same manner. He seemed to have endless sexual energy but very little imagination.

Rather than growing more docile and accepting with each instance, her anger had grown. She felt like a puppet, at his beck and call. If he said bend over, she had to comply. It was the most degrading experience of her life. She no longer exhibited the red flush, for she had ceased to find what was happening to her the least bit erotic. She wondered if this was how prostitutes felt after conditioning. Numb.

The disappearance of the flush annoyed DeMaio, as though it were some reflection on his prowess. The whole thing was ridiculous, and Kitty was ready to try anything to escape. His sleeping form presented the opportunity she'd been waiting for.

The door to her room locked automatically when he left. No key was necessary. But he always used a key on a ring that he kept in his pants to open the door when he arrived. This was to be their last time . . . at least for now. He'd made a big deal about how he had to leave this evening by chopper for a meeting in Halifax. Kitty wondered if he was tiring of her already.

She slipped silently into the small bathroom, which was where they usually disrobed. He liked to start with a joint shower. Gradually, she had formed her plan. She intended to take his key. She'd been thinking about it since the first time, but of course he would miss it the next time he came for her. So it would only work the last time. With luck, he wouldn't notice that it was gone until long after he'd left the oil platform.

She found the key and detached it from the rest, slipping it under the edge of the carpet. Her heart almost stopped as she heard him rouse and call for her. She went into the other room instantly. She was still naked and he motioned her over. He sat on the sofa and buried his head in her stomach, his hands gently stroking her thighs.

"All good things come to an end, Kitty," he said. "I won't be back, but I won't forget our time together."

"What happens to me now?"

He sighed, got up and went into the bathroom, then returned with his clothes and began to dress. He dropped the pants and as he picked them up, the key ring fell onto the floor.

Kitty's heart was in her mouth as he reached for them. She tried to distract him from examining them too closely.

"I enjoyed it too," she purred and went over and pretended to smooth out his trousers. "I'll miss you."

The bastard was such an egomaniac he actually believed her. How could he not satisfy a woman . . . any woman?

"I don't see any point in lying to you, Kitty," he said. "I've got to move on, which means so do you."

She stared at him. "You're sending me someplace?"

"No. But it's time for you to expand your duties. A number of foreign businessmen are coming to spend the next couple of nights. Your job will be to see that they are happy and content. Think of it as a business assignment. These men represent a consortium that's

228

going to buy three of our oil rigs. They'll be paying a fortune for them and so we're offering them a little bonus. You."

So. It was starting. She could hardly grasp what it would be like to be handed off from one man to the next. DeMaio had been cold and demanding, but he had been only one man, and he was generally only good for a single rape at a time. Soon, she would understand precisely what it meant to be *conditioned*. Soon she would know what it was like to be a full-time sex slave.

She felt her stomach turn. Her face must have looked bleak, for he put a hand up and stroked her cheek. "Don't fight it, Kitty," he said. "It will only make it harder. Do what they ask. You'll get used to it."

Then he was gone, out the door. She heard him try the knob to make sure it had locked. She went over, turned back the carpet, and took out the key. She sat on the sofa and waited until she heard the helicopter take off. She had no idea how long it would be before the group of new men arrived, and she had no intention of waiting to find out.

What she would do once she got out of the room, she had no idea. That it was just the first step, she was all too aware. She'd still be alone on an oil rig twenty miles from shore. It seemed hopeless, but anything was better than waiting to be handed around from one man to the next.

As the sound of the chopper disappeared in the distance, she got dressed. Her clothes were not terribly warm and she knew it would be cold and windy outside. But there was nothing she could do about that. Maybe she could find a coat somewhere. She was about to unlock the door after listening at it for several minutes to try to determine if anyone was outside, when the lock clicked.

She froze. Someone was coming in. Had DeMaio realized what she'd done and come back? No. He'd gone on the chopper. It had to be someone else.

She stared as the door opened and one of DeMaio's men entered. It was the short assistant who had introduced his boss at the press briefing. He was alone and smiled at her as he took off his coat.

"No reason for just the top SOBs to have all the fun," he said, looking at her. "Besides, what difference does one more make to you?"

He pressed himself against her and she felt his hands all over her. Something snapped inside of her. She wasn't going to let this little prick use her for his amusement. She stepped backward and he sensed she was backing up to lie down on the sofa. She put her arms around him and pulled him with her.

He was breathing heavily, completely focused on her. Kitty backed up more and whispered in his ear.

"Let me take your clothes off," she said. He stood back from her so she could undo his pants. He was already fully aroused. She pulled his pants down and unbuttoned his shirt.

"Turn around," she said. He complied, completely under her power, as she slipped the shirt off and ran her hands down his sides. He shuddered as they reached his bare hips. Then Kitty reached back and picked up the small lamp on the side table, whirled it around, and smashed the base as hard as she could into his scrotum.

He screamed and fell to the floor. She had to shut him up or the noise would bring others. She lifted the heavy lamp base again and brought it down on his head with every ounce of her ninety-eight pounds.

The screaming stopped as if a TV had been turned off. She stared at him. There was no question. He was dead. A portion of his skull was depressed and blood pooled out onto the floor.

She didn't wait around to take his pulse. She felt not a smidgen of regret. His warm coat was an unexpected bonus. With the

collar turned up, she might not be immediately identified by anyone seeing her from a distance.

She closed the door to the room and stood in the carpeted
hallway, listening. She could hear the wind outside but no sound
of voices. It was after dinnertime and starting to get dark out. She
took DeMaio's key, inserted it into the lock, then broke it off flush.
That would slow them down a little. They'd have to break the door
down and it was a solid, heavy door.

She moved down the hall, looking into rooms. Most were
empty bedrooms. Then she opened a heavy metal door and found
herself outside. She was on a catwalk. All around were pipes and
strange-looking masses of machinery. The place was an absolute
maze and she had no idea which way to go.

Keeping as low as possible, she skirted along one catwalk after
another. She crossed the empty helipad and dashed down a set of
circular stairs to another level, back into what appeared to be living quarters, then outside again. So far she hadn't seen a soul, but
she knew her luck on that front couldn't last.

The sea was relatively calm, but here, a hundred feet above
the water's surface, she could feel a strong wind. The sun was
beginning to set on the horizon, a huge, magenta ball she'd
have thought beautiful at any other time. Now, it only meant
she would soon be stumbling around in the dark. There were
lights on the rig, of course, but not knowing anything about
how the place was organized, she might wander right off into
oblivion. She had no illusions as to how long she'd last in that
cold water.

She tried to think. Where would they be least likely to search
for her? If she could just hide, Garrett might eventually come looking for her. But no. No one knew where she was. Hiding would do
no good. As soon as they realized what had happened and that
she'd killed one of their men, they'd search the place thoroughly.

They knew the rig much better than she did. They'd look in all the likely places.

It was hopeless. Then she heard voices coming toward her.

She turned and ran down a long grated steel platform and up a flight of metal steps, then stopped. Above her was what looked like a small room about ten feet square. As she stared at it, a door opened and two men came out of the room. She shrank back into a depression on the catwalk that appeared to be some sort of dead end facing an electrical grid.

In a moment, the men passed right in front of her on the catwalk. She heard one say to the other, "Better not leave the radio unattended for long. The chopper with the clients will be coming in soon."

"It'll be an hour at least," said the other man. "Plenty of time to get something to eat and bring it back."

They disappeared down a set of steps. Kitty was out of her hiding place in an instant and up the stairs into the little room. The place was filled with radio equipment and electronics, most of which she had no idea how to work. But her years in a TV production studio had given her a basic working knowledge of communications.

She sat in a chair and worked the dials of some sort of radio. She spoke into a microphone repeatedly, pressing various buttons and digital numbers.

"To anyone listening, this is an emergency . . . an SOS! My name is Kitty Wells. I've been kidnapped and am being held prisoner on Lighthouse Point oil rig several miles off the Eastern shore."

She could hardly imagine anyone who picked up her words would think it anything other than a hoax. Christ, she didn't believe it herself. She had no certainty if she was even broadcasting and wondered if someone elsewhere on the rig might be listening.

She kept at it for several minutes, then switched off and peered through the door. No one was visible, so she slipped back out onto the catwalk, where she stood in indecision. Maybe she should go back to one of the private staterooms. They were empty, and at least she'd be comfortable and out of the weather. But she knew it would only be a matter of time. The new arrivals would be given special rooms and once they asked for her and discovered her locked room, the search would be on.

Where to go? She looked up at the superstructure far above her. She'd never been good with heights and the thought of fighting her way across narrow catwalks hundreds of feet in the air in gale-like winds made her nauseated.

Instead, she went the other way. Down. Everyone who came to the rig seemed to fly in. But there had to be some sort of dock for boats to pull up to. It figured to be the last place anyone might look, if they assumed she was hiding.

She clambered down one flight of steel steps after another. It was incredible that she hadn't run into anyone. Maybe this rig wasn't fully staffed with roughnecks and was simply kept as high-end entertainment for the bigwigs. If that was true, then the odds might be a little less steeply against her.

She went down a long way, eventually coming to a steel-grated platform just a dozen feet above the ocean. The end of the line. There were catwalks connecting with each of the four heavy concrete anchors that disappeared beneath the surface. She spent some time exploring them, finding several spots where she could get out of sight if need be. She picked one and settled down in a corner. At least the wind wasn't so strong this close to the surface.

She pulled her legs up and wrapped her arms around them. She was cold. She was hungry. She was sore from having had sex with DeMaio. She had killed a man. But she no longer felt helpless.

She was taking action. She was free . . . as free as one could be in the middle of the North Atlantic.

The ocean rose and fell beneath her, spray occasionally finding her face. Thank God it was August. The temperature was almost bearable with the heavy coat. She stared at the water. It was mesmerizing. She'd been in some pretty tight spots during her years as a journalist, but this had to take the prize. She wondered how long she could hold out.

Then she heard the familiar sound of the helicopter returning.

41

ROLAND WOKE EARLY. IT WAS the pattern of a lifelong man of the sea. This morning, the sun pouring through his window was a most welcome reminder that today Grace would be home alone, sunning herself.

He rolled out of bed and rubbed his eyes. It was six a.m. Plenty of time to get ready. He'd have a leisurely breakfast, then call Rose and tell her he couldn't bring her home from the hospital till the evening.

He had no idea why he had so fixated on Grace. He'd seen lots of beautiful women, even had sex with a few unlucky prostitutes who were knockouts but had lost the lottery the day they met up with Roland. They would never give him their direct number afterwards. Once with Roland was enough, even for professionals.

Perhaps it was simply because Grace was so close and yet so unattainable. Her slim, willowy body and fine features swam before him in his nightly dreams. That he only caught glimpses of her once or twice a week just made her proximity all the more frustrating.

He put on a T-shirt and sweatpants, stained from years of use on his boat, and sat in front of the computer. He wanted to check the weather and make sure the sun that both he and Grace were anticipating would actually materialize. His years as a fisherman had given him an intuitive feel for the changeable maritime climate. Sometimes, he could almost smell changes in the systems that hurled themselves at Nova Scotia's rocky coast in bewildering and ultimately unpredictable patterns.

The early morning sun was no assurance that the fine weather would continue throughout the day. Indeed, the satellite image for the Eastern shore looked decidedly more iffy. A heavy fogbank sat just offshore and there was a gale forecast off Sable Island. Warnings were already out for fishermen and small pleasure craft, predicting four- to eight-foot swells.

Not a good day to go to sea, though he had experienced worse. But it just might be a good day for bird-watching . . .

By nine o'clock, it was warm if not hot, and he was already ensconced up in the trees with his binoculars, his camera, and his zoom lens. He'd even hauled a plastic chair up into the woods so he could be comfortable. At a quarter past nine, he heard the door to his neighbor's house open and close a number of times. Then he saw a car slip out of the driveway with Leo and Ingrid aboard, heading for Halifax.

It was just the two of them now. It almost felt like they were connected somehow. His anticipation was palpable.

At nine-thirty, she came out onto the deck, but he was surprised to see she didn't have her bikini on. Instead, she was dressed in warm clothes, pants, a long-sleeved top, and a shell jacket over that.

He stared at her. What was she up to? This wasn't what he'd had in mind.

Grace went back inside and reappeared in a few minutes with a backpack. She carried it down the porch steps and over to one of the solo kayaks they kept ever ready on the shore. She threw the pack and a water bottle inside, slipped on a life jacket, and pushed the boat into the water, where she clambered aboard and headed out to sea.

Roland couldn't believe his eyes. Where the hell was she going? He sat in the trees for twenty minutes, watching as Grace paddled straight out toward the first archipelago and disappeared into the maze of rocky spits and spruce-covered islets.

He was beside himself. What a day for Grace to decide to go for a paddle. She was home alone, the sun was out, and by all rights, she ought to be basking right now in front of him, maybe even slipping off her top to soak in the rays.

Could she be planning to sunbathe on one of the offshore islands? Maybe she and the others suspected what he was up to in the woods. That had to be it. Grace was heading where she knew she could have some real privacy.

Well, it wasn't going to work. He went back to the house and put together a few supplies of his own. Then he walked down to the wharf and fired up the boat engine. He was nearly an hour behind her and knew it might be hard to find her in the maze of islands. But he was determined. He knew where all the best places were for tourists to picnic and sunbathe. He'd taken enough groups out over the years. He would check them one by one. The bright orange kayak wouldn't be hard to spot unless she actually tried to hide it, and there was no reason for her to do that.

He'd find her. No problem.

He motored into the first maze of islands, throttling back so his boat would make as little noise as possible. The upgrade he'd been forced to give the engines following the sinking of his boat at the wharf had made them run much more silently than they used to. At least something good had come out of that fiasco. Still, he cut the engines back even further until he was just trolling along. They made very little sound, though out here in the quiet of the offshore islands, even a little bit of noise could carry a long way.

He maneuvered in and out of the endless collection of spits, rocky beaches, and plunging cliffs, checking several secret bays he knew about, each time easing around points, prepared to back off if he spotted her boat. After an hour of this, he'd still seen no sign of her. He decided to move on to the outer islands. She just might be crazy enough to go out that far, even though the weather and fog made it foolhardy.

The outer islands, called the Gull Islands, were two elongated, spruce-covered ridges. There were several rocky beaches where one could put ashore. Maybe that was where she'd gone.

As he cruised slowly along one of the islands, he suddenly caught sight of the bright orange boat, pulled up above the high-water mark in a small, rocky bay. It was no place for sunning oneself, and he almost hadn't seen the craft, for it was clear she'd made an effort to push it into the brush. There was no sign of her. He turned his boat around and made for a secluded bay nearby, where he anchored and took his dinghy in to shore.

After securing the craft on shore, he carried his binoculars and camera and began to cut across the interior, hoping to come across her from a direction she wouldn't expect. It was hard going. The woods were thick and full of roots that caused him to stumble continuously. His uneven gait through the tightly packed trees made for slow going. After just a couple of minutes he was wheezing heavily, his heart pounding. He was out of shape for this sort of thing. If he wasn't careful, he'd have a heart attack.

Finally, he came to a small fisherman's hut. He watched it for several minutes before deciding no one was around. Beyond the building was a trail that led up to the highest point on the island, from which, he knew, there was a spectacular view down a line of islands to Lighthouse Point in the distance. If Grace wanted a view and an open spot to sunbathe, this was the best one around.

He approached the top cautiously, stopping and listening continuously. He didn't want to stumble upon her. That would ruin everything. If she saw him, she'd pick up, put on her clothes and head for home.

But at the top, there was no sign of her. He cursed his luck. Then he saw another fishing boat pulled in close beneath him at the base of a steep, rocky cliff that plunged into the sea. He'd never seen the boat before, which was pretty strange. He thought he knew all the boats in the area. It bristled with antennas and was fitted out with the latest equipment.

He took out his binoculars and swept the boat's open deck, stopping abruptly. There she was. Grace stood on the deck talking to two men. One of them appeared to be a police officer. He wore the belt, hat, and gun and had a badge of some sort on his shirt, though it was difficult to make out clearly. It almost seemed like some kind of rendezvous. He stared at them, completely puzzled.

He could see Grace clearly. She still wore the shell jacket she'd had on when she left. She held her backpack and spoke earnestly to the men. They bantered back and forth for a while.

What on earth was she up to? He scanned the boat for a name or call numbers but there weren't any. That in itself was illegal.

Then, suddenly, it all became clear. One of the men handed Grace a small plastic bag. She opened it and stuck her finger in, then pulled it out and sucked a white powder off it, smiled, and put the bag in her pack. She took a tightly bound packet of something green and gave it to the men. They nodded and shook her hand. Then one of them helped her into a small rowboat and rowed her back to land.

Roland watched her head straight into the brush to cross the island back to where her kayak was. He put down the binoculars and stood, thinking. Unless he was completely nuts, he'd just witnessed a drug buy. He'd seen them before, on the waterfront in Halifax. There was no doubt what he'd seen. Grace had scored some serious drugs.

He could hardly believe it. For all the back and forth he and Rose shared about the women's druggy, city friends, he'd never really believed it. It was just an excuse to spread bad rumors about them. But here was the proof. He almost felt disillusioned. He'd never feel quite the same way about Grace. She was no better than the prostitutes he spent time with who were always drugged up. In fact, once they met him, many of them took drugs right in front of him to help them through the ordeal.

But the discovery gave him something else to think about. He had something on his neighbors now. Something serious. He looked down suddenly at his camera and zoom lens and swore. He could have photographed the entire exchange and hadn't thought of it.

Still, he knew their secret. He'd report it to Garrett, though absent proof, he knew the Mountie would do nothing. Gar would just think it was one more effort on Roland's part to discredit his neighbors. And there was one other thing. There had been an officer involved. Roland's forehead wrinkled as he tried to imagine the ramifications. It was hard for him. He wasn't a deep thinker.

He was still a little disappointed about not getting to see Grace sunbathing. But all in all, it hadn't been a completely wasted day. Not by a long shot.

He hiked back along the shore to avoid the dense spruce, rowed the dinghy back to his boat, and headed for home by the long way in order to make sure Grace didn't see him.

It was late afternoon when he got back to the house. The phone was ringing as he entered and he picked it up. It was Rose's doctor in Halifax.

"Mr. Cribby, I'm afraid I have some bad news. Your mother passed away about two hours ago. We thought she was making real progress with her breathing, but her heart just gave out. I'm very sorry."

Roland didn't hear another word. He stood motionless, holding the phone to his ear, as the doctor continued with further details and apologies. None of it registered. Finally, he put the phone down not having said a single word to the caller.

It was the moment he'd been dreading for most of his life. The only person in the world who cared about him was gone. He felt a wave of loneliness surge through him. Rose might not have been anyone's idea of good company, but she was virtually the only company he'd had throughout his forty-odd years. He knew there would never be anyone else, no matter how long he lived.

Suddenly, the house seemed deathly quiet. He'd enjoyed the quiet while Rose was away, giving respite from her constant wheezing and complaining. Now, the very walls seemed to close in on him. He walked into Rose's room and surveyed her space, the chair where she sat, the mounds of craft supplies, several projects almost finished, only waiting for final touch-up to the painting.

He placed one slim, callused hand on a partially painted wooden lighthouse and started to cry.

42

"THIS IS SO AWESOME," SAID Lila. She bounced up and down on the couch next to Ayesha, the first real friend she'd ever had. "We'll have a great time. You'll see."

"It's only been approved for a month," Garrett warned. "Then they'll do an evaluation. If anything negative comes up, it could kill the arrangement."

"We'll be the best-behaved girls you ever saw," Lila said. Then she and Ayesha went outside to walk along the beach and dig for clams.

Sarah watched them through the window, then went over and kissed Garrett. "I'm not sure this has helped our situation any, Gar. Now we've got to work around *two* live-in companions."

"The thought crossed my mind," he said. "But seriously, I think this will be good for both of them. Thanks for agreeing to it. My friend in Halifax has her doubts, though. She thinks girls like Lila are often lost causes."

"What about Kitty? Have you heard anything at all?"

He hesitated. He didn't really want to tell her his greatest fear, that Kitty was in the hands of some truly despicable people. But she read his hesitation instantly.

"You know where she is," she said.

"We're pretty sure Lloyd sold her to Madame Liu."

Her look was indescribable. "He sold her . . . ? What is this, the fourteenth century?"

"And then Liu sold her again to someone else. Someone we believe could be connected to or maybe even *be* the CEO of Global Resources."

"If you know all this, why aren't you doing something about it?" Her accusation hung in the air like morning fog.

"It's just not that simple. We think we know where they have her, on the offshore oil rig where you picked me up after the storm. But there are two problems. First, if we get anywhere near there, they'd probably just fly her out in a helicopter. Second, the rig is outside Canadian territorial waters. Technically, I have no authority."

She was shaking her head. "They kidnapped her for purposes of sexual slavery and you tell me there's nothing you can do about it? I won't accept that, Gar. Maybe she's outside Canadian territory now, but she was kidnapped on Canadian soil. That makes it a crime under Canadian law in my book."

He nodded. "I agree. I think we can get around the territorial issue once we have proof of what's happened. But we don't have proof. And if they fly her off somewhere, then we've just lost her again."

"Why can't you send in the entire goddamned Navy? Just take over the rig and have Air Force planes ready to prevent any helicopter from going anywhere."

He spread his hands. "I've been working on it. There are a whole lot of variables, though, and I don't want to get Kitty killed. Remember that the men who killed those four girls only did it because we came on the scene. These people are completely ruthless, and from what I've learned, those at the top of Global Resources are well connected politically. They could have ears anywhere, including in the military and RCMP. If I call in the

Navy, the people on that rig might know about it before I hung up the phone."

Sarah's face was anguished. "You can't just leave her there, Gar. How long has it been? Days already. She's probably been raped repeatedly."

"This may be something that will have to be done outside the law," he said quietly.

She stared at him. "You mean Lonnie?"

"I don't know. He's been strange about this whole thing. It started when I got him involved with the girls. He's seriously bothered by this stuff, by what's happened. I've been worried he might try to do something on his own."

"Well, *someone* ought to."

"Lon doesn't have any constrictions on what he does, Sarah. He's kind of like a force of nature, you know? But he's got a good heart. Not many people know that. It's why he helps me when I need it. More than just about anyone I've ever known, he really enjoys helping people. Especially if he perceives that they've been picked on. That's why he helped Lila and Ayesha, and right now, I think he's thinking along the same lines we are. That if he doesn't help Kitty, no one else will."

"What do you think he'll do?"

"For the moment, I think he's waiting for me to come up with a plan. But I'm not exactly having too much luck in that department. He sounded pretty frustrated last time we were together. He may be thinking about taking matters into his own hands. He understands where I'm coming from as a Mountie and puts up with my limitations most of the time, but . . ."

"I don't see what he can do, Garrett. From what you've told me, there's virtually no avenue that won't endanger Kitty. He must understand that."

"Remember I said the people at Global Resources were connected? Well, Lonnie's connected too, with some characters you wouldn't ever want to encounter. And he's helped a lot of people in his work, politicians, labor union leaders, military brass, powerful, rich people. I've always thought that if he ever decided to call in his chips . . . well . . . I wouldn't want to be the one he's after."

The phone rang. Sarah answered, then handed it to Garrett. "It's Tom," she said.

Garrett listened for a moment, then said, "When did it happen?" Then, "Okay, thanks for telling me, Tom. I'll go see him."

"What is it?" Sarah said after he hung up.

"Roland's mother Rose died."

"Oh."

Garrett sighed. "I'm not looking forward to it, but Roland hasn't any real friends. I need to go see him, at least offer my condolences. I think this will hit him pretty hard."

Her face held sympathy, but she couldn't let go of her fears for Kitty. "Gar, what are we going to do about Kitty?"

He noted her use of *we*. It was no longer what he was going to do but what *they* were going to do. It made him more than a little uneasy.

He spread his hands. "I simply don't have an answer yet. Until I do, I've got other responsibilities. This is what being an RCMP officer is really about. A sort of triage that I've had to do many times in my career. It's not possible to save the whole world, Sarah."

43

GARRETT DROVE THE HUNDRED YARDS from Sarah's house and pulled into Roland's driveway. For the first time in his life, he noted that nearly every light in the structure was on. Roland and Rose never wasted electricity, or anything else for that matter. Which explained the amalgam of junk in the front yard.

He got out and heard music and voices coming from inside the house next door. They were partying again, a seemingly never-ending activity.

He'd wondered for years what the effect would be on Roland when his mother died. The man had no social outlets. He worked with others on occasion, during scallop season and sometimes on carpentry jobs. But no one ever wanted to linger around after the work was done and go out to eat with Roland. Rose had been his anchor, the place he could go and someone would be there to greet him. Without her, there was going to be a difficult transition.

Garrett understood something about transitions. He'd had his own following his injury. Anger, depression, withdrawal from others, all the usual stuff. Lonnie had helped pull him through, but Roland had no one. It struck Garrett that *he* might well be the person who knew Roland the best in all the world. That was a pretty sad commentary, given that he hadn't even seen the man in the half dozen years prior to his return to the Eastern shore.

He went up and started to knock when the door opened. This had never happened before. Usually it took a couple of minutes of pounding to rouse anyone inside. Roland wore his trademark sweatpants and T-shirt. His eyes were red. He looked more gaunt than usual.

"Seen ya turn inta the driveway," he said. "Come on in."

It was the first time Roland had ever greeted Garrett with an invitation to come inside. Usually, the first words out of his mouth were "What can I do for ya?"

"I was awful sorry to hear about Rose," Garrett said.

Roland led him in to what had been Rose's room. The place was even more of a disaster than usual. It appeared Roland had been trying to organize his mother's stuff, boxing things up. But he had no concept of how to go about it, and the room was a shambles.

"Don't know what ta do with all Ma's stuff," he said, standing in the middle of the room. His face had a bewildered look.

Garrett looked through an alcove to a table that seemed more or less uncluttered. "Can we sit at the table?" he asked.

Roland just followed him and sat down heavily.

"It's hard to pack up after the death of someone close to you," Garrett said. "I had to do it after my mother died. My dad just wasn't up to it." He leaned over and squeezed Roland's arm. "It's good you're doing this. It's therapeutic to get about the business at hand, hard as it is."

Roland stared at the wall. "A'w'ys thought it would be nice ta clear this room out and put down new carpet and wallpaper, ya know? But Ma wouldn't have it. Said it would be too disruptive ta her routine." His eyes came slowly round to meet Garrett's. "Course there's not much point now. Ma's gone and no one else ever comes here."

Garrett studied the bleakness in his eyes. It looked familiar. Roland could see nothing ahead of him but loneliness.

"Something like this can jolt you out of your routines," Garrett said. "You're not going to have the obligations to your Ma that you've had for so long. You're going to have more time for yourself. That's not necessarily a bad thing, but it will take some getting used to. It took me three years after my accident to pull myself together completely. The most important thing was to have other people around. To talk to. To distract me from my own thoughts. You need to get out, be around people as much as you can."

"People don't like me," said Roland.

"That's something that is under your control, Roland. You need to reach out, be friendly, listen to people, help them when you can, don't criticize them so much. That's how you make friends. You might start with your cousin and his family."

The sound of laughter peeled across from the other house as the party broke up. Voices could be heard talking gaily, as car doors slammed and engines started. Then the sounds muted as the ladies went back inside.

Roland stared at the window as they listened. "I can't do that," he said. "I don't know how."

"Invite your cousin's family over next week after the funeral and things quiet down. They'll come and you make them a nice meal, clean the place up, talk to them about things. You've been cooking for you and your Ma for years. You know how to cook. The most important things in life are your family and friends, Roland. It will take effort, but you can learn."

Garrett took a deep breath. "And if you'll let me, I'll be your friend as well."

Roland's eyes teared up and he turned away. Garrett could see him struggling for control. "I—I'll try, Gar."

Garrett stood up. There wasn't any point in trying to do too much right away. This was way more progress than he would have expected so soon.

"All right. Good. You'll see. Things will look better. Maybe you should ask your cousin's wife if she would come over and help you pack up some of Rose's stuff. Ask her if she'd like anything of your Ma's. People want to help after something like this. This is the time to really make an effort."

The gratitude in Roland's eyes was evident. It was the first time Garrett had ever seen anything like that emotion from his old neighbor.

Roland stood up and put out his hand. "You're a good person, Gar. I'm sorry for all the trouble I've caused ya over the years."

Garrett shook the callused hand firmly. "It'll get better, Roland. You'll see. What you just said was important. It made me feel good. That's how you make friends, by telling them things that show you care about them. The more you can make that a habit, the better it will be."

Roland followed him out to the car and stood looking at the house next door. "I won't bother them none any more neither," he said.

"Don't do it for me, okay?" said Garrett. "It may be too late for you to bridge that gap, but lowering confrontation can only be positive."

As he drove away, Roland was still standing in his driveway, looking like he hadn't any idea what to do next.

44

GARRETT COULDN'T FIND LONNIE AND he had a bad feeling about things. At a loss over what to do and with Sarah's accusing glare over Kitty's fate hanging in the air, he decided to go back to Halifax. Maybe he could brace Big Margaret again and see what he could find out.

The sad-looking apartment house on Barrington Street hadn't changed. He rang the woman's bell, but there was no answer. Then he realized that the door to the hallway and stairs was ajar. He went in and up the stairs, his foot aching again. It hadn't really returned completely to normal following his ordeal at sea. The mechanism was functioning all right after Marcia's ministrations, so the soreness probably emanated from the long hours he'd kept his muscles tensed and working in the kayak.

Big Margaret's door was also ajar. This gave him pause. No way someone in her line of work casually left the place unlocked. That wasn't part of the business model for an escort service.

He pushed the door all the way open and called. "Anyone home?"

Inside, the place was a total mess, unlike his first visit when everything had been neat and orderly, even elegant, in contrast to the seedy exterior of the building. The place had been ransacked, as though someone had been searching for something. He saw no sign of the books filled with customer names and numbers. Something wasn't right.

He moved slowly through the room and into a small kitchen. Dirty dishes filled the sink. A box of Cheerios had spilled onto the table, little round circles everywhere. A saucer of milk sat on the floor, and a scrawny gray cat looked up at him and hissed, the fur rising on its back.

"It's all right, kitty," said Garrett. "Sorry to interrupt your meal. Where's your owner?"

As if in answer, the cat scooted past him and into the next room. He followed and stopped dead in the doorway.

Big Margaret's naked body lay sprawled on the bed. Her hands and feet were tied to the bedposts, a piece of gray duct tape stuck on her mouth. The entire bed was soaked in blood, now turned black as tar.

Garrett took in his breath. There wasn't much smell, which probably meant she'd been killed recently, perhaps within the last couple of hours. Someone had carved on her with a butcher knife that now lay on the floor, also covered in blood. Whoever had done this hadn't been concerned about leaving the murder weapon behind. Big Margaret had been tortured. It was about the worst he'd seen, and he'd seen a few prostitutes after they'd been cruelly beaten and abused by an unhappy pimp.

He wondered if Hank, the dead woman's sometime husband and business partner, had anything to do with it. The degree of pain inflicted here was the sort of thing one saw in crimes of passion . . . often performed by husbands. Or maybe the killer had been looking for something specific. Information? Clearly the house had been turned upside down.

He went back into the living room and picked up the phone. A moment later he was talking to Tuttle.

"You need to get forensics over to Big Margaret's escort service on Barrington. She's been killed."

There was a moment of silence. Then Tuttle's voice boomed in Garrett's ear. "What the hell have you done now, Barkhouse? Every time I hear from you, there's another dead body."

"I don't know why she was killed," said Garrett. "But it happened recently. And whoever did it appeared to want to inflict maximum pain. Someone wanted something from her. The names of her customers, maybe. I don't know."

"Be nice if the next time you call you have something more unusual than a dead body to report—like a suspect."

Garrett sighed. "I'm working on a few things. There seems to be a lot going on. Every time I think I've got a handle on it, something new blows up."

"Story of your life, Barkhouse. Next time? Don't call me. I'll call you."

He hung up with a thump.

Garrett didn't feel like sticking around till the police and forensics teams arrived. He had a lot to think about. He strolled down Barrington, then up Spring Street, through the Public Gardens, and on to Dalhousie University. School would be starting in a week and the campus was already humming with early-return students on athletic teams. A squadron of girls, dressed like cookie-cutter Barbies with bouncing ponytails, jogged past him. He watched them, remembering what it was like to be that age, until images of abused girls began to fill his head.

Marcia had called, asking him to stop by to try on something new.

"Garrett!" She stood up from her desk and gave him a peck on the cheek. "You're going to love this," she said, literally rubbing her hands together in anticipation.

"They've finally got a pill that will grow me a new foot," said Garrett.

"Better! I've got the latest prosthetic on the market. Actually, it isn't even on the market yet, but I wangled one for you by saying it would be tested by a Mountie under field conditions. The company loved the idea."

"Long as I don't have to give a testimonial on TV."

"All they want is your honest evaluation of it." She reached into a box on her desk, withdrew something that looked like a body part lost by C-3PO and handed it to Garrett.

"You are holding the most advanced prosthetic available in the world. Combines artificial intelligence with cutting-edge sensor technology. With this you'll be able to detect where your foot is in space, enabling it to identify slopes and stairs after the first step using artificial intelligence, instructing your ankle to flex in an appropriate manner. It reduces the energy spent in reacting consciously to the environment."

"Well, that's a good thing," said Garrett. "Usually I'm not reacting consciously at all to my environment."

She gave him a look. "That was my impression after you submitted your foot to a vat of salt water."

"It wasn't a vat of salt water, Marcia. It was the ocean."

"Whatever."

He turned the foot this way and that. It certainly looked like an impressive bit of technology. "How long will it take to fit me?"

"We can do it in an hour. It's very user-friendly. There's a fifteen-step calibration process, during which the device evaluates and memorizes your unique gait pattern. You'll be walking like Yul Brynner when you leave here today."

He stared at her. "Better than Walter Brennan, I suppose. Let's get started."

"One thing, Garrett. This is still a prototype. Two hundred thousand dollars' worth of technology. The developer wants the assurance of an active field test. But it would still be nice if you tried to . . . ah . . . keep it dry?"

45

K ITTY HUDDLED ON THE CATWALK far beneath the oil rig and listened as the chopper circled to land. She knew whoever was arriving was expecting her to be the welcomer-in-chief. Well, they'd get a surprise once they managed to break into her room.

The seas had picked up and were very choppy now. Even though she was twenty feet above the water, mist still sprayed her every time a big wave hit the base of the concrete anchors at the right angle. The longer this kept up, the more likely she was to eventually become soaked from the cold water. She knew hypothermia would be a real possibility.

Her choices were bleak. If she stayed where she was, she was going to be in trouble soon from the cold. Her ninety-eight pounds, which had long been a staple of her sexual allure and professional power, provided not an ounce of fat for warmth. But what could she do? There was no way off the rig. To climb back above the lower level would mean she'd be much more likely to be found.

Her one consolation was that the rig didn't appear to be operating currently as a working oil platform. There seemed to be remarkably few people on board. The place was so huge and such a maze of components that it would be hard for a handful of men to search it thoroughly. Slowly, she began to work out a plan.

If she climbed up far enough to get a view of the main platform, she might be able to see men looking for her once the search began. If she could then manage to sneak to an area that had already been searched, maybe they would miss her. It was a long shot, but the only one she had. She was already shivering. If she waited much longer, she might become incapacitated.

She steeled herself, got up, and began to climb the catwalk. Her fingers felt like little cubes of ice. Near the top of the walkway, the catwalk entered a hollowed-out section of one of the anchors. Here, she stopped to enjoy the warmth of being suddenly out of the wind and spray. There was a door, which she peeked through long enough to see that it led onto the main open floor of the platform. It would expose her terribly to go out there. Inside was another set of steps rising through the concrete tube that anchored the rig. She decided to stay inside for the time being and see where they went.

She climbed up to a small room at the top of the anchor. This seemed to be storage space, filled with cable and drilling equipment. Since the rig wasn't actually drilling, maybe no one would have reason to come here. But she knew once the search began, storage rooms would likely be among the first places they would look.

Still, the room had a single window that gave her a view onto the second level of the platform. She could see the approaches to her hideaway and would have some warning if anyone was planning to enter her space. She settled down to wait.

It was warm enough to take off her soaking coat. She squeezed as much water out of it as she could, along with some that had penetrated to her clothes beneath. Then she stashed the coat behind a pile of cable. She wanted to be able to move quickly when the time came, and lugging a heavy, water-soaked coat would only slow her down and probably leave a trail of water as well.

She explored her surroundings and found a heavy wrench. It was the only thing that might remotely be considered a weapon. She clung to it and then picked up a hard hat. It would make her less recognizable outside.

She was about to settle down and wait when a siren went off. It blared for thirty seconds and was followed by a voice over a loudspeaker that announced all hands were to begin a search for "our missing hostess" was how the voice described her. It almost sounded like a game. They knew there was no place for her to go and that she couldn't get off the rig. They had every expectation of finding her.

She thought grimly about the scene she'd left behind in her room. The man with his clothes off and his brains bashed in. It ought to give them pause. She wasn't going to be anyone's push-over any more. Having taken action, she no longer felt the sense of utter helplessness that had overwhelmed her ever since Lloyd had ordered her to take her clothes off. She'd fight tooth and nail if they caught her again, even if it meant being killed.

She peered out her window and saw a handful of men moving about the rig. A couple had climbed up into the superstructure and were exploring every crevice and cranny. Several others had begun to search the level outside her window. It would only be a matter of time before someone came into her room.

Directly in front of her was a steel ladder that ran up the side of a massive pipeline. About fifty feet up, there was a small steel platform that appeared to hold only an electrical box or grid center. It looked like a dead end, though she couldn't actually see the base of the area to be sure.

She watched as men moved around the rig. She'd been right about one thing. There didn't seem to be too many of them, though it was difficult to keep track as they appeared and disappeared. She counted only half a dozen within her limited sight range.

Two men started up the ladder, and she watched them climb to the open platform with the electrical panel. They only peered over the rim, then turned and went back down. She took this to be proof that the platform was a dead end, one they wouldn't be likely to bother searching again.

It was her chance.

As soon as the men disappeared to another part of the rig, she opened the door, hesitated only an instant, then raced to the ladder and scrambled up it as fast as she could.

The platform with the grid boxes was better than she could have hoped. As long as she kept back from the edge, she was totally invisible from any other part of the rig. There was even a small indentation between grid panels where she could wedge herself, comfortably out of the wind. It wouldn't hide her if someone else climbed up to look over the edge, but barring that, she felt a small degree of security for the first time since getting off the chopper.

She put her wrench and the hard hat on the steel platform beside her and settled down to wait, as men continued calling to one another all over the rig. They seemed excited at the search, something to help pass the time during their boring duty at sea. These men might be experienced roustabouts, but it was also clear they knew precisely what went on below decks on this particular oil rig.

She prayed DeMaio wouldn't come back. He had undoubtedly been informed about what happened first thing and would be furious that his aide had been killed and his important guests spurned. They'd have to come up with some way to explain how the man was killed, though head injuries from falling objects on an oil rig were undoubtedly not uncommon. In any event, DeMaio would assume, like the others, that there was no way for her to escape. Eventually she would be caught and returned to her duties.

She thought again about Garrett. Sarah would give him her message, but there was nothing she'd said to give a clue as to her whereabouts. At least she had mentioned Lloyd. That would give them something to go on, though if pressed Lloyd would almost certainly say that he and Kitty had been together but he didn't know what had happened after she left. Absent any proof, it would be a dead end for Garrett.

She lay on her back and stared at the clouds running across the sky far above. The sun felt warm and reassuring on her face. She could almost imagine she was lying in a meadow somewhere, without a care in the world.

Almost.

46

GARRETT SLAMMED THE PHONE DOWN for the tenth time in the past two hours. He'd been trying futilely to get hold of Lonnie and in between had tried Alfred Nichols, the intel man in charge of keeping an eye on DeMaio. Lonnie didn't answer, his cell phone turned off, and Nichols apparently wouldn't take his call. He'd even put in a call to Ecum Secum's Haven for Troubled Youth to see if Lloyd was around. Maybe he could squeeze something more from the scumbag. But no one knew where Lloyd was. He'd obviously gone to ground after his confrontation with the big man. That alone suggested he hadn't told Lonnie everything.

Sarah's insistence that he do something about Kitty put him on the spot. What the hell could he do? He wasn't sure she would be on the oil rig and if he called in support only to find her not there, all he would succeed in doing would be to make DeMaio and whoever else was involved very cautious. Kitty would be hidden and guarded even more closely, maybe even killed, if they thought the authorities were getting too close.

He'd about come around to the idea that his best bet was going to be another sleuth attack by kayak. At night. His stomach churned just at the thought. Marcia would kill him if he screwed up his two-hundred-thousand-dollar foot in salt water again.

Especially if the next time she saw the expensive bit of hardware it was attached to a corpse lying on a gurney in the morgue.

Where the bloody hell was Lonnie? He decided to drive back to the city to see if he could locate his cousin at any of his usual haunts. The hours-long drive seemed like a terrible waste of time. His mind was filled with images of what Kitty must be going through. He wasn't exactly fond of the reporter, but no one deserved such a fate.

He also thought about Roland. The odds the fisherman could really turn his life around seemed remote. It would require a makeover of near-biblical proportions. Since they were kids together, Roland had been a sort of outcast. No one at their small school befriended him. Garrett had felt sorry for him and made one or two attempts to be civil, but the efforts paid no dividends. Roland was just an unpleasant character. And nothing about that had changed in the thirty-odd years since. It was going to be interesting to see how it all worked out.

He hit the greasy spoon on Barrington Street, but Lonnie hadn't been seen since they'd been there together. He drove to a quiet residential neighborhood and located his cousin's house on Henry Street. It was an inner-city street, an easy walk from the waterfront. The house was an attractive Victorian with an apartment on the third floor that Lon rented out to the college-aged daughter of still another cousin in return for some housecleaning and keeping an eye on the place when he wasn't around, which was often.

The selection of the house had always seemed incongruous to Garrett. It was a neighborhood filled with young couples just starting out, lots of kids on the streets, a sort of Ozzie and Harriet environment. Lonnie liked it because it surrounded him with the normalcy he longed for in his own life. Garrett could hardly imagine what his cousin's neighbors thought of the frightening-looking giant in their midst.

But no one was home. Garrett sat in his car in the driveway trying to think what he could do next that would be constructive when he noticed a van parked across the street with two men sitting in it.

One of the men was looking at him. Slowly he raised what looked like some sort of walking stick and rested it on the open window. As Garrett stared at it in puzzlement, the stick suddenly let loose with a loud crack and his rear window, inches from his head, exploded. He ducked instinctively as three more shots were fired, then the van's tires screeched as it pulled in tight behind Garrett's car, blocking the driveway.

He leaped out of the car and ran into Lonnie's back yard, which consisted of a postage-stamp plot of grass surrounded by shrubs and flowers. The back yards of at least six other houses all intersected, with picket fences between each of them. He looked back to see if the men in the car were coming after him, but they appeared to have decided it was too much work to chase him through the warren of busy backyards with kids, barking dogs, neighbors mowing lawns and gardening. Too many witnesses. Or maybe this had just been a warning. The van backed out and roared off down the street.

By the time he got back to his car, his attackers had disappeared. He thought about what it all meant as he cleaned up the broken glass in his back seat and threw it in Lonnie's trash can.

An old man who'd been sitting on a porch across the street cackled loudly.

"Better than TV," he said, banging the porch with his cane, a demented grin on his face.

Garrett crossed the street and smiled at him.

"You know how long those guys were sitting there?" he asked.

The old fellow shrugged his thin shoulders and cackled again, revealing a mouth full of missing teeth.

"I jest came out ten minutes ago," he said. "Soon's *Law & Order* ended. Better show out here."

"Any idea who they were?"

"Nope. But it's not the first time. Big guy, my neighbor? I think he knows some pretty bad people. But he always rakes my leaves for me in the fall."

Garrett just nodded. Maybe he and Lonnie had been targeted by DeMaio. He wouldn't put anything past the CEO. A big power broker like that would think nothing of stomping out any little bugs that irritated him. Of course, given what Lonnie did for a living, the attackers could have also been from any of a dozen other interests that Lonnie had annoyed. Still, it seemed unlikely anyone would mistake Garrett for his cousin.

He retreated to his car and drove slowly down the street. He wasn't so sure it was a good idea for Lonnie to rent out an apartment to their cousin's daughter. She might get in the crosshairs by mistake. He'd mention it . . . if he ever found him.

Someone was playing for keeps. He wondered if Lloyd might have sicced the Global Resources people on them. But the more he thought about it, the more he doubted that scenario. Lloyd was too much of a coward and was well aware of Lonnie's reputation. He would avoid having anything to do with him.

That left DeMaio himself. It wouldn't have been hard for the CEO to determine who Garrett was, following the press briefing, though it was pretty hard to believe the man would actually attempt to kill an RCMP officer. Still, DeMaio had been more than surprised when Garrett said he'd been on the oil rig and seen the accommodations himself. If word reached the CEO that Garrett was a Special Constable with expertise in prostitution . . . well . . . that put Garrett with way more information than DeMaio would be able to accept. The CEO had too much to lose.

Things were heating up. He wondered again what was happening to poor Kitty. Then he slammed on his brakes in the middle of the street. A man in a sports car careened around him, cursing loudly out his window. But Garrett hardly heard him.

DeMaio would hire only professionals. One thing you could count on from the very rich was for them to always hire the best. If they had wanted to kill him, they would have done so. Which meant they were sending a message. One that worried him a lot more than just getting shot at.

He picked up his cell phone and called Sarah. By the tenth ring, he was already speeding down the highway toward the bridge, his temporary police light stuck on his roof. The message he feared was that someone close to him might be at risk—as a warning to him.

47

HIS WORST FEARS WERE REALIZED when he turned in to Sarah's little cottage. Milling around outside was Tom, along with his counterpart from up the shore, Arthur Parmenter. Even Alvin was there, in his Halifax patrol car.

Garrett just nodded at them and said, "Where is she?"

Before anyone could speak, Lila and Ayesha came running out of the house. Lila had an angry bruise on her cheek.

"Oh, Garrett," she cried, "Some men came and took Sarah away. We tried to stop them but they just knocked me down. One of them told me to tell you it was time to stop poking your nose where it wasn't wanted."

Garrett's heart sank. He put one hand gently on Lila's cheek. "They did this to you?"

She nodded, tears running down her face. But they weren't for the bruise. She'd been hit plenty of times during her years at Sweet Angels. The tears were for Sarah. "Why did they take her, Garrett? What's going on?"

"We'd like to know that too," said Alvin. "Tom here called it in to Tuttle and he sent me down to see if I could help."

"Thanks, Alvin. And you too, Tom and Arthur." He took a deep breath. "They took her to get to me. To get me to stop investigating this DeMaio character who runs Global Resources. They think they're more powerful than God."

"What do you want us to do?" Tom asked.

Garrett stared at the wharf. What would they do with her? Would they take her to the oil rig like Kitty? He didn't think so, or at least he didn't want to think about that possibility. They'd want to hide her away some place safe, where no one else would find or see her. Until they were certain Garrett would do as he was told.

He thought about Madame Liu's high-end Victorian house and that little barred bungalow where the girls were locked up at night on the island. "Tom, can you and Arthur check out Madame Liu's compound on the island in Lake Micmac? I've talked to Tuttle about it. He'll help you set up a raid."

Tom nodded slowly. "Okay. What about you?"

"Another possibility I'm going to look into. Alvin can help me." He looked at his friend, who nodded. He was glad Alvin had come. He was a short, wiry little guy with a chip on his shoulder, but he was a pit bull.

Garrett turned to the girls. "Will you be all right here by yourselves?"

"Of course," Lila said indignantly. "We're not babies. But isn't there something else we can do?"

"Yes," he said. "Can you tell me anything at all about Lloyd that might be useful? I've got to find him. He's in this up to his neck, but he's disappeared. Lonnie put the fear of God into him. I should have collared him when I had the chance. You have any idea where he might go to hide out?"

Lila looked defeated. "No, I'm sorry, Garrett. He has a house down the other side of Necum Teuch, but he wouldn't go there if he was hiding." She hesitated.

"What?"

"He used to take one of the kids at the home away with him sometimes. Said he had some yard work for him to do at his cabin. But the kid was gay, and we all kind of thought that had something to do with it."

"Lloyd is gay?" Garrett could hardly believe it. The man obviously relished his power over the young girls, and the way he looked at Kitty . . . it just didn't seem likely.

"I think he's bisexual," Lila said. "We got them sometimes at Sweet Angels. Even a few who would ask for a girl and a boy at the same time. Anyway, he was obsessed by sex. It's practically all he thought about. He liked for the guys to see him when he was naked just as much as the girls."

"All right, thanks, Lila. It's important to know. I want you to call anyone you can think of who might know something about Lloyd's whereabouts. In the city or at Lloyd's Haven. If you call the Haven, pretend you're a parent wanting to talk to your child."

She perked up. "All right, Garrett. I can do that."

He gave her his cell phone number.

Alvin said, "You have any idea at all where we're going to look for this guy?"

"We'll start at Lloyd's Haven. It's the only place I can think of. Lloyd knows more than he told Lonnie. I'm certain of it. He's the loose thread in all of this, and I'm going to pull it until his head explodes."

48

IT WAS A WINDY NIGHT on the ocean, signaling, perhaps, yet another storm moving up the Atlantic seaboard.

Lonnie lumbered along the Halifax waterfront. It was after eleven and the streets were mostly deserted. Only the requisite derelicts, a handful of hookers, and a police patrol car or two occupied the quiet byways. All of them watched Lonnie pass uneasily. The police knew who he was and had come to have a grudging respect for him. Some of that came from Lonnie's connection to Garrett. That he was often engaged in activities of borderline legality didn't escape the authorities, but they'd learned that the big man's word was good and that they could rely on him for an occasional tip when it came to pimps or the odd mugger.

But there would be no tips tonight. Lonnie was on a mission. He'd seen Kitty on TV a few times. She was a looker, and he knew she had to be deep into the worst nightmare of her young life. He couldn't really describe the way he felt. Anger that a promising young reporter should have to find herself in such a position. He felt a slow rage building deep within him, its source long ago primed by his grandmother.

His years in the business of enforcement on the docks of Halifax and Dartmouth had given him many contacts. Now one of them waited for him beside a deserted wharf in a speedboat with a powerful engine.

His intentions were still not fully thought out. But he was dressed in dark clothes and armed with a nine-millimeter Luger, a short-nosed .45 in an ankle holster, and an ugly looking knife with a six-inch blade. Normally a walking fortress of muscle and determination, the extra firepower made him an arsenal that no one in his right mind would want to come upon on a dark night . . . on the docks or anywhere else.

Garrett had his limitations being an RCMP officer. Even though he wore no uniform and drove his crappy old unmarked Subaru, Lonnie knew the supposed autonomy of action these things gave Garrett were superficial at best. He'd always tried to help his cousin whenever he could. Partly, he felt responsible for him after the injury in Iraq. There had been a lengthy recuperation period and several bouts of depression that Lonnie had helped Garrett fight through. Garrett was the closest family he had and he would do anything for him. Right now, however, what he wanted most was to try to rescue Kitty. And he knew Garrett was bound by rules and regulations that didn't apply to him.

He scanned the side of the wharf and saw the boat. It was sleek and fast-looking, painted black, with only a single running light. A low spray screen gave the skipper limited protection from the elements. The lone man on board saw him and waved an arm.

A moment later, they were motoring out past George's Island. Once out of the harbor, his companion pushed the throttle all the way out and they barreled up the coast, the craft taking huge, airborne leaps over the rising swells. It would take three hours to reach the oil rig. The pilot was an experienced navigator in these waters. Even at night in bad weather, he'd have no trouble avoiding the numerous shoals.

They exchanged few words. The man in charge of the boat knew from experience that Lonnie generally had little to say and was undoubtedly up to something unusual, if not downright illegal. Better to just pay his debt to the big man and keep his mouth shut.

Lonnie sat, filling the entire back seat of the craft, and watched the seas pass underneath, black and viscous, like riding on the sort of thick oil that might one day be sucked from beneath the ocean by a rig like the one beyond Lighthouse Point.

He hadn't put a lot of thought into what was going to happen. He was a born improviser and suspected the oil rig, still not producing oil according to DeMaio, would likely be populated by only a handful of workers, roughnecks who had no reason to be armed. Perhaps there would be some security, but whatever sort of low-level guards were employed by the company, it was certain they had never come up against someone like Lonnie. Besides, there simply hadn't been time to work out the details. Speed was of the essence. There was no telling how much time Kitty had.

He allowed his mind to wander as the boat powered through the swells. He almost felt like he was on patrol in Afghanistan and hoped, as he had on so many missions in that far-off country, that he'd be in and out quickly, with as few casualties as possible.

But that would depend entirely on the attitude of those he encountered. Only one thing was certain. He wasn't leaving the rig without her.

49

As THEY PULLED INTO LLOYD'S Haven for Troubled Youth, Garrett could sense Alvin's intensity. The little guy was wired.

"Take it easy," Garrett said. "He's not going to be here. We're just going to talk to the kids. See what we can find out."

"I just want to bust the guy one time in the chops," Alvin said, slapping his fist into the palm of his other hand.

"You might have to get in line," Garrett replied.

It was immediately clear that Lloyd wasn't around. In fact, it looked like the "troubled youth" had the run of the place. Kids lolled about everywhere they looked. Three tough-looking teens Garrett hadn't seen before sat on crotch rockets in the drive, bullshitting with one another. Others sat on the porch, which was a mess of food wrappers, empty beer bottles, and discarded clothing. No one was working in the gardens, and they saw no adults around at all.

Alvin was in uniform and his appearance caused some consternation as he and Garrett got out of the car. One of the motorcycle riders, a big guy with tattoos and a shaved head, looked at the diminutive Mountie and burst out laughing.

"It's a midget cop," he said to one of his friends.

Alvin was in the guy's face in a second, bracing him and pushing him off the bike onto the ground. The bike fell hard onto the pavement, breaking the mirror.

"You sonofabitch!" the big guy said. "I'll take you apart." He scrambled to his feet only to find himself staring down the barrel of Alvin's pistol. Alvin cocked the gun and put it right on the guy's nose.

"Back off, asshole," he said.

Garrett eased around beside Alvin and put one hand on his gun arm. Slowly, Alvin lowered the weapon, though he kept it cocked.

Garrett saw several kids he knew on the porch. "Why don't you guys beat it," he said to the bikers.

The three teens glared at them for a moment, then shrugged, got on their bikes, and peeled out with loud squeals, leaving rubber tire marks on the pavement.

Garrett went up onto the porch. The girl who'd been doing lip-locks with the overweight kid at the bonfire sat with two friends. She smiled at Garrett. "I was hoping you'd plug those shitkickers," she said. "Been trying to put the moves on us."

"Looking for Lloyd," Garrett said. "Guess he's not around."

"He was here earlier," she said. "Seemed pretty nervous about something. Only stayed long enough to pick up his boy toy and then they split."

"Who's the boy toy?"

"Reggie," she said. "Not the first time he's gone with our great and perverted leader."

"Any idea where they go?"

She looked at her friends, as if getting silent approval, then said, "Lloyd has a cabin back on a lake. He takes Reg there sometimes."

"Know where it is?"

She grinned. "Sure. He took me and some others there a couple of times to do yard work, clean house and stuff. He's a real pig and won't do any work himself."

She gave Garrett explicit directions, even drew him a little map. The place was at the end of a long dirt road that ran straight into the empty central wilderness of Nova Scotia, at least a two-hour drive. Garrett could see why Lloyd would go there. He'd feel secure in a place so hard to find, especially if he thought Lonnie might still be after him. But he couldn't resist taking along his boy toy, which had been a big mistake. It reinforced Garrett's opinion that old Lloyd wasn't the sharpest knife in the drawer.

The aging Subaru knocked around the potholed road for a long time, until Garrett began to worry the vehicle might come apart. They grounded out half a dozen times and the gears began to make unsettling noises. Most of the third-degree roads that traversed the interior of the province were lined with spruce and little else. They didn't pass a single house, crossed several rickety bridges over tumbling streams, and had to stop once to let a bull moose get out of the way.

"I just remembered why it was I moved to Halifax," Alvin said. "I grew up on a road like this. My dad was a logger and he loved living out in the trees. I always hated it. No one around for me to play with."

Garrett just nodded. He was uneasy about all the time they were wasting. Kitty and Sarah were in serious danger, and all he could think to do was chase down a sex pervert living in the freaking outback.

Finally, they rumbled across an old wooden bridge above a stream, banks overflowing from the wet summer, and pulled into an opening in the trees. A small log cabin perched on the edge of the stream, looking like something out of the movie *Deliverance*.

Garrett cut the engine and they sat in the car for a minute. The silence of the north woods was deafening. If anyone was here, it wasn't immediately evident. There was no car anywhere in sight.

If Lloyd was here, he would have heard the laboring Subaru for twenty minutes before it arrived.

Still, there was no other way out. Garrett got out of the car and walked over to the cabin. Someone had made a halfhearted effort to plant a few shrubs along the walls, and there was a small patch of yard that looked like it hadn't been mowed yet this summer.

Nothing ventured, Garrett went up onto the small deck and knocked on the door. Alvin got out of the car behind him and stood with one hand resting on his holster.

There was no answer. Garrett looked at Alvin. "Did you hear someone say 'come in?'"

"Clear as a bell," said Alvin.

The door was unlocked. Inside, there was only a single room. The space was furnished with about as much taste as a budget motel: a thin oriental-style rug on the floor, a queen-sized bed filled with tumbled blankets and sheets against one wall. Opposite the bed were cabinets, a sink, and a small refrigerator and stove that operated off of propane. In one corner, open to the room, was a chemical toilet.

"Not exactly the honeymoon suite," said Alvin. "I'm going to look around outside."

Garrett went over to the kitchen area. The little sink was filled with dirty dishes. A stick of butter, saturated with bread crumbs, sat on a small plate. On the stove was a cast iron frying pan with a residue of oil and bits of eggs. He put one finger into the oil and touched the bottom of the pan. It was still warm. Someone had been here in the last fifteen minutes at the most.

Suddenly, he heard a noise and scuffle coming from outside. He raced out the door and stopped. Lloyd was lying on the ground holding his cheek. Alvin stood over him with blood on his fist.

"Found him in the woods," Alvin said. "There's a little track goes back there. So he can keep his car out of sight."

Garrett went over and looked down at Lloyd.

"Hell do you want?" Lloyd asked, getting to his feet slowly. "You didn't have to sic your miniature schnauzer on me."

"Where's Reggie?" Garrett asked.

"Who?"

"Don't mess with me, Lloyd. I'm about two seconds from letting Alvin get on with it."

He shrugged, glanced at Alvin. "No need to get your nose in a knot." He turned toward the woods and yelled. "Come on out, Reggie."

A tall, thin boy came out of the brush. He had on jean shorts and nothing else and couldn't have been more than fifteen. He had a tousled head of blond hair and good features. Garrett guessed it was his misfortune to have a look that Lloyd found attractive.

"It's okay," Garrett said. "No one's going to hurt you. You're going back to the home, and old Lloyd here is going to have some explaining to do."

The boy started to cry. "He brings me here and rapes me," he sniveled.

"Shut your mouth!" Lloyd said.

Alvin punched him hard in the ribs. Lloyd gasped and doubled over.

Garrett said to Alvin, "I want you to use Lloyd's car and take Reggie home. I'll deal with Lloyd."

"I don't think that's a good idea, Garrett," Alvin said. "I can't leave you alone with him."

Garrett took out his handcuffs and cuffed Lloyd's hands behind his back. "I think we'll get along all right. We have a few things to talk about. I'll catch up and let you know how it goes later."

Again, Alvin hesitated, but Garrett just said, "Get going." Reluctantly, Alvin guided Reggie to the car in the woods. A moment later they drove off.

Garrett grabbed Lloyd by the scruff of the neck, dragged him over to the deck, and propped him up.

"I want to make sure you understand something, Lloyd. We haven't been able to find Kitty yet, but someone, and I'm betting you have an idea who, has also abducted my girlfriend. So I'm not in a mood to hear anything but straight answers from you on this."

Lloyd struggled to sit upright. The bruise where Alvin had struck him was turning purple. "What are you going to do with Reggie? Anything we did together was consensual."

"Even a scumbag like you ought to know there's no such thing as consensual sex with a minor. I can safely promise you your days exploiting those kids are over."

"I . . . I took care of them. We saved a lot of those kids from a life of prostitution."

"So long as they prostituted themselves to you, huh?"

Garrett reached over, grabbed his hair, and smacked his head against the porch railing. Hard.

Lloyd squealed. "Hey, you can't do that. You're a Mountie."

Garrett did it again.

"Ow! Damn it, that hurts. I told the big guy all I know. He said he was working with you. Why don't you ask him?"

"Here's the thing, Lloyd. I don't think you were entirely forthright with Lonnie. You made this personal for me. Now I'm the one asking the questions. Look around. You see anyone who is going to help you? Or maybe you'd prefer I hand you over to Lonnie? That's why you came here, isn't it? To hide from him."

"You think I'm scared of him?"

"If you're not, you're dumber than you look."

Lloyd struggled to sit upright. "You're nothing," he said. "You're dealing with people who will squash you and your ogre friend like eggshells."

"I assume you're talking about our Mr. DeMaio."

"Christ! *There's* someone to be afraid of. Whatever you've been doing, you got DeMaio's attention all right. Why the hell you think I'm up here? That son of a bitch has decided you're too close. He's cleaning up loose ends. He already did in Big Margaret. When I heard about that, I lit out."

Garrett stared at him. So that was it. DeMaio was getting worried about Garrett's interest in his special oil rig. It was the worst possible news. If DeMaio was ordering anyone who might spill the beans killed, then Lloyd was right to be worried. And Kitty and Sarah were at even greater risk.

"Where's Sarah?"

"I don't know anything about anyone named Sarah. Only thing I can tell you is if you've been looking for Kitty, then you probably pissed off the people at Global Resources and DeMaio in particular. They must be the ones who took your girlfriend. Trust me, you don't want to mess with these people."

Garrett stared at him. "Those people don't want to mess with me." He grabbed Lloyd, pulled him upright, hauled him over to the stream, and threw him in.

The water was only a couple of feet deep, but the current was swift. Lloyd went in over his head and Garrett let him flounder around for thirty seconds before pulling him out. He waited while Lloyd coughed and sputtered. His face was red.

"You can't do this," he said, still choking for wind. "I'll have your badge. This is torture."

"Glad you're beginning to get the message," Garrett said. He grabbed him and threw him back in the water. This time, he let him flounder around for a minute. Without the use of his hands it was very hard for him to get up on his feet against the current. Twice he got his head up and gasped for breath, then stumbled and fell back under again. After another while, Garrett pulled him out and put him on the ground.

"Where's Sarah?" he said.

"I told you. I don't have any idea." Lloyd coughed and spat up some blood.

Garrett grabbed him and began to haul him back to the stream.

"All right, all right. Enough. I'll tell you what I know."

Garrett waited.

"Like I told the big guy. DeMaio's the one set up their whole Club Med operation with freebies for the potential oil rig investors. I don't have any way to know for sure, but I'd bet good money Kitty is at Lighthouse Point. Your girlfriend is probably there too. If she's good-enough looking, that is."

"All right," Garrett said. "It's a start. Now, I want you to tell me everything you know about DeMaio, starting from the day he was born . . . or hatched. Whatever."

50

KITTY WATCHED AS THE SUN set and the stars came out. It was a black night on the ocean, with no moon. The display of the Milky Way was the most intense she'd ever seen, though the stars blinked out near the horizon and she suspected a front was moving in. The spectacular heavenly display almost made her forget how hungry and thirsty she was. Another day and night at the most and she'd be forced to go in search of sustenance.

Then she heard the sound of another helicopter thundering in. She cringed back as someone turned on extra landing lights for the helipad and watched as the aircraft landed almost directly below her. She hoped it wasn't DeMaio coming back to help look for her. Instead, peering through a slit in the platform, she gasped out loud as two men dragged Sarah out of the chopper and led her inside.

She fell back against the electrical panel and tried to think. Why the hell would they kidnap Sarah? A temporary replacement for herself to keep the investors happy? There had hardly been enough time for them to come up with such an alternate plan. At least DeMaio himself hadn't been on the chopper. Maybe Garrett was getting close and they grabbed Sarah to have leverage over him.

She was scared and didn't want to leave the relative safety of her platform. But she liked Sarah. She knew the feeling wasn't mutual. Kitty'd had no close women friends in her life. They were always uncomfortable around her, especially if they had their own men they were worried about. It was just something she'd come to expect. Men liked the way she looked. Women, not so much.

If Sarah was here to service the investors, who were no doubt seriously pissed off at the delay in their fun, then she was going to be in trouble very quickly.

Kitty got up and began to work her way down the ladder as quietly as possible. She felt almost helpless but was damned if she'd just sit by and not at least try to help another woman about to be brutalized.

The helipad lights had been turned off. Evidently the pilot intended to stay the night. The oil platform was mostly dark, and the search appeared to be over for now, maybe even for the night. She was right in her evaluation that there were few men on the rig. Still, she had to stumble across just one and the game would be up.

Outside a door that she knew led to an inside corridor, probably where Sarah had been taken, were a bunch of hooks where the roughnecks or whatever they called themselves hung their heavy jackets and hardhats. Most of the hooks were filled. It was dinnertime. Her stomach rumbled. She'd had nothing to eat in thirty-six hours.

Maybe she'd write a diet book when this was over. *The Sexual Slavery Diet.* Had a nice ring to it. Catchy. Kind of a variation on *How to Get a Man and Keep Him* or, maybe more appropriately, *How to Get a Woman and Hide Her Away.*

She put one hand on the door handle and hesitated. What the hell did she think she was going to do? How could she rescue Sarah? She couldn't even rescue herself. If she got caught, there would just be two women to pass around. Make the SOBs happy as clams.

Suddenly, the door opened. She was so startled she threw her entire weight against it. The door snapped back into the face of the man coming out and knocked him out cold. Fortunately he was alone.

She stared at the body at her feet. It was one of the men who had pulled Sarah out of the chopper. Now what? He'd come around any moment and raise the alarm, even if Kitty ran and hid. The search would start all over again in earnest.

She hadn't an iota of sympathy for these men. She was fighting for her life here, and Sarah's too. The more of them she could disappear the better. She still had her heavy wrench. But it would leave a mess. Better to dispose of the body outright. Who knew how long before the fellow would be missed?

She dragged the dead weight twenty feet to a railing, cursing her slight frame and grunting at the effort. She quickly went through his pockets and could hardly believe her luck. He had a gun. She stared at the thing for a moment. She knew nothing about guns, except that they were the great equalizer, and that was something she could definitely use about now. She slipped the thing into her jacket pocket.

Then, with some difficulty, she hoisted the man up and watched as his body cartwheeled to the water far below. Unconscious, he would drown immediately. Good riddance, as far as she was concerned.

She stood, breathing heavily at the railing. She'd killed two men in the past twenty-four hours. Far from guilt, she felt only a sense of exhilaration. She was rescuing herself, goddamn it.

She went back to the door into the corridor, opened it a crack, and listened. Nothing. She eased into the corridor, one hand firmly on the gun in her pocket. She walked quietly along the carpeted hall until she reached the door to the room where she'd been held. It had been smashed and broken open. The body of DeMaio's man was gone, a large smear of blood still on the floor.

She froze. There was a strange sound. She moved slowly down the hall and stood in front of another door. The noise was coming from the other side, a sort of scratching sound. She put her ear up to the door and could hear someone breathing heavily on the other side, someone trying to force the lock.

She hesitated only a moment. Who else could it be? In a harsh whisper she said, "Sarah, are you in there?"

The noise stopped. Then a voice said, "Who's that?"

"It's Kitty, Sarah. I saw them bring you here."

There was a moment of silence. Then, "Kitty? Are you okay?"

"More or less. Listen, can you get this door open?"

"I've been trying to pick the lock, something my husband taught me how to do. Hold on."

Kitty listened again as Sarah stuck something into the lock and twisted and turned. After what seemed like an eternity, the door suddenly snapped open.

Sarah hugged Kitty tightly. "Thank God you're alive. We were all sick worrying about you, trying to figure out what to do to help you."

"Let's bring each other up to date another time," said Kitty. "We've got to get out of here before they come for you. Did they say anything about what they were going to do with you?"

"I got the picture all right. They told me to take a shower and clean myself up, that I'd have visitors soon and I'd better treat them right."

Kitty stared at her grimly. "All right, come on."

"Where can we go?"

"I've got a hiding place. Don't know for how long. Once they find you're gone or that another of their men is missing, they'll probably turn the rig upside down. But there aren't too many men on board. It will take them a long time. And . . ." she reached into her pocket. "I've got this." She showed Sarah the gun.

Sarah's eyes went wide. "How . . . ?"

"Later," said Kitty. "Come on." She went down the corridor and opened a door she'd looked in on once before. It was some sort of storage room filled with food.

"Quick, grab a bag or something to hold stuff."

Sarah found a canvas bag and they stuffed it with whatever edibles they could find. Kitty also grabbed a gallon of water.

A minute later they were climbing up to Kitty's hideaway.

Sarah looked around the tiny space and said, "What's to keep them from finding us here?"

"Nothing, except I watched them search it once already. No reason for them to repeat it unless they decide to search from scratch all over again. All we can do is try to hold out. Look how this place is situated. There's no way for anyone to get above us. They can only find us by coming up the ladder. If they do that, I'll shoot them. Let's hope it doesn't come to that for a long time. With the food and water we can stay here a week if we have to. Maybe Garrett will think of something by then."

Sarah slumped down onto the grating. "When they came and took me, I could hardly believe it was happening. But they didn't take the girls, so Garrett will know what happened. Trouble is, he couldn't figure out how to rescue you either. I gather he's been talking to the government and to his own boss. But he was afraid if he moved on the rig, DeMaio would just fly you away somewhere, maybe even to another country. Or maybe kill you outright." She hesitated. "What sort of man is he?"

"DeMaio?" Kitty leaned back against the electrical grid box. "Like a lot of men, I guess. Sex-obsessed. But unlike most men, he has the power to actually pull something like this off."

"Did he . . ." Sarah started, then stopped. "No. I have no right to ask you that."

Kitty shrugged. "Did he rape me? Yes. There was no force used, but I had no alternative. I suppose I was fortunate that he took me for several days instead of just handing me over to a bunch of foreign oil executives. Before he left, he was already tiring of me and told me that I'd be turned over to others. That's when I escaped."

Sarah stared at her. "I want to apologize to you, Kitty."

She looked surprised. "What for?"

"For underestimating you and . . . for being jealous, I guess, of Garrett. I suppose most women would be jealous of you. I mean look at you. It's probably not an easy thing . . . to have that expectation from every woman you meet. I did the same thing when I first met you. Took your looks for everything there was to know about you. But you are one tough cookie. I don't know what would have happened to me if I'd had to go through what you did."

Kitty squeezed her arm. "We're not out of the woods yet. But if we do get away, would you do something for me?"

"What?"

"Be my friend?"

A tear rolled down Sarah's cheek. She leaned over and hugged Kitty tight. "For life," she said.

51

Garrett drove lloyd back to Sheet Harbor and turned him over to Alvin.

"What do you want me to do with him?" Alvin asked, after locking Lloyd in the rear of his patrol car.

"Take him to Halifax and give him to Tuttle. We've got enough on him to put him away for a long time, starting with raping a minor. Once we get Kitty back, I bet we'll have kidnapping and sexual trafficking to go with it." He headed back to his car.

"Where are you going?"

"DeMaio has raised the stakes. I've got no more time to waste. I'm going out to the oil rig, just as fast as I can. I want you to call Tuttle and also Tom at the Coast Guard and tell them what I'm doing."

"All right, Garrett. Be careful."

He drove through the black night as quickly as his back-roads-rattled Subaru would take him. He knew where he was going. The time for kayaks and sneaking up on the rig was past.

He pulled into Roland's driveway at four a.m. There was still a single light on in the back of the house, in the fisherman's private space. Garrett banged on the door and yelled until more lights came on. Finally, Roland appeared at the door, wearing nothing but a pair of sweatpants. His torso was lean and almost concave, with a sort of hollow in his chest. He had widespread acne scars on his back.

"Garrett?" he said, peering onto the dark porch. "What's goin' on?"

"I need your boat, Roland. And I need you to pilot it. Police business. Let's go."

Roland rubbed his eyes. "Are you crazy?"

Garrett nodded. "And getting crazier by the minute. Sarah's been kidnapped, taken out to Lighthouse Point oil rig. We're going after her."

Roland was struggling into a T-shirt and looking for his shoes. "Sure, sure, Garrett. Glad ta help. Why would anyone want ta take ya girlfriend?"

"Long story," Garrett said. "I'll tell you once we're on the boat."

Ten minutes later, they were motoring past the inner islands. Roland stood in the wheelhouse, talking to Garrett through the open window. "Ya say they're holdin' two women out there? What for?"

"To service Global Resources' international customers. They're running a sex ring off the rig. Conveniently in international waters."

Roland stared at him in disbelief and maybe a little envy at the perks held by the high and mighty. A world he would never have entree to. He also looked worried. "How many men ya think they have out there, Gar? Ya goin' ta get me killed?"

"You just drive the boat, Roland. When we get close, throttle down while we're still out of earshot. Then turn the engine off and we'll use the oars to get close to the dock. I'll jump off and you can drift off a ways and wait for me to signal you."

They motored for another hour without talking, moving across the black sea as if suspended in outer space, until the lights of the rig loomed in the distance. It was still dark enough to provide cover if anyone was up and about on the platform. There was the faintest hint of early morning light on the horizon and something else, a strange, pale bank of clouds looking like swirls out of a Van Gogh painting. The lights from the rig reflected off small whitecaps beginning to form on the surface. There was more weather in their future.

Roland said, "Somethin' else I found out t'other day, Garrett."

"What?"

"I followed Grace after she went out in her kayak."

"Be better if you left them alone, Roland. It's only going to get you in trouble. Remember you said you would?"

"It was before Ma died. Ya want ta know where she went or not?"

Garrett stared at the rig. It was still a mile off. Their engine wouldn't be heard over the wind and waves until they were less than a hundred yards from it. "Okay. I'll bite. Where did she go?"

Roland smiled. "I tol' ya they was all a bunch of druggies, but ya wouldn't believe me."

"What are you talking about?"

"Grace met up with a boat on one of the outer islands. She bought drugs from three men. Couldn't get close enough ta see what, but it was some kinda white powder. Cocaine, mebbe."

Garrett just stared at him. "Now's not the time to start this, Roland. I've had a bellyful of your little neighborhood war."

"I'm tellin' ya the truth, Gar. Hell, I hardly believed it myself. And I'll tell ya somethin' else. One of the men she bought the stuff from was a Mountie."

Garrett's head snapped up at this. "How do you know he was a Mountie?"

"You kiddin'? I know one when I see one, even if he was only in partial uniform."

It was something Garrett didn't want to have to think about right now. His mind was on Sarah and Kitty. They deserved his full concentration. Still, the fact that there was a bad cop some-where in all of this had come up before. Lila said some of the young girls brought into the escort services spoke about it. And it was probably a cop who set up Sarah's husband by planting heroin in their house.

"All right, Roland. We'll talk about it after." He turned toward the rig. "Time to turn your engine off."

52

THE RIG WAS EERILY QUIET as evening set in. A fogbank, nestled on the horizon all day, finally disappeared, only to be replaced by ominous-looking clouds. Still, they appeared far off, and it showed signs of being a calm night. That was a good thing, since neither of them was warmly dressed. Nothing had happened since the helicopter had landed and Kitty had secured Sarah from her room.

"They've got to check on you soon," said Kitty. "Maybe give you something to eat prior to the busy evening they have planned for you."

"I agree," said Sarah. "It's not going to be quiet much longer." She struggled to get comfortable on the steel deck. "You really think you can use that thing?" She gestured at the gun, which lay at Kitty's side.

Kitty picked the weapon up and juggled it in one hand. "So far I've killed two men," she said. "Bashed in the skull of one and threw the other into the ocean unconscious. Believe me, point and shoot will be lots easier."

Sarah stared at her with wide eyes. "I never asked," she said. "Was it really Lloyd who got you into all of this?"

"Yeah, he was the one. Garrett was right about him. I took a big risk playing him for information. Instead, he played me.

I was a fool to go with him. It was ambition, plain and simple. I wanted that big story, and I just never saw it coming, couldn't believe they would risk taking a well-known public figure. Boy, was I wrong."

Sarah squeezed her shoulder.

Suddenly, the chopper pad lit up, flooding the rig with bright light. Men poured out into the open. For the first time, Kitty got a sense of how many were on the rig. It was more than she'd thought. At least fifteen. And there was no doubt about their purpose. They knew Sarah was gone and probably that one of their own was also missing.

Kitty gripped the pistol tightly. She had only six shots. If their hiding place was discovered, they were going to be caught once she ran out of ammunition. No question about it.

As if reading her thoughts, Sarah said, "Better conserve your shots. Might make sense to just use a couple if they find us, then save the rest. They won't know for sure how many bullets we have. It may make them think twice about climbing up here."

Kitty nodded grimly and watched as the men fanned out beneath them. For a time, no one seemed interested in the ladder that led to their hiding place.

"What are they waiting for?" Sarah asked, on edge watching the search. "This platform has to be an obvious place to look."

"I don't know. Maybe whoever's in charge was one of the men who checked this place early on. But when they don't find us anywhere else, they're bound to come round to it again."

Kitty was right. After an hour of searching, the men gathered below them to discuss what to do next. A few minutes later, two men began to climb the ladder, as others went below to continue the search inside.

"I guess this is it," said Kitty. She crouched at the edge of the platform, the pistol firmly in her hand.

"Maybe we could just kick them when they look over the edge," said Sarah.

"No way. All it would take would be one of them getting a hand on my leg or arm. I wouldn't be able to break free." Her voice got lower as they listened to the men nearing the top. Kitty pulled back the trigger and waited.

When the first man looked over the rim, his eyes went wide as he stared down Kitty's barrel. His surprise lasted only a moment. Kitty put a bullet squarely between his eyes. His body cartwheeled backward, knocking the other man off the ladder. They both fell sixty feet, landing with a sickening crunch on the rig floor.

"Two for the price of one," said Kitty. "Saved a bullet."

Sarah could only stare down at the sight of the two mangled bodies, blood pooling beneath them. A cry went out, and the men who had disappeared inside came back out in a rush. Then they stopped and stared at their mates. One man pointed up to the platform.

Kitty leaned over the edge and shot at the pointer, missing him by at least a dozen feet. Everyone scrambled out of sight.

"Guess they know we're here," Kitty said. "So it won't hurt to reinforce the predicament of their situation."

"The predicament of *their* situation?" Sarah looked at Kitty as if seeing her for the first time. Whatever had happened to her new friend while under DeMaio's control, it had put some sort of steel in her. "In case you haven't noticed, we're the ones who are trapped. We're not going anywhere."

Kitty shrugged. "Maybe not, but they sure as hell aren't going to be climbing up here again any time soon. We just have to wait them out."

The waiting game began in earnest. There really was nothing the men below could do to get to them. Doubtless some of them had guns, but the steel floor beneath Kitty and Sarah was impervious to bullets and there was no way that anyone could get above them for a clear shot onto the platform.

Then the rig plunged into blackness. It was as if someone had pulled the main switch for the entire facility. Even the tiny lights at the top of the superstructure designed to warn off planes went out.

"Holy shit!" said Sarah. They literally couldn't see their hands in front of their faces. She felt a surge of vertigo. The stars seemed to reach right down to their feet, and the sensation was one of floating in mid-air, as though totally disembodied. "What the hell are they doing?" she asked.

"Keeping us from being able to shoot at them would be my guess," said Kitty. She hesitated. "But there's another possibility. They might feel safer sending someone up the ladder in the dark." She lay down full length on her stomach, her head just inches from the edge. "Only way we'll be able to tell is if we hear them."

Sarah grasped the heavy wrench in one hand and lay down next to her. They listened with every fiber of their being. The only sound was the distant lapping of the waves far below. If anyone was attempting to climb up, they were being as quiet as possible.

Finally, Sarah thought she heard something. It was the faint but unmistakable sound of heavy breathing. The exertion of climbing the ladder combined with their pursuers' undoubted nervous anxiety had given them away. She gripped the wrench tightly. Kitty stuck one hand over the top rung of the ladder and left it there. She couldn't see a thing, but the man's head would touch her hand when he reached the top and give her a moment's warning and a target to shoot at.

Sarah couldn't see what Kitty was doing and neither of them dared to speak. From the breathing, they knew at least one man was close. Then Sarah felt a sudden rush of movement next to her. The man had reached Kitty's hand and a moment later a gunshot split the darkness, the sound so loud that Sarah cried out. An instant later, they heard the body hit the deck below. Another man had been just behind his friend; he went down the ladder as though doing a fire drill. They heard him grunt when he hit the bottom and run for cover.

Then, silence reigned. After several minutes, a voice called out from below.

"Listen, ladies," a man said. "This has gotten out of hand. There's no need for any more killing. We want no part of this."

Kitty called out, "You didn't mind being a part of it, as long as we were helpless. Well, we aren't helpless any more, and I'm personally going to kill as many of you sick bastards as I can. So come on. Send someone else up. Please."

There was a pause. Then the voice said, "Okay. Can't say I blame you. I wouldn't trust anyone if I were you either. But the point is, what do you think you're going to do? Stay up there till you bake in the sun like a couple of herring filets? You have no way to escape. You're going to get awfully hungry and thirsty after a couple of days up there. We can just wait you out."

"And I suggest you use the time," Sarah yelled, "to figure out how you're going to explain all the men who have been killed out here. You think you're safe because you're in international waters? Think again. The police already have an idea what's going on here. It's only a matter of time. Every one of you is going to spend the rest of his life in prison."

Sarah didn't know what effect her words had. There was no more communication. Maybe she'd struck a nerve with at least some of those below. They were facing a reality every bit as stark as she and Kitty. They could be shot if they made more attempts to capture the women, or they were going to face almost certain imprisonment. No way could they explain away the deaths of five men, some from gunshot or blunt trauma, as normal oil rig accidents.

The men went back inside and the rig grew silent again. The tension they were under was exhausting. They decided finally to take turns trying to sleep and so passed the night fitfully. Near dawn, they roused themselves and watched as the first rays of morning light made a dent in the total darkness brought on by the rig's electricity being shut down.

"What next?" Sarah asked.

"Guess we see who has the greater stomach for waiting," Kitty replied.

By six o'clock, the sun was over the horizon, though they couldn't see it. The light was heavy, diffused through thick clouds moving in from the south. The man who had spoken to them was right. They had no protection from the sun, and it would have been a blistering day if not for the growing cloud cover. Kitty rummaged in their bag and emerged with a package of cookies. She handed two to Sarah and offered her a sip from their gallon of water.

They ate while watching the haze that obscured the sun grow heavier. The wind also began to pick up.

"Can't say I like the looks of that," said Sarah. "There's another hurricane moving north. I watched a weather report on it just before I was taken."

"Damn maritime weather!" said Kitty. "If it hits, no one will be able to come after us by boat or helicopter. We'll be lucky to hold on and not be blown away."

Then, suddenly, they heard activity below. They peered over to see what was going on. Several men were making their way up a catwalk opposite them.

"What are they doing?" Sarah said.

"Beats me. That catwalk won't get them high enough to fire down on us."

But then the men entered an enclosed space and a moment later they heard machinery start up. An enormous crane rose above the enclosure. They hadn't associated it with the enclosure because the crane itself was cantilevered in the opposite direction. But now the crane began to lift more upright and to swivel toward their platform. They watched in dumb fascination as it turned toward them, then stopped and began to lower a large hook. The hook went all the way to the platform floor, where two more men attached something to it.

"What are they up to?" Sarah asked again.

It was immediately evident. The men had attached a large weight to the hook, almost like a heavy plumb bob. It was about six feet high and obviously weighed a lot. The crane began to lift the weight up into the air.

"I've got a bad feeling about this," said Kitty.

Once the weight was roughly the same height as their platform, the crane began to move toward them, the weight swinging back and forth. Then it zeroed in on the platform and the man operating the crane let the cable out suddenly. The weight slammed into their platform with a crash that reverberated through their bodies.

Sarah and Kitty cringed back as far as they could from the edge and watched as the big weight came around again, smashing into the platform. Then the man began to get a rhythm, swinging the weight back and forth. Several times it swept across the surface of the platform like a bowling ball.

"Can't you shoot them?" Sarah cried.

Kitty looked over the edge in between sweeps of the weight but she had no view of the man operating the crane. He was clearly skilled at what he was doing, raising and lowering the boom and causing it to sweep over their platform again and again.

Then it stopped. The weight swung silently in the air. The same voice from before called up. "That was just a sample, ladies.

Harry's an artist with the crane. You have nowhere to go. He'll sweep you right off your little perch or else smash you where you lie. The choice is yours. Give up, throw the pistol over the side, and come down, or we'll finish the job."

As it sank in that they had no clear way out of their predicament, Sarah watched a strange transformation come over Kitty. It was as if she'd lost her will, reverted back to that sense of helplessness she'd so hated when she was at the mercy of Lloyd and DeMaio.

Kitty looked bleakly at Sarah. "I'm not going to be abused by them again," she said. "I'm going to jump."

Sarah cried, "No, Kitty! As long as we're alive, there's a chance. We have to submit to them. Every minute we stay alive is another minute that Garrett has to find us. I know you've been through far worse than I have. You know what to expect. Maybe I don't. But I don't want to lose my new friend after just one day. We'll face them together, okay?"

Kitty looked completely drained. She knew what was coming all right, and the thought of more submission and sexual abuse was almost too much to bear. But she also realized she couldn't leave Sarah to face that awful fate alone. One didn't do that to a friend. Her shoulders slumped.

"All right," she said, her voice empty of emotion. She threw the pistol over the side and for a moment the two women hugged each other. Then they turned and began the climb down.

53

ROLAND STOOD ON ONE SIDE of the boat with an oar and Garrett on the other. As silently as possible, they paddled in to the docking platform. It was slow going, moving the big boat with two oars. The wind had picked up and there was a good swell, which only made things more difficult.

"We're goin' ta bounce off that steel platform hard," Roland grunted. Paddling the big boat was more exercise than he'd had in years.

"We can't hit the thing," said Garrett. "It will make too much noise. Maybe they won't hear it up above, but we can't take that chance."

As they closed to within a few feet, Garrett shipped his oar. The boat was rising a dozen feet with every swell. In a harsh whisper, he said, "I'm jumping off, Roland."

"Ya'll end up in the drink," Roland wheezed, but he leaned against his oar, trying to counterbalance the boat.

Garrett stood on the open rear deck where there was no railing, designed to allow lobstermen to pull the heavy traps aboard. He tensed, trying to time the swells. Marcia had said his new foot was the best ever at anticipating his movements. He wasn't so sure this applied to leaps from the deck of a rolling boat. They wanted their contraption field-tested? This probably qualified.

Over his shoulder, he said, "You drift off a few hundred yards and make like you're fishing. I'll signal you with a light. Two quick flashes followed by a long one."

"See that sky?" Roland waved a hand. "It's a hurricane sure as I'm standin' here makin' a fool of myself. No one's goin' ta believe a fisherman would be out here in that." As far as he was concerned, Garrett was mad, trying to take on an entire rig full of men. Courage was not a big part of Roland's makeup. It was why he folded whenever confronted directly, especially by the authorities. Still, Garrett was his new friend, and he was going to help him save his girlfriend if he could.

At the top of a large swell, Garrett held his breath and launched himself. His timing was off. One knee hit the side of the steel platform and he cried out, scrabbling for something to hold onto. He grabbed a steel railing, his feet dangling over the water for a moment before he finally pulled himself firmly onto the surface. He turned and waved to Roland, who had already shipped his oar and was back sitting in the pilot's enclosure as the boat drifted away into the rising wind. Garrett wondered how long he would wait if the weather got much worse.

He began to climb the long ladder to the main platform, trying to get his bearings and remember how the rig was set up. Kitty and Sarah were probably locked in one of the fancy staterooms he'd seen on his last visit. But it was hard to get oriented. There were no lights on at this lower level, and the early morning rays from a sun still below the horizon were dim at best beneath the thick clouds.

Where the ladder emerged onto another platform, Garrett stood for a moment, flexing his foot. He was totally disoriented. There'd been lights when he reached this point the last time. Where were the damn lights?

But then that particular problem went away.

He was bathed in a sudden wash of bright light. Half a dozen men stood all around him, several holding guns. One looked familiar. It was Craig, the man who'd given him Tylenol and a hard hat. He didn't look anywhere near as welcoming this time around.

"You lost again?" Craig asked.

Garrett stared at him. "I think you know why I'm here."

"More the worse for you, mate." He signaled to the men with guns. "Take him below, lock him in one of the staterooms."

"There's only three staterooms with locks and no windows," said another man. "We put the girls in separate rooms. The third was busted when we had to break it in."

Craig hesitated a moment. "All right. Put him in with one of the girls for now, till we get things sorted out. His roommate won't be there for long anyway. She's got a date." He laughed.

As the men led him away, Garrett cursed his incompetence. He'd been aboard all of two minutes before being captured. Some rescuer he was. He stared out at a sea that was growing more turbulent by the moment. He could just make out Roland's boat in the gloom, several hundred yards off, fishing lines ostentatiously out. But he couldn't expect any help from that quarter.

They moved inside and down the familiar corridor, then stopped in front of a door. One of the men took out a key and opened it. "You got company, lady. Take my advice and don't waste your energy on him. The line forms after breakfast." He shoved Garrett in and slammed the door.

Sarah stared in disbelief, then fell into Garrett's arms. "Oh my God, Garrett. I thought I'd never see you again. But I told Kitty you would come. I *knew* you'd come."

He held her tightly, pressing his face against her hair, inhaling the presence of her. "Yeah," he said tightly, "RCMP Special Constable Barkhouse to the rescue. Only trouble is I'm as much a prisoner as you are. I'm sorry, Sarah. It was like they knew I was coming."

He pulled her down onto the bed and sat beside her, one hand on hers, the other stroking her hair. "Did they hurt you?" He had difficulty getting the words out for fear of her answer. The thought of her being abused made his blood boil.

But she shook her head. "Not yet, though it's clear enough what they have in store for me . . . for us."

"Have you seen Kitty then? Is she here?"

"Yes, and I'm so scared for her, Garrett. The men were very angry at her. She killed five of them. You should have seen her. She was fighting back until they forced us to give up. She was completely drained by being back under their control. Her will just seeped away. She's already been raped by one of those bastards. The one named DeMaio. I don't know if she'll be able to survive going through that again. I pleaded with the men to put us in together but they wouldn't. We've got to help her, Gar."

Garrett could hardly get his head around what Sarah was telling him. "Kitty killed five of them? I can't believe it." He felt his estimation of the willful reporter turning on its head.

Sarah proceeded to fill him in on how Kitty had escaped, helped free her, their ordeal on the platform, and how they were finally forced to surrender.

He shook his head and stared at her in dumb admiration. "Don't know how the hell you ever got designated as 'the weaker sex.'"

"It wasn't me, Gar. It was all Kitty. I was scared to death."

"You were the one holding that wrench, weren't you?"

"Yes, but I don't know if I could have really used it. Thank God Kitty had that gun, and she helped me get away, probably minutes before they were going to come for me. Now, they're poised to use Kitty again. And me. We have to do something, Gar."

He got up and surveyed their room. No windows. The walls were so solid he suspected they had steel studs. They were in a luxuriously furnished prison. The door was thick and firm. Outside, they could hear the wind picking up to yet another level. The platform vibrated as the gale whistled through and around the superstructure.

"I picked the lock the first time," Sarah said. "But they placed a guard outside and warned me not to try anything like that again. There's probably someone outside right now."

Their position seemed hopeless. And Kitty was probably suffering God only knew what sort of abuse.

Garrett finally sat down on the bed again. "Nothing we can do till they decide to let us out. Then we'll see. But I won't kid you. It doesn't look good."

Her face was bleak. "Doesn't anyone know you're here?"

"By now, Tom and Tuttle should know. I had no time to arrange backup myself once I realized where you probably were. I don't know what Alton will do. Aside from the fact he has no jurisdiction out here, the last time I tried an assault on this rig, he thought I was brain-damaged."

"How did you get here?"

"Roland. I commandeered his boat. He's still out there, floating a ways off, pretending to fish. But he won't stay long in this weather."

"Maybe it's best if he leaves. He'll call someone when he gets back to land, won't he? Hell, he's got a radio on the boat."

Garrett shrugged. "Hard to say what Roland will do. He's not real big in the initiative department. But . . ."

"What?"

"There's always Lonnie."

54

KITTY SAT ON THE SOFA in her stateroom, legs pulled up, arms tightly clasped around them. She'd been sitting that way for over an hour. Every time there was the slightest sound from the hallway outside, she shook.

She was ashamed for acting this way but utterly incapable of controlling her fear. After her brief sojourn as an escapee with a gun and an anger that seethed at what had been happening to her, it was all the more humiliating to be thrust back into abject terror. She never would have thought she was capable of killing someone. But something had snapped in her when DeMaio's underling tried to take advantage of her. Once she'd killed the first time, she felt strangely liberated and powerful. Each subsequent killing had been easier. There was no question in her mind that she was justified in what she'd done.

Once she'd been captured, however, the sense of helplessness reasserted itself. She stared at the door. Whatever came through it next was going to be extremely unpleasant. And the men would be taking no chances this time. After the deaths of their comrades, she had little doubt she would be accosted by several men at once, with some ready to hold her down if necessary.

There was a sudden click in the lock. She froze, her fingers white against her knees. They were here.

Three men came into the room and closed the door. She'd seen two more outside, waiting their turns, no doubt. The man named Craig stared at her. "Two of those you killed were good friends of mine," he said. "I've spoken to Mr. DeMaio about you and what's to be done. He said to teach you a lesson. Little bonus for us. We don't normally get the cream of the crop, if you know what I mean. I'm going to enjoy this."

He began to take his clothes off. He didn't bother to tell her to remove her own garments, just nodded at the others, who moved forward and lifted her off the couch. She hung in their arms, totally defeated and limp. One of the men grinned and began to unbutton her blouse.

Kitty felt her mind start to go away. She wanted no memory of what was about to happen. Complete amnesia would suit her fine. Her earlier decision that she would fight tooth and nail if ever caught again had evaporated. Try as she might, there was no blocking out the man in front of her, who now stood naked, waiting for the other men to undress her.

Then there was a funny sound from outside the door, almost like eggshells cracking, followed immediately by the door opening. Lonnie stood in the entrance. He held a pistol lightly in one hand as he stepped over the two men in the hall, whose bodies lay tangled and unconscious at his feet.

Kitty stared at this new menace. She'd never seen Lonnie before, and anyone who saw the man for the first time never forgot him. The wedge of his neck rose from thick knots of muscle on his shoulders. He was huge and filled the door frame.

"Who the hell are you?" said Craig.

It was perhaps the wrong thing to say. Lonnie stared at the man's naked body and then at Kitty, still being held by the other men, everything in a frozen tableau. Then he kicked Craig in the groin in a move so quick that it seemed to be over before it began.

The security chief screamed and went down as though poleaxed. Lonnie paid him no more attention, stepped over his prostrate and writhing form, and dispatched the two other men, who barely had time to open their mouths and gape. In a moment, all three were down, the two holding Kitty out cold, Craig still groaning on the floor.

"Are you all right?" Lonnie asked.

She stared at this huge man as though the archangel Gabriel on steroids had suddenly appeared on her doorstep. Then her knees buckled, and she began to slump to the floor. Lonnie caught her and picked her up carefully, like she was a rare flower he might damage.

"Who . . . ?" said Kitty.

"I'm Lonnie, Garrett's cousin. We've been tracking what happened to you. Sorry it took us so long."

Slowly, Kitty placed her arms around his huge neck and put her head on his chest. She felt safe for the first time in many days.

"Thank you," she said in a voice that was a whisper. Then she lifted her head. "Have you found Sarah?"

Lonnie stared at her. "Sarah's here?"

She nodded. "DeMaio's men took her right from her house and brought her here. Probably to get leverage over Garrett, but also to replace me for their sex clients after I escaped. We've got to find her."

"No argument from me. Can you stand up now?"

She nodded but clung to him a moment longer. Then Lonnie put her down, though she kept one small hand on his arm.

"Sarah must be in one of the other rooms," she said. "I heard them walk her away and it wasn't far."

Lonnie took several plastic wrist locks out of his jacket pocket. He cuffed all three men's arms behind their backs and around a heavy steel heating duct that ran floor to ceiling through the room, effectively immobilizing them. From another pocket he took a small roll of duct tape and slapped a piece across each man's mouth. Then he and Kitty moved down the hall, opening one door after another. When they came to one that was locked, Lonnie leaned against it for what seemed like only an instant before the door gave way.

Inside, sitting on a couch and staring at them with their mouths open, were Sarah and Garrett.

Garrett recovered first. "What took you so long?"

"Thought I was making pretty good use of my time," Lonnie said. "No Deputy Commissioners and the like wanting me to get permission to blow my nose."

Garrett slapped his cousin on the shoulder and grinned. "Hoped you might show up," he said. "My own rescue efforts weren't going so well."

Lonnie nodded at Sarah, who had gone over at once and hugged Kitty. "You all right?" he asked.

"I am now." She stood on tiptoe and kissed him on the cheek. "Question is, what do we do next?"

"Any idea how many more men there are?" Garrett asked.

"There were at least fifteen we actually saw," said Kitty. "I killed five. Lonnie just took care of five more. That leaves maybe half a dozen. But there could be others, including some oil executives who came in to enjoy their special privileges. I haven't seen anything of them." She glanced back down the hall at the two men still lying silently in a tangle. "What about them? Shouldn't you cuff them too?"

Lonnie shook his head. "Hit them together pretty hard. They'll be out a while and will be pretty concussed when they wake up. They're not going to be doing much more than staring cross-eyed at the floor for a couple of days. Still, I'll drag them into the room and close the door, so they won't be stumbled upon."

Garrett said, "The men who captured me had plenty of weapons. Not something you might expect on a simple operating oil rig. We could try to take over the platform, but I think the risk would be too great, especially with Sarah and Kitty here."

"I agree," said Lonnie. "I sent the boat that brought me away. He would have been too conspicuous hanging around the rig and he was at the edge of the craft's ability to withstand the storm. How did you get here?"

"Roland. He's sitting a ways off pretending to fish. Or at least he was before the weather began to deteriorate. But maybe it's time to bring in reinforcements. We've certainly got proof now of what's been going on here. Cell phones haven't been reliable, but they must have a radio communications center."

"I've been there," said Kitty. "I can take you."

"First, we should try to call in Roland's boat and get you two out of here," Garrett said.

"No way. I'm not going to leave you here," said Sarah. "We finish this together."

Garrett looked exasperated, but Kitty sided with Sarah. Lonnie's presence had given her, indeed all of them, new confidence. As far as Kitty was concerned, Lonnie was the Army, Navy, and Air Force all rolled into one.

"I agree—we stick together," said Kitty. "But we're not going to finish anything here today. DeMaio's not on board."

"And he won't be easy to get to," said Garrett. "Wherever he is. He has foreign ties and spends most of his time abroad, from what Alfred Nichols told me. For all I know he may have dual citizenship somewhere. Some place you can bet doesn't have an extradition treaty with Canada. He had to figure a day like this might come."

The wind suddenly picked up, as though someone had turned a switch. It howled through the rig, banging loose parts and blowing anything that wasn't tied down swirling off into the near blackness of the storm. Then a tortuous, rending sound split the night, like metal being ripped apart. It rose above the wind, dominating the nighttime cacophony.

"My God," Sarah cried. "What's happening?"

"Come on," said Garrett. "Let's take a look."

He led the way down the corridor and opened the first outside door they came to. The wind almost tore it out of his hand. The rig's lights were back on, and they gathered at the opening and stared at a mind-numbing sight.

The enormous crane that the men had used to force Kitty and Sarah to give up was swinging in the wind. In all the excitement the operator had evidently not battened it down sufficiently. Even as they watched, the wind swung the crane back and forth, screeching metal protesting the ill treatment. Then, suddenly, the support gave way and the entire crane collapsed onto the rig with a sound like a Boeing 747 crashing into a metal scrapyard.

The entire rig shook from the impact and they were barely able to keep their feet. Across from them, another door opened and several men stood, wide-eyed, peering out at the devastation.

Kitty stared at them with daggers coming out of her eyes. Every last one of the men working on this rig was aware what went on here and what had been happening to her. If it had been in her power, she would have killed them all. "You should have put a bullet in the others while you had the chance," she said to Lonnie. "Someone will find them, and we'll have to deal with them all over again."

"Maybe," Lonnie said, gently. "But we're talking about five men. I wasn't ready to kill that many just for the pleasure of it." He raised one massive hand. "Believe me. I understand where you're coming from. None of us have gone through what you have.

Maybe it was a mistake to leave them alive. It could stiffen the odds against us again."

The men spotted them. One gestured animatedly, clearly urging his companions to go after them. But no one was in a mood to go out onto that platform. Who knew what was going to come crashing down next?

Lonnie closed the door, which only minimally lowered the sound of the wind. "No one's going anywhere in a boat in this," he said. "And communications are probably down too."

"I agree," said Garrett. "Roland must have taken off as soon as things began to really deteriorate. I hope he makes it home. I wouldn't want to be out in this weather in a small fishing boat."

"He may be better off than we are," said Lonnie. "He's a good seaman, and who knows if this rig can withstand a full hurricane. Looks like we'll be testing Global's engineering, and given the rest of their operations, that's not a reassuring thought. More than one oil platform has gone down in something like this."

Kitty and Sarah looked at him with new horror in their eyes.

"What are we going to do?" Sarah asked.

Garrett put an arm around her shoulder. "I don't think we're in any immediate danger from the rest of the men on this platform. They've got to be as worried as we are about being out here in this blow." He looked at Lonnie over Sarah's head. "Anyone know enough about oil platforms to have any idea where the safest place to be is in a storm?"

"Back in Halifax?" Lonnie suggested.

Garrett stared at him. "That's not entirely helpful."

The big man shrugged. "If this thing topples, there *is* no safe place."

Kitty said, "When I was hiding in a storage room, I saw survival suits and what looked like some sort of emergency rafts or flotation devices. If you really think this thing might blow over, they may be our only hope. They were located inside one of the concrete piers, which should be about the safest place to be, short of a catastrophic failure of the rig."

"All right," said Garrett. "Can you take us there?"

She nodded and they all looked simultaneously at the door to the outside. Going out into that maelstrom was not an attractive idea, but they had no options.

"I'll lead the way," said Lonnie. "Hold onto one another. I don't want anyone blowing away out there."

Then they were outside. Kitty was almost at once disoriented and unsure of where to go. The collapse of the crane had turned the entire floor area into a mass of tangled steel, cables, and collapsed smaller structures. There were still lights, fortunately, though it was unclear how long they would last. Every so often, they flickered ominously.

Holding on to one another, they were blown along by the gale-force winds.

"Will it get worse than this?" yelled Kitty, not quite believing the violence of the wind.

Sarah had been in hurricanes before. "This is nothing," she yelled back. "Barely hurricane force. Maybe seventy-mile-an-hour winds at most. If we get hit directly, it could get twice as bad."

Kitty led the way, skirting around the jumble of metal parts, looking for a way through to the storage room. Lonnie held onto her, clearly worried that the wind might pick her tiny body up and simply blow her away.

The night was black, the wind cold, and icy spray from a hundred feet beneath them whipped high into the sky, only to fall back on their soaking clothes. In addition to the howling wind, there were periodic crashes all around them of unseen objects that had come loose from far above and plummeted to the platform. Every so often, the electrical grid simply went away for a few seconds and they were plunged into blackness. Then they stood, unmoving, fearful of taking a step that might throw them over the side into the swirling maelstrom until the lights flickered back on again.

Finally, to their universal relief, Kitty found the entrance to the storage room. Once inside, it took all of Lonnie's strength to push the door shut against the wind. Garrett turned on a powerful flashlight he'd picked up from the debris on the platform. They stood like a pack of drenched rats and surveyed their surroundings. "At least we'll be able to see," he said, "if the lights go out permanently."

Sarah found a rack of hard hats and handed one to each of them, except Lonnie, who looked at the thing like it was a child's toy. No way would it fit his enormous head. Then they set about the business of inventorying the survival suits and rafts that Kitty had mentioned. There were lots of immersion suits, at least twenty hung up in rows.

"Should we put them on?" Sarah asked.

"Can't hurt," Garrett replied. "No telling if we'll need them but if we do, there probably won't be a lot of time to get prepared."

Kitty eyed the big red suits skeptically. "These are man-sized garments," she said. "I don't think they cared about providing outfits for *guests* like me. I'll be swimming in one of these. Sarah too."

"They didn't have me in mind either," said Lonnie. "No way I fit into one of those things."

Garrett found a roll of duct tape. "We can modify to a certain extent. For the women, we can tape the arms and legs for a tighter fit. Not sure how we can modify for Lon, though. Maybe if we had a sewing machine, we could stitch two suits together."

"I'll take my chances," Lonnie said. "The rest of you should get into the suits now. Sounds to me like the wind is picking up even more. We may not have a lot of time."

His words were sobering. They could feel the rig literally vibrating in the high winds.

Suddenly, the door to the storage room opened and three men burst in. They struggled to close the door, not realizing there was anyone else inside. They were there for the flotation devices and survival suits and turned immediately to the equipment, only to find Lonnie facing them, holding a pistol.

Unarmed themselves, the men stared at this almost supernaturally imposing figure and halted in their tracks. Slowly, they registered the others as well.

"Whoa! Hold on," said one of the men. "We're not after you, just some of the safety equipment."

"Might not be enough to go around," said Lonnie casually. The men suddenly looked frightened.

"Look," said the one who had spoken. "We're all in this together now. If this storm picks up to full force, the rig won't take it. This is DeMaio's special rig. He wanted it built quickly for purposes of entertaining his international customers. I was here during the construction and they cut corners everywhere." He pointed to the concrete shell of the piling that made up the walls of the storage room. "See that concrete? It's way substandard. I'm amazed it's held up this long. We'll topple in winds anywhere close to a hundred miles an hour, maybe a lot less."

They stared at the man who had just, for all intents and purposes, pronounced their death sentences.

"Is it your intention to get off the rig now?" asked Garrett.

The man and his two companions exchanged looks.

"The others haven't figured it out," said the leader. "They're still inside talking about how to capture you, for God's sake. It's madness. They found Craig and the others. But Craig is just security. He doesn't have any experience with oil rigs. Only thing he's afraid of is doing anything that might displease DeMaio. But I worked rigs in the Gulf for twenty years. I know what a storm like this can do. We need to get off this thing as fast as possible, before it's too late."

"What exactly is your plan?" said Garrett.

The man shrugged. "Get in the suits, haul two rafts down to the docking platform, and climb aboard. And I mean now. I'll take my chances in the sea before I would on this rig, held together with chewing gum and substandard reinforcing rods."

It was enough for Garrett. The tense, frightened demeanor of the men was all the proof he needed that they were in serious trouble as long as they stayed where they were. A glance told him the others felt the same.

"All right," said Lonnie. "Those that can fit, grab a suit. We'll work with you for now," he said to the men. "But I see one wrong move from any of you and I'll personally break your necks. Understood?"

55

ROLAND HAD HUNG HIS NET line to the overhead winch on his boat. It was all for show. There were no fish in this particular area anyway. Fished out years ago. He eyed the rig a quarter mile off his bow. Garrett had been gone for a while now and the winds had picked up considerably.

He was a lifelong fisherman and had experienced high winds and tortured seas many times. But this blow showed every sign of getting a lot worse. And soon.

He didn't really want to leave Garrett and his girlfriend. He'd always had a thing about obeying authority that grew out of his lifelong feelings of inadequacy on so many levels. Garrett knew this and played on it, and Roland knew he played on it. But it didn't anger him anymore. He understood it was simply his nature.

Still, what could he do? How long should he wait? If he was going to get back safely to the wharf, he needed to leave now, before the wind picked up any more.

Maybe he was too far off and had missed Garrett's signal. He throttled the engine up and began to move closer to the rig. Though it was well into daylight now, the gloom from the approaching storm kept things much darker than normal and he doubted anyone on the rig would see him unless they were really looking for him. If they did, they'd simply see a working fishing boat . . . granted, one run by a madman to be out in these seas.

A hundred yards from the rig, he hove to and stared at the enormous monolith. The waves were six to eight feet and the boat wobbled like a top in its final throes. The huge concrete posts embedded in the sea floor towered over him, the waves breaking against them with great sprays of foam.

There was something strange about one of the towers. He maneuvered closer and saw that as each wave hit the pylon, pieces of concrete broke loose. Not pieces. Chunks. He looked around and saw the same phenomenon on each of the other piers. Roland sat back in his pilot's chair and pondered this.

Abstract thinking wasn't his strong suit. He'd always been a poor student, though he had an innate ability to pick up those things that he needed to know. Thus, he was well versed in carpentry, engine mechanics, and GPS, and had taken especially to computers over the years.

That pieces were coming off the rig seemed unusual. The waves hitting the piers were not particularly massive. He could hardly believe there was any problem with the engineering. After all, Global was a huge, immensely wealthy international company. The sort of authority he put faith in. They would have done things right. So the chunks of concrete falling into the water seemed interesting but hardly anything he would have thought held larger meaning.

His instruments showed wind speeds steady at fifty miles per hour with gusts occasionally up to seventy. This was not good. He watched the rig closely for another ten minutes without seeing any signal from Garrett. It was all he could afford. The boat was especially difficult to control in heavy seas while drifting or trolling slowly. He needed speed to counter the combined forces of swell, wind, and waves. Only his skill as a skipper had allowed him to stay this long.

He took down his nets and secured the winch, then throttled up the engine and headed for home. He'd done what Garrett asked of him for as long as possible. No one could fault him. Besides, at this point, kidnappers or not, Garrett was undoubtedly safer on the rig than Roland was out in a hurricane on the high seas.

The boat trimmed more evenly once he was under power. He thought about Grace on the trip home. What her drug habit might mean. He was more than a little disillusioned with the former focus of his desires. Garrett obviously didn't believe his story. Well, that was all right. Besides, maybe she didn't actually have a habit. Maybe she sold the stuff to help pay for the high lifestyle they all maintained. They obviously had lots of friends in the city, which gave them the contacts necessary to sell to an upper-class clientele. He wondered if Grace's housemates knew what she was doing.

He smiled. Somehow, his new information was going to change the dynamic in the cove feud. Then he remembered his promise to Garrett that he'd leave them alone. He sighed. A promise was a promise. Too bad.

He could never in a million years have imagined the manner in which his new-found information would transform life in the cove.

56

GARRETT TORE OFF A FINAL piece of duct tape and wrapped it around Sarah's leg. The ladies were indeed swimming in the survival suits. Between strips of tape, the suits still billowed out in pouches.

"I feel like the Pillsbury Doughboy," said Sarah.

"You look like him too," said Garrett. "But I bet he could float. That's a tradeoff I'd take about now."

The men were also in suits, all except Lonnie. There was no way he could fit unless he cut holes in the thing, which effectively negated both the flotation and insulation functions.

The three rig workers were ready. Lonnie motioned for them to lead the way to the lower boat launch. They knew the rig better than any of them.

Outside, the platform was a confusion of flying objects, stinging rain, and frigid mist from an icy sea whipped to a froth. Collapsed crane parts had torn loose catwalks, ripped off safety railings, and generally made moving through the debris like negotiating some fantastical Mad Max landscape. The lights were still working but continued to flicker ominously, giving the entire scene a kind of stop-action strobe effect.

"Christ, it's like being in a cartoon action flick," Kitty said to no one in particular.

Several times, the men leading the way got lost and had to backtrack, looking for a way through the debris. Briefly, they were inside, then they quickly passed through another of the pylons and out onto the first of the catwalks that led lower.

Garrett held onto Sarah, while Kitty had a death grip on Lonnie. He had a long length of nylon cord over his shoulder and held one of the still-folded collapsible rafts in his free hand. The rig men carried another. Each raft was rated to hold four people, though Lonnie would stress that limit.

"This looks right," said Kitty. "I came this way when I escaped. There's a platform a dozen feet above the water. We can launch the rafts there."

Garrett shouted to be heard over a sudden gust. "That's where I landed my kayak, but it'll be rough launching in these seas."

Now that they were outside experiencing the full fury of the storm, he wasn't at all certain they were taking the right course of action. Maybe the rig would fail and collapse. But maybe it wouldn't. If they stayed and it did, then they were dead. If they launched themselves into that cold sea in tiny rubber rafts and the rig didn't collapse, they'd have left the only safety there was. The odds that someone might find them bobbing in the black ocean in the middle of a hurricane had to be vanishingly small. Garrett hadn't forgotten the anxiety he'd felt in his plastic boat as he contemplated floating to Ireland.

At least they wouldn't face the danger of an overturning kayak. The rafts were state-of-the-art, designed to be totally enclosed and virtually impossible to tip over. Seasickness was another matter.

It was quieter this far down on the rig. The monolith above them seemed to muffle sound, and the whistling of the wind through the superstructure was farther away. Sarah and Garrett were the last to begin the climb down the final ladder to the launch platform. Sarah said to Garrett, "Are you sure about this?"

He shook his head. "Not a bit. We may be committing suicide by leaving the rig. We only have the word of these three men. Granted, they know oil rigs better than we do and obviously want to get off as fast as they can. Still, they're part of DeMaio's crazy network of sex traffickers and can't be the brightest bulbs in the socket."

"I'm scared, Garrett. I don't want to go floating around in that blackness. The rig feels much safer to me, even if it's only an illusion."

They joined the others on the platform and everyone gathered around in what appeared to be a brief lull in the storm. They were all looking to Garrett to make a decision, though his uncertainty was obvious.

"This is how I see it," he said. "It's a gamble either way. You men who work here are experienced with this sort of operation. But I guess I agree with Sarah that the rig sure feels safer than being tossed about in those seas in what looks like a toy raft."

"It may feel safer, but believe me, you don't want to be here if she topples," said the leader of the men. "We've made our decision. We're getting off. What the rest of you do is up to you."

Garrett was perplexed. All of their lives depended on making the right decision. "What about riding out the storm down here on the boat launch? If we see any signs of failure with the pylons, we might still be able to get off in time."

The leader of the workers shrugged. "You might get some advance warning if huge chunks of concrete begin to fall away or if the whole thing starts to sway. Maybe. Or it could go in an instant, with a big gust from the storm. There wouldn't be time to drop your drawers and kiss your ass goodbye." He stared at the little group. "I've told you our decision, and we're not willing to wait. Good luck to you."

The three men turned away, clambered down to the lowest level, and began to deploy the raft, which was designed to inflate on its own.

Garrett looked at Lonnie. "You haven't weighed in on this. What do you think?"

"Being the only one without a survival suit, I might be a little biased." He looked at Kitty and Sarah, then out at the tumbling cold seas. "Guess I lean toward waiting a while. Maybe the storm will abate. Maybe the platform is stronger than those men think. Maybe I don't know what the hell I'm talking about."

"Join the club," said Garrett. "We could take a vote. Too bad we have an even number of voters."

But Kitty and Sarah had already made up their minds. "We vote to wait," said Kitty. "I can't get away from this waterlogged Sodom and Gomorrah too fast. But being out in that"—she gestured at the blackness and froth all around them—"is every bit as terrifying as the thought of being here when the rig falls over."

So they waited. The platform was periodically swept by the ocean swell, so the little party climbed higher and found a spot on one of the catwalks where they could watch and wait. Meanwhile, the three men from the rig had successfully inflated the flimsy raft. It almost blew away in the wind, but they finally managed to crawl inside, zipper themselves in, and wait to be lifted cleanly off the platform by a swell.

When it happened, the supposedly untippable raft immediately flipped over. They could see a tumble of bodies pushing against the sides, like a Cub Scout pack inside a pup tent. But then the craft righted itself again, which it was designed to do. Garrett directed his flashlight on the contraption, and they watched as it swirled away into the darkness. Just before it left the halo of light, someone inside turned on a rescue beacon. A bright red strobe flashed at the top of the raft.

"Someone should see that," Sarah said.

"Won't be anyone to see anything till this storm passes," said Lonnie. "By then, they could be a hundred miles away."

"Maybe they'll blow up on shore or on an island," Sarah suggested.

"Good to look on the bright side," said Garrett. "But we should consider our own situation."

He played the light along the sides of the concrete pylons. They could clearly see where chunks of concrete had worked loose and fallen into the sea. The damage didn't look good, but it also didn't look like the rig was on the verge of catastrophic failure. Only time would tell.

As it turned out, not very much time. Almost immediately, the storm surged to yet another level. The wind increased in intensity until the tops of the waves were lifted and blown straight into the sky. They were dry and reasonably warm in their suits, with the exception of Lonnie, who looked like the largest wet rat any of them had ever seen.

"Bet you wish you were back in Kandahar now," said Garrett.

He just grunted, but the others huddled around him, sharing what warmth they could.

"Maybe we should go back inside, get out of this," Kitty said.

"It's an idea," said Garrett. "But I don't much cotton to being inside when this thing decides to give up the ghost. I say we wait it out right here."

They were quiet for a while, listening to the howling storm, faces turned away from the stinging rain as much as possible.

"It can't last forever," said Sarah. "Can it?"

"Longest hurricane on record was Puerto Rico in 1899," said Lonnie. "It lasted twenty-eight days."

"Jesus," said Kitty. "Not in one spot, I hope."

"Nope. They tend to move along, but we could have a lot more to go through before it leaves."

Above them, they saw lights flashing.

"Now what?" said Sarah. "Are the lights failing?"

"Those are flashlights," said Garrett. "Maybe more of DeMaio's men have decided to get off."

"Or decided to come after us," said Lonnie. He shook himself and pulled out his gun, cradling it in icy fingers.

"How crazy can they be?" Garrett said. "Worried about us in the middle of a hurricane."

"Maybe they see it as an opportunity," said Kitty. "They can say we were lost in the storm—blown right off the rig. No one could ever prove otherwise."

They watched as the lights moved lower. Then they picked out Craig leading the men. It was also clear that no one was wearing a survival suit or carrying a raft. Which meant they were there for another reason.

"What do we do?" said Kitty, a hint of panic in her voice.

Lonnie said, "My bet is they intend to get rid of us. But like you said, the best way would be to throw us into the drink so we drown. Any bodies found later won't have bullet holes to explain away."

"I suppose that's meant to be comforting," said Garrett, "but I can't quite see how."

"Just this. If that's their plan, they'll say anything to get us to believe they won't hurt us. They don't want a firefight. I think we can safely assume that guns are not going to play a role in the outcome here."

Garrett smiled.

"I don't see what's so bloody funny," said Sarah.

"What's funny is someone trying to get the best of Lonnie in hand-to-hand combat," Garrett said. "I'd almost pay to see that. Anyway, one thing's for certain. They may not want to shoot, but I don't have any compunctions along those lines myself."

"Neither do I," said Kitty.

They watched the lights bobbing along the catwalk, moving lower. When they got within twenty feet, Lonnie lifted his pistol and fired a shot that ricocheted off the steel catwalk above their heads. The men all ducked and then froze. There was no place to hide, no cover at all.

Lonnie said, "That's far enough. Next man who moves gets a bullet that's a whole lot closer than the last one."

Craig stood up, showing his empty hands. "We don't want any more trouble," he shouted. "Let's talk this over, see if we can come to some sort of agreement."

"We'll give you an agreement," Kitty yelled. "We agree you're a sick bunch of assholes!"

Lonnie put one hand on Kitty's arm. "Couldn't put it better myself. I suggest you men go back topside and wait out the storm same as we are."

"Looks to me like you intend to leave the rig," said Craig. "Unless you're wearing those suits and carrying that raft for exercise. We can't allow that for obvious reasons. Mr. DeMaio wouldn't be happy. Put your guns down and we'll let you back inside out of the cold. You've got no place to go down there. We have you pinned down just as much as you have us, but we've got more firepower. You don't stand a chance."

"He has a point," Lonnie said in a low voice. "They've got the high ground. It all depends on whether you buy the theory that they don't want to shoot us."

Suddenly, an intense blast of wind shrieked out of the night, the strongest gust so far. A loud cracking sound split the wind and darkness. Everyone stared at the pylon closest to them. Flashlights from both groups played over the huge concrete pier, searching for the source of the sound.

"There! Look!" Sarah cried.

A crack appeared along the entire length of the pylon and grew before their eyes. In a few seconds it extended from the ocean all the way to the platform. Then enormous chunks of concrete began to peel off. Pieces of pylon thirty feet in length and probably weighing several tons separated and plunged straight down into the ocean like missiles firing in reverse. The sea erupted in a boiling froth as more and more chunks broke away.

Craig and his men stared at the awesome sight in complete disbelief. They clearly hadn't held the same concern as their fellows who'd left, floating off into the dark night. Then the entire platform shuddered and seemed to lurch slightly.

Lonnie and the others watched as the realization came over the men above that the rig was failing. They were a hundred feet below the main deck and hadn't bothered to bring survival suits or rafts.

The next thing that happened was sheer panic. The men broke upwards, heading for the storage rooms as fast as they could go. No one was worrying about making a target for Lonnie any more. They wanted a way off this contraption and suits to protect them against that freezing, black water.

"Time for us to go too," said Garrett.

"No argument from me," Lonnie replied. They worked back down to the launch platform, where Lonnie picked up the nylon cord he'd brought and tied one end to the steel ladder. Then he broke open the raft and inflated it on the deck surface.

"Everyone in," he said. "We'll tie the raft off to the deck and let the wind take us out as far as the rope allows. Should be over a hundred feet. That way, if the rig doesn't fail completely, we stay close. This is where any search will focus. Better if we don't disappear into the storm."

"What about Craig?" said Garrett. "If they come back down with their own rafts, they'll untie us and hope we don't survive."

323

Lonnie shrugged. "One catastrophe at a time. My sense is they're going to be so panicked by that time they won't even notice our line. They'll just assume we launched as soon as we saw the pylon failing."

"Are you sure a hundred feet is far enough away?" said Kitty. "The rig is much higher than that. If it topples it could roll right over on top of us."

"It's a gamble, all right," Lonnie said. "I'm still betting this thing will stand longer than we think. There's an awful lot of concrete and engineering here, even if DeMaio's contractors did cut corners. If we get any warning at all that the entire thing is going to topple, I think we'll still have time to cut the line and let the wind carry us out of reach." His eyes swept the bedraggled group. "I'm open to other suggestions."

There were none.

Everyone climbed into the contraption. Lonnie attached the line to a steel ring on the side of the raft and barely had time to throw himself inside before a huge swell lifted them off the platform and sent them swirling out into the darkness.

57

ROLAND FOUGHT THE STORM AS though it were a living thing. The wind spiked just minutes after he turned for home. Waves crested at fifteen to twenty feet, and the little fishing boat bobbed like a rubber duck making its way down the Niagara rapids.

Again and again he came close to losing control of his craft, as huge waves rolled across the bow, the water slowly draining away through the scuppers, only to be immediately replaced. One fierce gust collapsed the pole holding the antenna and radar controls. Most of his fishing gear, which he hadn't had time to properly tie down before the sudden surge in the weather, washed overboard, a huge financial loss.

Fortunately, though he'd lost his communications and radar, he still knew how to pilot using dead reckoning. He was as familiar with these waters as anyone alive. After what seemed an eternity, he finally made out the outline of the Gull Islands looming ahead in the gloom. Once he was in their lee, the wind subsided, at least a little.

As he entered the more protected bay of the larger island, he saw something blinking off his port bow. A tiny red light flashed right at water level. Whatever it was attached to was invisible in the big waves, and he almost didn't bother to check it out, but something made him pause and consider the light again.

It was likely just a buoy, blown loose by the storm. Still . . . it could also be some small craft, a skiff or motorboat with its normal running light. But there was nothing normal about a boat out in this weather. Whoever it was had to be in trouble, assuming there was anyone aboard and it wasn't just an empty boat blown out to sea. As a lifelong fisherman, steeped in the rituals of the sea, Roland would never pass by someone in need. He began to carefully tack into the wind and against the huge waves until he came close to the light.

At last he could see it was just a small kayak that appeared to be empty. Its owner no doubt would like to have it back, but Roland wasn't about to risk his neck for a tiny plastic boat.

He began to turn away when he saw a hand rise up limply from the bottom of the craft and then disappear.

Someone was inside. He could hardly believe it. He turned the fishing boat back and edged in cautiously. It wouldn't help if he ran into the thing and sank it. The wind wasn't as strong here in the lee of the island. He motored as close as he could, then managed to snare the boat with his gaffing hook and pull it to the side. He could see someone lying in the bottom of the boat. Whoever it was didn't answer his calls.

He couldn't pilot his boat and pull the kayak out at the same time. Instead, he snagged the boat's bowline with the gaff, tied it off, and then guided his own craft farther into the protected cove.

Once out of the worst of the wind, he dropped anchor and immediately went to the little boat. He pulled on the line and managed to haul the tiny craft up and onto his deck. The effort nearly killed him. If he was going to be doing air/sea rescue, he thought grimly, he'd better get in better shape.

He stared finally into the boat's cockpit and got the shock of his life. Lying in the bottom of the boat, soaking wet and seemingly unconscious, was Grace. He stared at her in disbelief. What on earth was she doing out here?

He lifted her up. She weighed not much more than a hundred pounds, though the soaking clothes probably added a fair amount to that. He carried her into the cabin and put her on the tiny built-in bunk. He removed her wet clothing and covered her in blankets. Somehow, the reality of holding an utterly naked Grace didn't seem to affect him as he'd always thought it would. She wasn't shivering, and that worried him. She might be in the last stages of hypothermia. He needed to get her to shore.

He pulled anchor and started his engine. They were still some miles from the wharf. He kept one eye on the wheel and the sea and the other on his guest. Halfway in, she woke up. Sort of.

She spoke incoherently, her speech rambling. She was hallucinating. Roland tried to talk to her in a soothing voice, for she seemed terrified even in her sleep or whatever her state was.

The wharf loomed at last and he breathed a huge sigh of relief once he rounded the wooden bulwark and secured the boat with his lines. He probably should call for an ambulance, but knew it would take time before one could get here all the way from Sherbrooke in the bad weather. Instead, he carried her to her home and banged on the door with one foot until Ingrid came and opened it.

She stared at him in disbelief. Here was her nemesis, soaking wet, his hair windblown, standing on her doorstep holding the naked body of Grace, barely covered by a blanket. It was hard to say what sort of thoughts ran through her head. Roland could well imagine what they might be.

Instead of saying anything, he pushed past her into the living room and laid Grace gently on the couch.

"Ya got any more blankets ta cover her with?" he said. "She's right hypothermic. Ya need ta take her inta the hospital."

"What happened?" said Leo, coming down from upstairs. He grabbed several caftans from a rack and wrapped them around Grace.

"Found her out ta the Gull Islands," said Roland. "Floatin' in her plastic boat. She was unconscious. Bloody miracle I found her. What the hell was she doin' out there by herself?"

"I don't know," said a worried-looking Ingrid. "When we got home, she wasn't here. We thought she'd gone to visit someone."

"In this storm?" Roland looked incredulous. "In a kayak? How crazy is that?" He took one of Grace's hands and felt her fingers. They were like ice. "Ya got an electric blanket?"

Ingrid went immediately and got one, plugged it in and wrapped it around Grace, then layered the caftans on top. Her shivering stopped and her color began to return. Before they could decide if it was wise to move her and take her to the hospital, she woke up. This time she appeared to be lucid.

Ingrid sat beside her on the couch, one hand against Grace's cheek. "How do you feel?" she said.

"T-tired," came her one word answer.

"She should be all right," said Roland. "I've seen lots of hypothermia. Get some warm soup inta her."

With that, he turned and left. He felt decidedly uneasy being in the women's home. He didn't relish facing a fully alert Grace, wondering what had happened to her. It wouldn't surprise him if they decided he must have had something to do with her physical distress and state of undress. He knew what they thought about him. The whale.

Back in his own home, he put on dry clothes and puttered around for a while. The place was several degrees cleaner than it had been when Rose was around. His mother had been so helpless that it made keeping up with things just overwhelming at times. And the distinct odor of her had begun to dissipate.

Suddenly, he stopped cold. Ideas descended on Roland's brain like autumn leaves falling from the heavens and usually with less impact. Sometimes, though, he paid attention. Garrett and Sarah.

They were still on the rig. He should do something. The thought simply hadn't surfaced until this minute, so focused had he been on getting Grace to safety.

He got out the phone book and looked up the number for the Halifax Regional Police. It took him ten minutes to track down Garrett's boss, RCMP Deputy Commissioner Alton Tuttle.

"He's where?" Tuttle asked.

"I tol' ya. He went on board Lighthouse Point rig ta look for his girlfriend. Said she'd been kidnapped. I think ya should send the Coast Guard out there ta pick 'em up."

For some reason, Roland didn't mention what he'd discovered, that Grace was involved in some sort of drug trafficking. Roland didn't like drugs and had previously determined that he was going to use the information against his neighbors. But he couldn't see his way clear to turning Grace in in her current condition. Instead, he simply outlined how he and Garrett had approached the rig and how Garrett had gotten off.

Tuttle was quiet for a moment. "You're talking about international waters," he said. "I don't have jurisdiction. All I have is your word that someone was kidnapped. I'll pass the information along. The Feds seem to be interested in Lighthouse Point, but I can't say what their reaction will be. Besides, in case you haven't noticed, there's a hurricane going on. No one's going anywhere for a while."

Roland hung up and went back to his cleaning. The process, he had discovered, was actually therapeutic, taking his mind off his troubles. He hauled out the little vacuum cleaner and began to sweep the carpet. Ma hadn't run the vacuum in ten years. He was amazed to see color return to the worn rug as he passed over it again and again.

He stopped. Turned off the vacuum. His fisherman's instincts told him the storm was abating. The decibel level of the wind was down. Just maybe Garrett was due for a break.

58

THE TINY, ENCLOSED RAFT JERKED to a halt at the end of its tether. The abrupt stop sent the inhabitants tumbling on top of one another. When they had rearranged themselves, Garrett turned on a tiny battery-operated lantern.

They were a bedraggled bunch. The survival suits kept them from being cold, but Garrett could see that Lonnie was shivering. He took off his own suit and wrapped it around his cousin's shoulders. Kitty also shed her suit and used it to cover his legs. Soon, his shivering stopped.

The raft's movement was chaotic. Struggling at the end of its tether, subject to the whims of the weather, it jerked and bobbed in the huge waves and swell. Sarah began to get seasick. She huddled beside Garrett near the zippered flap, ready to lean out and vomit if it became necessary.

Suddenly, somewhere out in the darkness, they heard a cry. Garrett unzipped the entrance, leaned his head out, and played his flashlight back and forth. Almost at once a small flotilla of rafts, all bound together, flew by, just feet from him. He caught a momentary glimpse of Craig, wearing an immersion suit, as he was carried off by the wind. For some reason, the men were in open rafts. Maybe he and Lonnie had taken the only enclosed rafts that featured that particular life-saving innovation. Another one of DeMaio's cost-cutting maneuvers? Garrett wondered.

He zippered himself back in and told the others what he'd seen.

"Wouldn't want to be out in that maelstrom in an open raft," said Lonnie. "Bad enough inside this coffin."

"Do you think everyone got off?" Sarah asked, her face white from nausea.

"I doubt the bastards concerned themselves with the foreign executives on board," said Kitty. "They were in full panic mode when they left us, headed for the storeroom. They wouldn't have given the bigwigs huddling in their staterooms a passing thought." Her face took on a look of grim satisfaction. "Instead of the evening of carnal pleasure they were expecting, courtesy of yours truly, they got a full hurricane instead." She snuggled in closer to Lonnie for warmth. "Suits me fine. I hope all the bastards go down with the platform."

As soon as she said the words, they heard an almost indescribable sound, similar to the noise when the crane collapsed. They all held their breaths, not certain what was happening.

"Shit," said Kitty. "I take it back about the platform."

"What's going on?" Sarah cried.

Garrett leaned out the entrance again. When he did, he became almost immediately soaked from the waves and stinging rain. He craned his neck to look up at the platform. It still had lights, though they flickered ominously. That wasn't the thing that worried him. He could see the pylon closest to them, or what was left of it. He stared in astonishment, then pulled his head back in.

"One of the pylons is gone," he said.

The others stared at him. "Gone?" all three said in unison.

Garrett nodded. "Completely. Must have totally collapsed. That was the sound we heard. I think we need to cut loose. I don't have any idea how long the rig can stand on three feet, but it can't be long in this storm. Also, the pylon that went down is on the side closest to us. Makes sense that when the rig goes, it'll fall toward the weak link. That would be us."

"What do you think?" Kitty said to Lonnie.

"I think I should have gotten a longer piece of rope. Look, I still don't like the idea of blowing off into the dark. The rig might hold, but the decider for me is that missing pylon. If it could collapse so suddenly, it has to mean the others are at serious risk of doing the same. When the pylon we're tied to goes, it'll drag us straight to the bottom. I say we cut loose and take our chances."

Garrett played the light over their faces. Everyone nodded in agreement, so he took out his knife, reached out the opening and prepared to slice through the rope. At the same instant, there was a low groaning sound, and they all peered out the opening.

The rig was shaking, literally twisting in the wind, and beginning to lean slowly toward them. Even as Garrett sawed frantically at the rope, they watched the platform pivot and then pause, like Baryshnikov at the top of his leap. Then it began to tumble. With lights flickering and the sound of tearing metal, it bore straight down on them.

Finally, Garrett sliced through the rope and they were abruptly whisked into the night by the wind. Through the opening in the tent wall, they saw the rig's lights go out for the last time, leaving them only with the image of the tilting rig engraved on their retinas. A moment later, there was a huge blast as the mass of equipment, steel, cranes, and concrete hit the ocean surface just yards behind them.

It was as though a small meteor had struck the ocean, instantly raising a tidal wave, which caught them and threw them forward. Garrett barely had time to zipper the flap before they tumbled over and over in the surging sea waters. He couldn't tell which direction was up. For what seemed like an eternity, there was nothing but a jumble of legs and arms and bodies bouncing around inside their little pup tent. Lonnie landed heavily on Garrett several times. If it hadn't been for the give of the water beneath their float, the full weight of his cousin landing on him might have broken some bones. He heard Kitty and Sarah cry out as they were also struck by tumbling bodies.

Then the enormous wave passed and they were floating again, completely at the mercy of the wind.

"I'd say that qualifies," Lonnie said, "as cutting it a little close."

"You think?" said Garrett.

They tried to get comfortable, all rubbing sore spots from their pummeling. Lonnie insisted that Kitty and Garrett put their survival suits back on.

"I'm not cold anymore," he said. "And if anything happens to our raft, you need to have those suits on."

They could feel themselves being whisked along the ocean's surface, pushed by the fierce winds.

"Maybe we'll blow up on one of the islands or the coast," said Sarah.

"Be nice," said Garrett, "but hardly likely. We're too far out. Almost no islands out here. It's conceivable, I suppose, that we could be blown toward shore rather than out to sea, but . . ."

He stopped in mid-sentence. There was a sudden lull in the storm. The wind declined noticeably, and the rollicking, nausea-inducing speed of their helter-skelter retreat into the night slowed.

Lonnie unzipped the flap and played the torch back and forth. Swells and whitecaps were down. Even the stinging rain seemed to have stopped. "I think the worst is over," he announced.

Then Garrett raised one hand and the others grew silent. They all heard the same thing.

"It's a plane," said Sarah, incredulously. "What's a plane doing out here?"

"Got to be air/sea rescue," said Garrett. "The storm must be clearing for them to brave this." He reached up to the top of their raft and flicked on a switch that caused a red beacon to flicker.

"Can they possibly see that?" Kitty asked.

"That's what it's designed for," said Lonnie.

The plane went away, then came back and began to circle, proof they'd been sighted. An hour later, a Coast Guard cutter hove to beside them and pulled them aboard.

"Find any others?" Garrett asked first thing.

The cutter captain shook his head.

"There are a bunch of men in rafts out there somewhere," said Garrett.

The man nodded. "If they're out there, someone will find them. We've got a dozen boats looking for survivors, along with the plane and two rescue choppers. But right now, we've got you to take care of. Our medic will check you out and then we're heading for the hospital in Sherbrooke."

"Someone by the name of Alfred Nichols wouldn't be behind this, would he?" Garrett asked.

The captain smiled. "The spook? I never heard of him."

59

THE COLLAPSE OF LIGHTHOUSE POINT oil rig was front-page news around the world. Immediately following the storm, the Canadian authorities mobilized a huge effort to look for survivors and to contain any environmental damage. As it turned out, there was very little of the latter, since the rig hadn't actually been drilling for oil.

After a week, no survivors beyond Garrett and company had been found. One Coast Guard cutter picked up a tangled, deflated mass of open rafts tied together nearly forty miles out to sea. There was no sign of the occupants. A few days later, the bodies of several young girls were found floating far off the coast. Garrett speculated they'd been prisoners on the rig at the time it went down. One final horror in the lives of those poor unfortunates.

The reappearance of Kitty Wells also became front-page news. Her TV station welcomed her back with an extensive interview about her experience. Her tale of kidnapping and sexual slavery on the high seas held a prurient and fascinated Canadian public spellbound for days. True to her profession, Kitty held back nothing about her experience.

The Board of Directors of Global Resources scrambled to get ahead of the metastasizing scandal. They denounced their former

CEO and declared they had no idea what had been going on. Public outrage went viral and in less than forty-eight hours, Anthony DeMaio became public enemy number one. Interpol placed his picture in every major newspaper and on every television station in the world.

Of course, no one had any idea where he was.

Garrett was also besieged by the press. Tuttle ordered him to take some time off until the hubbub died down. An RCMP officer who worked mostly out of uniform and undercover wouldn't be helped by massive public exposure.

So Garrett was sitting on his porch one Sunday morning two weeks after the hurricane, nursing a cup of coffee and watching the whiskey jacks in his front yard, when Lonnie came up the lane. He hadn't seen much of his cousin since the incident.

Lonnie sat beside him on the little porch and stared at the birds for a couple of minutes without saying anything. He took a chunk of Garrett's bagel, broke it up, and threw it on the ground. The whiskey jacks ignored the offering.

"I was eating that," Garrett said testily. "This isn't the Public Gardens and those aren't the tame ducks you usually feed."

Lonnie grunted, then finally met Garrett's eyes. "Something personal I've been wanting to ask your advice about."

"Sure," said Garrett, though it was probably the first time his cousin had ever said such a thing. Lonnie wasn't a touchy-feely sort of guy, even to those who knew his true personality.

Again, the big man said nothing for a while, leaving Garrett wondering what was going on.

Finally he said, "Kitty's moved in with me."

Garrett's face lit up. "Lon! That's wonderful." He squeezed his cousin's huge bicep.

Then Lonnie gave the first sheepish look that Garrett had ever seen from him.

"Can't quite believe it myself," he said. "Something happened to her out there, Garrett. She equates me with her personal safety." He gave a long sideways glance. "Tell you the truth, I'm pretty tired. She's voracious in bed. Says what we're doing is so antithetical to what happened between her and DeMaio that she can't get enough of it."

"Uh . . . so your problem would be . . . what? Sounds like you're doing just fine on your own."

"That's it. I don't know if I can trust it, Gar. This is something I never thought would happen for me. She wants to get married, as soon as possible."

Garrett leaped to his feet. "That's fantastic! Who knows, maybe her being little and you being big, you'll have perfect-sized children." His pleasure at Lonnie's news couldn't have been more obvious, and his cousin smiled.

"Still," he said slowly, "Her feelings for me came out of something awful. It's kind of like that Stockholm syndrome thing, you know, where a hostage begins to identify with his captor. Only in this case, Kitty has glommed onto her savior instead. I just . . ." He struggled for the right words. ". . . don't know if it will last."

"Hell, it's a better basis for a marriage than a lot of others I've witnessed, Lon. There's no guarantee in any relationship. No guarantee it will last any longer than it lasts, period. Just enjoy it in the moment." He shrugged. "That's my advice."

Lonnie nodded. Garrett could see there was something else on his mind.

"She'll never feel truly safe again until DeMaio is caught," he said. "The idea that that monster is running around out there keeps her on constant edge, looking over her shoulder. She says the man is vindictive and will come after her if he can. You and I both know he'll probably never come anywhere near Kitty, not if he has an ounce of self-preservation in his body. Hell, he can't even get into this country any more. But I can't just leave him out there."

"Interpol usually gets its man," Garrett said. "Sooner or later."

"I'm going for sooner."

Garrett stared at him. "You're going after him?"

He nodded. "I won't get married until this loose end is taken care of. Maybe it's one way of proving to myself that Kitty really wants me for anything other than protection."

"All right," Garrett said slowly, "I guess I can understand that. But if Interpol can't find him, how do you expect to?"

Lonnie gave him a hard smile. "How many times do I have to tell you Eagle Scout types that you have your limitations? Interpol has as many as the Mounties—maybe more. International boundaries, bureaucratic bullshit, jurisdictional disputes, budgetary considerations. The game I play has fewer rules and most of the ones there are have to do with paying off debts. A lot of people owe me, Gar. I'll find DeMaio. No question. He's hiding in my world, now."

Garrett spread his hands. "How can I help?"

"Most important thing I need is someone to look after Kitty while I'm doing this. She knows about it, is against it. But it's something I have to do. Kind of like my wedding present to her."

Sarah came up the lane and stopped when she saw them together on the porch. "My two favorite men in the world," she said.

She went up on the porch and kissed Lonnie, then gave a longer smooch to Garrett and sat next to them. "I've just been talking to Grace."

"How's she doing?" Garrett asked. "Leo told me about what happened to her. I was pretty surprised. Last time I spoke to Roland, he told me he'd found Grace doing a drug deal out in the islands. I didn't believe him."

Sarah hesitated. "Grace told me something I'm not sure I should tell you, Gar. But she didn't tell me not to, so . . ."

Lonnie exchanged looks with Garrett and they both waited.

"Anyway, maybe it's something you could sort of check out. I believe her but . . . it's hard to know about people. Maybe you already know. It's sort of your area, after all."

Garrett looked blank. "What on earth are you talking about?"

She took a deep breath. "Grace says that what Roland told you was the truth. Sort of. She says she works undercover for the federal government. She's been trying to get close to some dealers, get trusted enough to trap them in a major bust."

Garrett's eyes went wide. "I don't believe it."

She nodded.

"I know nothing at all about it," Garrett said. "And I'd bet my limited bankroll Tuttle doesn't either. It's almost too fantastic. She's the least likely looking agent I could imagine."

"Kitty doesn't look much like a woman who could kill five men and help me escape from an international sex ring either," Sarah said.

"Pretty good disguises," said Lonnie, "for both of you. Slime balls in the profession see women like you and Grace and Kitty in two ways only, as potential customers for their drugs or money-makers as prostitutes. Preferably both at once. They would never expect any trouble from that quarter. They're so used to women being victims, period. Might make it easier for Grace to get close to them. Her story rings true to me."

"Something else," said Sarah. "Grace is grateful to Roland. He saved her life, after all. Evidently the bad guys figured out who she was. They pumped her full of drugs, put her in that kayak, and set her adrift. By the time her body was found, if it ever was, the drugs would be out of her system and the assumption would be that she got caught kayaking in the storm. It was a miracle Roland found her."

"Please God, don't tell me she's decided to marry Roland," said Garrett. "I can't take any more shocks this morning."

"Huh," said Sarah, her gaze washing over him. "Guess you're still recovering from the shock I gave you the other night?"

"That was more by the way of a systemic stimulus," Garrett sniffed. "You completely wasted me, not to put too fine a point on it."

She nuzzled him, kissed his neck. "Took us so long to get together, made it even better." She looked shyly at Lonnie, who was grinning ear to ear.

"Anyway," Sarah went on, "No way is Grace marrying Roland. Trust me. But she feels an obligation to him. And she says she feels sorry for him, since his mother died. He's all alone in the world, and she's decided to take him on. Kind of like her personal rehabilitation project. She's helped him clean and reorganize his house, taken him out to buy new clothes, bought him a membership in a health club so he can get in better shape, even taken him to see a dermatologist about his skin and a dentist to work on his teeth. She also helped him get fitted for shoes that will even out his gait. She says she's going to find him a wife if it's the last thing she does. Says there's someone for everyone in this world. It's just a matter of finding them."

"Unbelievable!" Garrett exclaimed. "I never thought there could possibly be any woman for Roland. I'd say Grace has taken on quite a challenge. But it's a good thing. You tell her next time you see her that I'll help in any way I can."

"Tell her yourself," Sarah said. "You're both invited to dinner tomorrow night at Grace's house. Roland will be there too."

Garrett's eyes widened. "That's a gathering I never would have believed."

"I have to admit, I'm still trying to absorb it myself," said Sarah. "Leo, and especially Ingrid, I think, are having a hard time with the new order. But they're committed to Grace and are grateful that Roland saved her. Anyway, I thought it wouldn't hurt to have the law, so to speak, attend the dinner, just in case there are any lingering areas of dispute."

"It's all good to hear," said Lonnie. "But I'm going to be tied up."

"Look," said Garrett, "before you plan anything, I think we should visit Alfred Nichols. See what he says. Maybe the intels can at least point you in the right direction."

The big man snorted. "That would be a first." But he shrugged acceptance. He'd take any help he could get if it meant putting Kitty's mind at ease.

60

ALFRED NICHOLS'S OFFICE WAS IN a towering high rise and offered spectacular views of the Halifax and Dartmouth waterfronts. Puffy white clouds scudded across the sky, and far in the distance the North Atlantic was pockmarked with whitecaps. Weather reports suggested still another hurricane might make landfall.

Lonnie stared out at the incredible vista. "Always wondered where my tax dollars went," he said.

Garrett didn't want to discuss his cousin's non-payment of taxes in this forum. Nichols sat behind an enormous mahogany desk that was completely empty, a sign of either bureaucratic efficiency or intel paranoia that he wanted no potential information inadvertently exposed to visitors. He wore a pearl gray vested suit that hugged a tight frame. The most incongruous aspect of his appearance, given his profession, was a ten-inch ponytail that began just above his neck. It was, in fact, the only hair on his head.

"Your meeting," he said. "Your agenda."

"We want to know what you know about Anthony DeMaio," said Garrett.

"Sorry, that's privileged information."

Garrett stared at him. "Don't fuck around with me, Nichols. We've had just about enough of Anthony DeMaio. We want to know everything there is to know about him."

Nichols stood up. "If that's what this meeting is about, I think we're done."

Garrett didn't move. "Okay, here's the thing," he said. "If you're not willing to help, I'm going to be interviewed on TV tonight. Miss Kitty Wells's show. I'm sure you've seen it. Audience share is right through the roof since she came back. You should see her mail. Tens of thousands of letters from sympathetic women all across Canada. She's going to ask me if we have any leads in looking for Mr. DeMaio and I'm going to tell her that the feds, and you in particular, have refused to cooperate in the investigation. That we're beginning to suspect you may have some link to Global Resources yourself."

Nichols blinked and looked from Garrett to Lonnie, who had a half smile on his face. "You can't do that."

"Eight o'clock tonight, you're going to be the most despised man in Canada," said Garrett. "I suspect your own wife won't be speaking to you."

After a moment, Nichols sat back down.

"All right. What do you want to know?"

Lonnie's smile blossomed. "The power of the press," he said.

"For starters, I want to know about Grace Finney. Does she work for you?"

Nichols looked out his window, though he didn't seem to register the spectacular view. "Yes," he said.

"How long?"

"She's part of a special task force set up over a year ago to investigate drug smuggling along the Eastern shore. We'd had rumors that someone in the RCMP might be involved, and she was also looking into that. One reason I hesitated to give you any information is because, frankly, it could have been you."

"She find out anything?"

He shook his head. "Some leads, but nothing I'd want to put out there. Even a rumor could destroy a Mountie's career."

"You manage to tie DeMaio into this?"

"To the drugs? No. Looks like he was strictly into the sex trafficking thing. Guess it was good for his business."

"Yeah, the whole bonus package thing for foreign buyers," said Lonnie, with an edge to his voice that made Nichols look at him uneasily. The spook dealt with unsavory characters on a daily basis, but even he could see that this giant was not someone you wanted to annoy.

"So here's the 64,000-dollar-question question," said Garrett. "Where is he now?"

Nichols drummed his fingers on the desk. Then he reached into a drawer and pulled out a file. He opened it and pushed it across the desk. "Man jets between at least four countries that we know of. He holds Canadian, Saudi, and Colombian passports. Probably others. So far, we have no leads as to his current whereabouts."

Lonnie snorted. "I could find out that much on the waterfront in a couple of hours," he said. "Never could figure out how you fellas manage to spend so much money." He looked around the office. "Or maybe I can."

Garrett tried another tack. "RCMP has Lloyd in their custody. Have you questioned him about all of this?"

"You haven't heard?"

"What?"

"Lloyd got his solicitors lined up quicker than Don Corleone. He was released for lack of evidence. His body turned up three days ago in a dumpster off Barrington."

"Shit!" Garrett looked out the window. "How was he killed?"

"Let me count the ways. There were similarities to the death of Big Margaret. Suffice to say, he was tortured. His Achilles tendons were severed, along with another of his favorite body parts."

Garrett swallowed hard. He'd done a modest amount of behavior modification on Lloyd himself. The man appeared to bring out the worst in people. Clearly, whoever got to the self-proclaimed naturist was considerably more thorough about it than Garrett had been.

"Seems slime-bucket DeMaio has a long reach," said Lonnie.

"Cleaning up more loose ends," Garrett said. "You got anybody on Kitty?"

"Two men, and the TV station has its own security. She's safe."

"You connect Lloyd with DeMaio?" Garrett said to Nichols.

He nodded. "Through Big Margaret and Madame Liu both. Your favorite public servant in charge of *troubled youth* got around. He was pretty well positioned to provide girls that eventually ended up with DeMaio, though our current thinking is Lloyd didn't deal directly with the executive. We broke Madame Liu's organization night before last. We think DeMaio got nervous after you appeared asking questions, so he had Lloyd killed by way of insurance. Probably did Big Margaret in too. Madame Liu had a stronger sense of self preservation. When she heard what happened to the others, she agreed to cooperate in exchange for protection. Unfortunately, she has no more idea how to find the scumbag than we do."

"You think he could still be in the country?" Garrett asked.

"Wouldn't be if it was me. Way this thing's blown up, courtesy of Miss Wells, I'd be hunkering down somewhere south of the border, in one of the countries we don't have an extradition treaty with."

"Doesn't mean he can't get people to do stuff for him," Lonnie said. "Long as he's got money."

Outside, they walked along the waterfront and considered what to do next.

"You think Nichols was telling the truth about not knowing where DeMaio is?" Garrett asked.

Lonnie shrugged. The waterfront was full of tourists. They veered out in a wave around the big man, then surged back behind him. It was a phenomenon Garrett had witnessed whenever he moved about the city with his cousin.

"Maybe. Maybe he just wants to see what we can find out on our own. You put the fear of God into him with that bit about appearing on Kitty's show."

"What are you going to do?" Garrett asked.

"Talk to some people. See what the word on the street is. DeMaio's careful, but he deals with lowlifes, people would sell out their own mothers for a Tim Horton's cheese biscuit. I'll know more in a few hours than Nichols's whole crew got him in a year."

"All right. Call me when you need me." He looked at his cousin. "I'm serious, Lon. Will you at least let me know if you decide to do something?"

He nodded. "Make my excuses to the ladies about tomorrow night. Love to be there and see the chemistry between Roland and his newfound friends."

They separated and Garrett watched him move off, a stationary wave in a sea of wide-eyed tourists.

Before going home, he decided to check in with Kitty and make sure she was all right. If Lon was happy with her security, then he knew there was nothing to worry about. But he was curious to see her in action at her place of work.

The station was a small, squat building bristling with antennas from its flat roof. He had to show ID to a guard at the entrance and then wait while another man went to see if Kitty would see him.

She returned herself, stood on tiptoe to give him a kiss, and waved him past the guards. She was made up even more carefully than normal. Her working clothes, her hair and makeup were all perfect. She was gorgeous.

"Security seems pretty good," he said.

She pointed across the street where two men sat in a car. "Station guards handle stuff when I'm inside. Those two in the car are Lonnie's men. They go with me whenever I leave."

"How do you feel about that?"

"It helps. I was getting pretty jumpy thinking about DeMaio out there somewhere. I killed five of his men, after all, and pissed off his investors, though I guess they aren't going to be complaining from Davy Jones's locker."

She took him to her office, which was small but comfortable, and they sat on a leather couch.

"I've got twenty minutes till I go on the air."

"Lonnie told me you two have moved in together."

She smiled. "Kind of a surprise, huh? But I really love him, Garrett. He's a big, lovable teddy bear. And besides," she gave him a wicked grin. "He's big all over."

"You're making me blush. I bet that's the first time anyone ever described Lon as a teddy bear. Anyway, he seems real happy. And I'm happy for both of you."

She grew serious. "Did he tell you we want to get married?"

He nodded. "He's a little nervous about it. Lon hasn't had much luck with women, you know. His size scares them away."

"One of the things I like, besides the blush factor. Maybe opposites attract or something."

"How do you feel about his going after DeMaio on his own?"

"Scared shitless. I know Lon can take care of himself. But DeMaio's filthy rich and has no moral compunctions of any kind. I told Lonnie that. Not to take the man lightly. With his resources he could be anywhere." She looked at him. "Where do you think he is?"

"Like you said. He has the whole world to hide in. My bet is he'll lie low for a long time. I don't think you have to worry about him, and I seriously doubt he's in Canada. Still, it can't hurt to be cautious. He can hire people to do his dirty work for him."

Garrett looked about Kitty's office. It was small but fashionable, done in muted pastels. He suspected it would be highly effective in impressing important guests. "Have the authorities given you any trouble about those men you killed?"

"I've been questioned several times about it. So far, they haven't found any bodies, which makes any sort of prosecution a moot point. But I've been totally up front about what I did and why. With the publicity and the shows I've been doing, I don't think anyone questions my motives."

He nodded. It was what he would have expected. She had a right to defend herself in such a situation.

"All right." He stood up. "I'm going home. Little dinner party tomorrow night with the ladies and Roland. I've been invited as security, I think." He smiled ruefully. "They wanted Lonnie too, which may be a sign of the possible level of need."

Kitty bounced out of her chair and put her arm through Garrett's. "I can do this now, Garrett," she said with a big smile. "We're going to be relatives."

"Fine by me," he said. "You're one gutsy reporter, Kitty. I've revised my earlier assessment, and I'm happy as a clam to have you in the family."

"Funny," she said, walking him to the door. "I *was* a pushy bitch. Felt like I had to be to get noticed for anything other than my looks. I just don't feel that need anymore. Maybe what I went through helped put things in perspective. Maybe it's having Lonnie in my life. Probably both."

She looked away from him, her face suddenly showing real pain. "I . . . I want to apologize for that crack I made a while back about your handicap. It was awful and I feel absolutely humiliated every time I think about it. You know, it's the strangest thing . . ."

"What?"

"People don't believe it, but I've always felt like my looks are my own handicap. They put me at a disadvantage with everyone I meet because they instantly classify me as a certain type. Over time, I just decided if that's how people were going to see me, then I might as well take advantage of it. Use what God gave me, if you will. Anyway, the need is gone, and I'm sorry."

Garrett unhooked her arm and held her by both shoulders. Then he leaned forward and kissed her on the cheek.

"Welcome to the family," he said with a smile.

61

LONNIE STOOD OUTSIDE THE LAW offices of Wanbolt, Hart-less, and Noseworthy, the firm that did much of Global Resources' legal work. He'd begun checking his sources and had found one interesting bit of information already. People were reluctant to talk about Anthony DeMaio.

This was unusual, since the average source he consulted would generally throw over his firstborn in exchange for a bottle or maybe even just to get Lonnie to go away. It suggested that DeMaio might still be around and close enough to make people nervous.

Why would he still be in Canada? It would be a huge risk. Was it some sort of hubris? The man had been invested with such immense power for so long, perhaps he felt invincible. Or perhaps he intended to get even. With Kitty? She'd said DeMaio was vindictive and maybe borderline psychotic as well.

The thought made him more than a little uneasy. It was a new feeling for him to be in love with someone. The possibility of harm coming to Kitty simply seized his emotions to such an extent that he had to fight being paralyzed by it. He'd never experienced anything like it before. Even the fear he'd felt for Garrett's life in Afghanistan couldn't compare.

A foppish-looking fellow exited the law firm and began walking toward him. Lou Liotino. The solicitor Lonnie and Garrett had confronted about Global's unusual Club Med facilities at Lighthouse Point. Lonnie had felt at the time that Garrett hadn't gotten everything out of the man that he could have. And he'd immediately recognized Liotino's fear of him. It was visceral, something he'd seen often enough in his line of work. Liotino would tell Lonnie anything he wanted to know. The man was a complete coward.

As Liotino crossed the street, Lonnie moved in beside him, matching him step for step. The man did a classic double-take and his eyes went wide as recognition suddenly came.

"What do you want?" he asked.

"I want us to keep walking into that park over there," said Lonnie. "Sit on a bench and feed the ducks." He put one immense hand on the solicitor's arm and directed him. He could feel the man wilt and begin to perspire right through his thousand-dollar suit.

"Hey, what is this?" Liotino said, but his voice betrayed more fear than outrage. Lonnie plunked him down on a bench and sat next to him.

"Damn," he said. "Forgot to bring corn for the birds." He considered the man cowering next to him as though he were some sort of rare bug. Of course, there was nothing at all rare about solicitors in a city the size of Halifax. As far as Lonnie was concerned, bugs were considerably higher on the evolutionary scale.

"Where's Anthony DeMaio?" he asked.

Liotino shook his head. "I have no idea. I'm not a full partner. I don't know everything that goes on inside the firm."

Lonnie nodded slowly. "That's going to be a real problem for you. Because you see, I don't believe you." He raised one ham-sized hand to forestall the man before he could offer another denial. "Interesting thing. Last man who refused to tell me what I wanted to know also happened to be a solicitor. Same sort of scumbag you are. It took me all of three days to uncover a list of the scams he was involved in and hand the information over to a special prosecutor. He's doing eight to twelve in Halifax Central Correctional Facility. Well, actually, he only did six months, because solicitors are not the most highly regarded people on the inside. He was so badly abused sexually that he died."

The color drained from Liotino's face. His eyes darted back and forth, looking for escape or rescue, anything to save him from this frightening giant sitting next to him.

Lonnie continued conversationally. "What I'm asking is really quite simple. I want to know where DeMaio is. I don't believe he disappeared without anyone in the firm being able to contact him. Frankly, I think he might still be in Canada. I'm not going to ask you again. Where is he?"

"They'll kill me if I tell you," he said.

"I'll do worse if you don't. And don't even think about lying to me."

Liotino was sweating profusely. "All right, all right. Just please don't ever tell anyone where you got this from, okay?"

"No problem. We'll call it attorney/client privilege, so long as the information is accurate."

"Well, I don't know exactly where he is . . ." He raised a shaky hand at Lonnie's look. "But he's in Canada, I'm certain of it. I know he's communicating with the board. They're scared of him and have been trying to distance themselves from him publicly, but DeMaio's still calling the shots within the company."

Lonnie stared at him. "That's too incredible to believe. Are they nuts? The man is probably one of the most wanted men in the world. How could they possibly allow him to continue to control the company?"

"He's got something on every board member. It's how he operates. And they all know that if they go off the reservation, he can get them arrested for any number of illegal acts and maybe even have them killed. So while they denounce him publicly, something they have undoubtedly cleared with DeMaio, they continue to supply him with money. It's all a mess. I don't think the company can survive if this comes out. I'm one of three members of my firm who deal directly with the board, and we've all started looking for other positions, because if this thing falls apart, it'll bring down not only Global but my own firm as well."

"You still haven't answered my question. Where is he?"

"I don't know . . . not for sure. But I have an idea. DeMaio is very close to the Chairman of the Board. A man named Wade Preston. If I had to guess, I'd bet Preston is hiding him."

"Where?"

"I was invited once to a private meeting with Preston. It was a sensitive personnel issue at the time. I was the only one dealing with it. He sent a helicopter to pick me up at the corporate headquarters and flew me to his private island, about an hour from Halifax by chopper. Very luxurious—huge compound, numerous outbuildings, a dock big enough for an ocean-going yacht and heliport. If my life depended on it, I'd bet that's where DeMaio is staying."

Lonnie stood up. "Your life does depend on it," he said. Liotino looked ill. "All right, let's go."

"Go where?"

"To the train station. You're taking a trip to Ottawa for a few days."

"What? I can't do that. I have a job."

"Not for long, if my guess is right. Besides, from what you've told me, you don't want to be around when the shit hits the fan. I'm doing you a favor. I want you out of town, just so you don't accidentally run into Preston or DeMaio. You got your phone on you?"

"Yes."

"Call your office. Tell them a family emergency has come up and you have to go out of town at once. Don't say where. I'm not going to stay around to make sure you do this right, because believe me, if something goes wrong, I'll know it was because of you and I'll find you." He stared at Liotino. His big hand gripped the smaller man's shoulder like a vise. "Do you believe me?"

The look on Liotino's face said it all. This time tomorrow morning, he'd be taking in the nation's parliament buildings and wandering through the ByWard Market. No question about it.

62

GARRETT STROLLED AROUND THE COVE, picked Sarah up at her house, and they arrived at Roland's neighbors' house a little after six. Leo greeted them at the door with a nervous look on his face.

"I don't know how this is going to go," he said. "Especially with Ingrid. She's having a lot of trouble with the new order."

He led them into the living room where they could see Ingrid, Grace, and Keith sitting outside on the deck. There was no sign of Roland.

Garrett said, "Something I want to ask you before we go outside. Did you and Ingrid know what Grace was up to? About working undercover, I mean."

Leo shook his head. "Not a clue. Grace said she wasn't assigned to the job until after we moved here, and then she was ordered not to tell anyone. We always thought there was something a little odd about her schedule. She'd take off at strange times without explanation. We wondered if she had a lover she didn't want us to know about."

"And you had no idea she was a federal agent?" Garrett asked incredulously.

"None. We both knew her in Halifax and assumed she came from a well-to-do family. She always had money, which made her a welcome addition when we decided to invest in this place."

They went out onto the deck and greeted the others. Keith was undoubtedly present for moral support, of a kind, for Roland. As another longtime resident of Misery Bay, he'd always gotten along with Roland as well as anyone. Garrett and Sarah offered congratulations to Grace again for her narrow escape.

"Nothing narrow about it," she said. "I was as good as dead until Roland came along. I've been trying to get Ingrid to understand how I feel. I owe my very existence to Roland."

Ingrid gave out an extended and, Garrett thought, theatrical sigh. "I still don't see why it means we have to invite the whale to be our best buddy," she said.

Grace shot her a piercing look. "I told you not to call him that anymore. He's got enough baggage to deal with."

Garrett accepted a Manhattan from Leo and sat down.

"What do you make of all of this?" he asked Keith. Garrett had never known anyone more at peace in his own skin than his neighbor. Keith's family was close-knit, and while he didn't make a lot of money working as a postal clerk, he was so completely fascinated by genealogy that he was always in an upbeat mood. Nova Scotia was a crucible of history, after all, a result of being at the center of the world's maritime stage for over four hundred years. Keith was like a kid in a candy store, surrounding himself with books, maps, diaries, weather analyses, tide charts, and mariners' logs. It was all he needed to amuse himself for a lifetime. Garrett had often wished he might feel as passionate about something.

Keith gave his usual infectious smile. "The winds of change are blowing in Misery Bay. You seen Roland yet?"

Garrett shook his head. "I've been trying to lie low till the press furor dies down."

"Well, prepare yourself for a shock, that's all I can say."

Before Garrett could quiz him further, the doorbell rang and Grace went to answer it. A moment later, Roland appeared on the deck.

Garrett and Sarah stared at him in disbelief. It was the first time they'd ever seen Roland looking clean and dressed in anything other than a stained T-shirt and sweatpants. His hair was a tousled mat of ringlets, obviously professionally coiffed. He looked like some sort of gaunt version of Paul Newman playing a Roman centurion. When he walked over to them, the limp was noticeably diminished.

He had on a pale gray shirt under a leather vest and matching, pressed slacks. His rough fisherman's hands were scrubbed clean and he had clearly used some sort of hand lotion to make them look smoother. There was even a hint of cologne. When he took in Garrett and Sarah's open mouths, he looked sheepish.

Sarah was the first to recover. She stood up and gave him a little hug. "You look terrific, Roland."

"Feel a little silly," he said. "But Grace says she knows what she's doin'. And I gotta admit to ya, people look at me differently. Even . . . girls."

"Women," Grace corrected him.

"Sorry," said Roland. "I forget sometimes. Women."

They settled back into their chairs. Garrett thought even Roland's posture had improved and wondered if he was wearing some sort of girdle or body cast. The thought was almost too much to absorb.

Periodically, Roland sneaked a peek at Ingrid. Obviously, he had taken to Grace's remake program, but Ingrid was the unknown factor in all of this. She'd been the one who despised him the most.

Garrett said to Grace, "I talked to your boss the other day. He confirmed to me that you'd been doing a good job and were extremely brave to be out there all alone."

She smiled. "We'd been building up a case against some of these drug traffickers and then I began to see that at least some of them were also involved in moving young girls for the escort agencies. It's the most despicable thing, Garrett. Some of the girls are just babies, eight, nine years old. They find it easier to train them when they're very young." She shook her head. "It just breaks your heart."

"Did you ever come across anything about DeMaio?"

"No. I'm pretty sure he wasn't into the drug trade, though. At least as a dealer. He could have been a buyer, I suppose, for personal use or to control his own women. But he probably considered the drug business beneath him. I gather money wasn't his issue. He had plenty of that."

It was more or less what Garrett had come to believe. DeMaio was a businessman. He sold multi-billion-dollar oil rigs and provided sexual favors to his customers. It was all about influence and power.

"So how did they get on to you?" Garrett asked.

She frowned. "I haven't really worked it out. I don't think I slipped up. Nothing I can put my finger on anyway. When I went for my last buy, they just grabbed me, held me down, and one of them said, 'this is what happens to people who double-cross us.' I didn't know what he meant, but then they pumped me full of drugs and set me loose in my kayak in the middle of the storm."

"Were you conscious?" Sarah asked, leaning forward.

"Semi. I could barely move and drifted in and out. I remember being cold and wet and managing to turn on my emergency beacon somehow, but most of it's still a blur. I do have a foggy memory of Roland picking me up, though, and putting me into a warm place." She smiled at her rescuer.

Garrett looked at Roland, who watched Grace with an expression on his face Garrett had never seen before. It wasn't desire, not even infatuation exactly. It was more a sort of puzzlement, as though he were trying to absorb a feeling he'd never experienced before. How an attractive woman might consider him a friend.

Ingrid stood up abruptly and stalked off the deck, leaving an awkward silence. Grace put one hand on Roland's knee. "Give her a while," she said. "She'll come around."

Roland said, "Can't blame her, ya know. I was pretty mean ta ya all. I want ta say somethin.'"

Everyone looked at him.

"I . . . I never really had any friends. Not one my whole life. It's goin' ta take me some time ta get used ta this, same as Ingrid. But I will. With Ma gone, I thought I was goin' ta be alone for the rest of my life. I never thought somethin' like this would be possible. And I'm goin' ta make it work. Grace has done somethin' no one 'cept Ma ever did. She cared about me."

Grace leaned over and gave him a hug.

Tears welled up in Roland's eyes. There was no question that what he was feeling was real and transforming. After a moment he appeared to get control of himself.

"Sorry," he said. "I din't mean ta embarrass ya."

"One other thing I wanted to ask Grace about," said Garrett, trying to move the conversation away from the awkward moment. "Did you ever come across anyone dressed in a Mountie uniform, maybe working with the drug runners?"

She nodded. "There was someone I saw a couple of times. I was never introduced to him, but I gathered he had inside connections." She shrugged. "It was hard to know his role, exactly. He came and went. I never saw him in full uniform, but he carried a Glock and always wore at least the hat. It was kind of strange." She got up, poured herself another Manhattan, and clinked glasses with Roland.

Sarah said, "Have you got any leads at all on DeMaio, Gar?"

He spread his hands. "Nothing. Which is only slightly more than what Nichols has. DeMaio holds passports for several countries and is bound to have planned for a day like this. Probably got plenty of money socked away in Swiss bank accounts or the Caymans. Probably got a home . . . or homes . . . under assumed names. Hard to believe the CEO of one of the world's biggest oil companies could disappear without a trace. But he'd be a lot bigger fool than I would think possible if he was still moving around inside Canada. I suspect we may never hear from him again."

"I disagree," said Grace. "He's so used to having power and influence, he's not going to be able to give it up. I can't imagine him simply slipping away to become a beachcomber for the rest of his days. Hard to give up what he had."

"Maybe you're right. Anyway, Lonnie's looking into it. If anyone can find the man, it's him."

Conversation turned to the collapsed oil rig.

"The incredible thing," Keith said, "is that there's been almost no oil spilled by this whole business. Do you think the real reason for it's being there was simply to serve as a sort of floating brothel?"

"Hardly makes sense," said Sarah. "That rig probably cost upwards of a billion dollars. Hell, you could pay thousands of professional women top dollar to service your clients if that's what it was all about."

"I think DeMaio got off on having women from all walks of life forced into servitude to him," said Garrett. "I mean, imagine the chutzpah to buy a television anchorwoman, for God's sake. He liked the conquest aspect of the whole thing. I also think the rig was intended more for show to potential buyers than as an efficient operating platform. Anyway, the money spent on the rig wasn't his. It was the company's.

"And don't underestimate the lure of being in international waters. That sort of freedom from legal scrutiny was huge and made it nearly impossible for DeMaio's protégés to escape. He set himself up with every man's dream. A steady crop of beautiful young women for his personal pleasure at virtually no risk. Probably hasn't been anything like it since the days of the hareem ... maybe Hugh Hefner. I'm sure it fed his ego to know he had what every other man could only dream of.

"As for bargaining power . . . he had something to dangle in front of legal assistants, employees, members of the board, police, politicians, you name it. A lot of men would bend over backward to not risk losing access to that ultimate fantasy."

The room was silent as they all contemplated the incredible world of one Anthony DeMaio.

63

THE ROOM WAS LUXURIOUS, PERCHED on the edge of the sea, all mahogany and stone and glass. The view to the western sunset was perfect. Though isolated, the space contained a large desk and computer, satellite hookup, and fax lines that connected instantly anywhere in the world.

The central compound was crisscrossed with carefully laid-out walkways surfaced with imported red clay from France. There was a red clay tennis court, a large heated swimming pool, and a dining room with crystal chandeliers, run by a world-class French chef. There was a fully equipped gymnasium and even a small medical center. Supplies and carefully screened foreign workers were flown in by helicopter daily, along with fresh lobster, Russian caviar, and the latest Toronto and New York papers, including the *Wall Street Journal*.

Anthony DeMaio sat in a leather armchair and stared at the lowering sun, brooding. So far as he was concerned, the magnificent surroundings were nothing but a glorified prison. For three weeks he had restlessly paced about the island, his lean face taut with frustration.

Global's Chairman of the Board, Wade Preston, had convinced him that he should ensconce himself at Preston's secluded island rather than try to get out of the country.

"No way you can get out under the radar," Preston had pleaded. "Everything's being watched too closely; every plane, ship, and border in the world is displaying your picture. You need to hunker down and wait this out."

Now, however, DeMaio wasn't so sure. He seemed to be living in his own personal purgatory. Granted, it was one any normal person would give their eyeteeth to reside in. But for a man used to flitting around the world at his leisure, the inability to move was stifling.

The Halifax papers kept up a steady drumbeat of reports about the sinking of the rig, the exploitation of young girls, and always, always, the traumas of Kitty Wells. It would be ironic if it weren't so painful. It was because of him that Kitty Wells had achieved national fame, maybe international. Her star rose as his own languished in his luxurious gulag. That blasted woman had killed five of his men, with many more lost at sea, destroyed his floating brothel, killed off his potential investors, and taken his reputation and freedom. He would never have believed such an outcome possible from such a tiny slip of a woman.

His days were filled with brooding and visions of revenge. To add insult to injury, he had no access to the beautiful young women he was used to having at his beck and call. For nearly a decade, he had indulged his sexual desires at whim. Hundreds of beautiful women had been forced to submit to him. His sexual frustration after just three weeks of celibacy was nearing explosive levels. He couldn't conceive how he would ever survive such abstinence if he went to prison. The very idea horrified him. The possibility of sex with men, possibly forced, disgusted him.

Preston refused to bring girls to the retreat. It was too great a risk with the entire world looking for DeMaio. Global's board was also under constant scrutiny. Women had to go on hold for the time being.

It was a rare example of the chairman standing up to his guest. For the members of the board feared DeMaio. The man held a knife at all of their throats. Each of them was compromised by a carefully constructed web of financial ties and illegalities. There was no doubt the man's reach could extend even beyond the grave, should anyone be so foolish as to try to dispose of him, much less turn him in.

DeMaio paced about his glass cage. His anger at being effectively imprisoned here by one of his own conquests drove him to distraction. Finally, he stopped and stared out to sea.

Enough.

It was time to fight back. Already he had dispensed with Lloyd, the imbecile who had kidnapped Kitty Wells to begin with. Though he'd enjoyed the woman, it was now clear that the selection of such a high-profile victim had been the cause of his downfall. His men had been slower to get rid of Madame Liu, who was now under police protection and, no doubt, interrogation. He wasn't worried about that. Liu had no idea how to find him.

With access to his communications center and to his foreign bank accounts, his reach was still considerable. His fury at Wells was mixed up with a sea of emotions; sheer outrage that she had gotten the better of him combined with fantasies of their sex together, now that he had no other outlet. When the reporter's availability to him had been assured, he'd quickly tired of her, as he did with all women. But now, he thought of her incessantly, desired her even as he fantasized about the ways he would cause her to suffer.

He sat in front of his computer and worked the keys. Preston had tried to dissuade him even from this, for computer activity could be traced, even the most secure of systems. No matter. Nothing would keep him away from Kitty Wells.

64

L ONNIE CALLED GARRETT AN HOUR after his conversation with Liotino.

"Got a probable location on DeMaio," he said. "Highly likely. And Garrett, he's in Canada."

"No way!" said Garrett. "He really must be crazy. How sure are you?"

"Had a little talk with your buddy, Lou Liotino."

"Damn. There goes another source. I knew it was a mistake to talk to him with you in tow. Lou's not exactly the bravest lion in the pride. Word gets around you work with me, it's going to stifle my reputation on the street. I hope you didn't kill him, at least."

"Just a few coaxing words."

"I'll bet."

"We need to move, Garrett. No telling how long he'll stick around. You up for another kayak trip?"

"You can't be serious. Where is he?"

"Island three miles offshore, an hour from Halifax. Belongs to Global's chairman of the board, a man named Wade Preston."

Garrett thought quickly. "Give me twelve hours to set something up."

"Twelve hours could be more time than we have, Gar."

"Look, I'm going to light a fire under some people. We can't go in there with just the two of us. I want Tom and the Coast Guard in on this. Nichols too. Maybe he can get the Navy on board. I'll inform Tuttle as well. You don't know what sort of setup they have on that island. They may have a lot of security. Remember, Global's got more money than God."

Lonnie grumbled some more but finally agreed and left to make his own arrangements.

It only took six hours to line up the cavalry. Tom and Nichols were both excited to hear that DeMaio might actually be within reach. Garrett knew Lonnie would double-check Kitty's protection before the shit hit the fan. But he'd been thinking that Sarah might also need protection. She'd been Kitty's comrade in arms, after all, and if DeMaio really was feeling vindictive and couldn't get to Kitty, he might turn his attention elsewhere. Lila and Ayesha were away for several days attending a special program for girls set up by Protective Services. Sarah was alone in the house. Garrett called Tuttle and asked for Alvin to be sent down to stay with Sarah while the operation was on. Selling it to Sarah would be another matter, but there was no time. He'd leave that to his former partner.

Ten minutes after his third call to Nichols setting up the operation, his phone rang. It was Grace.

"I'm going with you," she said.

He didn't hesitate. "All right. You've earned it. This whole thing's moving quickly. Nichols is sending a chopper to pick us up in an hour."

He could tell she was excited. Nichols must have had a lot of confidence in her to tell her about the operation so quickly.

"You really think he's going to be there, Garrett?"

"No telling. Lon usually gets reliable information. If there hasn't been a leak somewhere, I'd bet on it."

An hour later, a chopper set down next to the wharf in front of Roland's house. The neighbors stared out their windows in disbelief as a woman, a man, and a giant scrambled on board, then rose quickly into the late afternoon sky. Garrett caught a brief glimpse of Leo and Ingrid standing on their deck, holding on to one another and staring somberly at the aircraft.

Grace looked down on her friends and sighed. "They're scared out of their minds for me. I always knew a day would come when I'd have to tell them what I do."

"Take them a while to get used to it," said Garrett. "But they will."

Lonnie sat next to them in a rumble seat. He looked like some sort of toy action figure, belted in and ready for a commando raid. He bristled with small arms and carried an Uzi as well. For all his years working at the very edge of the legal system, the big man somehow managed to have permits for a wide variety of weapons. Garrett knew he managed this via his extensive military and political contacts.

"What's the plan?" Lonnie asked.

Garrett pointed out the small window next to him. Lonnie and Grace leaned over and looked out. Below on the ocean surface were two Canadian destroyers, their white foam trails a sign of how fast they were moving.

"Holy shitkickers!" said Grace. "That's awesome."

"The plan," said Garrett, "is dead simple. We land and *persuade* DeMaio to surrender."

"Personally," Lonnie said, "I hope he resists. Be nice to have him permanently out of Kitty's hair. Life in prison would be too good for that asshole."

"Try to keep things in perspective, Lon," said Garrett. "It won't do Kitty any good if you get yourself put away for unnecessary use of force. Just let things play out, okay?"

Lonnie looked unconvinced. It was a look that worried Garrett, one that suggested the big man just might have plans of his own.

The expansive estate appeared on the horizon thirty minutes later. It was an elongated island with vast, rocky beaches. One end rose to a bluff that overlooked the sea. Here were rambling buildings, manicured lawns, and a sparkling blue pool. Next to a tennis court was a helipad. Their pilot had been in constant communication with the destroyers, which now floated offshore. Garrett could see two amphibious landing craft, bristling with armed men, churning toward the dock. It was going to be an exciting dinner hour for Wade Preston and company.

The chopper landed and cut its engines at the same time the men from the landing craft swarmed up to the house and took up positions encircling the main building, their commander barking orders. Nichols and Tuttle were there as well. No way was either man going to miss out on the most important arrest in Nova Scotia history. Tuttle probably expected to ride this straight into the Commissioner's office.

As Lonnie, Garrett, and Grace approached, a number of people came out of the building to stare at the uproar. Most appeared to be maids or groundskeepers.

Lonnie led the way onto the rambling deck and closed immediately on the bewildered people clustered there, staring numbly at the guns pointed in their direction. Then Wade Preston came out. He had both hands in the air.

"I'll come peaceable, boys," he said, a grin on his face. "Always wanted to say that."

Lonnie went up to him with a look that would have sent Genghis Khan crawling under his bed. Preston cringed and his demeanor changed instantly. His upraised hands turned suddenly to palms forward as if expecting Lonnie to charge straight into him.

"No trouble," he said. "What is it you want?"

Nichols came forward, looking around at the disposition of his men. He had on a dark blue jumpsuit and protective vest and carried a pistol in one hand. His ponytail bobbed as he looked back and forth. He stopped next to Lonnie and stared at Preston.

"We have a warrant for the arrest of one Anthony DeMaio. Present him at once or we'll search the premises." He leaned in to Preston and said, "We know he's here, so don't try to con me, sir. You and the rest of your board members are on thin ice already. Harboring a fugitive makes you all accessories here."

Preston stared back, eyes wide, then seemed to crumble. "Had to happen sooner or later," he said. "The man's a walking nightmare. I always knew he'd bring this company down and probably all of us with it. We were all being blackmailed. It couldn't go on. . . ." He shook his head.

"Where is he?" Lonnie asked sharply.

Preston looked unhappily at the giant in front of him. Not someone you wanted to deliver bad news to.

"He's gone," he said simply.

Everyone stared blankly at him. Garrett was the first to speak. "Gone where?"

"One of the grounds people just told me. It was an hour before you got here. He took off in one of our cutters."

"Alone?" Garrett asked.

"Yes. No one here would have gone with him. Everyone hates the man, even the cooks and maids."

"What direction did he go?"

"He was headed southwest toward Halifax, but of course he could have changed course any time, or even landed. We have a private boat landing a few miles up the coast where we keep several vehicles. That might have been his destination."

"All right. He's on his own now," said Nichols. He immediately turned to one of the armed men, a communications specialist, and told him to inform the ships to proceed to Halifax, searching every bay and landing for a small cutter and boarding any vessels that looked suspicious. He also told them to check the landing where Preston kept his cars.

Lonnie pulled Garrett and Grace aside. "Someone tipped him off. He's going after Kitty. I'd bet the farm on it. It's all falling apart for him and he wants his revenge before he either gives himself up or goes down shooting. I've got to call and warn her and get my men fully alerted."

"No argument from me," said Garrett. "I want to check on Sarah too. She could also be a target, though I got Alvin sent down to be with her."

"The midget cop?" asked Lonnie.

Garrett grimaced. "Don't say that in front of him. He'd take a pop even at you."

Grace was listening to them. A strange look crossed her face. "What's this about a midget cop?" she asked.

"Alvin used to be my partner," said Garrett. "He was pretty short for a Mountie and he was sensitive about it."

"Son of a bitch."

"What?"

"The cop I ran into a couple of times during my drug runs? Only distinctive thing about him was his size. He was very short. And I heard at least one of the men say he was sensitive about it."

Garrett's eyes went wide. "You don't think . . ."

She just nodded. "I bet he's the one, Garrett."

65

LVIN TURNED INTO SARAH'S DRIVEWAY, parked the car, and stepped out onto the lupine-lined walkway. Across the road, the wharf was being pounded as whitecaps picked up by a stiff breeze barreled down the length of the bay. He'd never met Sarah and would have to rely on the RCMP cruiser and her faith in the uniform to put her at ease.

"Are you Sarah Pye?" he asked when she answered the door. She looked down on him, as many women did.

"Yes. Can I help you, officer?"

"My name is Alvin. I used to work with Garrett in Halifax. He sent me to take you to a safe place until Anthony DeMaio is caught."

A worried look crossed her face. "What's happening that he needs to do this?"

"They think they know where DeMaio is holed up. They're going after him. Kitty is well protected, but Garrett was worried about you, if DeMaio should somehow get tipped off and slip past them. It's too exposed here in the cove and a dead end to boot. All DeMaio has to do is look you up in the phone book. Better all around if you get out of Dodge for a while."

She bought it. No reason not to. She climbed into the cruiser, content that she was under Garrett's protection. As they drove inland, however, it niggled at her that being hidden from DeMaio also meant being hidden from any help should they get in trouble.

Two hours later, they turned onto a long dirt drive that climbed through thick spruce woods and then opened up to a rambling two-story house set in a meadow of uncut late-summer hay. There was a spectacular ocean view and Sarah realized that for all the sense of isolation, they were actually close to Halifax. The city spread out below them, appearing and disappearing as a light fog drifted in from the North Atlantic.

"Nice place," Alvin said. "Private, but you can be on the Halifax waterfront in ten minutes."

The hay was overdue for cutting and flitted from gold to auburn and back again as the breeze whispered across the field. An SUV sat in front of the building with writing on the door. Sarah got out, took a breath of spruce-perfumed air, then read the writing. It said GLOBAL RESOURCES and had the company's logo.

She stared at it. "Why is that here?"

Then the front door opened and DeMaio came out and stood on the porch. Sarah had never seen him before, yet she knew instantly who he was from Kitty's description. She whirled around to see Alvin now holding his pistol loosely in one hand, pointing it generally in her direction.

"Shouldn't you be pointing that at him?" she said, gesturing to the cold-faced man on the porch. "What's going on, Alvin?"

The diminutive Mountie ignored her. "Where do you want her?" he said.

"Put her in the front room," said DeMaio.

Sarah began to back away, but Alvin stuck the pistol in her side and pushed her forward.

"You?" She said. "*You* are the bad cop?"

"Depends on your point of view, I guess. Hard to make a decent living on a cop's salary," he said. "Global pays a whole lot better."

"You're the one who got my husband killed." Sarah's eyes blazed and she slapped him across the face just as hard as she could. His cheek turned red and he instinctively started to strike back.

"That's enough," DeMaio said. "She owed you that. Get her inside."

Five minutes later, Sarah sat alone across from the man who had raped Kitty. Alvin had gone back outside.

"What are you going to do?" she asked. "Why did you take me?"

"Leverage," said DeMaio. "And maybe, after a while, a little fun. Your friend Miss Wells has got herself pretty well protected. I can't get to her, so I got to you instead. Now we'll see if she's as good a friend as you think."

Sarah was mesmerized by his face. It was distinctive mainly for being devoid of expression. The eyes were calculating and black, like those of an animal.

"You must be mad," she said. "The whole world is looking for you."

"Why I stayed in Canada," he said. "No one expected it."

He stood abruptly and moved closer to her. He put one hand on her hair and stroked it.

Sarah stiffened.

"Haven't had a woman in three weeks. Longest drought of my life. You'd think my body could use the rest. But I guess no man ever really gets enough. You any idea how many women I've been with?"

"None that count," she replied. "No woman would ever be with you voluntarily. It's small wonder you can only get them by force. You're a pathetic excuse for a man."

His eyes blazed and he struck her with the back of his hand, sending her sprawling onto the floor.

He pulled out a cell phone and dialed a number. When some-one answered, he asked to be put through to Kitty Wells. He listened for a moment, then said, "She'll want to talk to me. Tell her it's her old friend Anthony." Then he turned the speakerphone on. "You might as well hear this," he said.

After a moment, Kitty came on the line. "Who is this?" she asked.

"Surely you haven't forgotten me so soon."

Kitty felt the hairs on the back of her neck stand straight up. After a moment, she said, "I don't know what you think you're doing, but trust me, you won't be doing it for long. Every law enforcement officer in the country is after you."

"Yes. Thanks to you and your pathetic little TV show. But no one's found me yet. Been kind of lonely staying out of sight for so long. Thought you might like to come entertain me."

"Your cellmate will entertain you soon enough, you sick bastard!"

"Got a friend of yours here," DeMaio said. "Why don't you say a few words, Sarah."

"Sarah?" Kitty said. "Is that you? Are you really there?"

"I'm sorry Kitty. They tricked me. It was Alvin, Garrett's former partner. He was the bad cop." She hesitated, then said in a rush, "Don't you come out here, Kitty. He'll rape you and kill you. You can't help me."

"I can't leave you there, Sarah."

DeMaio turned off the speakerphone. "Now that's a sensible attitude, Kitty. You've caused me a lot of trouble the last few weeks. I'd like to bring things a little more into balance. Here's what you need to do if you ever want to see your friend alive again. You're to slip out of the station right now, avoiding any bodyguards you may have. I know you can do it, and Sarah's life depends on it. Give me your cell number and you'll be told where to go. Until you get the call, just walk. When Alvin is in place, he'll direct you to his police car. Get in and he'll bring you here. Tell anyone and Sarah is dead."

"If you want me," said Kitty, "you have to give up Sarah. Only way I'll get in that car is if Sarah gets out of it first."

"That can be arranged," said DeMaio. He took down Kitty's cell number, then looked at his watch. "Get going. I'll be in touch. Don't carry anything. Don't put on a coat or even a sweater. If Alvin even thinks you might have a gun, the deal is off and Sarah's life is over. I don't want your friend, Kitty. You know that." His voice took on an even more lifeless quality than usual. "It's you I want."

Kitty hung up the phone. She was shaking. It took a minute for the adrenaline to begin to drain out of her system. Hearing DeMaio again had been paralyzing. The last time she'd listened to that awful, toneless voice, it was to respond to his commands to bend over.

She tried to consider her options realistically. He'd ordered her to leave the building immediately. Maybe he already had someone outside, waiting to report her movements. She wanted to tell security. Perhaps they could follow her. But it was no good. If Alvin got even a whiff of a double-cross, he simply wouldn't show, and Sarah would be as good as dead. Though Kitty had little doubt it would only be after DeMaio used her first.

She'd be damned if she would let that happen. The last thing she wanted was to be back under DeMaio's control. But there probably wasn't anything he could do to her he hadn't already done. Except kill her of course. But if she could save Sarah, she was going to do it.

There was no time. She tried to call Lonnie but he didn't answer. If she didn't go now, they'd probably figure she was trying to plan something. She looked at her purse. Lonnie had given her a pistol to carry in it, but it was a bulky thing. There was no way she could hide it on her person. She rummaged quickly in the bag and took out something else Lon had given her: a tiny locator device. She turned it on as he had shown her and clipped it inside the waist band of her pants. He'd made her promise not to go anywhere without it. The last thing she did was to kick off her heels and put on her running shoes.

Making sure no one saw her, she slipped into a storage room at the rear of the station. A window opened onto a back alley. She opened it, leaned out and looked both ways, then sat on the ledge, swung her legs over, and dropped to the ground. She moved quickly away from the building, avoiding the front, where Lonnie's men sat in their car.

Not having a direction, she walked slowly. There wasn't a lot of traffic in this part of town and only a few pedestrians. She stared at each car that went by, wondering if someone was tracking her. After ten minutes, her cell rang, making her jump six inches. She answered and listened to a voice she assumed belonged to Alvin.

"You're doing fine," he said, as though he knew precisely where she was. "Take your first right up ahead." He hung up. Thirty seconds later, he called again. "Now you're approaching a small street on your left. Turn on to it."

When she did, Kitty saw the police cruiser sitting next to a large trash container, its engine running. The site was perfect. It was lined on both sides by tall, windowless warehouses, and there was not a soul anywhere in sight. As she approached the car, the driver's door opened and the shortest Mountie she'd ever seen got out. He held a gun down by his side, his eyes sweeping the alley.

Then he pointed the gun at Kitty. "Stand right there," he said.

She stopped. He opened the rear door of the cruiser and Sarah got out.

"Kitty, I'm so sorry," she said. "I wish you hadn't come."

Alvin motioned Kitty forward. "Get in," he said.

Kitty squeezed Sarah's arm as she passed. "Thanks for being my friend," she said. "It will be okay."

Then Alvin jumped in the cruiser and they sped away, leaving Sarah staring after them.

"Some friend I am," she said out loud.

66

THE MOMENT KITTY CLOSED THE car door, she began to think about how she could escape. Sarah was safe. Now she had to find a way to save herself.

The back seat of the cruiser was impregnable, designed to keep prisoners as securely as a holding cell. This left the driver as the sole object of her focus. She could talk to him through a wire mesh that separated the front and back seats.

"Why are you doing this?" she asked. "You were Garrett's partner. You must have been willing to give your lives to protect each other when you worked together. What happened to you?"

Alvin turned slightly and glanced at her over the seat. He said nothing for a minute. Maybe she was imagining it, but Kitty thought he looked uncomfortable and maybe even a little guilty. There was a code between RCMP officers and it was only stronger between partners.

"Did Garrett ever do anything to you to justify your kidnapping his girlfriend?" Kitty pressed.

"He was actually a pretty good guy," Alvin said finally. "I feel a little bad about all this, you're right, but I made my bed a long time ago. There's no backing out once you enter into an agreement with DeMaio. Or Global Resources, for that matter."

"I can't believe you were a part of that sex trafficking business," Kitty said, though she could quite easily believe it. "You worked with Garrett *against* prostitution. You must have seen what happened to girls caught up in that system."

"Going to go on regardless of what I did. Or Garrett. Prostitution's been around since men started walking upright. It'll never go away. I just decided to get some of the money for myself. You any idea how many drug busts I've been involved with? I've only been on the force two years, but the money floating around would just blow you away. Why work for twenty years and a miniscule pension? I'd walk into a room that had hundred-dollar bills tied up in bundles the size of suitcases. The fourth or fifth time, you start to wonder, 'Who's going to miss it if I take one of these?'"

He shrugged, made a turn, and they started up a steep dirt drive. "Once you take the first one, everything gets easier and you see reality more clearly. After a while, I worked my way into Global's organization. They liked the idea of having their own cop. Can't say I blame them."

"Why don't you just stop the car and let me go?" Kitty said. "You don't have to do this. I won't bring charges. I give you my word and I can speak for Sarah too."

He shook his head. "I don't think so. I'm the guy who made the plant in her house that got her husband sent up. That makes this my last job. How else could I let Sarah go? No way I could do that and expect to stick around. Garrett would have my hide, one way or the other. DeMaio's offered me a nice bonus to go with the money I've already salted away. Soon as I deliver you, he pays me and then I disappear. Forever. I've been planning it a long time. No one will ever find me."

Kitty looked at him in complete incomprehension. "You arranged the murder of Sarah's husband? Why would you do that?"

"Call it my final exam. The only way DeMaio would accept me into the Global family, so to speak. By setting up Sarah's husband, I took a step I could never undo. It gave DeMaio something he could always use against me if I ever strayed. It's how he operates. He doesn't trust anyone he doesn't have something on."

Kitty looked out at the rambling house looming ahead, surrounded by spruce and a large meadow. They were only minutes from downtown Halifax. All around, people were going about their lives, unaware that Kitty Wells, their local newscaster, was about to be brutalized for the second time in a month. She reached down and checked the locater on her belt. It might be her only hope.

The car pulled up in front. Alvin got out, opened her door, and directed her up onto the porch. The door opened just as she got to it and her heart nearly stopped as she found herself face to face with DeMaio once more.

The sophisticated and relaxed demeanor he'd displayed in their earlier encounters was gone. Now, he was all business. He grabbed her by one arm so tightly she cried out as he pulled her inside.

Alvin followed and watched as DeMaio pushed Kitty into a chair and told her to stay put. He carried a gun that he stuck in his pants.

"Give me my money," Alvin said. "I don't want to be around when Garrett or that Frankenstein cousin of his show up."

DeMaio took a long, appraising gaze at Kitty that made her heart go cold. "One last bit of business, Kitty. Then I can devote my full attention to you. We'll have even more fun than we did a few weeks ago."

He disappeared into the next room and returned in a moment with a sack filled with cash that he handed to Alvin. "Plenty more where that came from," he said. "If you want to stick around."

"No way in hell," said Alvin. "Sarah's probably already reported me. I'm going to dump the cruiser and pick up a vehicle I liberated during one of our drug busts. You won't see me again." He looked at Kitty. "Sorry, Miss Wells. For what it's worth, I enjoyed your news show. You were a real professional."

He left and Kitty heard the cruiser drive away. She could hardly bear to look at DeMaio, but knew she had to try to connect with the man in some way, if only to delay the inevitable. Every second she survived was a second that Lonnie could use to find her.

She was puzzled that he hadn't tied her up. He seemed preoccupied. He watched Alvin drive off, then gestured for her to go ahead of him into the kitchen, which was at the rear of the house.

"I'm hungry," he said. "Make me a sandwich. You'll find stuff in the refrigerator."

It felt completely surreal making a sandwich for this monster. He appeared, now that he had her, to be in no rush to exact his revenge. He clearly craved her company and not just sexually. He wanted someone to talk to.

She put his sandwich on the table and poured him a glass of milk, then moved away and sat in a chair by the window.

DeMaio put his gun on the table and sat down. He began to wolf down his food. "You're a smart woman, Kitty," he said, waving one hand holding half a sandwich. "Probably one of the smartest I ever had. Lots of beautiful women out there, but not too many you can carry on an intelligent conversation with."

"Am I supposed to be flattered?" she asked.

He shrugged. "Just stating a fact. We both know the main thing you are good at. I missed it when you stopped doing the flush. Maybe we can work on that."

She shuddered at this reminder of their recent past. Somehow, she forced herself to maintain her composure. If there were ever a time in her life that she needed to think clearly, it was now.

"How . . . how did you come to set this whole thing up?" she asked. "I mean with Global Resources."

He considered her. "Ever the reporter, eh? Truth is, it was so long ago, it's almost hard to recall precisely. I started out pretty far down on the totem pole. Worked my way up to CEO. By that time, I'd pretty much figured out how things worked in the power game. It was absurdly easy to get a hold on the board members. They were all corrupt to begin with. I just started documenting what they did. In time, I had complete control. No one dared to oppose me."

"That when the brainstorm of using an oil rig as a brothel came to you?"

He didn't answer. He finished eating, got up and went over to the door, opened it, and looked out on the expansive meadow. It was twilight. The sun had set and the shadows of the trees ran like accusing fingers across the hayfield. He held the gun in his hand.

"I had a pretty good run," he said. "Aren't many men who wouldn't have traded places with me if they could. I underestimated you, though. You ruined it all for me." He closed the door. Three weeks without a woman had been an eternity. "Time to pay the piper for that, Kitty." He went back to the table and began to finish his glass of milk.

Kitty suddenly realized two things. First, that the door was not locked and second, that what he wanted more than anything was a reprise of their sex together. He'd actually missed her. Which meant there was no way he was going to shoot her until he'd had his fill of her.

The moment this sank in, she moved so quickly DeMaio was surprised and dropped his glass, which shattered on the floor.

She was out of her chair and through the door in an instant. She bolted straight across the big meadow. There was a cry of rage behind her and she expected to feel a bullet in her back at any instant. But she'd been right. He wasn't going to kill her before he enjoyed her.

He came after her, but Kitty felt more sure of herself now. She'd been a runner her whole life, track in high school and college, lots of miles at lunchtime along the streets of Halifax. She was good. Tireless. Not many men could keep up with her.

But she didn't want him to realize this too soon. If she started to leave him behind, he might decide he had to shoot her as his only option. So she slowed just enough to make him think she was tiring. She cursed that she'd bolted out the rear door of the house and run in a straight line, her only intent to get away from him. The only way out of the secluded spot was back down the front drive. Now, she could see in front of her nothing but the approaching edge of the meadow and thick spruce all around.

Once she ran out of meadow, she'd lose the advantage of her speed. But there was nothing for it. The meadow narrowed toward the back and if she turned to circle around, the angle would make it easier for him to catch her.

She hit the woods at full speed and practically dove into the underbrush. The trees were close together, a maze of branches grabbing at her clothing and piercing her skin. She cried out as a sharp branch hit her in the forehead and she staggered, looked back. He was coming.

She twisted and turned, trying to find a way through. Her size helped. She could make it through tighter spots than her stockily built pursuer.

Suddenly, she was at the edge of a steep hill. She lost her footing and tumbled down the slope. When she recovered, she looked back and couldn't see DeMaio.

She tried to catch her breath. Running through the obstacle course of the trees was more work than just running on the flat, and the adrenaline coursing through her system made her heart race. Then she saw him.

He didn't know where she was. He was standing still, looking away from her, trying to listen for her. She held her breath, tried even to stop her heart from its frantic and seemingly drum-like beating. She flattened herself against the ground, moved to take advantage of a fallen tree to hide her further. The light was dimming, and it was becoming harder to see in the dense woods. She just might pull this off, she thought.

Then her heart sank as he turned and began to angle back in her direction. He'd clearly decided she must have gone down the hill. She watched him like the chicken watches the fox. She gauged the path he would probably take, slightly to one side of her, to take advantage of a small opening in the trees. He'd be looking for her to be standing or moving, not lying flat. She hugged the ground tighter still.

He was going to come very close to where she was. She groped with one hand and it closed on a thick branch. There would be time for only a single effort.

Then he was right beside her. She could smell his sweat from exertion. He stared intently at the ground a few feet to her right, then turned slightly to look back up the hill.

She leaped to her feet and swung the branch as hard as she could, hitting him on the side of the head as he swiveled, hearing her move. He grunted, staggering, arms flailing. The gun flew off into the brush. Then he fell and lay still on the ground.

67

WHEN SHE STUMBLED BACK TO the meadow, Kitty was uncertain what to do. DeMaio was still unconscious. She couldn't move him. He was too heavy. If she'd had any sense at all, she would have hit him with the branch until he was dead or at least far enough along in that direction that she needn't worry about him coming after her again.

As she stood in the near darkness, a figure suddenly loomed up in front of her. She cried out and took a step back before she heard a voice.

"Kitty? Is that you?"

Lonnie. She cried out, ran to him and fell into his arms. He held her so tightly she couldn't breathe and she didn't ever want it to stop.

"I'm sorry," he said. "Sorry it took so long. The damn GPS locator got me to the house, but then I couldn't figure out which way to go. I'm sorry I ever left you. I should have known DeMaio would find some way to get to you. He's a master manipulator. I just never thought he'd go after Sarah." He stopped and looked at the woods. "Where is he?"

"I'll show you," Kitty said. "I don't know if he's alive or not. I hit him over the head."

Lonnie smiled. He looked like a gigantic Cheshire cat in the late twilight. "You'd think the asshole would have thought better about facing off with you and Sarah again. I guess some men never learn."

It took Kitty a few minutes to find her way back. DeMaio was where they'd left him. Lonnie knelt and felt for a pulse. Then he grunted. "Good," he said. "Still alive."

"What's good about that? Even after all he's done, the man's still got enormous resources. He'll hire the best solicitors in the world. He might get off, like O. J. Simpson." She stared down at the silent body. At this moment, she wanted nothing more than to hit him again and again until there was no doubt.

Lonnie picked the body up like it weighed nothing, but then had to struggle to get his massive girth through the tightly packed spruce. It took half an hour to get back to the house, where he deposited his load on the couch in the living room. By this time, DeMaio had begun to stir.

Lonnie drew Kitty aside. "Do you believe in retribution being given to those who deserve it?"

She nodded.

"I could kill him now," he said. "I'd have no regrets, but it's not enough for him. Robs him of his just punishment."

She stared at him. "What are you saying?"

"I mean there's another way."

"What other way?"

"A way that doles out punishment, definitively and over time. Without having to inconvenience the legal system."

"I still don't understand."

"You remember what you told me DeMaio said to you after he'd raped you for three days and was about to turn you over to a string of men?"

"I'll never forget it. He said I should accept it. That I'd get used to it." She frowned at the memory. "But I still don't understand . . ."

"Life in prison, even if it was certain, would be too good for this guy. Killing him outright would be even less just. He doesn't deserve a quick death after the hundreds of women he's abused."

"What other way is there?'

He stared at her. He couldn't believe how much he loved this tiny firebrand of a woman. "There's my way."

"Which is?"

"You go home now. My car's in the driveway. Keys are in it. I'll take care of everything else."

She realized she was holding her breath. She let it out and went over and hugged him. "You won't get in trouble will you?"

"Who—me? Of course not." The big man smiled.

"I don't think I want to know about it right now," Kitty said. "But will you tell me some day when I'm ready?"

"Scout's honor."

She grinned. "You were a Boy Scout?"

"Lasted two weeks. Always had a thing about authority."

Epilogue

I T WAS LATE OCTOBER. THE last hurricane of this busy season had come and gone. Bits of Lighthouse Point oil rig continued to wash up on shore and the outer islands. Roland had developed a side business scavenging the most marketable pieces. Global Oil's Board of Directors had been purged, and Wade Preston was under indictment for harboring a fugitive.

The Eastern shore drug pipeline dried up. No more young girls washed up on shore either, or were found in the holds of fishing boats. Garrett knew it was only a temporary reprieve. Someone else in the business would soon take up the slack.

Ecum Secum Haven for Troubled Youth tottered, but remained open under new management. The parents of several children under Lloyd's thumb brought suit against the province. It was uncertain if the establishment would survive the publicity of an extended, and very public, lawsuit.

Life went on in Misery Bay. Roland agreed to sell the spruce-covered hill behind his house to his neighbors. Garrett hired a general contractor to level the floors in the old house. While the work was going on, he moved in with Sarah, an arrangement that soon felt like it might outlast the contractor. Lila and Ayesha started school in Sherbrooke. Their first report cards were good, and both girls were granted permanent status to live with Sarah. Ayesha's father appeared uninterested in spending money for a solicitor to get her back.

Old Man Publicover buried his fifth wife.

Garrett enlisted Lonnie to help him put down yet another layer of roofing over the central part of the old homestead, which still leaked when it rained heavily. It was a leisurely pursuit, consisting of nailing a few rows followed by a break and a beer and then a few more rows.

Lonnie had no more trouble with heights than he did with claustrophobia. In truth, Garrett had never known anyone with fewer phobias. Still, he consigned his cousin to being gopher, to hauling flats of shingles up the ladder and only working on rows he could reach without actually getting on the roof.

"Roof's too old," Garrett said. "Won't take your weight. When Roland and I were teenagers, my dad hired us to put on some new shingles. First time Roland got up here, the rafters gave way and he fell right through onto the kitchen floor. You can still see the dent in the linoleum where he hit."

"That's an image I'll always treasure, Gar. He'd probably be even more likely to fall through now."

Roland had put on twenty pounds since Grace started teaching him how to cook more interesting meals. And he went to the gym and lifted weights as well. He looked good, not great, but he was making progress.

"Not sure weight was the problem," said Garrett. "It's a matter of being careful where you step. Roland has always been accident-prone."

Lonnie lifted the final row of flats onto the roof. He paused at the top of the ladder and stared across the meadow. "I told Kitty what happened to DeMaio the other day. She said she was ready to know."

Garrett ceased pounding and looked down at him. "Wouldn't care to share it with the rest of humanity, would you? Whole world's still looking for the creep. It's as if he disappeared off the face of the earth."

"I could never get past what he told Kitty about becoming a sex slave, that she should just accept what was happening to her. That she'd get used to it."

Garrett shook his head. "What a crazy thing to say . . . or even think."

"One good thing came of it. It gave me an idea about the sort of punishment the man deserved."

Garrett stopped, hammer poised in the air. As a police officer, he wasn't sure he was going to like this.

"He's in prison, Garrett."

Garrett's eyes widened. "Prison? Where, for God's sake?"

"Turkey."

"What? How on earth did you manage that?"

"Called in a favor. I once helped out the current president of the country before he went into politics, back when he was still in the military and got into a little trouble on shore leave." He looked away for a moment, as though briefly considering the vagaries of life. "So, DeMaio has been disappeared into the Turkish prison system, one of the most notorious in the world."

"You never cease to amaze me. What was the length of his sentence?" Garrett asked, knowing the silliness of the question before he posed it.

"Indeterminate," said Lonnie. "Some last a long time. Some not so long at all. Sex between men is rampant in the Turkish prison system. DeMaio, sad to say, went in with the reputation of a child molester."

"I wonder who told them that?" said Garrett.

"Hard to imagine. I told him where he was going and why. Last thing I said to him before I delivered him, clandestinely, to Turkish sailors from a warship passing through Halifax was that he should try to relax and accept his fate. I told him he'd get used to it."

Garrett swallowed hard and looked away. When it came to balancing the scales of justice, Lonnie marched to his own drummer. He'd suspected his cousin had arranged a special resolution to the DeMaio problem. It wasn't something Garrett could openly support given his years as a Mountie, but Lon had a history of dealing with difficult problems in creative ways. To change the uncomfortable subject Lonnie knew was difficult for Garrett, he asked, "Anything new on Alvin?"

Garrett shook his head. "Disappeared like a ghost. DeMaio should have taken lessons from the man."

"How does Sarah feel about that?"

"Pissed off. He's the one who got her husband killed, after all. All we can do is keep after him. He'll make a mistake some day and we'll pick him up in Saudi Arabia or on some remote island."

"No extradition treaty with Saudi Arabia," said Lonnie. "Maybe I'll look into it."

Garrett started to say something, then thought better of it. At the far edge of the meadow, a doe appeared, picking her way through the blueberry bushes.

He slid a shingle into place and began to hammer it in.